PRIME AMBITION

A Novel

by

P.J. Ralls

DORRANCE
PUBLISHING CO
EST. 1920
PITTSBURGH, PENNSYLVANIA 15238

Dorrance Publishing Co
585 Alpha Drive
Pittsburgh, PA 15238
Visit our website at *www.dorrancebookstore.com*

ISBN: 979-8-8860-4255-9
eISBN: 979-8-8860-4526-0

This book is dedicated to my dad.

I would like to thank everyone who has helped
make my book a dream come true.
A special thanks to Mr. Michael Tellier;
Maisie McIntyre, my project coordinator; and Mr. Zeolla.
As well as many thanks to the editors, page designers, and artists.

Special thanks to Jenny,
for her continued encouragement and support
during the writing of this novel.

"Every Night and every Morn
Some to Misery are born.
Every Morn and every Night
Some are born to Sweet Delight,
Some are born to Endless Night."
—William Blake

"Ambition has but one reward for all:
A little power,
A little transient fame,
A grave to rest in, and a fading name!"
—William Winter

CHAPTER ONE

"The Shooting"

For Ruth, this morning started just like every other morning, very early. Ruth and Charles owned Pointer Enterprises in Braxton, Missouri, and that made them pioneers of their community. Charles was a proud man, and he fell in love with that nineteen-year-old jet-black-haired beauty the moment he saw her, and now almost forty years and four children later he's still intoxicated by her. His wife, now fifty-eight years old, has not lost her striking beauty. When Ruth enters a room, men and women alike naturally gravitate toward her. Charles is eleven years older than his wife, and he boasts about like a peacock when given the opportunity to say, "Allow me to introduce you to my wife, Ruth."

Thanks to his vision and a little inside information, he knew this was the place to be. The main highway that ran through the town was the settlement's lifeline to putting this place on the map to becoming an entertainment capital. It was once a beautiful little town tucked away in the Ozarks that didn't have much going on. As the highway expanded, so did their brick-and-mortar, along with their wealth. Its geography and location would be this little town's salvation after all. From gospel singers and country singers to fine dining and fun parks, it was growing. Charles had the vision, and Ruth had the ambition, and together they had been unstoppable since their marriage and formation of Pointer Enterprises. Now being three generations of Pointers, Ruth believed they would soon shed their stigma of "New Money." Well, maybe not be known as old money, but at least some earned respect as legitimate new money with integrity.

Charles married late in life and had resigned himself to the fact that he may never have a family of his own. Unlike her husband, Ruth came from a family of four brothers and five sisters experiencing the pangs of poverty. Clawing her way out of that impoverished life, she promised herself she would never suffer the dire straits of poverty again. She had married well. Her ambition of owning all the brick-and-mortar on the main highway that led to Springton, the queen city of the Ozarks, was well within her grasp. *Their* grasp. She had become the face of their enterprise, and he was the money man. Anyway, Charles never gave much thought to the animosity and fighting over the old money versus the new money. To him it was silly; besides, he had enough money and didn't care. It never made sense to him, money was money, and as far as he was concerned, after WWII, one war was enough for him. His family always had one foot in high society, but the whispers were always there chattering about how he and his family were nothing but opportunists. Regardless of the chatter and the gossip, he and his wife enjoyed the feast of accumulating great wealth after WWII.

And just like every other morning, Charles would remain sleeping while his wife started her day. Showered and dressed in her sophisticated but elegant style, she made her way to the dining room where Mathilda, their housekeeper and cook, whom they called Mattie, had her coffee and toast with the morning paper ready for her.

"Thank you, Mattie. Have I ever told you how happy I am that you're an early riser too?" She smirked.

"Yes, ma'am," replied Mattie, trying not be too transparent to the lady who had become the matriarch of the Pointer family. Mattie was loyal to Charles, and she had always been fond of him. But once Charles brought Ruth home that day in 1948, Mattie put her feelings aside and tucked her hopes and dreams away. Mattie thought Ruth was an emotionally absent mother and a manipulative wife. There wasn't a day that went by that she didn't think, *What a selfish woman!* Mattie did well to hold her tongue, remembering her position in the household that provided her with an above-average lifestyle, for a war widow with no children. It was easier for her now since Ruth and Charles's children were grown and out of the house.

"Mattie..." called Ruth, ignoring the table setting that was obviously set for Charles, with love and adoration. For years she had noticed these little things and always thought to herself, *"How sweet... futile...but sweet.* It was Ruth's habit to scour the paper every morning, preferably unobserved, just in case they made the headlines without knowing it.

"Yes, ma'am?" replied Mattie, being careful not to enter the room too soon, so Ruth would have time to tuck the paper safely away. It was so obvious to her what was important to Ruth. Charles, however, remained blinded all these years by his wife's charms and beauty.

"I'll be leaving for the office now. I don't think I'll be late, and I expect it'll just be Charles and I for dinner," said Ruth dismissively.

"All right, you have a wonderful day," Mattie replied. She had learned to ignore her tone over the years, and as far as she was concerned, Charles signed her paychecks, not her.

"Is there anything special you'd like for dinner?" asked Mattie as an afterthought.

"Not that I can think of, I know that's one decision I can trust you and Charles with, so I'll leave that up to you two!" Ruth answered, briskly gathering her purse and brief case heading out the door.

Mattie simply replied, "Yes, ma'am. Dinner will be at eight as usual." Then she quickly went about her daily routine thinking to herself, *What a selfish woman! And it's my job to be up early every day!*

The best thing about living in the Ozarks was the scenery, and it was a beautiful day for a drive. It wasn't hard for a local to take the scenery for granted. It was September, and the trees were changing their colors to the vibrant colors of reds, oranges, and yellows. The air smelled crisp, and some days would carry a chill. How stimulating and beautiful are the Ozarks! The best part about fall was the advent of the holiday season it was announcing. It was this time of the year Ruth would enjoy the glamour she longed for all her life. In the winter months the tourism would decrease, and business would slow, the Pointer family would take a nice needed break.

Arriving at the office Ruth parked her Cadillac in her designated spot, just like every other day.

"Good morning, Mrs. Pointer. How are you today?"

"Very good, Lauren, yourself?"

"Good, good. Thank you," replied Lauren, who had been with Ruth and Charles for many years and proudly held her title "Executive Administrator."

"Anything I need to know?" Asked Ruth.

"As far as I know, everything's right on schedule, and the holiday financials are prepared and on your desk," answered Lauren.

"Oh, excellent. Right on time," replied Ruth. She was pleased with Lauren and the confidence she brought to the administration. Her businesslike manner always kept Ruth at ease.

Ruth's office was comfortable. Those who entered would sink to their knees in the plush carpet. The walls were filled with plaques that spelled success. Hanging in their glory were awards from the restaurant associations, acknowledgements from charities, clippings of newspaper articles, and reviews from food critics. Pictures of her and Charles with the mayor, judges, bankers, and local politicians reflected their importance in society. Her mahogany desk was large, with an extension to the right side, making it "L" shaped. A high button backed burgundy leather armed chair completed its regal, intimidating presence.

Ruth began going over the financials and the progress of the budget for the Thanksgiving turkeys and Christmas bonuses. It took all year to prepare for the holidays, including the down time from January to March. There were a lot of turkeys to get smoked and sent out to the employees. The Christmas bonuses for the next year were something they would start talking about right after their own New Year's Eve family party.

Lauren buzzed Ruth's phone. "Mrs. Pointer, Sean is on line one, and it sounds urgent," she announced.

"Okay, Lauren, put him through."

"Son," said Ruth, "everything all right?"

"No, Mom, it's not!" he replied, struggling for the breath he needed to speak. "Robert's been shot, it was accident. You need to come right away. It's bad, Mom. It's bad."

"I'm leaving now," she replied, immediately hanging up the phone, collecting her purse and keys. "Lauren, please cancel all my appointments, I'll be out for the rest of the day." Before Lauren could reply, Ruth had disappeared from her sight in a frenzy.

The curvy and winding roads she knew so well were challenging for her to drive, and she did her best to keep her thoughts on the road. Her mind was racing, and she was hoping it wasn't as bad as Sean had made it sound. She saw flashing lights of the emergency vehicles coming upon Sean's house on that desolate dirt road, and her heart sank. There were so many flashing lights, they paralyzed her with fear, and she had to stop her car. For a moment she could only blindly stare at what was going on in front her. *Robert couldn't be dead!* Sean and his little family of four had to be in utter panic. Slowly, she drove closer to Sean's. Getting out of her car, she didn't see anyone she recognized. Jack and Joshua were nowhere in sight and must have been inside with their mother, Caroline. *Where is Sean? Who is here that can tell me what's happening? Who is here that could take me to my son?*

Sean and Caroline's house sat on a hundred acres down that dirt road. It was rustic and woodsy to its location but lacked none of the modern amenities. It was a four-bedroom log cabin, with two fireplaces and a wood burning stove. The beautiful home was tucked away from the outside world and nestled quaintly amongst tall, majestic trees that reached the sky. There was a wraparound porch that offered a perfect view of the whole property, including the enamoring view of the man-made lake, Marble Shores.

Ruth tried to make her way to her son, Robert, and she couldn't get close to him. The paramedics were urgently tending to him as he lay there on the ground, and their gloved hands were covered in blood. They were hooking him up to IV's, hanging bags and talking with the doctor over the radio for instructions. Her son looked lifeless.

She wandered aimlessly for a moment, her vision blurred as uniforms and gold badges were hurriedly moving to and fro. Looking around at everything that was happening around her, time seemed to have shifted.

The shift caused her to feel like she was moving in slow motion, and she couldn't keep up with the pace of those around her. With the talk on their radios and all the static, her hearing was muffled and everyone else was talking as fast as they were moving. She was looking for a familiar face, looking for Sean. Having difficulty just putting one foot in front of the other, she heard someone shout, "Get that woman outta here!"

One of the paramedics said to her in a matter-of-fact tone, "Ma'am, you must step back!"

"I'm his mother!" she cried. Neither her words nor her tears seemed to resonate with the paramedic.

"Ma'am, you must step back!" he repeated, guiding her to the front porch.

She felt helpless, she could do nothing to control this situation. Hoping to escape for just a moment, she opened the front door of Sean and Caroline's house to find her grandsons sitting with their mother. Just like her, they were trying to come to terms with what was happening in their driveway.

"Mom, what happened? Uncle Robert's going to be okay, isn't he? The hospital will be able to make him okay, won't they?" Ruth heard Joshua asking his mom.

"Mom…" said Jack.

"Jack, honey," said Caroline, interrupting him upon seeing Ruth open the front door.

"He's going to be taken to the hospital, we'll know more later on today. Right now there's nothing for you to say, okay?" Jack went silent.

Caroline's pleading eyes looked at Ruth, and she returned her pleas with the same horror that Caroline had reflected.

"Boys, your mother is right, you stay here inside. It'll be okay, you just wait and see," Ruth said to her grandsons.

Jack and Joshua remained close to their mother, and she gathered her boys closer to her in a huddle, and they all tried to gain strength and comfort from one another. They could hear the movements outside and heard an authoritative male voice say, "Bring that tape over here and block off this area."

Inside the house, lights of red and blue continued to project through the windows onto the walls, swirling in their circular motion and highlighting the wall hangings and family pictures, like a light switch that was being turned on and off, on and off. Ruth wished they would turn those damn lights off: they did nothing but bring more anxiety. They continued to swirl back again and again, increasing their panic and fear. They brought an unknown anticipation of something not good with each swirling interval, and she could see that her grandsons were frightened.

Gathering as much courage as she could, Ruth stepped outside on the porch and saw the paramedics urgently continuing to care for her son to get him stable for transport. The police officers were there starting their investigation and asking questions. She watched in horror as the paramedics lifted her son from the ground. The pool of blood was thick his head was lying in and dripped from his thin hair as they placed him on the stretcher. Chills ran down her spine and left her gasping, seeing the reality in front of her. A mother, helpless to protect and save her son, left with fear and vulnerabilities to rely on others to save him. Powerless. Her mouth filled with saliva, and she moved because she needed to, her stomach began feeling sick. Immediately she closed her eyes, but it did no good, the vision was still there.

"Whoa, steady there, ma'am," said a police officer who helped her support herself when her knees buckled and her legs wouldn't hold her up.

"Thank you. I'm not sure what just happened," said Ruth.

"You almost fainted," said the officer. "Are you okay? Do you need to sit down?"

"I'll be all right, thanks again," answered Ruth.

"Might I ask, ma'am, are you related to the young man, Robert Pointer, who was shot?"

"Yes, he's my son," she answered sobbing quietly.

"Oh, I see. And Sean Pointer, is he your son?"

"Yes."

"I'll need your phone number and address in case we have any further questions," replied the officer with a look of bewilderment.

Finally, she saw her son, Sean, and he was covered in blood. His brother's blood, her youngest son's blood.

He had done his best to stop his brother's bleeding, and for a moment felt like he was back in Vietnam field dressing a gunshot wound to the head.

The ambulance was getting ready to transport Robert to the hospital.

"Officer," said Ruth, queasy and unsteady on her feet, "we have to go, we'll answer all your questions later, but I have to be with my son, and Sean needs to be with his brother."

"I'm sorry, ma'am," replied the officer, "but Mr. Pointer, Sean, will need to stay here and answer a few more questions."

Ruth wanted to say to the officer, *Do you know who we are? I can have your badge!*

"Sean, I'll meet you at the hospital," she said, doing her best to ignore the blood on Sean's hands and clothes. Unknowingly she was pushing herself into a state of denial so she could do what she needed to do.

Sean was full of anxiety, and his face had grown pale. "Okay, Mom, I'll be there as soon as I can. Be careful," he replied and gave his mother a kiss on the cheek.

While her best efforts to ignore the vision of her son standing before her had served her well, the fetid smells she inhaled when he leaned in to kiss her cheek almost suffocated her. She was overtaken by smells of sweat, an irony metallic smell and a sickening sweet scent, she could no longer block the vision. The smells of blood and sweat made it all so vivid, her youngest son being lifted on the stretcher and her oldest son standing before her covered in his blood. She immediately turned away and stumbled a few steps over to the side of the driveway in the grass and fell to her knees gagging and retching.

"Get someone over here right away and block off this vomit... Dammit!" Ruth heard a strong, dominating male voice bark out as an order that continued to echo in her head.

"I'm sorry," cried Ruth. "I'm so sorry. I tried not...I couldn't help it." Sean made an effort to go to his mother who had crumbled to the ground, but an officer stopped him before he took a second step.

With help from another officer, she was taken to her car. "Ma'am, it's okay. We understand, and please pay no attention to his tone of voice, we just have a situation here we need to contain. It's okay. Are you planning to drive? Are you in any condition to drive?"

"I just need to sit for moment, I'll be able to drive. I have to be with my son."

She had every intention of following closely behind the ambulance as their sirens screamed through those winding roads, and she didn't even realize that, as she drove, the vibrant colors of fall were fading fast in her eyes. Everything was turning gray. It was a mother's worst nightmare: she didn't know if her son would be alive when they reached the hospital.

She found herself unable to keep up with the swirling red and blue lights of the ambulance on those Ozark roads, and her leg would shake when she pressed the gas pedal for her Cadillac to go faster. With every twist and turn she tightly gripped the steering wheel. An eerie silence had replaced the sounds of the sirens. Increasing the speed of her car caused her heart to pound so hard, she thought it might explode. *My son, my son!* She was alone, twisting and turning along those curvy and winding roads.

The image of the big red sign that said "EMERGENCY PARKING" broke through those racing thoughts in her mind and she turned left on auto pilot and followed the sign. Entering through the automatic doors of the emergency room, more of her new reality appeared in front of her. Everything from clothing to counters seemed to be either white, green, or made of metal, shiny stainless steel. There were smells of antiseptic and other smells that smelled of medicine. There were machines making beeping noises, patients in beds in the hallway up against the walls, black resin chairs scattered against the walls in no particular order, and the elevator doors were opening and closing. No one knew who she was or why she was there. Distraught and disoriented, she approached the front desk hoping to find out any information.

"Nurse, my son Robert Pointer has been brought in with a gunshot wound; can you tell me where he is?" she asked in hysterics.

"Mrs. Pointer, the doctors are with him now. If you would please have a seat, as soon as the doctors have any news, they'll be with you directly," replied the nurse while leading her to a waiting area close to the nurses' station.

"Is there anything I can get you?" she asked.

Ruth stood still in shock for a moment.

"Ma'am, is there anything I can get you?" the busy nurse prodded.

"Uh...a glass of water?" answered a shaky Ruth.

Time seemed to have stopped while she sat in that waiting room. She took a seat in one of the many hard padded-covered armchairs. There was a table next to the chair with a lamp and a coffee table that was strewn with magazines that sat in front of her. The walls were hung with cheap wall art of flowers in vases painted in pastels and looked like they were done in watercolors, designed to create a calming space. The air was stuffy, and the antiseptic was strong. Even in the stuffiness of the room, with the heavy smell of antiseptic, the fetid smells from earlier were still lingering, still with her. Most of all her sense of smell filled her with fear, she smelled fear. There wasn't anything that could have calmed her at this moment right here and right now. She abruptly crashed with her emotions of the morning. Over the intercom echoing through the halls, she heard, "Dr. Carsman to ICU, Dr. Carsman to ICU."

Ruth paced the floors and looked outside of the waiting area occasionally to see if there was anything she could observe that had to do with her son. The fluorescent lights were harsh and unforgiving in the sterile hallway, reflecting blindingly off the highly waxed floors. She was almost dizzy starring at the floor's reflection trying to compose herself while waiting for Charles. Not only was she waiting for Charles, she was waiting for the news, news that her son was going to be all right, and it wasn't coming to her. The doctors and nurses were jetting around the halls like she wasn't there, and it sounded like they were talking in a foreign language. There wasn't any news coming to her at all. In a situation that would bring most to their knees to pray, she wouldn't pray for her son. She couldn't pray for her son because she didn't believe in God, or a higher power for that matter. She believed in the power of her money, the persuasion of her beauty, and instead paced back and forth some more and then took her seat again, vowing to herself that she would get the best doctors and the best medical care that money could provide for her son.

When Charles found a shaky Ruth, he didn't know the details of what happened and decided this wasn't the time to press his wife for answers. Sitting in the chair next to her, "Ruthie," Charles said, quietly reaching for her hand, "Rose and Cassandra are on their way. Where's Sean?"

With tears in her eyes and tightly holding his hand, she answered his question the best she could muster, "He's…he's with the police giving a statement."

Charles tried to speak and instead found himself gasping for air. He could see the anguish on his wife's tear-stained face. Her tears continued to roll down her face through the dark smudges of her mascara, leaving their streaks behind. Her once made-up face was now blotchy and red.

"Mr. and Mrs. Pointer?" asked Dr. Carsman.

"Yes," replied Charles.

"I'm Dr. Carsman," he said, standing, "your son, Robert, has a gunshot wound to the head comprising of what appears to be made of pure lead pellets that have disbursed primarily within the right side of his face and brain and that will be challenging to remove, but based on the CT scan we're going to be taking him into surgery immediately. As soon as we know more, we'll let you know."

Ruth nor Charles could speak and shook their heads in a way trying to thank the doctor as he turned away quickly to prep his patient for surgery. Dr. Carsman's body language said what his words didn't, that his patient, their son, was fighting for his life.

Rose and Cassandra joined their parents in the waiting room with many questions. Cassandra looked right through her father, he wouldn't have anything to say because he wouldn't know the truth or admit it even if he did. Rose went right to her father's side and sat beside him offering her support. Cassandra couldn't help but glare at her sister for a moment and wonder how someone so smart could be so…stupid. In

Cassandra's opinion, Rose's intelligence had not served her well outside of the office.

"Mom, what happened?" asked Cassandra in an accusatory tone.

Before Ruth could answer the question, she looked up to see Sean and Caroline walk into the waiting room. Out of habit the whole family turned to look at Caroline, and even though Sean was oblivious, Caroline was not. Caroline did what she always did, stood by Sean and kept her head and eyes down. A beautiful girl she was, with big, brown doe eyes, but clumsy.

Sean had a few scratches and looked like he'd been in a fight, his right hand was swollen and wrapped in white gauze from his wrist to just over his knuckles with a hint of blood bleeding through. None of this went unnoticed, especially to Cassandra.

As composed as she could be, Ruth began to try to tell the family what had happened, and her voice was weak and filled with uncertainty.

"There was an accidental shooting..." she said, doing her best to try and explain.

Sean saw how horrific this was for his mother and wished he could turn back the clock... but he couldn't.

"Mom, please let me explain what happened," said Sean.

The horror of what happened brought devastation to the whole family, but it seemed that Sean was the only one who recognized his mother's devastation, other than Charles, of course.

"Robert and I had a disagreement..." said Sean.

"Disagreement, Sean?" seethed a scared and upset Cassandra, standing nose to nose with her brother.

"A disagreement is an argument between two people, Sean. A difference of opinion. You don't have disagreements, you have fights! Robert has been shot, shot in the *head,* he could die, Sean! This is what you call a fight?"

Cassandra was crying uncontrollably, with her arms folded in front of her maybe trying to give herself a hug, or physically hold herself together, and you could barely understand her last words...*He could die!*

If Ruth had the strength she would have stood up and faced her daughter, but she didn't, and just said her words with as much authority in her voice that she could find. "Cas-san-dra, now is not the time, watch your tone with your brother. We're all worried and upset."

Charles and Rose remained quiet in their seats and leaned back in what almost seemed to be defeat.

Sean began again. "Cassandra, I'm not going to do this with you right now," he said, blasting her.

Cassandra's big blue eyes full of distrust met his, "Oh, really, Sean? What, this place not public enough?" she barked back.

Ruth raised only her eyes over to her youngest daughter, "Cas-san-dra!"

Charles's relationship with his youngest began to derail when she was barely a teen, and he wasn't exactly sure what had caused her to become so indifferent and reclusive, it was like it happened overnight and seemed they would remain divided. Charles would remove himself from many of her emotional outbursts, mainly because he didn't understand her. However, considering the grave situation the family had found themselves in, he wasn't going to allow it.

Charles stood up. "That's enough!" he said, loud enough to get their attention and quiet enough not to make a scene. His small beady blue eyes blazed at Cassandra. He then turned to Sean. "Son, please, what happened?"

Once again Sean began, "Robert and I had a disagreement."

Cassandra rolled her eyes but stayed silent.

"Our *disagreement* turned into a fight, as Cassandra so pointed out. Robert took a swing at me, and I had the shotgun in my hand, and not because I grabbed it to shoot him..." Sean immediately turned toward Cassandra, his hand held out in Cassandra's direction, saying to her, "Let me finish." He was nervous and upset as he continued, "I was taking the gun to my truck to put it in the gun rack. When Robert hit me, I fell to the ground and the shot gun went off."

All Sean could see in his mind was the image of his brother lying there on the ground, his head in a pool of blood and remnants of what appeared to be broken teeth and fragments of bone. His skin on the right side of his face was dimpled, violently torn, and ripped where the lead pellets penetrated his skin. There were pits and holes in his neck, and his ear was badly damaged where the buckshot had peppered his face; his blood pooled into his pores and then profusely spilled out on the ground like a bubbling spring. He couldn't say any more; like his mother, he was left to crash with his emotions. The blood-stained gauze on his hand stood out like the center of a target and was another reality check to all of them: they were in the waiting room of the intensive care unit.

Cassandra knew at this moment, in this family of secrets, that it was Sean who was harboring a secret now. No one would believe the shot gun went off when it hit the ground, that didn't happen. Even she knew that.

Trembling and meek, Caroline sat next to Ruth. "How's Robert? Have you heard anything?" she asked softly.

"No, he's been in surgery for almost two hours," answered Ruth.

Time was now out of sync, and the family sat in that eerie silence while they waited. Charles needed to know what happened, preferably sooner rather than later. Rose was thankful she lived a comfortable distance away from the toxicity of all that was Pointer. Sean was in the worst position of his life, and he knew it. Caroline was a mother worrying about her sons. Jack was an impressionable fifteen years old, and Joshua a young thirteen years old. The waiting room was filled with fear and anxiety. A familiar untrustworthiness loomed in the atmosphere.

CHAPTER TWO

"The Golden Child, Daddy's Little Girl, Sacrificial Lamb, and The Scape Goat"

Robert was not only Cassandra's brother, he was her best friend. They shared their struggles within the Pointer family, searching for a sense of belonging, validation, and emotional support. The preconceived notions of how things should be, could be is what Robert and Cassandra had a hard time letting go of. Things they had heard about families attending church every Sunday and brunch afterwards. Mom and Dad sitting down to help with homework, playing board games and such things. These ideals had turned into a fantasy instead of a reality for both of them. Cassandra believed that if she willed it hard enough it would become so, and Robert believed that if the truth be told it would become so. What they really needed was for all of them to come together. Robert and Cassandra painfully learned, over and over, they were kidding themselves pretending that within the Pointer family would one day be a safe place. No matter what they did to change their reality, it wasn't happening. With that horrifying truth slapping them in the faces, they were leaving Braxton and leaving everything Pointer behind. *And now this,* thought Cassandra.

Rose had always been daddy's little girl, and Sean had always been Ruth's golden child. That left little room in the family for Cassandra and Robert. The relationships between the siblings were strained and delicate at best. Robert lived in the shadows of his older brother Sean, and Rose imagined that she lived in the shadows of her younger sister, Cassandra. Being born to very wealthy parents, they never wanted for anything materialistic and had always received the best. Yet each one in their own way desperately needed a connection to their roots to help them fight a loneliness within. All deeply yearning for the unconditional love and support of family. The family's wealth only intensified the longing for nurturing family ties, rendering them feeling even more disconnected. A cycle that repeated itself throughout their childhood. Imbalance and instability. These were the feelings the silence brought to Cassandra.

Caroline began feeling claustrophobic in the waiting room and was grabbing onto anything that would get her out of this place. She felt like she was trapped in a maze and couldn't find her way out. She wanted Robert to be okay, she needed Robert to be okay. Caroline decided to go home and check on the boys: she needed her sons and knew they needed her. Alone, she made her way through the white sterile halls. The intercom was still busy with chatter. There were other families waiting just as they were, there was crying and loss. Lives of those changing instantaneously with each breath that was taken and for some it was their last. When the elevator made its distinctive "ding" announcing the doors were about to open, she barely heard it.

It was four hours later when Dr. Carsman finally came into the waiting room, and many emotions were lingering; he looked solemn. Anxiety, fear, anger, shock, and disbelief. Even shame and guilt that were buried deep within was starting to surface.

"Mr. and Mrs. Pointer," immediately Cassandra sat forward in her chair and attentively focused on the doctor. Ruth and Charles looked up and in unison said, "Yes."

Dr. Carsman began to explain, and the family held onto his every word. He spoke quickly and as a matter of fact, "Robert is out of surgery and will remain in intensive care. He has a penetrating head wound, and we believe we have removed all the lead pellets. He's receiving antibiotics and we'll continue to keep him sedated for several days as we monitor his brain activity and vitals. We've done everything we know to relieve any pressure inside the skull. If the shot would not have come from such a far distance and had been a direct shot, we wouldn't be having this conversation. The next few weeks will be critical in determining the severity of the injuries to the brain, and he will remain in a medically induced coma so his brain can rest. He miraculously survived the blood loss, his vitals are weak, but stable. So right now it's touch and go. I recommend quiet visitation and not a lot of activity in the room during visits. Do you all have any questions for me?"

The room was silent, no one could find their voice. Then, Cassandra spoke through her tears, "He's going to be all right, right?"

Dr. Carsman remained steadfast in his tone and answered Cassandra's question the best he could. "It's too soon to tell. You're all welcome to stay here and we'll let you know of any change. Please remember, Robert needs to rest, and I'm sure you all could use a rest. You can plan to see him tomorrow, but not tonight." Dr. Carsman turned and left the family in the waiting room to gather their thoughts and come to terms with the news they had just received.

Ruth and Charles decided to go back home and wait by the phone and come back in the morning to check on their son.

"Charles, I'll drive Sean to his house and meet you back at home," said Ruth.

Charles was usually fine with being dismissed, but this time was different, and he didn't want to be *dismissed*.

"Ruthie, I'll follow you to Sean's, I'd like to check on Caroline and the boys too," he replied.

Ruth just nodded her head in a "yes" motion.

Rose had decided she would stay with her parents until there was more certainty about Robert's condition. After all, he was her brother too, and her parents, well, her daddy would need her. She headed back to the big house on the hill. Cassandra wanted to stay and see her brother, but the doctors weren't going to allow that, so she decided to head back to the marina, Scenic Waters. She was going to have to tell Mary what happened.

It was dark when they left the hospital to head to Sean and Caroline's, and the words the doctor said kept echoing in her head, *If the shot would not have come from such a far distance and been a direct shot, we wouldn't be having this conversation.* What did that mean? That shot would have come from about six feet, it was a close shot. Ruth was trying to put the pieces together as she tried to remember what she wished she could forget, and she couldn't get them to fit. She had no tears left to cry and just stared out the window, seeing nothing as Sean continued to drive. They rode in silence, not even the car radio was turned on.

Turning down the road to Sean's house Ruth remembered making the same turn earlier that morning. Her head throbbed, her chest was tight, and her stomach was in knots. She didn't wish the last several hours on any mother to have the worries of this day's horror. Her son was fighting for his life. Approaching the driveway, it was hard to ignore the yellow tape in black lettering instructing, **DO NOT CROSS.** For a fleeting moment Ruth wondered why Sean and his family were allowed to stay here by the investigators.

Sean parked the car on the side of the road, and he and Ruth walked toward the house where Caroline met them at the door. Charles was close behind, and he parked his car behind Ruth's.

Ruth could hear the movement of the water. The water even seemed restless, maybe feeding off the emotions of the day. The water was rustling in so effortlessly and gently caressing the rocks at the edge of the shore, only to retreat. And tonight, for whatever reason she noticed the movement and the sounds of the water. Maybe she just needed to connect with something that wasn't human. Her senses were heightened, but her emotions prevented her from interpreting them.

Charles and Ruth got Sean and his family settled in; Jack seemed particularly upset, and Joshua didn't seem quite sure of what was happening around him.

"Caroline," said Ruth, "you're all welcome to stay with us for a while if you wish. If you think it might make things easier."

"Thanks, Ruth, I appreciate that, and we may stay with you. But for now, or for tonight at least…we'll see what's best for the boys and go from there. That's what I'm trying to say, I'm sorry. I'm, um, uh, just having trouble putting my words together," answered Caroline.

"I understand," replied Ruth, hugging her daughter-in-law goodnight.

"Thanks, Mom. Thanks, Dad," said Sean, and hugged his parents goodnight.

"Call us no matter what time, day or night, if you need anything," said Ruth, while she and Charles were walking out the front door.

"We will, Mom, promise," said Sean closing the front door.

They didn't stay long, just long enough to give assurances to Sean and his family, and of course tuck in their grandsons. Jack and Joshua thought they were too old to be tucked in, but tonight they welcomed the security and comfort they felt in the togetherness.

Driving home, the silence hovered and threatened. Time confirmed the fact, the sun had set just like every other day. Time was announcing that according to the natural order of things, it would rise again in the morning to debut a new day. Time being out of sync was promising Ruth this day would be endless. Endless to ensure enough light for many secrets and betrayals to manifest themselves from the darkness to truth in their own time.

CHAPTER THREE

"Tragedy Takes Control"

Charles and Ruth arrived home to find Rose preparing dinner and the table in the formal dining room set to perfection, customary of owning a five-star restaurant, The Medallion. Rose hoped the evening could comfort their pain and distress. Most of all, she hoped that her and her mother could remain cordial. It didn't matter if you walked into the dining room from the panel doors of the sitting room or from the panel doors of the kitchen, it was a vision. At first sight there was the magnificent dining room table, which sat twelve, made of cherry wood. High-backed chairs with intricate scroll work in the center of the backs, with cream-colored thick velvet padding. There were usually flowers on the table, but tonight, there would be no flowers. Two beautiful chandeliers hung above the table, from the finial that looked like glistening ribbons hanging down showcased the crystal pendeloques cut in wide teardrop shapes with diamond facets. These pendeloques hung in midair dancing with the light and had a mesmerizing effect on those who entered. The room was carpeted in a light brown with a subtle abstract pattern woven in cream colors throughout. Above the fireplace on display was a captivating oil painting of a gentle flowing stream in a serene woodsy setting. The painting could draw one into a place of peace and tranquility. This was one of Rose's favorite rooms, and she was looking for something, anything to keep her busy.

Rose was a great restaurant manager, she exceled at both positions she held at Pointer Enterprises, but she lacked charisma and natural charm that was so necessary in the entertainment business. In the entertainment business, lacking charisma and natural charm was a nice way of saying, smart but unattractive.

Nonetheless, Ruth was sad the day Rose quit and walked away from Pointer Enterprises to be, just a wife.

Charles was happy to see Rose. After she had gotten married and quit managing The Medallion, she rarely left Springton other than to come home to visit for holidays. He had always hoped that Ruth and Rose would be able to get along better one day, and he was still hoping.

"Rose, where's Mattie?"

"Daddy, I went ahead and sent her home. I thought under the circumstances it might be best," she answered.

Charles had known Mattie since his return from WWII and instead of putting her to work for one of his upcoming companies, he hired her for his housekeeper, and she had been with the Pointer family since it was just a lonely household of one.

Ruth shot a quick disapproving glance in her daughter's direction and wanted to tell her that was not her decision to make, not her house, and she only comes around a couple times a year…but Charles saw that coming and kept his wife in check.

"Yeah, that's probably best, don't you think, Ruthie?"

Rose quickly went back into the kitchen to finish making dinner and avoid any confrontation with her mother.

"Sure, Charles, we haven't seen her since our last family New Year's gathering, she would *know* what is best, I guess."

Charles's thin lips were tightly pressed together, and his beady blue eyes turned cold; he couldn't hide the fact that Ruth's words upset him. He was well aware she was the reason Rose didn't come around much.

"Ruth, give it a rest. She's here and staying with us to help us get through this, just accept it. She's your daughter, your flesh and blood!"

"Charles, I love her, don't think I don't. She's the one who walked away not me," flared Ruth.

Tilting his head and looking in her direction with his eyebrows raised and the wrinkles in his forehead deepening, "Ruth, she got married and has a family of her own. There's nothing wrong with her wanting to be a wife and maybe a mom one day."

When he and Ruth got married he was a multi-millionaire and her ambitions not only birthed their four children but also extended their wealth with the creation of Pointer Enterprises, expanding them from Tanton County into Ridge and Greenco Counties. Ruth wasn't going to let Charles have the last word no matter what was going on around them, she never did.

"Charles, she doesn't have to be just a wife and a mother. She could have so much more. We've worked hard to build Pointer Enterprises and provide a good life for all our children. Does she not want it? Pointer Enterprises is our children's and our grandchildren's legacy."

Charles could not deny that Ruth's ambition had taken him, *them*, further than he ever imagined but he felt that he could separate family and business better than she could.

"Ruth, I'll say this again, she left Pointer Enterprises, not our family. A quick reminder, Pointer Enterprises is our company, not our family," he said firmly.

"Charles, Pointer Enterprises is a family business, hence the word 'family,' and our children have no idea what it took to get here. Running an entertainment business is like living in a fishbowl, and a business needs an owner! The community has to like you to patronize your businesses," replied Ruth.

Charles was gentler in his tone hoping to prevent any further disagreement. "Yes, Ruthie, I agree, but just try to keep in mind that she didn't abandon her family, okay?"

"Fine!" said Ruth, rubbing her forehead and then her eyes.

Dinner was quiet and just the three of them. "Rose, dinner is delicious, and your mother and I are glad you're here," said Charles, trying to set a mood of contentment.

Rose had baked three boneless chicken breasts wrapped in bacon from The Smoke House, and topped them off with Provel cheese, a baked potato, green beans, and dinner rolls. All in all, a simple dinner.

"The table setting is beautiful as well, dear, thank you," said Ruth.

The pleasant aroma of baked chicken and bacon had gone unnoticed.

Rose knew her and her mother would never be close, but she wanted to make an effort too. There was just so much conflict between them. Out of the four children Rose was the closest match to her mother's intelligence and possibly surpassed it. But she wasn't in the pretty people circle and didn't share her mother's ambitions.

During the time she worked for the family business she was stuck in a much coveted corner office with payroll and tax rolls, and even though coveted, she was glad to have given it up and didn't miss it. If there was ever any catting around to be done or a face needed for a Pointer event, Ruth would always take Cassandra. So, to Rose, the perfect coveted corner office was nothing more than a pity move on her mother's part. A payoff, compensation of sorts. That's just how it worked in her family. She felt left out, and her intelligence could never bring her to a logical place of understanding to help her overcome the rejection she had felt in the past. Rose knew that her mother would never understand that she got so tired of hearing, "Oh, aren't you Cassandra's sister?" Or "Look, there's Cassandra's sister. What's her name again?"

The only dance floor Rose was ever twirled around on was the night of her wedding when she and her husband danced. Her thick red hair was fire red, wavy, and unmanageable, almost wiry. Her frame was narrow, and she was tall and skinny. Her face was oblong and her nose, though small, was pointed and broke any smooth lines from her forehead to her chin. In school she was picked on because of her pointy nose, and she hated it. Her pale cheeks were peppered with freckles, and her brown eyes were strong and piercing like her mother's and her lips thin like her fathers. There was no denying that Rose favored her father in looks more than her mother. She never took to wearing much make-up despite her mother's attempts of scheduling makeovers and giving cosmetics for gifts. Neither Ruth nor Cassandra would dare step outside without their perfectly made-up faces.

Even Rose had to admit that her sister Cassandra was beautiful. Cassandra was taller than both of her parents and stood five feet seven inches tall with long black silky hair, that didn't fly away everywhere. Her cheekbones were high, and like her mother her smile was big and bright, her lips full, and she had a small waist. Curves, Cassandra had curves. Her skin tone was smooth and there weren't any freckles on Cassandra's face. She was the spitting image of her mother except Cassandra had deep blue eyes. Many had said that Cassandra's beauty surpassed her mother's, and it was in the eyes. Cassandra's combination of her jet-black hair and blue eyes were undeniably captivating.

All the boys except Matt would pretend to like her to try to get to know Cassandra. Rose fell hard for Matt; he was the love of her life.

Over the years, Rose had coined the phrase, "pretty people." She was insecure in the circle of the "pretty people," and she intimidated those who prided themselves as above that of an average intelligence. It was often hard for her to find a place that she fit in, but it was her struggle, and she did her best not to hang onto those feelings. There was no need really, she was happily married and making a life of her own.

"Any new updates on Robert's condition, Mom?" asked Rose, attempting to break up the obvious tension.

"No, we're hoping he makes it through the night; just seeing him lying there so still, all wrapped up not knowing what tomorrow will bring or how long it will take for recovery, if he'll recover. I just don't know." Ruth's bottom lip quivered when she spoke, and Charles placed his hand on top of hers in silent support.

"Did Sean say what they were fighting about?" asked Rose.

Ruth was moving more food around on her plate. "No, we don't know any of the details yet."

Rose's thoughts moved to her nephews, and she didn't mean to speak out loud but the tragedy was controlling her. "Jack and Joshua were there when it happened, weren't they? Those poor boys," she said.

Neither Ruth nor Charles commented and kept looking down at their plates of food, which had still remained full. Throughout dinner they nibbled, going through the motions.

"Well, Caroline looked good, didn't she?" said Rose, intending for that to be a rhetorical question.

"Rose, if you were a little less judgmental and more ambitious you would be more than just a wife and not have so much time on your hands! I really don't want to talk to about this," said Ruth like those were magic words to stop the conversation.

"Oh really, Mom? So, you're telling me that you haven't seen the bruises on Caroline's face at times and on her arms too? You're telling me that you can deny that Sean has a temper? Accidental or otherwise…"

"That's enough, Rose!" she said with more anger in her voice than she meant too, slamming her fork into her plate making a startling *clanging* noise that caused Rose to shudder. The tragedy was controlling Ruth too.

"Oh, that's right, Mom, we don't talk about that, and if we ignore it, it hasn't really happened, right? And just because I don't sit in a corner office means I have no voice in this family and cannot speak about what I've seen in the past, the not-so-distant past!"

Charles was hoping the conversation wouldn't lead to this, but it was hard for the two of them to be in the same room without some conversation coming up that Ruth didn't want to have. As calmly as he could, Charles spoke up, "Hey you two, let's not do this right now; our focus needs to stay on Robert. We've all had a long day and we're worried out of our minds. We'll find out what happened. Let's just go to bed and start again in the morning."

"Fine!" protested Ruth. "I'm going to draw a hot bath and go to bed. I will not sit in my own house listening to my daughter tell me again how Sean undeservingly gets all the glory, how Cassandra gets paid well to simply throw parties, and how bad she is treated! Not on the day that my son has been shot! I won't have it!" Crying, she threw her napkin in her plate and stormed out of the dining room and marched up the curved staircase while Rose held back tears of her own.

Rose cleared the table and went into the kitchen to wash the dishes and Charles dried, just like when she lived at home and Mattie had the night off.

"Rose, your mother has a lot on her mind, she's really worried about Robert, Sean, Caroline and the boys too. With Thanksgiving coming up and the holiday season, there's a lot to do at Pointer Enterprises. Just go easy on her, okay?"

"Fine, Dad, but this isn't about Mom or Pointer Enterprises, but somehow it always becomes about her and then about the business. No one wants to ask her questions or talk about what happened between Robert and Sean because that was in the past and we must move on. Now, here we are years later, Dad."

Those words stung Charles and he was just as worried as she was.

"I know, my child," he replied. Trying to make his daughter feel better, he quickly added, "Hey, I got a 'fine' from your mother and a 'fine' from you, so that must mean that everything's fine, right!"

Rose laughed a bit at his sarcasm, but her tears still came, and she turned to sob into her father's shoulder. "Will it, Daddy, will it?"

Charles consoled his daughter the best he could and tried to convince himself at the same time answering his sweet Rose, "It will."

After they finished the dishes, Rose turned in herself. For most of the night she lay awake revisiting history and wishing she was back home with Matt in Springton, her safe place.

CHAPTER FOUR

"A Secret Still Kept"

Charles found Ruth the next morning at the breakfast table with her coffee and toast. "Good morning, dear," he said, and kissed her on the cheek. "How you holding up this morning? You tossed and turned all night, not much sleep, huh?"

He poured himself a cup of coffee while Ruth tried to hide the fact she was scouring all the newspapers in print for any scandalous articles about the shooting. It was mentioned in all the major papers but wasn't front page news, and for that she was thankful.

Folding up the newspaper she replied, "No, not really. How about you? You tossed and turned yourself throughout the night."

Nodding his head in agreement he replied, "We both tossed and turned, I guess. It was a hard day," he answered with enough sadness for both of them.

Charles sat down to join her for breakfast and studied his wife for a moment.

"Ruthie, have you found any articles in the newspapers about the shooting? Is there a scandal looming?" he said sarcastically with a mocking twist, making it known to her that he knew what she was doing.

Ruth ignored his tone and answered his question. "No, nothing other than the police had responded to an accidental shooting at the residence of Sean Pointer, Local Business Owner of The Smoke House. You know, Charles, why do they always have to say 'Local Business Owner of such and such'? That just infuriates me. Even if you're not well known in this town but own a business, just have some tragedy happen and it will be announced what business you own. Then everyone can drive up and down the strip and point the finger at the owner's shingle and say 'Hey, did you read about their family in the newspaper this morning!'"

"Now, Ruth, calm down, we have more to worry about than what they print in the papers. At least they said 'accidental shooting,' maybe that means that the police have closed the investigation."

Rose came into the kitchen and sat down for breakfast with her parents.

"Daddy, did I hear you say that it's been ruled an accidental shooting?" she asked with some skepticism.

"No, no. I hope that'll be the case, but that's what was written in the morning papers. I was just telling your mother, who wasn't going through the papers front to back," giving Ruth a quick glance and a wink saying that she had already been forgiven, "that it could be a good sign they reported a response to an accidental shooting."

Rose poured herself a cup of coffee and took the last two pieces of toast on the table. *Who would believe that story about the gun falling on the ground and going off? The golden boy still reigns,* she thought.

"Daddy, are we riding to the hospital together?" she asked, slowly buttering her toast.

"Sure," he answered, and then looked to his wife. "Ruthie, do you want to ride with us?"

Ruth poured herself another cup of coffee. "I do, but I need to go into the office for a bit. How about I meet you both back here?" she replied.

Rose hated feeling this way, but she was glad that it was just going to be her and her dad.

"That all right with you, Rose?" asked Charles.

"Sure, Dad, that's fine."

"Fine, huh?" said Charles.

Rose gave her dad a small smirk. "Yes, Dad, fine."

No sooner than Ruth heard the door close, she grabbed the newspapers again to make sure she had read everything written about that tragic day. Even though the article was short, the office had to be buzzing with gossip.

Thankfully, not even a headline stating "Son of Tanton County Business Man Shot and in Critical Condition" or any other headlines she could see flashing in her mind, "Brother Shoots Brother." The more she thought about this, the worse the headlines got. The worst thing that could happen would be for the newspapers to print a blast from the past and report about the shooting at The Medallion that resulted in a death almost twelve years ago. She wasn't going to overthink this matter, there was nothing in print so nothing to think about. So far, no charges had been filed against Sean, but if that were to change, the Pointers and Pointer Enterprises would see how fickle *her* society could be.

At Scenic Waters, Cassandra had just finished with the high school homecoming parties and was preparing to book their Halloween Party on *The Eclipse* and then move onto Christmas. Scenic Waters found themselves in more of a time crunch during the holidays than The Medallion or Pointer's Inn: they had more activities and shows to contend with. The yacht, christened as *The Crimson Rose*, would host the majority of the Christmas parties. And the river boat, which was really a three-deck showboat christened as *The Eclipsed Entertainer*, would focus on the Christmas shows with headliners. In town the locals called it *The Eclipse.* The Lake Girls were busy with cleaning, maintenance on the boats, food orders, liquor orders, organizing the headliners and stage preparation. Candace, whose nickname was appropriately "Candi," would take the lead and organize the real parties, oversee the amenities and events that made the real money. She would enter the underground and make sure there were enough ludes, cocaine, and matchboxes. She would also check out the latest fads on the party scene that made Scenic Waters the place to be. The Lake Girls were exceptionally busy.

Mary, who was Cassandra's best friend and right-hand girl at the marina, was reading the papers too. Last night was a difficult night for Cassandra, having to tell Mary that Robert had been shot and they weren't sure if he was ever going to be okay. The three of them had bonded over similar childhoods and, before the shooting, were close to leaving everything Pointer behind, and Mary didn't take the news well.

Mary grabbed the newspaper and a pot of coffee and ran to Cassandra's cabin.

"Cassandra, Cassandra, get up!" she hollered, continuing to bang on her door.

"Hang on a minute! For Pete's sake, what time is it, Mary?" yelled back an annoyed Cassandra, and then she immediately felt horrible, her friend was hurting too. Mary's life had been turned upside down.

"Open up, it's about nine a.m.." hollered Mary, still yelling through the door.

A groggy Cassandra opened the door. "Mary! We're never up this early! You better have coffee!" she grumbled.

With a coffee pot in one hand and the newspaper in the other, Mary walked into Cassandra's cabin.

Cassandra poured herself a cup of coffee with one eye open.

"You didn't sleep well, did you, Mary?"

"Of course I didn't! I guess you chased down ludes with bourbon and passed out instead of going to sleep?" Mary spat.

Cassandra rubbed her eyes, yawned, and took a drink of coffee.

"Yeah, that's exactly what I did."

"How many times do I have tell you, Cassandra, that drugs and alcohol, no matter how much you drink or how many pills you swallow, isn't going to change the truth of reality! It'll still be the same when you wake up!" said Mary, lecturing and scolding her friend at the same time.

"I know, I know. I'm sorry. What's happened?"

Mary sat the morning paper on the table pointing to the article she had read. "Look at this, the paper reports the police responded to an accidental shooting at the residence of Sean Pointer. An *accidental* shooting, are you serious?"

Cassandra took the paper to read the short article that had been written.

"See, Cassandra, see? Does that mean the police are going to rule this as an accidental shooting and close the investigation?" asked Mary nervously while Cassandra quietly read the article.

"I don't know about you, Cassandra, but I don't believe for one minute that shotgun hit the ground and went off. I just don't. You said no one would believe that story. Well, it looks like they do! I'm sorry, and I know he's your brother, but I just don't care for Sean. He's arrogant and seems angry all the time. He has everything and a beautiful family. Why does he have such a chip on his shoulder? It makes no sense to me, what's wrong with him!"

Cassandra feared that her friend was right. She was doing her best to hide her anxiety that was creeping into every part of her being. At that moment Cassandra wanted to go back to bed, hide in a bottle of bourbon, and pop ludes until the reality disappeared and she could quiet her anxiety. Her first thought was, *What if the past is repeating itself?* She feared her and Robert wouldn't survive a second round being between their mother and her ambitions.

It was more than Cassandra could bear, and she and Robert both agreed that Mary wouldn't be harmed or affected by the evilness in their family. There must have been something more about this God she always talked about…relied on and believed in, for she had retained her hopefulness and never lost her sweetness. The only thing Cassandra was sure about was the fact Sean had lied about what happened the day of the shooting. It was the lie that he told, and why he told that lie that made Cassandra skittish and unforgiving. She was exhausted and scared to sleep. She was just as scared to be awake for fear of what was coming next. She believed that deception and exploitation were sure to follow.

She glanced over at Mary. Mary had laid her head on her cradling knees, sobbing and rocking back and forth. Cassandra was sure she was praying. Normally Cassandra would interrupt her and tell her to ask her God why they're still suffering and why he allowed all this to happen if he was a good, kind, and loving God. Why won't *her* God deliver them from this life they were born into since they were the innocent ones? Today, Mary was too distraught for her needling.

"Mary, I know it's hard, please try to calm down. If it makes you feel any better, I don't trust Sean either. We're related by blood, but we have nothing in common, or at least I hope we don't. I promise I'll do my best to find out what happened."

"What are we going to do?" cried Mary.

"Hey," said Cassandra, trying to bring her friend back from her downward spiral, "I need you to schedule me all the free time you can. Give some of my clients to the other girls if you can and let them know they can keep them if they want to. I need to be at the hospital."

Mary grabbed the after-party schedule book to begin rearranging.

"Oh, and Mary, I'm going to need you take over my duties such as the payroll and things like that, okay? So, maybe you should give away some of your clients too. Plus, it'll help the girls make a little extra cash to save up for their move. Be sure to stress to them to be prepared to leave. Also, make sure that all the underground purchases are paid in full, we can't have any debt."

Mary looked up from the party book with tears in her eyes. "I can't go see Robert yet, can I? Not without your parents and my parents finding out about me and him…oh, Cassandra! My place is with him, not yours!"

Cassandra circled her arms around Mary's shoulders and Mary let her head fall on her shoulder and her tears roll down her face.

"I know that your place is with Robert, not mine. I'm so sorry, my friend. I'll take you with me to the hospital today and you can see him."

Mary sat up straight and wiped her tears. "No, you're right. I trust you with my life and I trust you with Robert's too. I have to believe he's going to recover, and then we're gonna get the hell outta here like we planned. It just can't happen any other way, it can't…" Her words turned into sobs. "Oh, how I wish we'd left earlier, then this would've never happened to him! I hate everything Pointer! I hate PECC, and I hate this boat!" she screamed.

Mary saw immediately she injured Cassandra with her words. Cassandra was shocked; she never heard Mary speak of so much hate.

"Well, everything Pointer except you and Robert. I'm sorry, I'm so sorry, I didn't mean that, Cassandra, my friend."

"It's okay, I understand. Me and Robert hate everything Pointer too and wished we didn't. We wished there wasn't anything to hate," whispered Cassandra.

In order for there to be nothing to hate, the family clock would have to be turned back many years. Like Mary, she was wishing they'd moved earlier too; they had waited too long.

Mary stood up and had both party book schedules in her hands.

"Cassandra, you go do what you have to do for all three of us and I'll take care of things here. And don't forget, I have some wonderful surprises for you and Robert in our new place!"

Cassandra giggled a bit. Mary had gotten them a house but didn't tell her where and immersed herself in the details of the move. It was Mary's happy place, and she would go there mentally when things got to be too much. Her happiness always overflowed to Cassandra, and then she would pretend to be annoyed by all Mary's chatter. In turn, that just gave her more reason to go on and on. Sometimes Mary's little guessing game would go on for what seemed like hours, dropping hints and giving clues about what it looked like and what she had done lately in preparation for the big move.

"I know, I know, my friend! Now let's get to work on those schedules and be ready when Robert's released!" said Cassandra with some newfound hope.

All of Cassandra's free time that Mary could schedule for her was spent at the hospital with Robert. Caroline was staying close to Jack and Joshua. Rose spent her time between the hospital and the big house on the hill. Sean would spend his time between home and the smoke house. He seemed a little more relaxed now that the police tape had been removed from his driveway and he wasn't getting a daily visual reminder of the accident.

As fate would have it, according to the police report, it was ruled an accidental shooting, and that too brought Sean and the family relief.

Cassandra, however, was drowning in fear, and her paranoia was fueled by family history. No matter what anyone told her, she knew this was no accident.

The family continued to do what they had always done, working and avoiding any real conversation of any matter that would stain the family's public reputation. The entertainment business and its presentation seemed to be second nature to all of them, even if they didn't realize it. They had learned to hide what they didn't want to be seen.

CHAPTER FIVE

"Haunted By Past Emotions"

Ruth could hear the whispers approaching her corner office. "Mrs. Pointer, I'm sorry about Robert. I, *we* all hope he'll be all right," said Lauren.

Ruth was adjusting to her and her family's new reality, but still hoping to get a full day's work in.

"Thank you, Lauren, I appreciate that. Has Sean come in yet?"

Lauren was nervous trying to hide her obvious distraction and did her best to switch her focus back to business.

"Oh, yes, he's waiting for you in your office."

Sean was standing at the window when Ruth walked into her office.

"Good morning, son," she said, standing next to him, looking over the property of The Medallion.

"How's your family holding up?"

Sean continued to look straight ahead at the end stages of The Medallion's construction.

"The best that can be expected, I guess. How about you and Dad, how you two holding up?"

"Same as you all, the best that can be expected."

"Well," said Sean, changing the subject, "the expansion of The Medallion is almost done, isn't it?"

"Yeah, next year at this time we'll be hosting ballroom dances, festive and holiday parties, private parties, and wedding receptions," she answered with pride.

"Well, it's been a long time coming, and I'm sure you'll be relieved when it's complete. The French doors were a nice touch, I like 'em," he replied with approval.

"Yeah, the French doors were one of my favorite touches too. The fountain for the center of the patio will be installed tomorrow. The light fixtures will be here this week, and the fireplace will be put in early next week. Oh, and just wait, son, until you see the chandelier that's going to be hung."

Sean knew this had been his mother's baby for the last five years, and she spared no expense. It was a nice set up sitting in the square of town. The third floor of The Medallion was the massive living space, which Robert and Cassandra called the penthouse. The second floor hosted the corporate offices of Pointer Enterprises, and the first floor was, of course, the restaurant and all its glory.

"I'm really excited about it, Sean. This expansion is going to give The Medallion amenities that no other restaurant has in town, and the woodsy grounds behind here provides the perfect back drop for an evening on the town, don't you agree?"

Sean scanned the woodsy grounds and he could see the path that led to the two commercial icehouses; they too had been remodeled, added onto for meeting rooms. They looked more like little houses these days with porches. Rustic and nostalgic, they added nicely to the grounds. Sean chuckled a little as the icehouses held his gaze.

"You know, Mom, I still remember all the fighting you and Dad did over the restoration of those icehouses. Dad wanted to demolish them."

"Oh, I remember that all too well myself. But see how well it turned out? It's going to do nothing but bring a certain charm and ambience to the place."

Sean shook his head. "Yeah and don't forget that our construction company did the remodel as a testament showing what that company could do," he replied mockingly.

"Knock it off!" she said, playfully slapping him on the shoulder. "You know I'm right, and your father knows it too! And yes, it was a nice start up to the construction and excavating side of the business!"

"Okay, yeah, Mom, whatever you say!" Sean said with a chuckle.

"Well, I say!" replied Ruth.

They got down to business and signed bonus checks and checked timelines for the smoking of the turkeys. Finalized the delivery schedule and then both decided to call it a day.

"I'll see you later, Mom."

"All right, son, I love you, and give my love to Caroline and my grandsons."

"I will," he replied, walking out the door.

This was supposed to be the best time of the year for Ruth, for the whole family. This tragedy with Robert was heart wrenching. In these past few months, she was having a hard time being the vice president of Pointer Enterprises and being a mother. Good sleep was hard to come by, and the stress was beginning to take its toll on her physically. She was fatigued, noticing weight loss, back pain, and swelling in her legs.

Ruth needed to slow down, and she knew it. The winter months were important for her and her family. This year, more so than any other year, she would need the winter to recuperate from the tourist season and come to terms with the shooting of her youngest son. Retirement was something she had been contemplating over the last couple of years and passing the torch to Sean.

It was difficult to keep her mind on the Christmas parties, ball gowns, fine jewelry, furs, crystal stemware, and champagne. This was her favorite time of year, she got to mingle in society and reap the spoils of her work. The Medallion was the most sought-after place in town for company Christmas parties, and Robert was the chef in the kitchen that had made it happen these past few years. At that thought, she jotted down a note to schedule a meeting with the kitchen manager about a chef. She didn't want to think on that thought any further, she knew Robert would never be returning to The Medallion and wasn't ready to face that reality yet.

Now sobbing, she stepped out of that world into the future she was so ambitiously building and imagined the property decorated like a mini winter wonderland all the way down to the ice houses. It was time to begin preparing for the holiday decorations. It was time to begin planning The Pointer New Year's Eve Party that was held each year in the "Queen City," Springton at Pointer's Inn. It was a formal event, and everybody who was anybody was at this party. Politicians, bankers, and attorneys were comped and bought and through all the glamour none were the wiser.

Times were continuing to change, and she was getting older. The harder she worked, the more things she found she had to do, and she was exhausted. It wasn't often that her desk would be cluttered. The inbox that sat on the left corner of her desk was so full it was overflowing, and her outbox contained only what had to be completed. It was the wrong time of year for a scandal, and the time had come that would prove whether or not her children could take hold of their legacy. It was still unknown what her fickle society would think about another shooting in the family. Surely, it wasn't forgotten. Would they condemn or console? Would the holiday parties and their glamour be able to mask any gossip and prevent the possibility of being ostracized in the business community and her society? After all, Rose had washed her hands of working for Pointer Enterprises, and even though she was the brains behind Matt, he was the face of Pointer's Inn. Cassandra hid from reality in drugs and drink. Sean was obviously still hot headed and reckless, and Robert may never be the same again if he survived. *What were those boys fighting about this time?*

When Ruth arrived home, Charles and Rose were in the sitting room playing a game of chess and Mattie was busy in the kitchen. Ruth took comfort in the fact Mattie was still there, it might help curb a bit of conversation and help to avoid any unwanted questions or comments from Rose. The panel doors of the sitting room were open, and Ruth watched the two of them for a moment, remembering all those years ago when Charles tried to teach their children to play chess. Cassandra wanted nothing to do with it, she preferred to spend her time playing the grand piano that sat in the bay window. Sean was a hurried boy and didn't have the patience to sit and strategize, he preferred being outside hunting and fishing. Robert was indecisive as a child and chess over-challenged him. Rose, the valedictorian of her high school class and Phi Thetta Kappa president for four years, took to the game like it was made for her to play; her and her daddy would bond over chess for many years. The chessboard was an antique chessboard made of rare combinations of black wood, red woods, and walnut. The design of this beautiful board and its pieces were just as complex as the strategy of the game, and Rose and Charles were really the only two who appreciated it.

"Hey, Ruthie," Charles said over his shoulder. "Looks like Rose is going to beat her old man at this game!" Rose beamed; they were both good strategists.

Ruth smiled a small smile. "Well, darling, that is the plan in life, is it not? That eventually the student surpasses the teacher?"

Charles chuckled. "Yes, dear, that's when you know you have succeeded!"

He looked at Rose with his blue eyes twinkling, he had been contemplating his last move for quite some time now knowing he had lost this game. Never would he admit it, but he was really trying to decide how he wanted to lose. He made his move, and then Rose excitedly made hers, "Checkmate, Daddy! Oh, the sweet taste of victory!" exclaimed Rose with delight, reaching both of her arms high above her head as all champions do.

"Ugh! All right, all right, but I demand a rematch, little girl!" replied a proud father, adopting a demeanor that he let her win, which was not the case.

There were no new updates on Robert, he was still weak but stable. "Hey you two, are we going to ride to the hospital together tomorrow? Sean is going to visit Robert."

Rose continued to place the chess pieces back in their original positions, and even though that was the loser's job, she enjoyed doing things for her dad. Besides, she never had the heart to make her dad put the pieces back in their original positions after she had won. She couldn't help but think, *It's been weeks and now Sean wants to go see Robert?*

She decided to keep her thoughts to herself and instead just said, "Sure, Mom."

Charles was pleased that his daughter had decided to ride to the hospital with them in the morning. Rose knew there wasn't a car in the world big enough for her and her mother and wasn't looking forward to it. It was obvious her dad was pleased, and he did just lose at chess. One day, one ride. That would be *fine*, she would endure. After all, it wasn't about her, it was about Robert.

Dinner was just sub sandwiches that night, something quick and light that didn't require all three of them to sit at the dining room table, meaning less conversation. At nine p.m. the Pointer household turned off the lights and went to bed. All tossing and turning, struggling to sleep and then waking again.

Ruth was the first one up as usual the next morning, and when Charles and Rose entered the dining room they found her drinking her coffee and scouring the newspaper again. Charles just went to the coffee pot and didn't say a word.

Rose couldn't help herself and decided to start the day off with her mother, head to head and toe to toe.

"Anything interesting in the paper we should know about, Mom?" she asked like she was an announcer making a subtle dig at her mother.

"No, Rose, and now don't you start in on me too. Someone has to make sure what is being said out there for the public to read. As much as you would like to think it doesn't matter what other people think, it does. And that's for you to hear too, Charles!"

Charles chimed in so the conversation could be ended before it began, "C'mon, ladies, drink up! Visiting hours are starting soon, unless you prefer to drink that crappy coffee at the hospital." Mother and daughter took their cue, gathered their coats and purses to leave. On that crisp and cold morning as fall was turning to turn to winter, they set off to the hospital.

Cassandra had sat quietly by Robert's bedside throughout the night and wondered if this God she heard Mary talk about was watching over him. Cassandra knew of church and Sunday school, it was hard not to growing up in the Bible belt, but it wasn't part of her life as a child or even now as an adult. The last time she was in a church was when Rose and Matt got married, and before that was when Sean and Caroline got married. She was pretty sure the church weddings were really for the public image of her family and nothing else. Their public image of being a religious family was based on the amount of money they contributed to the local church and its causes; it appeared the Pointer family was very religious. Cassandra was confused about religion; to her it seemed something like a grocery list, items that were bought and paid for. On the list you would find things like forgiveness, gratefulness, humility, joy, miracles, and peace. Right now she wanted to purchase a miracle for her brother.

Cassandra was tired, and it showed when she looked up to see her parents and her sister enter the room. Her beautiful blue eyes were red and puffy from crying, and the dark circles under her eyes brought about a grayness dampening their vibrancy. Good sleep for Cassandra was hard to find, and when she found it in ludes and bourbon, it still wasn't a good sleep. She would awake in a fog having to piece her reality together again, causing herself more pain.

"Cassandra, honey, when was the last time you got a good night's sleep?" asked Ruth.

Cassandra looked at Robert lying there, his head still wrapped in bandages, and you could see his belly slowly moving up and down as the machine pushed air into his body. The ventilator was mechanic in its operation and its noises were startling. Just when you thought its mechanical operation wasn't going to bring the oxygen fast enough it would beep a steady tone that mimicked a flatline tone. Then, it would lead you to think the whole machine shut down and quit working. Right before your panic would be able to overtake you, there would be a startling loud, slow *whoosh* of air, then nothing. Again, another slow *whoosh*, in perfect timing. Then nothing. That was the only movement Robert made, and he was in perfect rhythm with the machine. Cassandra sat next to his bedside many nights and the startling tones of the ventilator would fill her with paralyzing fear. The alarming sound of the *whoosh* of air shocked her own heart to pound and flutter and her throat would become tight. Then, she would breathe a sigh of sweet relief, only to be paralyzed again with fear. Abruptly, she would be shocked back to reality and hurled deeper into her nightmare of what happened and the wonder of what's still to come.

Cassandra looked up at her mother. "I'm okay, Mom. The doctor should be in shortly."

The family gathered around his bedside and they all had so many questions. Ruth loved both her sons so much and wished there wasn't all this hostility between the two.

The door of Robert's room opened, and it was Dr. Carsman. Behind Dr. Carsman followed Sean and Caroline.

"Good morning," said Dr. Carsman.

Cassandra looked up at Dr. Carsman with her big blue eyes that had dimmed. "How is he? Do you have any news?" she asked.

Dr. Carsman stood looking at Robert's medical chart and reviewing scans. He started to speak, and he was speaking slower than he had before.

"Well," said Dr. Carsman, "he's been in a medical induced coma for fourteen days. He's stable, and we feel it's time to reverse the process. Today we'll begin to withdraw the drugs and continue to monitor his brain activity and vitals. He's suffered a severe trauma, and as we bring him out of the coma we'll begin to know more. He'll continue to remain in intensive care and visitation will be restricted."

Cassandra felt like she was just punched in the gut; she knew that meant her visitation would be even less. *Oh, Robert, will we ever go swimming again? Will I ever get to be maid of honor or best girl when you marry Mary? Will you and Mary ever see the sunset over lake, sharing a bourbon again? Why did this happen? How did it happen? Why did Sean lie? Please, big brother, please wake up to be your old self.* These thoughts ran through her mind and she didn't hear the rest of what Dr. Carsman had to say, she had descended deeper into the darkness.

Caroline felt there was hope, hope that Robert would wake up and make a full recovery. He was so still and was one with the breathing machine. She was scared to death of every tomorrow. She wanted more than anything for Robert to be whole again.

The color disappeared from Sean's face and he couldn't make eye contact with anyone in the room. Since the day of the shooting he hadn't been able to face Robert either. He had the Pointer name, but he was a haunted man. The feelings of anger toward his mother ran deep. His animosity toward his father who forced him to marry a pregnant Caroline or be disinherited had festered over the years; and yet still today, his bewilderment of the man he called "Dad" always left him with more questions. Some days he wanted to scream, *Who the hell are you, anyway?* It's not that he didn't love his children or his family, he did, there just never seemed to be a choice. He wanted so desperately to wake up from this nightmare, and when he would wake up, his anger and rage wouldn't be part of who he had become. To turn back the hands of time is what he wanted to do. Since he couldn't do that, he had to do what he had to for his family.

Charles was speaking out loud and not to any one person, "This is good news!"

The sprits in the room had lifted.

Cassandra thought it was good news too, but that should also mean visitation shouldn't be restricted.

"Dr. Carsman, when will he wake up?" asked Ruth with an abundance of hope in her voice.

Dr. Carsman ignored the hope that was in the room and remained steadfast in his matter-of-fact language.

"It could be anywhere from forty-eight to seventy-two hours, we just don't know. For now, I ask that you all go home and let him rest, or you're all more than welcome to remain here in the waiting room and as soon as I have an update I'll let you know."

Cassandra spoke up and asked the question everyone was afraid to ask, "Dr. Carsman, he's going to wake up, right?"

Ruth, Charles, Sean, and Caroline sat very still, not knowing how to prepare themselves for the answer and wondering if they could handle the answer if it was something they didn't want to hear.

"It's still touch and go. I'm sorry I don't have better news," Dr. Carsman replied. With that, he turned and left the room, and the family made their way to the waiting room.

Sean and Caroline left to go home that afternoon to be there when the boys came home from school and the rest of the family stayed into the evening.

"Cassandra, honey," said Ruth "why don't you come back to the house and get some rest and we'll come back in the morning."

"Thanks, Mom, but I'm gonna go ahead and stay here for the night. I just don't want to leave him."

"I know, sweetheart. All right, you stay here then, and call if you need us?"

"I will, Mom," said Cassandra.

The last place Cassandra wanted to be was under the roof at the big house on the hill with her parents and her sister.

It had been four days and Robert still had not come out of his coma. Throughout the night, Cassandra would sneak into his room and sit quietly in the dark. She wasn't going to abandon him now and was hoping he wouldn't leave her, that he would fight to come back. Cassandra talked with her brother, saying his name and holding his hand. She would give him a hug and kiss his bandaged forehead every morning and every night, hoping he would wake up to touch, but he didn't. Robert and Cassandra were devoured by their mother's ambition. Robert was fifteen, and she was a young fourteen. Cassandra nodded off, and Robert lie just as still as he did before. Without the ventilator and its startling noises, it was quiet in the room. Some nights Cassandra would be startled awake hearing the sound of the ventilator in her dreams.

The bandages he was covered in left her to her own visuals of her imagination. Torn and ripped skin discolored, a color gray mixed with olive green because of infection and lead poisoning. A sagging cheek, droopy jaw, and shattered teeth. A shaved head and deep, deep wounds with bloody staples to hold his head together. The deep wounds would be the color of red, almost black from the drying of the blood and maybe some scabbing. There would be heavy bruising that caused the blackness of his skin. Though, no matter how hard she tried, she couldn't imagine what his eye looked like. Surely, they could replace that with a glass eye? He could just wear an eye patch, it would add to his rugged good looks, maybe? It didn't matter where Cassandra's imagination took her, the bandages couldn't hide the brutality he'd endured.

Cassandra was in a dead sleep and jolted awake by a raspy groan, or maybe a cough? It took her a moment to determine if she was dreaming of the sounds of the ventilator that she went to sleep to so many nights or other sounds that had started to haunt her sleep. *Oh! Was he waking up?*

Immediately at Robert's side, "Robert, it's Cassandra, I'm here, I'm here! Shhh, shhh, don't try to talk. You've been in a coma," she whispered, placing her hands on top of his and patting them gently.

"Don't try to move, okay? You're in the hospital, in the intensive care unit. Do you remember what happened? Robert, you were shot. You have a patch over your right eye and you may be deaf in your right ear. Take it easy, I'm going to go get the doctor and I'll be right back."

His one was eye was darting back and forth; he couldn't focus and the sounds he heard painfully echoed. It looked like he was still wanting to move. Cassandra was afraid to leave him at that moment. Again, he tried to move his arms, and the more she tried to make him lie still, the more agitated he got. His flailing arms were weak and shaking because of the muscle loss and they fell hard to the bed, and his IV was pulled out.

"Robert, please! Oh please, be still. Hang on, I've got to get the doctor. I'll be right back! I promise"

In a frenzy she ran out into the hall to get a nurse, to get the doctor, to get anybody! *Robert was surely awake, wasn't he?* she thought.

"Nurse, nurse! It's my brother, I think he's waking up!"

The nurses came running, and once again you heard throughout the halls, "Dr. Carsman to ICU, Dr. Carsman to ICU."

It wasn't long and Dr. Carsman was walking at a fast pace down the hall to Robert's room, his white doctor's coat tails trailing in the air behind him.

"Ms. Pointer, please go to the waiting room and I'll be with you as soon as I have an update," ordered Dr. Carsman.

The nurse took Cassandra by the arm and escorted her to the waiting room. Cassandra thought maybe the doctor wasn't pleased she had snuck into Robert's room that night. While she was being ushered to the waiting room, she could hear Dr. Carsman's matter-of-fact tone speaking loudly to Robert. "Robert, it's Dr. Carsman. I know you're agitated, and you may feel like you're between two worlds right now and that's normal, okay? We're gonna give you something for the pain and to help you rest."

Exhausted and confused she sat in the waiting room trying to catch her breath. In most families loved ones would be ringing everyone's phone giving them the good news or at least calling with an update. Cassandra struggled deciding whether or not to call her parents. Apprehensively, she walked to the payphone down the hall and deposited a dime and heard it drop, deposited the second dime and slowly dialed her parents' number.

Charles and Ruth were lightly sleeping, tossing and turning, and both were jolted awake when the phone rang so early. Ruth immediately thought the worst, that Robert had died. She was having difficulty connecting to her reality and was in fear of who was on the other end of the phone.

Charles immediately picked up the phone, "Hello."

"Dad, it's me, Cassandra. I think Robert's trying to wake up, the doctors are in there with him now," she said all in one breath.

"All right, we're on our way," he replied back just as quickly with his words.

Charles hurriedly put the phone back onto its cradle and threw his covers off.

"Ruth, get dressed. That was Cassandra and she thinks Robert's waking up."

Ruth let out a sigh, not realizing she had been holding her breath during the time Charles was on the phone.

"Thank goodness," she said, exhaling in a raspy voice.

"Yes, this is good news. I'll get Rose and bring the car around and meet you downstairs."

Ruth was breathlessly rushing around grabbing clothes and getting dressed, "Okay, I'll be right down."

Upon arrival, Charles, Ruth, and Rose found Cassandra in the waiting room. The doctors were with Robert. Cassandra and Rose barely spoke when in the same room together unless it involved a Pointer Enterprises matter, and this grave situation didn't change that.

Ruth rushed to her youngest. "Any word yet? Is Robert awake?"

"I think so, I hope so, I, uh, surely he is. Did anyone call Sean and Caroline?"

"No, it's best to let them sleep and stay with the boys. When we know more we'll let them know," quickly answered Ruth.

The four waited in the waiting room and time was still out of sync for the Pointer family. Again, they were so anxious but sitting so still; the eerie silence had returned. No one really knew what was happening in Sean's little family of four, and their absence was conspicuous. It was the early hours of the morning and they were trying to meet the new day amongst all the darkness. Ruth was feeling the devastation of a mother watching her son fight for his life and was hoping for the best. The last place she ever wanted to be was in the middle of her two sons, and she was afraid she had found herself in that same position again. Her fight-or-flight response was raging within. Charles was crushed. Robert was his son that was most like him. Robert looked like him and they shared many of the same mannerisms. Their time as father and son was cut short when Robert was only fifteen and he became a man without his guidance. Charles had felt robbed of his youngest son and struggled with that for many years. Charles's pride had controlled his thoughts and actions in the past. Now, in the future, there was no way his son would be taken from him a second time. As for Rose and Cassandra, their thoughts were on Sean, and both had many questions. They wanted to know why Sean lied, and they wanted to know what the fight was about. They all shared the same feeling of relief that Robert had awaken, but what was coming next brought much uncertainty. They were all lost in their thoughts of what the future was going to hold for each of them, drowning in emotions that felt all too familiar.

It seemed like an eternity had passed before Dr. Carsman finally found the family in the waiting room of the ICU.

"Mr. and Mrs. Pointer, your son is awake. He'll be groggy and a little confused for the next couple of days, but I see no reason why he can't have visitors. Keep your visits short, he'll be heavily sedated. For the next few days we'll be running several tests to determine the next course of action. We're fearful he has the potential of a possible stroke so we're going to continue monitoring him closely. Again, as we know more, we'll let you know."

Before leaving the room, "Cassandra," said Dr. Carsman, "Robert seems to be trying to say your name."

Not saying a word, she immediately got up and walked toward Robert's room. Ruth went to follow her and Dr. Carsman stopped her. "One visitor at a time, please."

Rose watched her mother closely. Knowing this had to be infuriating to her and yet she found it amusing that not only had Cassandra surpassed her mother in beauty and had youth on her side, now she was the first one to visit her son... *Interesting,* she thought to herself. Then she saw it, Cassandra turned and looked at her mother. It was intense when Ruth and Cassandra's eyes met. It was almost like both of them had *checkmate.* For a fleeting moment her mother and her sister eclipsed, and Rose was sure that Cassandra would do what she always did and back down when up against her mother, but she didn't. Hiding what she didn't want to be seen, Ruth returned to her chair and sat down next to Charles.

What just happened? thought Rose. Cassandra had her mother's aggressiveness, but whether or not she had her resolve, only time would tell.

Robert seemed calmer when she entered his room, and his one eye tracked her movements all the way up to his bed. She thought she saw some recognition in his eye. "Robert, it's me, Cassandra. Are you in any pain?" she said softly.

His left eye full of uncertainty, and fear was wandering around the moderately lit room, and he was having a hard time keeping his eye open, but the signs of confusion and agitation were lessening. Pieces of the shooting were playing in his mind like a filmstrip, just fragments of the last couple of months were in his memory.

There wasn't much to see in the hospital room. The walls were beige and bare. There was no television, and the room was smaller than the others, equipped with machines and stainless-steel carts.

Her brother, once so strong now couldn't move and was so weak. He was trying to talk and his speech was raspy, slurred, and broken, "Soe, om, Sean…"

"Robert, please don't try to talk yet."

"Ja Ja, Ja oe." Robert continued to try to get his words out, causing him pain, and his frustration was growing.

"Are you trying to say 'Joe'? You mean Uncle Joe?" she asked, confused.

Is he trying to tell me what the fight was about? But what did Joe have to do with it? she thought.

"Robert, I need you to remain calm, okay? I'll be here every day, I promise, and we'll get through this together. Joe, Anne, and Piper are back in French Town at Grandma and Grandpa's. You rest and regain your strength."

With that promise from his sister and some obvious help from his medications, he began to quiet. He did his best to keep his one eye open, struggling to stay in his awakened state. He would look around trying to get an awareness of what was happening around him. Bits and pieces of information and then thoughts would flood his mind that couldn't be real, but it was right in front of him. He couldn't figure out why Optimus Prime would have a front green housing, when it was normally red. Maybe because he bled so much it turned red. The one who saved him had to be Optimus Prime. Optimus was wearing green the last time he saw him, he was sure of it.

Cassandra noticed he was blinking rapidly, and she held his hand hoping to bring him some comfort.

"Robert, what is it? Are you in any pain?"

He was able to steady his gaze on his sister and his head fell a little closer on his pillow in her direction. Then the fragments of his reality began to play in his mind again, he did his best to stay in his reality to remember. He would succeed for short periods, but his mind wasn't completely his own. Heavily medicated, he began to drift off. Cassandra had been his one constant for the last few months, and he did recognize her.

Still holding his hand, Cassandra did her best to gain control over her emotions and hide her anguish. "Robert, tomorrow will be better, I promise. Mom, Dad, and Rose are here and they want to see you."

Robert lay still and closed his eye and Cassandra held his hand until he was asleep before telling everyone else to come in and see him.

There he lay, innocent in the past and paid a price for the guilty. He lay in this bed today innocent and vulnerable. When the guilty and responsible would enter his room, there he would lie.

CHAPTER SIX

"Thanksgiving Day"

Thanksgiving Day was here, and with Robert in the hospital Charles and Ruth decided the family should spend Thanksgiving morning at the hospital. Rose's husband Matt came to Braxton and joined Rose for the family Thanksgiving. Cassandra spent the night again at the hospital and was looking forward to seeing Sean visit her brother. The sisters were disappointed when there was no sign of Sean and Caroline.

Rose sat back and decided if Cassandra didn't ask where Sean was, she was going to. Neither sister believed their brother's story, and both were curious to see the two of them interact. However, both sisters also knew this was one of those things that shouldn't be talked about. The differences between the sisters were obvious and their similarities overlooked.

"Mom," said Cassandra, "where's Sean, Caroline, and the boys? Didn't you tell them we were meeting here before going to the house?"

Ruth was sitting by Robert's bedside holding his hand, and Rose was curious to hear the answer just like her sister.

"I did tell them we'd be meeting here, but we have to be understanding, this is hard on Sean and his family too," she indignantly answered her daughter's question.

The two sisters shared a glance of the same sentiment and Cassandra thought to herself, *And here we are worrying about the golden boy.* She decided to let that go for now and was thankful her brother had awoken, and that was really all she wanted for Thanksgiving.

Rose thought to herself, *Interesting.*

It was an exhausting day for Robert, and with his medication he drifted off to sleep and the nurses said it would be best if he were left to rest. He may not have grasped the fact it was Thanksgiving Day, but he knew he wasn't alone. He also knew that he was vulnerable. The only one missing was Mary and he hadn't forgotten his one true love. The family had been given hope this Thanksgiving. There were still many unanswered questions, but Robert's prognosis seemed to be better than the day before and the day before that.

Thanksgiving Day at the big house on the hill was set to start around four p.m. that afternoon. Holidays were big in the Pointer family, and this year there was an emptiness that was stirring in everyone: The desolate absence of Robert. The void in the atmosphere during the holiday season had been countered with the gleam of hope they'd all received this morning. He was awake and had survived the shooting. Usually, the Pointer family Thanksgiving entailed boasting about sales, profits, projections, and plans for the upcoming year. They would talk about the parties, holiday shows on *The Eclipse,* and the big Christmas party to come at The Medallion.

Sean was always prideful about his work at The Smoke House and what a man's man he was managing their campground, Cornerstone Campground. Jack and Joshua would hang onto every arrogant word and snide remark their father would make, and each year it seemed they were getting to be more and more like their father.

Matt even joined in the competition with the success and hosting the New Year's Eve party each year in none other than the "Queen City" of the Ozarks. Being in Springton, he felt like he'd been pole vaulted to the top of the food chain. Matthew, too, had married well.

Cassandra never boasted much about Scenic Waters, her numbers were always high.

Thanksgiving told who was who in the family and "who was better." Cassandra thought it was all really appalling. Appalled they were all born into a position and yet had to fight for it. Appalled they were loved based on merits and not being a daughter or a son, an individual. Appalled they were part of a plan, not part of a family. It seemed Cassandra was always destined for the job at Scenic Waters. It was always planned for Rose to sit at the right hand of the president of the company, and one day that would be Sean. What Robert's position turned out to be was to save the golden boy at his own demise.

The holidays were the time of year that successes and failures were announced for all to hear and then followed by a promotion or demotion. It didn't make any sense to Cassandra—this conflicting viewpoint was hardly selfless and always had nasty consequences. It left her with insecurities and unable to determine her own self-worth or explore her individuality. Hopefully, there wouldn't be any of that healthy competition this year. That's what *"Daddy"* called it, *healthy competition*. None of the children could fail, that would reflect badly on Charles and Ruth. On the other hand, the children couldn't be too successful and upstage their parents. It was a delicate balance.

They would always have drinks and appetizers in the sitting room. It had gotten chilly in the Ozarks quickly and the fireplace in the sitting room was blazing. It was beautiful really, and created an atmosphere this family just couldn't. Ironic in a way, thought Cassandra, *A fire is so beautiful and warms you when you are cold. Calms you as it brings tranquility and pleasantries to the senses. Speaks to you as it cackles, but if you get too close, you'll get burned.*

Cassandra would usually play a few tunes on the piano that showcased many photos of what appeared to be a close-knit family, all with their commanded but natural-looking smiles. With Robert being in prison for so many years, there were few pictures of him after the age of fifteen. This year she had no music to play, it had left her while she watched her brother fight for his life, and no one asked her to play. She would have foregone these family parties if she felt she could, but it wasn't in her best interest, and she knew it.

Rose and Matt were sitting by the fireplace catching up on the time they had spent apart. Matt was a handsome young man with thick flowing dirty blond locks that would tease you when it brushed against his collar. His light-colored brown velvety eyes seemed to look into your soul, and he could connect with anyone. Matt was a preppy dresser, and a suit and tie fit him well. For Cassandra's taste he was a little too cocky, but he was smart to marry Rose. He doted on her, her connections and her money. Then when she vacated her coveted corner office, Matt moved in. Regardless of the "just a wife" snubs that Rose would receive, it appeared she was content these days, finding her place, her niche. Rose had her own big house on the hill, but she didn't have the marina. It confused Cassandra that Rose still felt slighted in any way.

Ruth and Charles were sitting opposite of each other sipping brandy on the ivory-colored couches. A glass coffee table with solid brass legs sat between the two couches creating an elegant gathering place. The room was formal but comfortable, yet there was no denying it had a stiffness and a sophistication to it. It was a room where music was played, chess games were commenced, and the fireplace danced.

Cassandra remained seated alone looking out the bay window. *I wonder if humiliation to be served cold and jealousy to be served hot is on the menu this year?*

"Oh, look! Sean, Caroline, and the kids are here," Cassandra said walking to the front door. Opening the door, Cassandra hollered out, "Happy Thanksgiving!"

Jack and Joshua ran to their aunt and gave her hugs; she hugged them back and kissed them on their cheeks. Joshua was thrilled, and so was Jack, but he was at the age that he was almost too old for kisses on the cheek from his aunt. With all that had been going on with their Uncle Robert, today they were well received.

Caroline hugged Cassandra, and as awkward as it was, Sean bent down and kissed her on the cheek and went into the sitting room. They all said their "Hello's" and greeted one another as they gathered. The conversation was kept light, and the focus was on what the boys had been up to in school and a lot of mastered small talk.

Sean poured himself a brandy and sat next to his mom.

"Mom, any news on Robert?" he asked without explaining his absence earlier that morning.

Ruth looked at Sean for a moment, wondering why he hadn't spent more time visiting his brother at the hospital. Maybe he made the right decision. After all, he was the one that accidently shot him. A terrible tragedy the whole family would have to come to terms with eventually. Swirling her brandy and trying to make sense of her confounded thoughts, she decided it was best she not ask why he and his family didn't join them at the hospital that morning.

"Yes, this Thanksgiving brings us hope. Robert is out of his coma and is responsive. He has a long road ahead of him, no doubt, but for the first time in weeks we have something good to hold onto. They're watching him now in case of a stroke or something like that; hopefully that won't happen and he'll continue to get stronger. Isn't that wonderful?"

It took Sean a moment to understand what he'd heard, not that he wasn't happy that Robert had survived and was continuing to get stronger, but he had to wonder just what would Robert remember. Would he remember? Sean looked over at his two boys proudly telling grandpa, their aunts, and Uncle Matt what they had been up to in school, enjoying a moment of normalcy. Sean's eyes reflected regret looking across the room at his two boys. He felt like he had the world on his shoulders and knew he was a man in a terrible position.

"Sean? Son, you look like you're a million miles away."

Sean realized he may have been lost in his thoughts for too long.

"I said isn't that wonderful news?"

"Yeah, Mom, that's great news," he answered.

"I know it's hard, but we'll get through this, I promise. Are you doing all right? Is there anything I can do for you?" Ruth asked.

"Not right now, and yes, it's really great news that Robert came out of his coma and I hope he'll be all right," replied Sean.

"I know that, dear."

"I was just happy to see genuine smiles on my sons' faces," said Sean, doing his best to explain his distraction.

"Me too, son. Me too. It's amazing to see how my grandsons have grown. Look at Jack, he'll be driving soon and had a wonderful season of varsity football. What an accomplishment. And Joshua, sweet Joshua. He may just be the valedictorian of his class! Wouldn't that be something?"

"Yeah, following in the footsteps of his grandma, huh?"

"And what would be wrong with that? You're looking at the future of Pointer Enterprises, you know," said Ruth playfully.

"Okay, Mom, whatever you say!" he responded back in the same manner.

"Well, I say!" said Ruth, using her magic words again that would make it so.

They headed into the dining room and sat in their same seats as the year before and the year before that. Ruth at one end of the table, Charles heading up the other end of the table. Rose, of course, to her Daddy's right, then Matt, then Robert's chair, then Cassandra. Sean was to his mom's right, then Caroline, Jack, and Joshua. In Robert's absence, Cassandra took his chair.

The hanging crystals from the chandeliers danced with the light, and the buffet table of desserts brought forth smells of pumpkin, cinnamon, and ginger. Calming and comforting smells to warm them within while the candlelight burned itself out trying to bring togetherness.

A familiar *clang, clang, clang* filled the room as Charles tapped his glass and got everyone's attention and stood up to make the traditional Thanksgiving toast.

"This year has been a great year for Pointer Enterprises, as you all know from your dividend checks," he said, chuckling, "the excavating and construction company is beginning to grow as we hoped it would, and Cassandra, Scenic Waters is doing well."

Cassandra didn't even acknowledge what her father said—he had no idea about *Scenic Waters* and what it did. Charles, too, felt that his sweet Rose was held back by not receiving the marina to run and, in second place, treated like she was less than when Cassandra was the one chosen to manage the marina. To Rose's humiliation that was one of the decisions announced many Thanksgiving dinners ago, and the jealousy within Rose was like a burning inferno. However, Cassandra knew, if the truth be told, Rose would have never survived how it came about that she became the manager or "glorified hostess" of Scenic Waters. Besides, Rose was still on the payroll, received dividend checks from Pointer Enterprises, and had Matt to do her bidding for her. From Cassandra's point of view, Rose had prevailed, and yet the rivalry between the sisters raged on as dangerous as an undercurrent.

Rose leaned up a bit and looked past Matt in Cassandra's direction, remembering her mother's words when she told Cassandra that *...her beauty would take her further than her brains.* Maybe her mother was right after all.

Charles went on continuing his toast, "The Medallion has been chosen again, already for next year, 1986, to be the official restaurant of the awards presentation to give out the 'Hillbilly Medallion Award' and has maintained its five-star rating. For that I thank my beautiful wife, Ruthie, and my son Robert."

Charles paused a moment to regain his composure: Robert's absence was clearly upsetting to him.

Clearing his throat he continued, "Sean, The Smoke House is in full swing and on projection, and from the looks of this smoked turkey, I know I for one am excited about the Christmas hams. The campgrounds are doing terrific. There's no stopping you, son."

Ruth chimed in with a "Here, here!" hoping to give Sean all the assurances he needed to believe that his family was there for him and he wasn't out of the fold. It was a tragic accident, but the Pointers would prevail.

Rose looked over at Sean and couldn't help but hear, *...and all the glory goes to...Sean William Pointer and the pretty people.* Rose continued to stay quiet; she was leaving tomorrow with her husband for Springton and took comfort in that.

Charles turned toward Matt, continuing his toast, "Matthew, Pointer's Inn never has a high vacancy rate, and the banquet rooms are always full. We're all excited to see what you have planned for the Pointer New Year's Eve party, so good job, Matthew."

Rose proudly patted her prideful and confident husband on the back, and Charles continued with his traditional Thanksgiving toast.

"For the Pointer family, as we all know, we have suffered a great tragedy this year. It was an accident, and this year we toast to the empty chair at our table knowing it won't be empty next year. Here's to hoping for and wishing Robert a full recovery."

Underneath the beautiful chandeliers dancing with the candlelight, they all commanded their Pointer smiles to their faces and met each other with their glasses.

With pride, Charles proudly carved the turkey, somehow believing the carving action reinforced his position as head of the family. It was hard for Cassandra not to laugh every year when he would pick up the carving knife and the big three-pronged fork to hold the turkey while carving. Cassandra saw a shell of a man who thought he was more important than he was, but if sitting at the head of the table twice a year in charge of carving a Thanksgiving turkey and slicing a Christmas ham, more power to him.

Proudly carving the turkey, he turned to his son. "Sean, this turkey is smoked to perfection as usual." Sean and Caroline finally managed to smile.

"Thanks, Dad," replied Sean.

Charles began to pass each dish around the table, and everyone started to fill their plates.

"It's good to see you again, Matt," said Cassandra, taking the dish of sweet potatoes.

"You too, Cassandra," replied Matt.

Rose had just realized after these last few years how grateful she was that Robert sat between Matt and Cassandra. *How silly*, she thought, that it bothered her that Matt and Cassandra were sitting next to each other—she knew she was smarter than that. Rose knew she would never be able to overcome her insecurities between her and Cassandra. She called them insecurities because that sounded better than out right admitting she was jealous and envious of her sister's beauty and position. But her *insecurities* and feelings of rejection from her younger years that scarred her emotionally were left unresolved and had moved with her.

After everyone filled their plates, "Daddy," said Cassandra, while the rest of the family fell immediately silent and tense. They all knew when

Cassandra used the word "Daddy" it was meant to demean and insult their father. All they could do was wait in anticipation of the words that would spew from Cassandra's mouth.

"You didn't mention anything about The Station at 76, why not? Isn't the station vacant since Uncle Joe and Aunt Anne left and went back to French Town?" she asked.

Charles glanced uncomfortably at Ruth and gave a simple reply, "The station is vacant and will most likely be sold, but it won't affect Pointer Enterprises negatively, and it doesn't involve you, Cassandra," he answered almost too abruptly.

Rose darted a sideways glance to her sister. *Oh! Little sister, look at you all grown up thinking you can play with fire!* Looking down at her wedding ring and twisting it around her finger, she wanted to blurt out, *Better stay within the bounds of your beauty, Cassandra!*

"Very well, *Daddy*," replied Cassandra.

Rose decided against speaking those words, composed herself, and turned in her father's direction and instead said, "Happy Thanksgiving, Dad."

Ruth remained rigidly still, keeping her eyes focused downward, worrying that her younger self may now be her nemesis. A nemesis who has never been so close and seated across from her at her own dinner table. Cassandra's commanded Pointer smile was just as beautiful and natural as her mother's, and between the two of them there seemed to be an understanding. Ruth understood that Cassandra had come into her own… but she was still her mother.

With that, there wasn't another word mentioned about The Station at 76. Cassandra now knew what she thought was nothing and unrelated was something, and Robert knew what that something was.

Sean and Caroline left immediately after dinner, not staying for dessert. Their little family was clearly still reeling from the accident. Everyone was worried about Jack and Joshua and understood if they wanted to go home. Those poor boys, they had witnessed a horrific event at such a young age and the experience of the second generation knew and understood the boys' plight.

Cassandra left heading back to Scenic Waters, leaving Matt and Rose to stay with Ruth and Charles, relieved she wouldn't be under this roof again until Christmas.

Cassandra was the only one who visited Robert that Friday after Thanksgiving and it brought her some serenity. It gave her time to just be with her brother. Scenic Waters was closed, and there were no immediate worries hanging over her. Robert recognized her and spoke in broken weak words and his focus was scattered.

"Ell Ary I ove her. I ember Coss, I ember," he said, struggling to get his words out. His eye indicated that trying to speak was still causing him pain.

Sitting next to her brother's side, she was gently holding his hand, trying to hang on for dear life, his life.

"Oh, Robert, Mary loves you so much. We're still getting out of here, you know," she said, pledging, vowing, and promising.

That calmed Robert, but he still had something to say and he needed her to figure it out. Although his mind was foggy and he was slower to put things together, he remembered.

"Coss, ish is inorant, reates in I desk, get ose to Ja Ja oe," he said, managing to speak through his pain.

It made no sense what he was trying to say, and left her no choice to figure it out. He was restless and would get frustrated with her when she didn't get the words right.

"Hang on, Robert, give me a minute and calm down. Our visits are supposed to be quiet and calming. What you are telling me is important?" she repeated, wanting desperately to get it right.

Robert was getting weaker, and he did his best to respond, "Es."

"Okay, okay," she replied and was having difficulty with the word *reates.*

Robert made a hissing sound. "Sssssseattts."

"Robert, I love you, but this is like playing a game of vocal charades! Be patient with me, please. This is important to you, so it's important to me, okay?" she whispered.

That seemed to have calmed him and at the same time brought some amusement to him, and she giggled at his response. Then Robert hissed again, and she mimicked him, "Reatessss?"

He was still restless; she knew she didn't get it right and tried again.

"Ressssates? Resssssseats? OH! It's receipts, is that what you're trying to say?"

"Es," he answered, and his body relaxed.

"There are receipts in your desk that you want me to get to Uncle Joe?" she exclaimed like she had won a game of charades. But sadly, this wasn't a game, and she knew it.

"Es," responded a weak and exhausted Robert, with his one eye full of encouragement.

"I promise I'll go to your apartment first thing in the morning and look for the receipts."

He squeezed her hand a little, drifting in and out of sleep.

"Happy Thanksgiving, big brother," she whispered, and kissed him on the forehead. Cassandra felt Robert's hand lightly squeezing hers. *Amazing,* she thought. Then she had a cot brought into the room, surprisingly without much resistance from the hospital staff, and lay next to his bed. They both drifted off to sleep.

CHAPTER SEVEN

"Truth and Manipulation"

"Charles, do you remember when I was pregnant with Robert?" asked Ruth, remembering the good times. The days before things got so desperate and convoluted.

Charles put the paper down, Ruth had already read it anyway, so he knew he wasn't missing anything.

"Well, of course I remember. What kind of question is that?" he asked, seeing the darkness creep over his wife's face.

"I'm just remembering when the boys were young and things seemed easier," she answered.

Charles chuckled a little. "Well, you didn't think it was that easy back then with your swollen ankles!"

A sweet smile came to her face. "I carried Robert for nine months and all you remember is the swollen ankles?" she said, kindly chastising him.

"Well, dear, I may not remember those days exactly the way you do!" Charles couldn't help but laugh out loud. What he really remembered was that, when she was pregnant, she could be even more demanding and driven than she normally was.

"Charles!" She tried to hide her laughter—she remembered those days too! "Seriously, he would move around and kick but there was no morning sickness, and yes, other than the swollen ankles there was little discomfort."

"Yeah, he was even quiet as a baby, and he sure loved his momma!" exclaimed a proud Charles enjoying the memory of Robert as a baby.

Ruth lightly smacked Charles' shoulder. "You're not saying that he's a momma's boy, are you? Because I would never say that Rose was a daddy's girl!"

"No, dear, not at all. Why, I would never say Robert or *Sean* were momma boys!" he said with his light blue eyes dancing. "And yes, Rose and Cassandra are both my girls. Granted, Cassandra is a little more spirited than Rose, and her and I may not connect like Rose and I do, but I love Cassandra and I believe she knows that."

"I know you love all your children. They are the best of us Charles, and I love them all so much," she replied.

"Do you remember how Robert always greeted everyone with those sweet coos and little smiles? He would stretch out his little legs and fling his arms up in anticipation of being picked up."

"Yeah, I remember, and that's how he learned when doing that, you would always pick him up, and Mattie was guilty of that too!"

"Oh, Charles, I'm not saying that he didn't have his moments, but they were few and far between. And I don't know what you're talking about, if it wasn't me or Mattie picking him up, you were picking him up!"

Charles folded his arms in front of him and leaned back with a sheepish look on his face. "Yeah, I know. He's still a soft soul, always was." Charles blinked trying to keep the darkness from engulfing both of them.

"Do you ever wish we could still pick him up and hold him?" she asked. "I do, Charles, I wish it so bad."

Ruth took a sip of her coffee and somehow seemed to be seeking validation when she asked her husband, "The boys did get along at one time, didn't they?"

"Oh, I think so. Sean was always restless, even in the last month of your pregnancy with Sean you were confined to bed rest. He was just a strong baby. See, Ruthie, I do remember."

Those were bittersweet memories for Ruth and Charles.

"Yeah, I know. Sean has always been strong willed and stubborn. Why do you think my sister Dorothy ever said anything about Bruce Bordure to him? It changed everything. Charles, Robert has to come through this, he has too. We have so much to make up for!"

Charles watched the darkness overtake his lovely wife. It was a devastating place and in the time period of the original sin. She knew she had always been a conflicted mother. For herself, she struggled and looked for the opportunities that presented themselves to her so she could pull herself out of poverty. She had succeeded for them—it seemed natural to her that her children would continue her work and each generation would embrace Pointer Enterprises bringing it into the future. Her original sin could be buried, and her company and her children would grow and thrive together in harmony. Charles saw she was struggling again thinking about the "what ifs." He couldn't deny that he, too, had revisited that place the day of the shooting.

"Damn Dorothy!" Ruth blurted out.

"Well, Ruthie, Dorothy's not all there, and we know that. Hell, I've said before that I think she's almost criminally insane and absolutely certifiable. She scared the hell outta Cassandra, and Rose never took to her either, and frankly, I'm glad. I didn't and don't want her to be a part of our life. None of our children really understood that she was their aunt. All the kids were there that day when she shook Piper like a maraca screaming she would kill her, and she was only two. Remember that awful day?"

"Yeah, I remember that," answered Ruth.

Charles was shaking his head in disbelief. "Do you remember who got Piper away from her?"

"No, I think it was Joc. By the time everyone came running and was gathered around, I'm not sure."

"Ruthie, thinking about the past isn't going to do us any good. They say every family has 'one of those,' you know. I guess our one of those is Dorothy," he said with bitterness.

Charles took a sip of coffee while he and Ruth toggled between the past and present. Charles was remembering a past of only half-truths believing it to be the whole truth. Ruth knew the whole truth and was believing she had no choice but to do what she had to do.

"I know it's hard, sweetheart, but we need to remain focused on Robert. It's understandable that we always come back to this because of what Sean did that night after Dorothy made her innuendos known that I wasn't his father. Maybe if we would've just talked through it with him, Sean's anger wouldn't have grown to the magnitude it did. Maybe he wouldn't have shot out the windows of The Medallion and that man wouldn't have died. Maybe, I don't know, I guess we never will."

He paused for a moment and took Ruth's trembling hands in his.

"I know that doesn't change the facts that we did what we did. We thought that Robert being fifteen was the answer and that Sean going to Vietnam would teach him a lesson. We never dreamed that by telling Robert to say he was the shooter would lead to him being tried as an adult and that he would go to prison."

They sat in silence for a moment at the kitchen table, their hands still clasped together, desperately fighting those memories so they wouldn't have to live them yet again. Ruth was lost in her thoughts, confused by Sean's stubbornness to embrace his life and legacy. Stubbornness that had turned to rage quickly.

"You know, Ruth, I truly believe Dorothy was jealous of you, and when the factory in French Town closed, she knew she wasn't going to get another job. That's why she came to you. Sadly, when we had nothing to offer her, she threatened you, and who would believe any of her ramblings anyway? Everyone in the family knew she was a brick short of a load. She was desperate and we had no idea Sean would fall into that."

"Charles, I should have known better. She chased Lydia with a knife, and if Landon hadn't been there, I don't know what would've happened," she replied, trying to bury the past and put it back where it belonged. When Ruth left her past behind her she felt victorious. *Will I ever be able to get the past to stay in the past?* she wondered.

Charles got Ruth another cup of coffee seeing she had mentally gone somewhere else, somewhere he didn't recognize.

"Hey, hey, come back here to the present with me. It isn't your fault."

"Well, I should have just sent her a monthly check and let it go. I regret not giving her what she demanded," she said, and then cradled her face in her hands.

Charles sat back straight in his chair; just talking about Dorothy raised his blood pressure off the scale, and he would immediately get angry at the mention of her name.

"For God sakes, Ruthie, Dorothy pulled the same shit with Joe and Anne and told Piper she had a half-brother and a half-sister out there somewhere! Your own brother Brandon told us that last time he was here."

Ruth felt the past squeezing the life out her, blinding her fore vision and complicating their family dynamics with a magnitude of details.

"I know, and apparently that was true. That poor little girl. Oh, Charles, I wish we could've kept Piper here with us. At least until Joe got more settled. We were wrong to allow a child to be put in that household. I just wish Joe would've been able to go some other place than back to Mom and Alfred's. We just allowed Piper to live with Dorothy!"

"I know, but Joe and Anne weren't going to allow that under any circumstances; they made that clear. Your brother Joe will never trust us again," he replied with a shrug of his shoulders. One less Tarlson to deal with, was one less problem for him.

"Ruthie," said Charles, clearing his throat, "we better get going."

"Yeah, you're right," she replied, packing up the past and putting it away, once again.

Ruth got up and took her coffee cup to the sink and rinsed it out.

Neither one of Robert's parents would admit when they left the big house on the hill that day, they both took the same memory with them. The memory of a young fifteen-year-old boy, their son, frightened, crying and reaching out so desperately for his mother and father. Robert didn't really understand what was happening as they took him to prison. This wasn't supposed to be happening; his mom had told him that everything was going to be all right, that he was fifteen and fifteen-year-olds don't go to prison.

Robert thought he was helping his seventeen-year-old brother, and happy to do so because he would be safe. If Robert didn't help Sean, he was going to be in serious trouble, and he could save his brother.

When the ten-year prison sentence was handed down, neither Ruth nor Charles could hug him. Ruth had her arms stretched out and she couldn't reach him—the court wouldn't allow it. That day, Charles had his heart ripped out. He wanted to beat Sean to a bloody pulp and drag him into the court room and force him to tell the truth and stop this madness! He blamed Dorothy and Sean. Ruth was conflicted between her two sons, and the only one connection to a piece of the past she had left. The fear and the fright in her youngest son's eyes was again a vivid memory. The same fear was on Sean's face when he witnessed his parents signing on the dotted line for his early enlistment to Vietnam. Ruth blamed her sister, Dorothy for the plights of both of her sons.

With a sadness in their eyes and heavy hearts, Charles and Ruth got in the car and rode in silence to visit their son. Other than the fact Cassandra would be at the hospital when they arrived, Charles and Ruth weren't sure what to expect. The anxiety and stress were maddening. Anger was beginning to creep into their emotions. Anger that Robert was shot, knowing it was a terrible accident. Guilt would follow for feeling angry, and it was a never-ending cycle of emotions. It was Robert's turn, it was his time, and once again it was cruelly ripped away from him.

Robert had recognized Ruth and Charles and knew who they were but had difficulty in making the connection to their relation. His recovery was going to be lengthy. Dr. Carsman entered the room to see Cassandra, Ruth, and Charles.

"Good morning," said Dr. Carsman. "Today's the day. How's everyone holding up?"

Ruth was hoping this was the moment, the moment when she was going to be receiving the good news that Robert was going to make a full recovery.

"We're doing the best we can," answered Charles speaking for all of them.

Dr. Carsman went to Robert's bedside. "Robert, you're going to take a ride today. You're going to a rehabilitation center and work on building your strength to prepare for the necessary upcoming surgeries. I'll be there and checking in on you, okay?" Robert's eye looked at Dr. Carsman in acknowledgement.

"Mr. and Mrs. Pointer, if I may speak with you for a moment before we go to meet the ambulance?" said Dr. Carsman, motioning for them to step in the hallway with him. Ruth and Charles followed him to the hallway while Cassandra stayed with Robert.

"Robert has lost his right eye and he will be permanently deaf in his right ear," said Dr. Carsman. "Reconstructive surgery will be necessary to rebuild his cheek bone and jaw to correct the droopiness of the right side of his mouth, and this will involve skin grafting. He has a long road ahead of him mentally and physically. They'll have more information for you at the rehab facility. I thought it would be important for you to know, so you both could begin to prepare for what is ahead for both of you and your son."

Ruth and Charles took a minute. Questions flooded their minds coming fast and furious; neither Ruth nor Charles had the mental capability to hold onto their thoughts. The color drained from their faces and tears welled up in their eyes. Dr. Carsman led them to the other side of the hall to sit down in the chairs against the wall.

"Doctor" said Charles, "when you say mentally—"

Dr. Carsman interrupted, "They'll have more information for you on that aspect at the rehab facility. He'll be working with a psychiatrist. More and more we'll begin to have more information for you, but right now it's just one day at a time."

"Charles, what does this mean?" Ruth asked her husband with her quivering lower lip.

"Ruthie, honey, it means we take it one day at a time. Other than that—"

"NO! I want to know if my son is going to recover and if he's going to be all right. Someone has to have an answer! Dr. Carsman, what exactly do you mean?" asked Ruth in more of a demanding tone, repositioning herself in her chair to sitting strong and tall.

"I would like for both of you to keep in mind it's important that you don't get ahead of yourselves with your expectations of Robert's recovery. If you could look at it like this, each day is a new beginning for Robert with new challenges to face," explained Dr. Carsman.

Charles and Ruth were non-responsive to Dr. Carsman, and he believed he was seeing complete denial in Robert's parents.

"You must understand," continued Dr. Carsman, "that your son has suffered a severe trauma not only physically but mentally as well. With his predominant injuries to the right frontal and temporal lobe, he must undergo neuropsychological testing. That is why he'll be working with a psychiatrist."

A nurse and two orderlies that walked past them broke up their conversation entering Robert's room. They were getting him into a wheelchair and arranging his IVs. Ruth's heart sank, and the hope she had been filled with over the last few weeks was slowly deflating within her, torturing her. Sadness had overtaken Charles as he sat watching the nurse and the orderlies. *Why did this happen to my son?*

Ruth turned to Dr. Carsman, and with a weak voice she asked, "Doctor, is he going to recover?" Thinking this should be a *yes* or *no* answer. Still wanting to hear so desperately that her son would recover so all could be made right. One day there would be encouraging news about her son, and then the next day always presented another challenge.

With his steadfast matter-of-fact tone he replied, "There are things we cannot know yet, which is why one day at a time is how we proceed. The ambulance is ready."

Cassandra and her parents walked with the nurse who was wheeling Robert from his private room down those familiar white sterile halls of the hospital to the elevator. The halls were much quieter than in the intensive care unit, and there were no beds against the walls and no black armless resin chairs scattered about in the hallway.

"Mom, on the way I'm going to stop at Robert's and pack him some clothes and things. I'll meet you there," said Cassandra.

Ruth just nodded to Cassandra feeling she should have already done that and she couldn't rationalize why she didn't think of getting his things earlier.

When Sean was discharged from the army and Robert was released from prison, this was supposed to bring new life and new beginnings for the family, and for Pointer Enterprises. Ruth's family should be coming together, and now they seemed further apart than ever. She felt herself losing control and coming undone.

It had been Ruth's intention to give The Medallion to Robert. With the kitchen under Robert's management and the construction completed, it was a given that it would be a success. Having Robert take his rightful position in the family would bring the unity she longed for over the last ten years. She was having difficulty seeing the future over this tragedy. Never in her life had she not been able to see or plan for the future; she had no fore vision, and this caused her to panic. The emotional and mental anguish was taking its toll. Physically, her head and back ached and she couldn't keep her legs from swelling. This tragedy had literally begun to suffocate her. *What on earth could have happened between these boys that they were willing to destroy each other over? What could have caused them to throw away their futures, their security, and their positions in the community?* She wondered.

Today, frantic and frazzled, she found herself following an ambulance transporting her son to a rehabilitation facility. Protecting so fiercely her link to the past that may be the downfall of her future. It never dawned on her that both worlds wouldn't be able to co-exist.

Over the last couple of months Charles had been struggling in silence like he had always done. He found himself again wanting to beat Sean to a bloody pulp to teach him a lesson. A lesson he should have learned years ago at the age of seventeen. Even if he did beat him to a bloody pulp today, the point would be moot. Charles had to cope with the fact he had lost his youngest son during his adolescent years, and now, before they even got to know each other again, he had to prepare himself to lose him again.

Charles found his world turned upside down, and even found fleeting moments when he was proud of Cassandra and felt admiration for her, but he never acted on it. Instead, he continued to judge his youngest based on her past behavior, never seeking any answers to his questions. Never making an attempt to know the true person she had become. The person she had to become.

CHAPTER EIGHT

"Another Piece of the Past"

Cassandra turned into the parking lot of The Medallion and drove around to the front entrance to the penthouse. The Christmas decorations were still being placed about, and the bright white lights for the front of the restaurant were already hung and looked like a winter wonderland. Christmas wreaths adorned the double entrance doors and poinsettias embellished the tables on the wood-planked front porch. The stair railings were intertwined with silver and gold garland. For the final touch, mini lighted Christmas trees transformed the sidewalk into a runway. Even though December was cold, the front of the restaurant glowed in an elegant warmth, inviting all to eat, drink, and be merry. For a moment, Cassandra got lost in the beauty of it all, believing its presentation. Driving around the back of the restaurant, she parked her car and turned off the engine. She looked up at the front door of Robert's penthouse and the silence quickly snapped her back to reality and reminded her that its presentation was a facade for others, make believe. The elegance of the white lights on the front of The Medallion were no longer enchanting, but a spotlight. A spotlight that shone through the beauty and ambience exposing the unspeakable.

The closer she came to Robert's front door, her anxiety increased and her hands trembled while unlocking the door.

When she walked into the penthouse she called out, "Robert, are you here?" She knew he wasn't and hardly recognized her own voice at that moment. *It's finally happened, I've lost my mind.*

Not wasting any more time, she gathered up Robert's suitcases and began packing his comfy clothes. Cassandra had found if she kept moving, she could focus better.

Walking through the penthouse she remembered how excited she was the day Robert moved in.

"From a prison cell to a penthouse, not bad I guess!" Robert had said, laughing to Cassandra.

"No, big brother, not bad at all! And well deserved," Cassandra replied.

Robert's laughter faded and his pale blue eyes that were so much like his father's looked around room, seeing what freedom looked like. It was fear, fear that he wouldn't be able to adjust, that he wouldn't know how to live on the outside. For he never had, not really.

He walked around the apartment that he and Cassandra had mockingly named the "penthouse." It had four bedrooms, three full baths, and was modernly decorated. By the time Cassandra was born, they were already living in the house in Springton. Sean and Robert lived a few years of their early lives here in this penthouse.

He was not only living in the penthouse, he was also the highest paid chef around, and he deserved it. All of this was Robert's compensation, a payoff. She couldn't help but admire Robert: he was part of a work release program in prison and went to culinary school and graduated at the top of his class. He was a chef, and he could cook, bake, broil, grill, and fry anything to perfection. His prepared dinners not only aroused the senses by their aromas, they were also a work of art.

"Robert, you okay?"

"I'm not sure, sis," he replied.

"Oh, Robert, why didn't you tell me sooner that you weren't at some prestigious boy's school? I knew something was wrong when you could never come home, and that's why I pressed you so much in my early letters for you to tell me where you really were. Do you wanna talk about it?"

"No. I will tell you that prison is no place you wanna be. Time is not your own and choices are few and far between. You learn to sleep with one eye open. Apparently, Mom and Dad must have paid for my protection, so I was luckier than most. Things got better when I became the chef for the warden and his family. I'd also bet that every guard was on the Pointer's payroll and has a job for life if they want to retire early as security for the company. You were too young, and I didn't want you to freak out or have the stigma attached to you of having a brother who was in prison."

"I love you, big brother," she said softly.

They were both silent for a moment; their eyes were clouded and their emotions ran high sitting there, starring into the Pointer abyss. Their pain that reflected back from one another awakened their own shame and guilt.

"Oh, the hell with it! The shame belongs to Sean and our mother," flared Cassandra.

"Yeah, maybe. Then when I found out what happened on your birthday, I thought I was going to go mad! Our lives haven't been that much different, have they?" replied Robert, shaking his head.

"No, I guess not. You had nothing to do with what happened on my birthday that year. All of this is on our mother! You know, one day Rose and I woke up and we were told that you had gone to a boy's school and that Sean had been sent to Vietnam. There were no goodbyes, no nothing. On Wednesdays I would come home after piano lessons and you and Sean would be in the back yard. Sean would chase me and pull my pigtails, and you would protect me. All that was just gone. One day things were just different. I'm glad that you finally told me the truth, and I did keep your secret. I don't know how Rose found out. I'm guessing *Daddy* told her."

Robert gently smiled and hugged his sister. "Well, it doesn't really matter. I don't know how long Mom thought she could have kept that secret anyway, especially with all the news coverage. We've lost ten years, sis. I don't wanna lose another minute," said Robert softly.

"Yeah, that's true, and you're right, we're not gonna lose another minute! Going to school wasn't easy—everyone knew the truth except us, I think. For whatever reason, we defended that lie until we couldn't anymore," replied Cassandra.

"We all did," said Robert.

Embracing his newfound freedom, Robert lightened his heart.

"Hey, what do you think the higher society would do if they knew that a *learned-in-prison chef* was cooking their dinners?" Robert said to Cassandra. "Why, they'd be appalled!" he said, answering his own question, mocking his mother's priorities.

Cassandra laughed and replied, "Well, according to the rumor mill, big brother, I think they already know! We should put an announcement in the paper, don't you think?"

"Wouldn't Mother love that," he replied back. "Can you imagine Mom scouring the papers and seeing that headline, 'Tragedy Turns to Triumph for Parolee.'"

"However, I prefer something that says, 'Wrong Pointer Brother Convicted…' or 'Charles and Ruth Pointer, Parents of the Year!'"

"No," said Robert. "There'd be a traffic jam on the strip with everybody pointing at the Pointer shingles, and we don't need that," he said, grinning, giving it just a quick second of real thought.

"Let's not poke the bear as they say, sis! The best thing we can do for ourselves is to get outta here. Take the money and run. Shut down that horrific charity 'PECC' that bears my name. How could she have done that?" he asked, hanging his head to hide the horror in pale blue eyes.

"I don't know," answered Cassandra.

"And why you?"

"I don't know," answered Cassandra again.

"You were forced to survive, just like me. And we have survived, and now we're leaving! Me, you, Mary, and the 'Lake Girls,' as you call yourselves these days," Robert declared.

It was then Cassandra realized that Robert and Mary had made a connection. They immediately began making to plans to leave everything Pointer behind. As they worked on their goal to leave in the near future, their visions of what should be or could be now became *it will be*.

From the time he moved in, Cassandra helped him get his driver's license and they went clothes shopping. She even took him to get his first haircut after being released, showed him the town and its growth. She was the one who introduced him to Mary; yep, she did that.

Tears were rolling down her cheeks and she was choking on her uncontrollable sobs. She took solace in remembering their conversations. It was the first time since the accident Cassandra had found herself alone and could confront some of her emotions. Once again, Sean and Robert had been caught in the crosshairs of rising ambitions.

Before Robert had a driver's license, he had a prison record, and Sean the golden boy was deemed *honorable* by the United States of America. The older Cassandra got, the angrier she got; this just all made her sick. Now, it appears that fate raised the stakes between her two brothers. Now, here in his home she was packing his suitcase and he was on his way to a rehabilitation facility, uncertain to his recovery, his future hanging in the balance.

Cassandra resumed her packing and put one of the suitcases on the bed, having to sit on it to get it closed. The other suitcase closed fine. Maybe she was bringing too much, maybe there wasn't enough.

What if Robert doesn't make it? What will happen to Mary? Will I have to remain at the marina? What are my mother's plans for me as I get older?

It never dawned on her that the other suitcase could have held more and saved her from the struggle of closing the other. All those things in the suitcase he needed, but what he needed the most couldn't be found in the penthouse. There were no miracles here, and nothing could reverse time before the trigger was pulled. Her tears continued to fall going through his bathroom. She packed toothpaste and a toothbrush out of habit and hesitated packing his razor. No one had seen Robert's face where he'd been shot, he was still in bandages. She stared at the razor for a bit, and sadly she knew it wasn't going to be needed, or was it…? She put the razor in the bag.

Usually when things would get rough within the family she would go home to the marina where she made her home in a stateroom on *The Eclipse*, take her vitamin "Q" with a swallow of bourbon for her lullaby to sleep. She looked down at her trembling hands and her stomach churned and gurgled. She heard Mary's voice in her head, *Cassandra, chasing ludes with bourbon is not going to make things any easier…and cocaine put in a capsule is still taking cocaine!* Her position at Pointer Enterprises was the party boats, and occasional drug use was just part of the job. Now, she needed to help her brother and try to figure out what he knew. Dismantling PECC and finding out Sean's truth was a priority.

I can't afford to drown myself in ludes and bourbon! This is really happening, and when I would wake up, it wouldn't be just a dream. It's a living nightmare, she told herself over and over when she was trembling and craving just one drink or just one lude.

She picked up the suitcases and headed to the door, turned, and gave the "penthouse" one last look searching for the life and the hope that could've lived here. There were so many voices in her head, so many memories vividly coming back to her scattering her thoughts. The memories, like time, were out of sync.

"Robert, you can't have the desk in the main room of the house! Use one of the bigger bedrooms for your office. By the way, why do you need an office again?" asked Cassandra, teasing him.

"Because I'm the 'kitchen manager,' the 'head chef'! It isn't the ideal restaurant to work in no doubt, but it's a start. If I can be a successful chef and run a kitchen such as this kitchen here at The Medallion, I can go anywhere, sis," said Robert, a young man with many hopes and dreams, and it was wonderful! It brought a smile to Cassandra's face seeing Robert so hopeful and making plans.

"You know, sis, you've already established yourself, and you don't even know it. You could run a bar, you could market for a huge company if you wanted to, and don't forget about your piano playing."

"Yeah, okay. Did you want to buy some ludes or ecstasy and sex while I play the piano for you?" she asked dryly.

"You know what I mean! Now, help me move *my* desk over here, please?"

OH! She had forgotten! Maybe the drug use and alcohol had made her senses dull and her memory short spanned! *The desk,* she thought. *Uncle Joe, receipts. What was Robert trying to tell me?*

Sitting the suitcases down, she frantically went to the desk and started going through the drawers. There was a strong box in the bottom right-hand drawer, and it was locked. *Of course it's locked!* Spending no time looking for a key, she got a hammer from the utility closet and broke the lock.

There must have been hundreds of thousands of dollars of receipts and one single propane gas bill marked "past due." These invoices were to Ruth, Charles, Sean, and Caroline for personal gasoline fill-ups and car repairs. There were invoices to Scenic Waters and Pointer's Construction and Excavating, and she had never seen these invoices. *Oh my God, oh no! No, no, no! These invoices dated back from when Uncle Joe first took over the business up to his recent eviction, and all bear the signature of Joe Tarlson, Uncle Joe. This must have been what the fight was about between Sean and Robert.*

Uncle Joe and Robert were always close—Uncle Joe was his favorite babysitter. Robert had dinner more times with Uncle Joe and his family than he did with his own family. Robert would spend time with Piper and was getting to know his five-year-old cousin more than his own nephews. Uncle Joe was good for Robert, and he helped him with life on the outside. Robert and Joe would spend time together in the garage building his GTO and he was given a wealth of mechanical knowledge. Robert had met all of Joe's friends and hung out with the boys at the shop and even attended their parties and gatherings. Robert learned how to race his GTO down at the dam and even had a few wins under his belt. Every time Joe's daughter Piper would see Robert, she would run to him with open arms yelling, "Cousin Robert, Cousin Robert!" Robert's eyes would light up when he saw that little girl, and Piper, well, nothing made her happier than seeing Cousin Robert. Next to Uncle Joe, their father appeared to be a mouse of a man with an underlying anger. Their mother appeared to be selfish, cold, and unattached. When Robert wasn't working at The Medallion, he could be found at Uncle Joe's or at the marina with Mary.

Family chatter said Ruth had no choice but to evict Uncle Joe from the station because it was failing and running in the red. Ruth had publicly blamed Anne for the failure of the business. It was said that Anne would steal petty cash from the office that Ruth so graciously provided, and she was always out shopping and what not. However, regardless of the dynamics of the relationships, Ruth was clearly swindling her own brother.

Joe and Anne were footing the bill for the gas at the marina, the construction and excavating company, and their personal car repairs and gas!

No wonder Uncle Joe was in such debt. In the box was also the contract that was signed between Ruth, Charles, and Uncle Joe. There was a bank note and a full deed of release showing the note was paid in full two years before the eviction. There was also a personal note between Ruth, Charles, and Joe for the equipment that was in the shop—it was a balloon note marked "paid in full."

She remembered Robert staying with Joe for two days helping him pack. Packing up that equipment was quite an ordeal. It was called The Station at 76 on paper, but the business was called "Joe's Garage." Joe had hung that sign with such pride. As the sign came down, everyone helping him pack up and move were witness to a broken man who just had everything stolen from him, and only forty-eight hours to relinquish it all.

Joe was paying Ruth and Charles's banknote on the property and paying rent to Ruth and Charles. The payments that Uncle Joe made to Ruth and Charles were camouflaged and ingeniously done. The garage was upstairs with their residence underneath, and that is how the two payments had come about and no one was the wiser. *But what business? Just the gas for the marina alone was a small fortune and should have come from the marina. Where was that money going?*

The eviction of Uncle Joe was so sudden, and the timing seemed odd. Anne had started a successful car detailing business, and it was doing well.

It was all so hard to remember, Cassandra was wishing she had paid more attention. Aunt Anne's best friend Emilie was Ruth's major competition in the restaurant business, and her family was from old money. It was for those people that Ruth would put her accomplishments and pictures in the paper each year, building her pedigree on her way to *age* her wealth. It was Emilie's father that sent Joe and Anne to their certified accountants.

Emilie's family owned J.J.'s, one of the few restaurants on the strip that wasn't a Pointer Enterprises business. The only business owners that weren't shaking in their boots about their business was the candy store across the street from the station, and that was only because Ruth didn't seem interested in it. However, the owner knew if his was the only business she didn't own on the strip, he might find his business devoured by Pointer Enterprises.

Cassandra remembered her mom giving Anne an ultimatum when they stopped at the station to get gas on the way home from school one day. Cassandra followed her mom into the office at the station to get her favorite candy bar; free candy was just too good to pass up!

"Joe, Anne, I'm glad I caught you both together," said Ruth. "I heard you were having dinner at J.J.'s the other night, is that true?"

"Yeah," answered Joe. "Does it matter where we eat dinner?"

"Well, when your sister owns The Medallion, and you, my business partner and his wife dine at J.J.'s, yeah, it matters. It doesn't send a good message to the community."

"Oh, I see," said Uncle Joe.

"So, end the friendship with her and husband. They need to find someone else to work on their Mercedes and J.J.'s trucks or never step foot in The Medallion again," replied Ruth. Once again, she believed her magic words would set things straight.

"Well, Ruth, they're *paying* customers, and last time I checked this was still a free country. Now, I do understand, so we won't be dining at The Medallion again. Are you going to extend us the same courtesy and never step foot in the station again?" Joe said in rebuttal against his sister, just as simply and sharply.

Angrily, Ruth grabbed Cassandra's hand, not saying a word and yanked her towards the door, and they left. Cassandra shuddered at that memory, knowing Uncle Joe made a grave mistake that day when he told her mother that!

This paperwork was all so confusing. Did Pointer Enterprises pay off that note and not tell Joe? It looked like Joe was never told the residence portion had prorated out and only one rent payment was to be made. Uncle Joe ran the station for several years, and it had been sitting vacant for almost two years. *Daddy* had mentioned at Thanksgiving to the family the business would be sold... *But if the business was to be sold, wouldn't its finances of its last operation be reviewed?*

According to this, The Station at 76 was carrying a lot of debt. If nothing else, it was clear that her parents pulled a two-time rent payment scam on Uncle Joe. Ruth and Joe shared a checking account for the deposit of the two rent payments and payments on the equipment. Joe was also contractually forced to use her banker and her accountant, but Uncle Joe didn't use her accountant for long.

Maybe that's what happened, and Joe knew what was going on? Maybe Mother didn't want anyone to know what she had done to her own brother? Maybe Uncle Joe knew more than he let on; maybe like her and Robert, he too was looking for a way out. She just wasn't good at these things, and she wasn't about to ask Rose. One didn't have to be an Einstein to figure out it was the shared bank account that was the hook that would or could come back and haunt Uncle Joe.

Oh, Rose! Rose had to know about this—she was working for Pointer Enterprises at that time, and after a huge fight with their mother, she decided to step out of the accounting part of the business and manage The Medallion. What did Rose know?

Right after she married Matt, she quit Pointer Enterprises and moved to Springton to begin her married life. That's what everyone thought, anyway.

Matt was such a twit, and why Rose couldn't see through him, she would never know. He was the love of Rose's life, and again, Rose's intelligence had not served her as well as it should have. Their mother was wrong about one thing, and that was the belief that Rose didn't have any ambitions of her own. Rose must have stood up to her mother this time, and look what happened, Matthew took her rightful position in the company, among other things. Maybe it was their mother that positioned Matt as head of Pointer's Inn, to teach Rose a lesson? Maybe Rose did want more than to be just a wife. *Although being just a wife was not a bad thing,* thought Cassandra with envy. However, it wasn't a far stretch that maybe *Daddy* was right and Rose was devalued too, just not in the way he thought. Maybe her own big house on the hill, remaining on the payroll, and Pointer's Inn was her payoff or compensation.

Cassandra had never really stood up to her mother, she would get emotional but never call her out on anything. She would have "emotional outbursts" as *daddy* called them! She had accepted the fact she was cowardly, but today she promised herself she was going to be strong for Robert. Just how she was going to do that, she didn't know yet.

She checked the time and realized she better get going—they may already be at the facility by now. It was hard for her to leave the "penthouse." It represented the hopes, dreams, and freedom of a young boy who spent the most precious years of his life in prison. It was the cold hard reality that to make up for the past was an impossible task. Wounds that would heal and turn to hardened scars. Scars of remembrance and vulnerability.

Forgiveness was ambition's catalyst. In Cassandra's and Robert's world, ambition would rely on forgiveness to continue to thrive, leaving broken hearts and broken spirits along the way. Taking any self-esteem and confidence with it in its wake. Ambition would allow the light in when necessary and cry when caught, having gone too far. It would hide its dirty deeds in the dark. Those that were struck by their mother's ambitions wouldn't realize it until it was too late. They were sucked up in a tornado of excitement, exquisite beauty, forbidden pleasure, and immense wealth. Then, sadly, ambition would justify itself in one's soul, confirming there wasn't any other way. Ambition would then rationalize and comfort that all would be well, until one was caught and trapped by it. Then, ambition would turn its back on the ensnared to save its good attributes and characteristics.

Cassandra's head was spinning out of control with all she had found, and even more so with all the unanswered questions and no one to ask but Robert.

Robert was right, she had to get these receipts to Joe; if he didn't have a record of all this, he may be asked some hard questions. Uncle Joe was under pressure, and this explained Robert's reborn anger toward their mother.

The long ride helped her get herself together. It was cold, and there was no warmth to feel from the sun and the skies threatened snowfall.

Here she was just a party girl who partook in drugs and alcohol to survive the days and endure the nights and now she understood her brother's belief in the truth; it would protect the innocent. Robert obviously put the pieces together, and Cassandra was afraid of what she didn't know. Maybe ambition was also smart. Maybe Rose's ambition was to get out too? Maybe she thought she had.

Pulling into the parking lot of the facility, she put away what she had just found and tucked it safely in the back of her mind for the time being.

It looked nice for a rehabilitation center.

"What took you so long? Did you pack the whole apartment?" fumed Charles.

Cassandra opened the trunk and pulled out three suitcases and one bathroom bag while Charles glared at her.

She took the heaviest of the suitcases and handed it to her dad, glaring right back at him, and he didn't take it. She sat the suitcase on the ground next to him instead of saying out loud, *Pick it up!*

"Cassandra, really, does he need all this?" flared Charles.

Cassandra took a deep breath, and Ruth recognized her daughter's body language, warning of an "emotional outburst" soon to follow.

"No, *Daddy*, what he needs is to not be here at all," she flared back at him. "What he needs are no buckshot holes in his face and brain. No lead poisoning. What he needs is to be able to talk, walk, and eat like we're all doing. It looks like he was safer in prison than he was here at home with his own family!" she spat viciously.

Charles looked wounded. Any other time Charles would have put her in her place, but he stood there in the cold, freezing, and remained silent. His beady blue eyes fixated on his youngest and the scowl on his face spoke loudly, without saying a word.

"Cas-san-dra!" said Ruth in her tone that Cassandra recognized immediately, telling her she was out of line and invalidated.

"Let's get his things and go inside!" demanded Ruth.

Charles grabbed two suitcases and Cassandra carried one suitcase and his bathroom bag.

Even in the winter the barren gardens were beautiful and bountiful pledging its promise of life to come after the winter had gone. The icicles hung from the barren branches and glistened. There were Styrofoam cones that had been placed over many flower bushes to protect them from the freezing temperatures of winter. The brochure showed pictures of the gardens, and from the placement of the cones, it looked like the rose garden was huge. The sidewalks were wide that wound through the gardens so that a wheelchair could easily glide through. There was a small pond off in the distance and huge weeping willow tree stood tall. Its leaves were mostly gone, and it was showing its skeletal make up and still encouraging those to let go of the pain and suffering and to forge on toward stability and healing. *It must be beautiful here in the spring,* thought Cassandra.

There was an outside patio for dining or just for sitting outside. They continued to tour the facility, and it was explained that Robert's room would be private and he had already been assigned a head nurse and three other nurses for round-the-clock nursing care. Also, there was a psychiatrist that would work with him to deal with the emotional trauma of being shot.

Cassandra still didn't like the place. She was thankful for the wonderful care her brother was going to receive, but as nice and safe as it was, she didn't like it. It seemed set up more like a permanent residence, and this wasn't where Robert was going to live. This is where he was going to get better and leave.

They were taken to an area set up as a meeting room where they waited to meet Robert's head nurse.

When Elizabeth entered the room, Charles and Ruth looked like they had seen a ghost.

At the introduction of Ms. Bell by the administrator to Ruth and Charles, Ms. Bell clearly said, "No introductions necessary, I know Charles and Ruth. I served in WWII with Mr. Pointer."

Nurse Bell took a seat facing all three of them.

"I never thought I'd see you again, Charles, and Ruth, you look well," said Nurse Bell.

Cassandra could see that Nurse Bell was nervous, and Ruth was shaken. Ruth couldn't help but notice that Elizabeth hadn't changed much; she had retained her youthful look and still wore her blonde hair pulled back. It was still the same as it was all those years ago when Elizabeth walked into a room—her presence just said she was smart, confident, and sophisticated. Elizabeth Bell was one of the reasons this world was a better place and no one had to speak those words to know that was true. Cassandra had never seen her mom so shaken before. Maybe it was all the stress she was under; still, there was an uneasy vibe in the room, and Nurse Bell was most definitely in the "pretty people" circle, as Rose would say. To Cassandra it appeared that her mother no longer owned the room, and she never remembered a time in her life when her mother didn't own a room.

Just like all those years ago when in the presence of Elizabeth Bell, Ruth felt smaller, she felt poor.

Nurse Bell spoke to all three of them to put everyone at ease, "I'm sorry to hear about your son, Robert. I've read his file, and what a tragic accident."

Ruth was slow to respond; she was trying to determine if she wanted Elizabeth to be her son's nurse, but this was one of the best-rated facilities in the Midwest. Yes, she did know Elizabeth from many years ago.

"Thank you, Elizabeth," said Ruth as elegantly as she could. "How long have you been working here?"

Elizabeth seemed to jump at the chance to answer her mother's question, and if Ruth could have retracted her words, she would have. She had just asked a question that she probably didn't want to hear the answer. Elizabeth always had an unintentional way of keeping Ruth off balance.

Elizabeth responded in a tone that was hard to put an emotion to, "Ever since Bryce Bordure died, I was his private nurse after his heart attack for his rehabilitation. You do remember the Bordures, don't you?"

Cassandra's ears perked up hearing the name *Bordure*. She'd heard that name before, and it wasn't as if Nurse Bell was asking her mom a question, it was more like she was making a statement.

"Charles, it was a shame that you lost contact with Bryce," said Nurse Bell with a sincere tone of sad regret. It was uncomfortable and awkward, and now Cassandra was wondering if *she* wanted Nurse Bell to be Robert's nurse.

Charles finally spoke to try and remove the awkwardness, "Elizabeth, this is my daughter, Cassandra."

Cassandra wasn't exactly sure who she was being introduced to and extended her hand. "It's nice to meet you, Ms. Bell."

"Likewise," replied Nurse Bell apprehensively. Cassandra's beauty had taken her back many years ago, and looking at her, trying not to stare, she saw a younger Ruth Tarlson with blue eyes, and was unnerved.

CHAPTER NINE

"Cassandra's Courage"

Charles, Ruth, and Cassandra listened to the realizations of seizures and the continuing possibility of a stroke. It was a lot to hear and complex to understand. Nurse Bell had given the family a little break to catch up emotionally and being experienced in such medical cases, she had coffee and small bite sized sandwiches sent up in an effort to provide some level of comfort. Even with all the talk and hope that came with the words of Nurse Bell, devastation was what they felt. They discussed the reconstructive surgeries, physical therapies, and reconciliation of the trauma that would begin in the near future. This brought to light the mental distress and realities of Robert's physical pain. They sat in silence for a moment taking courtesy bites of the sandwiches.

"As Robert continues to regain his strength we'll begin reading and writing assessments and slowly begin with hand and leg exercises, and then, of course, he'll be meeting with his psychiatrist regularly. Then we'll begin to help him adjust to the loss of his right eye and the deafness of his right ear. Are there any questions at this point?" asked Nurse Bell.

Like Mary would do, Cassandra immediately submersed herself in all the plans that were being made to leave. Looking for a happy place she heard Mary's voice, *Oh, just wait, my friend, I got us a place and have some surprises for you and Robert!* Charles's faded and hopeless blue eyes looked gray and locked with Elizabeth's. Without words he pleaded to her, *You saved my life once, please save my son's life.* He tried to hide the pain he felt hearing of his son's prognosis and his future struggles to come. She knew

Charles was searching for an answer that she couldn't give him, and she wanted so desperately to tell him that all the answers he was searching for was right here. Ruth stared at the floor knowing the past had come full circle, and she still wasn't feeling well. It was all so overwhelming, and she was doing her best to breathe through all of this. She was one of the wealthiest women in the Ozarks, yet so poor. She was a striking and beautiful woman, but her hidden inner self was getting harder to contain.

Ruth was feeling exposed and never looked up from the floor once, never made eye contact with anyone while they sat there in silence. Only Cassandra was holding onto the false hopes of leaving everything Pointer behind.

"That's all right," Elizabeth said. "The questions will come, and this is a lot to take in. When a question arises, please call to ask it, okay?"

"Yes, of course. Thank you," answered Charles, clearing his throat.

"Now," Nurse Bell continued, "it's important to remember there really isn't a timeline that we can place on this process as each case is based on the injuries, who he is now and who he was before. You can be assured that we'll strive for Robert's full recovery. I just want you to be aware it'll take time and we need to respect that, we need to respect the process." Looking over at Cassandra she concluded with saying, "The facility is very lenient with visiting hours, and we encourage regular visits."

Cassandra met Nurse Bell's eyes and without words her expression of gratefulness was expressed and received. Nurse Bell no longer felt unnerved by Cassandra. And Cassandra was sure that she wanted Nurse Bell to be her brother's nurse.

"Well," said Nurse Bell in an uplifting voice, "let's go see Robert and make sure he's all settled in, shall we?"

Ruth and Charles agreed and were anxious to see their son. Cassandra followed behind with Robert's suitcases placed on a luggage cart, timidly guiding the cart through the halls on the way to her brother's room. The room was painted a pale blue and there was a dark blue chair rail with flowers woven through that looked like lilies in soft pinks and white. The windows were large glass pane windows in a trio and could be opened to let in fresh air. There was a huge bathroom with a handicapped shower and toilet that had the same paint and chair rail as the room. The shower curtain was white, and its matching outer curtain was tied back in swags. Robert's bed was by the windows and the heater register sat below. There was a television that sat inside a built-in wall encasement. Within the room there was a couch and two recliners. Each recliner had its own table and lamp. A coffee table sat on an oriental decorative area rug that created a circle and invited a gathering. It mimicked a living room in one's home. Cassandra hated it even more now; it caused her an uneasiness that it may be a possibility he wouldn't leave this place and they had plans.

Robert's face was still heavily bandaged, with hopes of the bandages to be removed tomorrow.

"The ride has been very difficult for him. He's exhausted. We have pain medication going through his IV along with a sedative. He should begin to have some relief soon, then he'll most likely sleep for the rest of the evening into the morning," explained Nurse Bell.

Her trained eye observed Robert's indifference to his parents and the closeness between him and Cassandra. When Robert saw Cassandra, she noticed he welcomed her. His eye focused on Cassandra and she already had a chair beside his bed and was holding his hand before Nurse Bell even turned around. Seeing their closeness, Nurse Bell couldn't help but give a warm smile to the brother and sister before her. Once Robert gained some peace from his sister, his eye wandered around the room. It was strange for Nurse Bell watching this—his eye skimmed over Charles like he wasn't even there, invisible. Robert continued to look around the room with his bloodshot blue eye. His eye fell on his mother. His body stiffened up, his vitals raised, and his blue eye turned stoned cold.

Robert's in there just trying to get out. I bet he remembers what happened. Bruce never had a chance to explain what happened all those years ago, he died. By God, Robert will have a voice! vowed Nurse Bell to herself.

Before Cassandra knew what she was saying she said to Robert, "I'm going to stay a few days at the hotel next door, Robert, and I'll see you for breakfast tomorrow."

She worried if she had overstepped. Looking at Nurse Bell, wanting her opinion, added to her comment, "If that's all right, Nurse Bell."

Nurse Bell smiled sweetly. "That would be wonderful, Cassandra. You would be amazed at how having loved ones around helps to bring about a successful rehabilitation."

Nurse Bell was happy with Cassandra's decision. Ruth on the other hand didn't seem to be as happy with her daughter's decision but wasn't going to push the issue in mixed company, and certainly not in front of Elizabeth.

"Well, I'll leave you all to visit with Robert," said Nurse Bell, and closed the door behind her.

Ruth placed a chair next to the other side of his bed. She wanted to hold his hand, but she couldn't, the IV was pumping sedatives and pain medication into his veins. Charles sat at the foot of the bed. Ruth's bottom lip began to quiver, and with her shaky hand she rubbed his forehead. She wondered how this happened, how did it come to this, and she wished she could pick him up and cradle him in her arms, but she couldn't. It seemed fate had its own way of orchestrating the pathway of life. They sat quietly until Robert fell asleep.

Ruth and Charles were leaving the facility and Cassandra was headed over to the hotel next door and then came the confrontation she had felt brewing, knowing it was unavoidable.

"Cassandra," she heard her mother call. Cassandra stopped and turned around.

"Yeah?" she answered with an uncertainty, afraid she may say the wrong thing or handle the situation in a manner that would expose her and what she knew.

"I understand you want to be here with Robert," said Ruth genuinely, and then her next words betrayed her, "and your father and I do to, but the holiday season is the only time Pointer Enterprises has any real business during the winter season. Do you think it's wise to be away from Scenic Waters for so long?"

Charles watched his daughter's reaction very closely, and she could feel his eyes on her. Cassandra may be the mirror image of her mother except for her eye color, but Charles was curious to see how she answered that question and how she was going to prioritize Scenic Waters. He had the same question Rose did: whether or not Cassandra had her mother's resolve. He was a conflicted father, and if he knew his daughter's reality, it wouldn't be her resolve he would be questioning. Cassandra knew that her "Daddy" thought she had devalued herself by becoming a party girl. He had made it clear to her and the family that if the marina didn't make so much money, he would send her to rehab and she would never work for the company again until she was clean. Cassandra also knew that her "Daddy" would never do anything for the world to see that he didn't have the perfect life after all. He was the man who had it all and he was proud of that, no matter how humble he presented himself to be.

Anger began raging through her and she saw a smirk come across her Daddy's face—she was about to have an emotional outburst, and Charles knew it. Over these last few weeks some of Cassandra's anger had been replaced with confidence, and that helped to strengthen her resolve. That's what "Daddy" didn't know. What she really wanted to do was tell her mother she knew more today than yesterday. That she knew why Rose left Pointer Enterprises. That she knew the fight between Sean and Robert was most likely over Uncle Joe and the sale of The Station at 76. That a review of the books would show that Joe embezzled funds *and* she knew it was purposely done to make it look that way and he could still be set up to take the fall! She wanted to scream she knew her mother would sell her own daughter to make a buck, *and* she recognized the name "Bordure."

For the first time in her life she didn't speak without thinking, she didn't spew the venom on her parents they so rightfully deserved. For the first time in her life, without the use of drugs or alcohol, she commanded her Pointer smile and it came as she commanded. Cassandra was proud of herself and began to believe that she indeed, had her mother's resolve.

"Yes, Mom, I'm sure. *The Eclipse* is being checked over before we start the holiday shows, same with the *The Crimson Rose*, and all the house boats are in for maintenance and won't be rented again until spring. We have a few parties scheduled on the yacht and I'll be back for those," she answered.

Charles was standing with the car door open and leaning on the roof of the car facing them both, looking deep in thought. Once again, Cassandra had surprised him.

"Cassandra," said Charles, "do you want to stay at the house here in Springton instead of the hotel?"

Ruth hadn't thought about that: it was about forty-five minutes or so away, and that was better than her being right next door. She wasn't comfortable with her daughter getting to know Elizabeth Bell.

"Sure, Dad, that's a good idea," she answered, deciding at this time it was best to go with the flow and keep things as calm as she could.

Charles reached into his pocket pulled out the keys to the house and tossed them over to Cassandra and she caught them in midair.

"Thanks, Dad. Hey, Mom, Dad, how do you know Robert's nurse again? Wasn't that something running into someone you know here at the facility?"

Ruth was just ready to go home, and this was one of those conversations she didn't want to have. Things were beginning to unravel at the seams and quickly. *Cassandra's right, what was the chance we'd run into Elizabeth Bell again?* she thought.

Cassandra tried not to lock eyes with her mother and failed. Once again, they eclipsed, and both seemed to have checkmate. Ruth's pelvic and lower back pain had caused her to break eye contact with daughter and reposition herself to lean on the car.

Like Ruth, Charles was not without charm and was careful about his answer. "Elizabeth was a nurse in the war and that's where we met. For a few years after the war some of us would meet up and keep in touch, but then we all got busy, got married, had children and the like. The years went by quicker than we realized," he replied nonchalantly.

"Well, Dadd—" she almost slipped and called him *Daddy*. "That should give you some comfort knowing at least one person caring for Robert here."

Now it was Cassandra's turn to watch for a reaction. It was very rare that Charles's body language or facial expressions would betray him, and this made him very hard to read. Throughout the years, Cassandra learned when there wasn't a reaction from "Daddy," that was actually a reaction.

"You bet it does, doesn't it, Ruthie?" Charles replied, without missing a beat.

Looking at Charles, nodding her head *yes,* she answered, "Yes, it does." There was a shakiness in her voice that resonated possibly from the pain she was experiencing or from the name of "Bordure" being spoken in front of Cassandra. It was impossible for Ruth to determine what was heard and what was actually comprehended from today's overwhelming magnitude of information.

For Ruth and Charles, the ride back to Braxton was tense.

"Ruthie, are you okay?"

Ruth slipped off her pumps and let them lay on the floorboard; they had left their impressions on her swollen feet. She turned and looked at Charles and wanted to scream back at him. *Why do you ask such a stupid question? You surely know the answer to that!* Her envy, bitterness, and resentment of Elizabeth carried her through her pain, and her brown eyes glared at him. Charles remained silent—she seemed to have revisited that unrecognizable place from earlier.

I hate Elizabeth Bell and you worship the ground she walks on! Everyone worshipped the ground she walked on! If it weren't for her… Those were words she couldn't speak and emotions she had to keep suppressed. Unsettled. Elizabeth, again, had her unsettled, and she wasn't even present.

"Charles, what do you think? Elizabeth Bell is Robert's nurse!" she answered a little too harshly, hoping that she had hidden her emotions so they couldn't be seen. "She knew Bryce and Bruce, don't you remember when Dorothy told Sean to ask us if we knew Bruce Bordure? She blames me for Bruce's death, just like his father Bryce did. Just like our talk this morning, I try so hard Charles to let go of the past, but here lately it seems like every time I turn around its staring me in the face. I can't help but think about the past!"

Ruth propped her elbow on the arm rest and nestled her forehead into her hand and closed her eyes.

Before pulling out of the parking lot Charles turned toward her and gently touched her cheek. "Look at me, Ruth. That was a long time ago, and it was an accident, a terrible accident. It wasn't your fault."

"Are we just supposed to rely on her not to tell Robert or Cassandra the history of their mother, do you think she can be that professional?" she asked, looking to Charles for answers, which was something she hadn't done in years.

Pulling out of the parking lot and keeping his eyes on the road, "Yes, Ruth, I do. I know Elizabeth better than you, and she was born to be a nurse and help people, not hurt them." Charles knew if he had to look her in the eye when speaking, he wouldn't have spoken those words.

Ruth didn't even turn her head to look at Charles, she just kept staring out the window. She tried her best to hide the fact that Charles's comment left her reeling. This conversation confirmed that her and Charles were still not in agreement after all these years when it came to Elizabeth. If she and Charles were not in agreement, then he was against her. For many years she hid her dislike of Elizabeth. She and Elizabeth were in love with the same man, and he was in love with Elizabeth. It was complicated, it was in the past, and that's where Ruth needed it all to stay.

"Do you think Cassandra recognized the name Bordure?" Ruth quietly asked. That's what she really wanted to know.

He reached over and grabbed her hand. "No, I don't think so. That was so long ago and her focus is on Robert."

"Oh, Charles, I hope you're right. We don't need to rehash all this past history again and give merit to Dorothy's tall tales. Dorothy took away any opportunity we could give Robert. Sean cannot run into Elizabeth, he just can't."

Charles loved and adored his wife. He hated to see her in so much anguish and have more worries than she should. As the years went on, he'd painfully learned that, for Ruth, sometimes love wasn't always enough for her.

"Ruth, you have to keep in mind that we did what we had to do for our sons. Sean would still be in prison today, and we wouldn't have our grandsons. Maybe we should have let Sean take his punishment, and in a way he did. Vietnam was no picnic..."

"But Robert...," she replied.

"I know, honey, I know. That's in the past, and sadly we have new problems for our present time. One day at a time, all right?" replied Charles.

Ruth laid her head back against the head rest and closed her eyes and whispered, "All right, one day at a time."

CHAPTER TEN

"In the Darkness"

Time remained out of sync as the Pointer family continued to revel in the shooting of Robert. A son, a brother, a nephew, an uncle, a cousin, a friend, and fiancé. He was just one man, but he meant so much to so many.

The weeks had quickly gone by since Robert was taken to the rehabilitation facility. Cassandra was only going back to Braxton for the backroom parties. During the holidays, the backroom parties on *The Crimson Rose* would lessen, and the holiday shows on *The Eclipse* became more of a draw.

Cassandra made a stop at the grocery store on her way to the Springton house. It was starting to get dark by the time she reached the house. She grabbed the grocery bags from the backseat of her car, hearing only the sounds of the crunching of the snow with each footfall. Why she got groceries she wasn't really sure, but take-out was getting old. It was still the struggle of making simple decisions, looking for normal. Whatever normal *is*, and grocery shopping seemed like a "normal" thing to do.

Then she called Mary to catch her up on the latest news. Mary was in a daze walking down the heavily royal blue carpeted hallway to the office on *The Eclipse,* when she heard the phone ringing. She broke out into a run toward the office in case it was Cassandra.

"Hello," she said, quickly answering the phone hoping she wasn't too late.

"Mary? It's me, Cassandra. Are you okay, you sound like you're out of breath?"

"Yeah, I was down the hall when I heard the phone ringing and ran to the office hoping I wouldn't miss the call in case it was you. How's Robert doing?"

"He's doing better. Physical therapy is helping him adjust with one eye and he's learning how to manage his deafness. His right arm is still shaking, and he's had a couple of seizures, but no stroke. His shaking seems to have gotten better and he's eating better. They make his food in a blender, and he can use a straw now."

"That's wonderful to hear. Is there any way I could come and see him? Maybe it's time everyone knows the truth. We know too well what shame and guilt secrets bring, don't we?"

"We can't, Mary, there's a nurse here that knows my mom and dad. I'm afraid she'll tell them or mention you were here, and then Mom and Dad will figure it out about you and Robert."

Mary was quiet for a moment, not sure what she had just heard.

"Did you just say that your mom and dad know Robert's nurse?"

"Yeah, her and *Daddy* served in the war together, can you believe that? I don't think Mom likes her much—there's really a weird vibe between the two of them. I have more to tell you, I'll fill you in on all that later."

Cassandra and Mary were spinning in the chaos around them, holding back their tears of sadness and frustration. Both wanted to be strong for each other and say all the right things. Robert's release was the first time the girls had experienced real hope and finally felt that, after all, their lives did have meaning. Cassandra was trying to choose her next words wisely; she knew Mary was right. The waters ran deep at the marina.

"Mary, the secrets we have are only ours because we are the secret, nothing good can come of my mom and dad or your parents knowing about you and Robert. I want to tell the whole world, I really do. Can you trust your parents to allow you this piece of happiness?"

The truth scared her more than their secrets. They knew their secrets, and in them Cassandra, Robert, and Mary found safety, security, and stability. Most of all, the ideals of how three young children thought life should be would no longer be a fantasy, it would be their lives.

These were the moments Mary dreaded, never being able to find a place for the truth. They were all trying to gain control over their own lives, not watch it slowly fade away right in front of them. The truth was the only answer.

"No, Cassandra, I don't. Even though I haven't spoken to my parents since I came here, I don't trust them," answered Mary.

"Yeah, I don't trust my parents to tell them about anything that brings me happiness or peace, either. Their succubi, you know," replied Cassandra.

"Yeah, I know. I miss you and Robert so much."

"I know, Mary, I miss you too, and Robert misses you. He loves you very much, he hasn't forgotten you."

"Oh, Cassandra, I love him so much. I just wish we would've been able to leave earlier. If we would've just packed up and left, he wouldn't have been here and he wouldn't be fighting for his life right now."

"I know, I've thought about that a lot. As soon as Robert's ready to leave the facility, we won't go back to Braxton. We're almost out, Mary."

They both took solace in their shared secret. Together they found enough hope between them to keep their tears hidden and focus on Robert and their plans. This way of life was coming to an end. Soon PECC would be a thing of the past. With their discretion and no bad publicity for Pointer Enterprises, it would surely end once and for all with each of them going their own way to leave the past behind.

"I hate to ask this, Mary, but are the holiday shows and events going okay on *The Eclipse*? You're not too overwhelmed, are you? I know I put a lot on you."

Mary was sitting at Cassandra's desk that was once neat and organized, now covered with purchase orders, schedule changes, and the year's fourth quarter tax rolls. The inbox overflowed into the out box. The Lake Girls were showing some jealousy between the switching up of clients. It wasn't out of greed, it was out of fear of getting left behind. Fear of the changes they would soon be facing, and The Lake Girls were in a panic. Their once tight-knit circle was beginning to implode. To make matters worse, over the weekend there was a bar fight, and one of the bartender's got a broken nose from a patron that swung and missed his adversary.

"I stay pretty busy, and being without a car has complicated getting last-minute things we may run out of or what not and doing the bank runs, but Charles has been helping out with those things. Anyway, I need to stay busy, and knowing you're with Robert gives me comfort, even though I wish it were me instead of you. I really do, Cassandra. I know I harp on it too much and I'm sorry, but I just can't help it," answered Mary, pushing past her visions of the broken glass that resembled her life. Pushing past the laundering of blood-soaked towels from the bartender's broken nose that seemed to confirm to her this move wasn't going to end as they planned.

"I know, Mary. I know your place is here with Robert and that my place is at the marina, and if I could make that happen, I would in a minute."

Cassandra paused briefly, clearing her throat.

Mary knew what she was doing, retreating within herself. She knew because she was retreating in her own way, to the office to bury herself in the unfinished paperwork hoping that no one would bother her.

"I know this is how it has to be, but you must know that I'll need to see him eventually. He has to know I'm here for him and I've got to be able to tell him that I love him. He has to hear those words from me," replied Mary softly.

"I know, and I promise you as soon as the first opportunity comes up we'll get you in to see Robert. There's so much I have to tell you when I get back. I'll tell you everything I've found out. Okay?"

"Okay. I know you will, I'm just beside myself and so confused," answered Mary, praying for some inner strength and healing for Robert.

"I know, me too, Mary. I'll talk to you tomorrow. Goodnight, my friend."

"Goodnight, my friend. Oh, and Cassandra, I'm sorry. No one belongs here at the marina, and neither do you."

Cassandra sat on the couch sipping her merlot, looking out the glass patio doors up at the sky, wondering if God was really up there. It was a clear, starry winter night. Cassandra would have no answers to her questions. It would be four bottles of wine later when she finally cried herself to sleep.

Mary lay in bed starring at the stars over the lake praying for Robert and praying for God to deliver them from this life. She gave in and took a vitamin Q with a sip of bourbon to help bring her sleep.

Robert had stirred a bit in between the administering of his medications, and he, too, saw the same clear sky and the same stars with his wandering eye. He thought of Uncle Joe, Cassandra, and Mary. He remembered the shooting. The memories brought him agony that compounded his physical pain. The strange thoughts he had during his awakening from the coma would still cause him some confusion. The color green would turn to red. He would overcome that, without fail, and Robert's first and last thought each day was of Mary. With his medications flowing freely, a single tear drop escaped down his cheek.

CHAPTER ELEVEN

"Intertwining Pathways of Past and Present"

It was the early mornings and late nights that were most difficult for Ruth and Charles. Ruth woke early, showered, dressed, and made her way downstairs for coffee. Charles had become an early riser—he was too restless to sleep in and lounge these days.

Christmas was quickly approaching and the day of the Pointer Christmas party to be held at The Medallion was almost here. Both Ruth and Charles were showing signs of exhaustion.

"Good morning, Ruthie," said Charles, walking into the kitchen, and he kissed her on the cheek. "You're up early. Got a busy day, huh?"

Ruth looked up from the newspaper and took a drink of her coffee, not going to admit she was scouring the paper again to see if there were any articles written about Robert, which there weren't.

"Yes, I have a busy day at the office overseeing the preparations for the Christmas party, and now that all the major parties of our customers are done and over, it's time for ours! And Charles, I'm up early every day. It's you who's up early today!"

Charles was pouring himself a cup of coffee and ignored her snarky comment about his "lounging." Grinning, he said to his wife, "Oh yes, and we must make sure we outdo every party in town, and it's not just the last Christmas party of the year, but THE last Christmas party of the year!"

Ruth ignored his sarcasm.

"That's right, darling, and don't you forget it!" she said, confident she was going to prove him wrong again about the importance of providing glamour and the opportunities that a good party could bring.

Charles was playfully mocking his wife, but he also felt his wife deserved the glamorous nights out on the town.

"Oh, Ruthie, you so do love a good party, don't you? And you know what?" he asked with his baby blues twinkling.

Seeing that Charles was in a flippy mood, she raised only her eyes and playfully said back to him, "No, my dear, what?"

"And I love you!" he replied.

"Oh, Charles!" she replied with the innocence of a young girl.

"Are you doing better today, my darling?" Charles asked his wife, grinning from ear to ear.

"I think so. Robert's recovery is going well, and there's even hope he may be able to live on his own again. I know we still don't have all the answers and his recovery could be a year, maybe two. Like you said, one day at a time, right?"

He gently took her in his arms and they embraced. "Yep, one day at a time," he whispered lovingly.

Charles wasn't going to acknowledge what he knew about gunshot wounds to the head from his service in WWII. For this place and time, he was willing to get lost in an apparition of what they all wanted for Robert. They all needed this ray of hope to hang onto.

Ruth gently pulled away from her husband of thirty-seven years, lingering, still holding his hands. "Will I see you in the office today?" she asked.

"No, I'm going to head to the marina. With Cassandra's absence I want to make sure the place is still floating out there," he said sarcastically, but really meant it.

She couldn't help but giggle and gathered her purse and briefcase. "All right," she said, and kissed him on the cheek. "I'll see you later this evening?"

"It's a date!" said Charles, smiling at his wife.

The Medallion was turning into the winter wonderland, just like she imagined, and the two biggest Christmas trees that could be found in town were now at The Medallion. There was one in the dining room and one in the banquet room. It smelled of pine and poinsettias were scattered about in the colors of red and white. The bar was lined in red and white Christmas lights, and the fireplace in the dining room was roaring every night during the dinner hour. Stockings were hung on the fireplace mantle for collections for the local town charities. The VA Administration, The Salvation Army, Harmony House, CAM Forsyth, and Pointers Enterprises Children's Charity (PECC). PECC was a charity closest to Ruth's heart and she started it in 1967. The charity did many things and prided itself on the ability to provide young adults with work skills so they could learn how to provide for themselves and focused on helping downtrodden children. It was really born of ambition verses guilt. The charity was started when Robert went to prison and was incorporated as part of his legacy. If Ruth's ambition didn't devour her guilty conscience creeping in, it may have destroyed her. PECC seemed to fill the void of losing her sons for a period of time. The bonus was the outward appearance to the entertainment world said she did have the skills of a good mother and that remorse and redemption were also characteristics of the Pointer family. Each year Pointer Enterprises would match the donations, minus a small handling fee, of course. It was good public relations for the Pointer family, and their picture was in the paper each year boasting about the accomplishments of Pointer Enterprises and who was who and how much money was raised and what Pointer Enterprises had matched.

It was this picture in the paper each year that Ruth was able to make her statement to those who called her "new money" that whether it be old money or new money, both did good things. It wasn't that Ruth didn't realize she was being subtly reminded that regardless of her acquired wealth, she would never have a pedigree of wealth; nor would she ever achieve the social status that is earned through old money…she knew. The style of such lineage and class of old money could not be bought.

Poor people were wrought with ambition from the pangs of poverty, and rich people were engulfed in endless opportunities with a platform. It was for these reasons she was up early every morning having her coffee and working so hard.

Ruth usually worked with her door closed; sometimes the office would be so busy it was hard for her to finish a thought.

Knock, knock, she heard rapping on the door. "Come on in, it's open," she called out.

Sean stuck his head in the door. "Mom, do you have a minute for me and Caroline?"

"Of course, come on in. What brings you by?"

Caroline was quiet and Ruth could see she had been crying; her eyes were red and swollen and she looked like she hadn't slept in days.

"Sit down," she said, motioning to the two chairs in front of her desk.

"Mom, Caroline and I have something we need to tell you," Sean said with hesitation.

Ruth put the tax rolls down she was reviewing, and her dark brown eyes were full of anticipation. Leaning forward with her hands clasped together, "What is it, son?" she asked.

Sean stammered a bit, and Caroline would look at Sean, then at Ruth, and then to the floor.

"It's about the shooting…" answered Sean.

Ruth began to speak softly before hearing any more.

"Sean, Caroline, the police investigated the shooting and it was ruled as the accidental shooting it was. I know this has been hard on you both and my grandsons. I promise you, this is something you can all get past. Robert's doing very well, and he has the best medical care that money can buy; he's regaining his memory a little more each day, and we have hope."

Sean rubbed his forehead as he always did when he felt stressed and was wondering what to do about something.

"Mom, I didn't shoot Robert," he blurted out bluntly and quickly.

"What?" She gasped.

"If you didn't shoot Robert, who did, Sean?"

The eerie silence had returned and demanded answers. Ruth's eyes darted back and forth between Sean and Caroline, judging Sean and condemning Caroline.

"Who shot Robert?" she asked again, demanding the answer.

"Sean, I am talking to you, *who* shot Robert? I'm waiting for an answer, son!"

"Jack, Jack shot Robert," said Sean, almost in a whisper.

Caroline broke out in tears. "Oh, Ruth, it's true, it's true." She cried like she was in a confessional.

Sean was hurled back to the past when he was only two years older than his own son and in a similar position.

"What if Robert remembers it was Jack that shot him?" wailed Caroline.

Caroline could no longer contain the torment she had been going through for months.

"My son, Ruth! My son!" she said almost in a whimper. "He didn't mean to do it, he got scared and thought Robert was going to really hurt his dad."

Ruth took in a deep breath having the worst case of deja vu. *This was not an accidental shooting!* She fell back in her chair, rested her head against its high back, and closed her eyes.

Ruth hoped so desperately that it was different this time. Sean was angry, and Jack was angry *and* scared. Ruth wanted to cry, she wanted to scream, *My son! My son! What about my son! How could this have happened? How could you have let this happen? Didn't you learn anything! Didn't you teach your son anything! Caroline, this is all your fault, you are no good for my son, and you are weak!* She couldn't put words to her emotions. Blame. She didn't know where to place the blame. Her face was like stone, her demeanor distant, and her powerful piercing brown eyes loudly raged and expressed what her voice couldn't speak.

Sean glanced up at this mother—he had seen his mother look like this before and he was afraid of what was coming next. Emotions that Ruth had difficulty dealing with were rushing in and taking over. Feelings of anxiety and despair were causing her to want to react immediately, and the underlying anger she had been harboring on her own had begun to boil in her veins. For a moment a headline flashed through her mind. "Tanton County Businessman, Another Family Shooting, Like Father, Like Son."

A little more composed, Ruth decided it was not only time for the truth, but it was time for the unanswered questions to now be answered. She knew why she couldn't put the pieces together and she heard Dr. Carsman's words again. The words that had kept her up at night: *If the shot would not have come from such a far distance and been a direct shot, we wouldn't be having this conversation.* He was shot from a distance further away, probably the porch area; it was Jack! That's why she couldn't understand. Immediately she wondered if anyone else had figured this out. Obviously not, the police ruled it as an accidental shooting.

"Sean, what was the fight between you and Robert about?" Ruth directly asked her son, and her tone sent shivers down his spine.

Caroline looked persistently at her husband, needling him. "You need to tell her, Sean. This isn't something that's going to go away. You and I both know how this is going to go down and how it was set in motion to go down!" she said, continuing to challenge him.

Sean looked at his wife red faced and angry. If his mother wasn't present, this may have been one of those times he wouldn't stand for Caroline to be so taxing. He was standing up and pacing, his arms were straight down by his sides and his hands clinched in fists. Caroline noticed his body language and knew it well, but she didn't flinch.

"Well, Sean, what was the fight about?" said Ruth, commanding her son to come out with it. His mother was escalating, and Sean knew it was going to get worse before it got better.

Sitting down in the chair next to Caroline, Sean began to answer his mother's question.

"It was about Uncle Joe and The Station at 76," he said with indication that he was blameless in that affair, knowing how important it was that he try to proclaim his innocence early on. More importantly to proclaim his son's innocence.

Ruth held up her hands to push his words back. This wasn't a conversation she wanted to have.

"Sean, that deal has nothing to do you with any of you kids. I don't understand why this keeps coming up!"

Sean pushed the matter hard with his mother. "Oh, but Mom, it does: Robert found all those invoices that Uncle Joe made out to us and Pointer Enterprises."

"I have those invoices, there's no way Robert knows," Ruth confidently replied, opening the safe.

His mother's over-confidence didn't surprise him, but Robert's over-confidence the day of the shooting did surprise him.

"Mom, he knows about all the money that's rightfully owed to Uncle Joe, and he also knows I control the marina, and that it's not just a marina. He knows about PECC."

Ruth's face was expressionless when she didn't find the papers in the safe; not only were the invoices gone, but the contracts that were between her and her brother were gone.

The atmosphere in the room was heavy. Ruth turned her back to Sean and Caroline, looking out the window. They had no idea of what would come next. They sat still and quiet, afraid of what they would see when Ruth turned around.

Her brother Joe held a tenant status with Pointer Enterprises. Ruth remembered the day Joe asked about a health insurance policy for him and his family, he knew with the group rate it would be less expensive and better than anything he could get individually. She remembered telling him that he didn't qualify to be under the insurance plan of Pointer Enterprises because of that tenant status. She had taken every fringe benefit she could out of her brother's business and sucked it dry, making herself a half of million dollars in the process and withheld from him a basic need. This was no secret amongst Joe's employees, they knew as soon as they received their insurance cards and wanted to know why they weren't part of a corporate plan.

Sean was scared to break the silence and bring up the next point, but it couldn't go without saying.

"And now that the station is for sale..." Sean's words trailing off, as this is the part where it got messy with his mother. He wasn't up for challenging her over something that wasn't supposed to be his business, but it had become his business that morning when Robert showed up in his driveway bringing the sins of their mother with him.

Ruth and Sean were on the same page, and she didn't need him to explain to her how devastating this could be.

"Yes, Sean, I know the business will have to show its assets and its cash flow, and *it's* carrying a lot of uncollected debt," she said haughtily.

"Mom, there's almost half a million dollars that's going to be unaccounted for. How are you going to explain this when the new buyer starts requesting to see the books? Was Robert right, were you setting Joe up to make it look like he embezzled this money to save the sale? You do know that it's possible if this plan of yours works that Uncle Joe, your own brother, may be sent to prison?"

When he really saw his mom, who she really was it frightened him. Ruth remained silent.

In a whisper he continued, "The one thing I don't understand is that Uncle Joe doesn't have the money. We never paid him, did we?" Sean ran his fingers through his hair and took a much-needed breath.

Ruth never responded.

"Oh, Mom, Caroline is right, Robert was really angry. I've never seen him so angry and I wasn't even sure I was going to be able to defend myself against him that morning, and that's why Jack shot him."

Caroline's shoulders relaxed; now it was out and all she really cared about was her son. Caroline looked at Ruth, condemning her for the past and silently warned her that Jack is her son.

"Ruth, have you thought about what Robert may do if he remembers it was Jack that shot him? Jack's been living through hell these past few months, and he'll have to carry this with him for the rest of his life," said Caroline, digging deep into herself for courage. "He's your grandson, your fifteen-year-old grandson! One thing you can be sure of, Ruth, is that my son's will not suffer the same fate your son's did!"

Caroline was now face to face with her mother-in-law.

"Caroline!" said Sean, fuming. "Don't talk to my mother that way! She loves her grandsons."

Caroline stood up and faced Sean shocking her mother-in-law.

"She loves Robert and Cassandra too! But why do you think Robert was so angry Sean! Maybe another innocent person going to prison was more than he could stand for. Did you ever think about that? Let's get this straight here and now, both of you! This third generation of Pointers will not live as the first and second. Jack and Joshua are my sons!"

In a rage, Sean turned to Caroline. "They're my sons too, Caroline!" Caroline stood tall and continued to challenge Sean; her days of clumsiness were over. "I'm only gonna repeat myself one more time, Sean: they are *my* sons…"

She decided not to finish her sentence saying what she really felt, *that he didn't deserve his children*. There was no doubt that Ruth and Sean understood exactly what her words meant. Once again Sean's face was red with rage, and his neck muscles bulged. Sean turned his back to Caroline, and she didn't care what this may have cost her.

Ruth sat listening to her son tell her what happened, and in turn figuring out a big part of what had happened between her and Joe and even listened to her daughter-in-law threaten her and challenge her husband. It hurt her deeply that her children had found themselves in another precarious situation. This emotional roller coaster ride Ruth had been on these last few months had raised her anxiety level to a high peak; the pit in her stomach was anticipating the dramatic drop.

"Mom, money is the only thing you need or care about. Well, *your* money didn't keep Robert out of prison, and it didn't keep me from going to Vietnam, did it!" he yelled, channeling his rage toward his mother.

Caroline sat up straight and remained rigid in her body language, she looked at her husband and her tear-filled eyes pleaded with him to be quiet, to stop. It was her instinct to protect her children, and it took everything within her to come here today and be face to face with her mother-in-law, her children's grandmother, and she needed his support. Things were changing in Sean's world, and the power was shifting to his wife.

"Both of you will do well to remember it was your anger Sean that sent you to Vietnam and it was Robert that saved your ass! *So*, you say my money couldn't keep you out of Vietnam? You may be right about that, but it was you, Sean, who got yourself sent to Vietnam. As far as Robert going to prison, you have no idea what I did to try to prevent that, and *that* was also left over remnants from your anger!"

Ruth turned and looked at Caroline and her piercing brown eyes were now almost black with rage. Caroline knew if it was possible, they would have burnt a hole right through her. Ruth couldn't hold her tongue any longer and blasted Caroline, "What about my son, huh, Caroline? What about my son!" she said harshly. "You're not the only mother in this room worried about *her* son!"

"Ruth, neither Sean nor I meant any—" Caroline started to say.

Ruth cut Caroline off in midsentence, taking her control back.

"Caroline, I agree with you that my grandchildren shouldn't be plagued with the past sins of the generations before them. Let me remind you that I've been in this position before, between my two sons. Now, you can both sit in judgment of me if you want to, but the business dealings that went on between myself and your Uncle Joe has nothing to do with your portion of Pointer Enterprises that you manage, Sean. I'm not going to discuss it with you, and we aren't ever going to discuss this matter again, do you both understand?"

Caroline looked at Ruth and nodded her head yes.

"Caroline, I'm sorry, I didn't hear you," flared her mother-in-law.

"Yes, I understand, Ruth," she answered meekly.

Immediately Caroline was angry with herself, she felt she had just taken back her submissive position with Ruth. Sean was not as compliant at first, but eventually, he looked at his mother and simply replied, "Yes."

With that understanding Ruth asserted her control and continued on.

"Sean, I have listened to you and lived with this underlying anger and rage towards me thinking there was some big secret about your father. Now you know full well the things Dorothy has done. And you, my son, have heard all of this before, but yet you still chose to believe her over me and you took your anger out that dreadful night on this restaurant. Do you see any bitter irony here, Sean?"

Sean knew that was a rhetorical question and dared not interrupt. He knew that letting his mother continue on and on would be less painful than if he didn't. As far as the bitter irony of his situation, he had been reeling in it for months.

"Your father and I were in a precarious position, and to save you, we all made sacrifices. Especially Robert." She faltered for a moment, consumed with regret, but quickly recovered. "And now you and Caroline are ironically in a similar predicament that your father and I were in all those years ago. Now, I ask you both, what are you going to do?"

Neither Sean nor Caroline could find any words. Sean sat there hoping that his and his son's innocence had been proclaimed. Caroline sat there crumbling on the inside, hoping she at least appeared to have stood her ground. She knew she was no match for her mother-in-law. The silence had found them once again. Time was continuing to move forward, while their reality moved backwards, gravitating toward a familiar history, one agonizing minute at a time.

"Huh?" asked Ruth. "Go ahead tell me what you're going to do!"

Ruth reclaimed ownership over the room that was filled with an explosive revelation.

Caroline and Sean remained silent.

"Yeah, that's what I thought. Sean, your underlying rage and anger has negatively impacted this family from that dreadful day, and I realize the difference in this situation is that you didn't go looking for trouble this time, it came to you. My point here is that your anger and rage hasn't left you. You beat your wife, and your children are growing up with this anger and hate. Jack almost believes his mother deserves the hits! Although he's my grandson, he's disrespectful, too cocky for his own good, and growing up to be an angry young man! And, might I add, you both should remember that I've never stood in judgment of either of you. The ignorance of you both to think nobody knows this is appalling!"

Ruth made direct eye contact when she turned to speak to Caroline, her eyes still reflecting anger, but when speaking of her grandson her voice began to soften.

"Caroline, I'm not going to abandon Jack."

Then she looked at Sean and he feared that his mother would control them for the rest of their lives.

"Sean, you're never going to lay another finger on your wife, you're going to let go of the past and focus on being the head of your family, the man your family deserves. One that your family admires and respects and you'll continue to own and operate the smokehouse, the marina, and the campgrounds. You'll preserve your legacy and pass that down to your children. A legacy that was handed down to us by your grandfather. A legacy that your father and I continued to build on, to be handed down to our children and grandchildren."

Even if Sean and Caroline could have found any words, they wouldn't have been able to speak them.

"It's time, Sean," said Ruth looking directly at her son, "that you realize what you have and what's been done for you so that you could keep it. You, my son, have no reason to be angry. Can you do that, Sean, to save your family?"

Sean ran his fingers through his wavy light ginger brown hair again, and Ruth couldn't help but notice his hair hadn't even begun to gray, not even his beard. Oh, how she recognized the beautiful color and thickness of his ginger hair. He was part of her, and he was a part of her past that she wanted to hang onto so desperately.

"Mom, I'll do anything to save my family. I'm a shit, and I know that, but you're right, my sons don't have to be. I never wanted them to go through some of the things I've gone through."

Sean's face reflected sadness, and much regret, he knelt down next to Caroline's chair. "Caroline, can you ever forgive me?" he pleaded.

Caroline didn't want to, she wanted to run away as far as she could and take her boys with her. This wasn't a conversation she wanted to have in front of her mother-in-law.

She looked down at her husband. "Sean, do you really mean it?"

He closed his eyes for a moment and a tear ran down his cheek and lay glistening on his ginger beard and he looked up at her. "Yes, I do,

Caroline, I do," he answered, speaking the well-rehearsed words that he'd repeated many times before in the years of their marriage.

Caroline replied with a simple, "I want that too." She hoped she used the right voice of naiveté. She was stuck, and now she would be fighting for her sons.

Caroline had learned the hard way over the years and had developed the same second nature to the entertainment business and knew to how to hide what she didn't want to be shown. She hoped she had hidden it well enough.

Ruth seemed pleased and was hoping this was the epiphany Sean needed and that he really did realize how good he had it and how important and beautiful his family was.

"Mom, do you think Cassandra knows?" he asked cautiously.

"No, son, I don't. If she knew something like this, we'd *all* know it. Cassandra is the least of our worries, for now anyway. Oh, Sean, Caroline, Charles cannot know any of this."

It sounded more like an order than a plea. Sean and Caroline nodded their heads yes, and recognized they were being dismissed. Obediently, they left her office, closing the door behind them. It was the Pointer way to suppress a secret in the Pointer family with another one.

Ruth was worried about Cassandra, but not for the same reason that Sean was: she worried about that day at the rehab facility when Cassandra heard the name "Bordure." Maybe that was finally put to rest and wouldn't come up again to haunt Sean. And Rose, she was worried about her too. Rose did know, or had an idea about the business dealings with Joe. That day her and Rose fought, it was over this same matter: the eviction of Joe. Ruth had insisted she'd made a mistake in the calculations of the debt the station was carrying and confirmation of whose debt it was. Rose had already checked and rechecked her figures and she'd made no mistake. It was one thing for her mother not to allow her into the circle of the "pretty people," but another to insult her intelligence. Just as Cassandra surpassed Ruth in her beauty, Rose *had* surpassed her mother's intelligence. It was a unique situation that had presented itself for Joe and his family to move to

Braxton. Joe was an ingenious mechanic, second to none. It couldn't have come at a better time for Pointer Enterprises. The family element had made it possible for her to bridge her construction loan. In the past it had to be Joe, and in the future, it must be Jack. Jack will be the one who takes Pointer Enterprises into the future.

This deal had caused her some exposure and appeared to have the potential to blow up in her face. Ruth's worst fear had come true: the past had collided with the present.

CHAPTER TWELVE

"Preserving a Legacy"

After Sean and Caroline left her office, Ruth immediately made a phone call to the rehabilitation center. She was desperately trying to figure out how to save Robert, Jack, Pointer Enterprises, and not be sentenced to poverty. This scandal would surely ruin the Pointer name that was already controversial, and the third generation must be above reproach.

She was scrambling through the papers on her desk looking for the business card of Robert's psychiatrist. *Oh! Where is it?*

She frantically flipped through her rolodex, moving things around on her desk and looking under papers.

Oh! Thank goodness, there it is, it's a Dr. Marshall.

Clumsily, she dialed the phone number.

"Ozarks Rehabilitation Center, how may I help you?"

"Hi, this is Ruth Pointer and I'm calling to speak with Dr. Marshall regarding my son, Robert Pointer."

"One moment, please. I'll see if he's available."

Ruth felt like she was on hold forever, nervously tapping her pen on the desk.

She heard a click on the phone. "Dr. Marshall here."

"Dr. Marshall, this is Ruth Pointer."

"Hi! Mrs. Pointer, good to hear from you. What can I do for you?"

"I was hoping to get an update on my son, how's he doing?"

"He's doing really well. Each day he's emotionally stronger. I see no reason why he won't have total recall of that dreadful day and we'll begin to piece it all together and begin to come to terms with it. He still has a long way to go, but considering the circumstances, I have high hopes."

"That's wonderful news. I'm going to come see him tomorrow morning. Would you have time to meet with me?"

She could tell he was checking his calendar, hearing the flipping of pages turning.

"Would ten a.m. work?" asked Dr. Marshall.

"Yes, that sounds perfect, thank you."

"Very good, I'll see you tomorrow morning, goodbye," replied Dr. Marshall, hanging up the phone.

The next morning Ruth was up early, and Charles was back in the habit of sleeping late. Ruth had always wondered how he could sleep late with so much going on in one day. She would have every day planned to the last detail, to the last minute, and being late was unacceptable. There were managers, bankers, accountants, and lawyers that would need consulting from time to time. There were purchases, contracts, and loan closings that needed signing and approved, countered, or rejected. She had to make sure she was aware of any newcomers that may have joined the networks she worked within. More importantly, to make sure they knew her. She worked off lists with goals in mind, her behavior was purposeful. Her ambition was her driving force that empowered her to minimize family drama and maintain their lifestyle in the fishbowl. However, Charles's golf games with the mayor also proved to be beneficial more times than not, so she rarely mentioned or begrudged his lounging. After all, it was a man's world.

Walking down the stairs Ruth smelled the aroma of fresh-brewed coffee. It seemed to be the only constant these days. The smell of freshly brewed coffee used to give her confidence that her day would start like any other day. Now, the smell of fresh-brewed coffee was not only was how she started her days; it was a reminder of how important each day was. Robert and Jack weighed heavily on her heart. It would be best if Robert didn't remember, and Jack could forget.

She started having her breakfast in the kitchen these days because she couldn't face the vision of Robert's empty chair at Thanksgiving. A vision imprinted in her mind that appeared to her often. A vision she desperately tried to escape.

The kitchen floor was made of red-glazed brick tile. There was an oversized center island with a butcher block top that seated four. Shiny copper pots and pans hung from the island on display. Above the double stainless kitchen sink were large double pane windows that twisted open and faced the swimming pool in the backyard. The large windowsill was filled with every kind and color of orchids. When in bloom there was a beautiful array of light pinks, dark pinks, oranges, yellows, reds, and even blues. In the center of the orchids sat a healthy aloe vera plant.

In the back corner there was a bay window that overlooked the woods. It was a perfect setting for the large kitchen table that sat three on the padded window seat, three chairs opposite of the bay window, with seating on each end of the table.

Decorative baskets sat high on top of the white cabinets. The kitchen was homey and said "Welcome" to anyone who entered. It was on the padded window seat she would curl up, to drink her coffee and look out over the woods. The kitchen held many wonderful memories for her. Swimming, pizza nights, and the children's birthday parties. So happy and vivid you could almost hear the laughter of the Pointer siblings splashing in the pool. Beautiful sounds of music filled the house while Cassandra practiced the piano. Ruth walked to the window and looked out at the swimming pool; it was covered for winter and there weren't any children outside playing. Following the music in her head, she walked into the sitting the room. She no longer heard the songs that Cassandra used to play, and her daughter wasn't there.

No one was there, she was left with the memory of her sister Dorothy. When she was young, she, too, struggled with ideals of how things should be, could be. Being born in poverty with nine siblings and a father she called by his first name brought her much confusion, and she carried her father's secret all these years. No other family she knew called their father by his first name. Over the years Ruth and Martha would take on the role of being caretakers and raising their younger siblings. Ruth had grown up quickly.

It was just another oddity noticed by others causing teasing from her peers and judgment by her elders. Ruth and her sisters, Martha and Lydia, were beautiful and in the "pretty people" circle. Nadia died in her first year of high school in a sporting accident, and Yolanda died from fever when she was only two. More loss was suffered in the family when Bernie died at the same age of Yolanda from fever. A doctor was never called because there was no money for the doctor. Of Ruth's surviving brothers, Aaron, Landon, Joe, and Brandon were very handsome men. All born with jet-black hair except for Lydia and Landon; they were born with beautiful red hair. When their sister Dorothy was born, she was born with a speech impediment and mentally slow when it came to learning. Dorothy was smart, but it was difficult for her to learn in a standard routine scholastic setting. Growing up she would often be pushed aside at home and at school. She also wasn't in the circle of the "pretty people" in a family of beautiful people. As time went on, Dorothy lacked self-care and suffered from low self-esteem. She grew up with a rage inside of her that would cause fear in her siblings, and she was a very observant child. It was at the one and only family reunion that Dorothy taunted her nephew, Sean, with the *Bordure* name.

Aimlessly, with her memories fading, she walked back into the kitchen and curled up on the padded bench seat, looking out at the dormant woods. Mattie handed her a cup of coffee. "Thank you, Mattie."

"You're welcome. Would you like some bacon and eggs?"

For a moment Mattie thought she might be sincere, lost in deep reflection and genuinity.

"No, no thank you, toast is fine, but I'm sure there's no better alarm for Charles than cooking smoked bacon!" Ruth said with a little chuckle.

There it is! What a selfish woman! thought Mattie, and decided not to engage in a back and forth with Ruth and just handed her the paper and went about her work.

Ruth still wasn't feeling well and having difficulty eating full meals. And now, just finding out that Jack shot Robert took her into more darkness than she could ever imagine and the biggest scandal she would ever encounter.

She scoured the newspapers and gathered her thoughts before making her long drive this morning. If it were to get out that Jack shot Robert, the headlines would be brutal.

What would Robert do if he remembered that Jack shot him? Would he tell his story to the police and try to ruin his young nephew's life, as his was ruined all those years ago? I lost him when he was young boy and met him again when he was a young man, he wasn't the same person. To him, he might just be setting the record straight for once and for all. If he told his story of what was a mother's betrayal in his eyes, would that ruin me? What would that truth do if it got out?

Saddened, she got in her car and headed out to the rehab facility; only she knew where she was going today. Once again, she was driving alone on those curvy Ozark roads, hoping the drive would bring some bring clarity to the questions that plagued her at breakfast. Ruth was not happy that her son had grown so close to Joe. Today brought to her the reality of a truth she always had to push to the back of her mind for the last ten years. She did what she could do to make it not true and struggled to ignore it. The little boy that loved and adored his momma so much was no longer there, and after his release from prison, he never tried to connect with her.

It was the cold hard fact that if Robert had some other place to go, he would've been there instead of working at The Medallion and living in the apartment above it. If her son never had to lay eyes on her again, he would've been happy, and that hurt her deeply. All Ruth wanted when Robert came home was to be his mom, give him everything that was rightfully his, and make up for those long-lost years. She turned up the radio hoping that would bring the desperately needed distraction she was looking for. The past was the reason she was in her car driving to The Ozarks Rehabilitation Center, in the present.

A long time ago back in that little Ozarks hill town, she made herself a promise she'd never be plummeted into poverty again, and even still, she intended on keeping it. She had come too far to ever be referred to as a hill person or from a family of hill people; she and her family were pioneers of the town of Braxton. Charles was considered a founding father of the town, and if she weren't a woman, she would be too. Her ambitions of wanting more and more were no longer fueled by her accomplishments, instead they drove her to attain more and more. Her ambitions over the years began to blur the balance between greed and generosity. She grew more and more emotionally unattached and found herself left with tunnel vision. Tunnel vision that left her clinging to what she could see and count, not always what she could feel. Her selfishness was intertwined with self-sacrificing and self-preservation. As complex as the situation was and Joe being her brother didn't change the fact that The Station at 76 had to be sold; she *needed* the money.

Relieved when she finally turned into the parking lot of the rehab facility, she took a moment to compartmentalize herself. It wasn't that she was happy to be there, she was ready to get rid of those thoughts that were running wildly around in her head. Cassandra's car wasn't in the parking lot and she hoped she had missed her. Today of all days, she was not prepared for a confrontation with her youngest.

Today she had to be prepared to come face to face with Nurse Elizabeth Bell, just in case. Ruth armed herself in a smart-looking long-sleeved pale blue suit with sensible navy pumps and twisted her hair into a sophisticated French roll. She had taken extra time with her make-up, and her jewelry announced her entrance. Nurse Bell wasn't going to be able to make her feel insignificant or poor today, or ever again.

The bitter cold slapped her in face getting out of the car. Being careful not to slip and fall, she walked as quickly as she could to the front entrance. When she opened the door, she felt the immediate warmth from the radiated heat.

"Hi, may I help you?" asked the receptionist.

"I'm here to meet with Dr. Marshall, my name is Ruth Pointer."

"Yes, ma'am, he's expecting you. Follow me, I'll take you to his office."

"Thank you," replied Ruth.

Together they walked down the hall to Dr. Marshall's office without encountering Elizabeth. Dr. Marshall's office door was open, and he was reviewing Robert's case file. "Dr. Marshall," said the receptionist, quietly knocking on his door, "Mrs. Pointer is here."

He quickly stood up from behind his desk and met her at the door, "Mrs. Pointer, thank you for making the trip. I know it will mean a lot to Robert to see you as well." Ruth nodded. She didn't know if she could face Robert today, and she missed him so much. A familiar feeling of guilt panged her heart and her stomach felt sick. Still, to this day it never dawned on her that she was, again, in a moral dilemma. A moral dilemma rejecting salvation from the past and the deep-seeded need to hang onto a piece of it: a part she felt she couldn't live without.

"Let me take your coat, come in, come in, have a seat. Can I get you a cup of coffee or a cup of tea?" Ruth took a seat across from his desk and hung her Chanel purse over the back of her chair.

"Yes, please. A cup of coffee, black, would be wonderful. Thank you for taking the time to see me today," she replied.

"Not at all. What do you wish to talk to me about?" said Dr. Marshall, handing her a cup of coffee. Ruth crossed her legs and took a sip of her coffee. Her diamond wedding ring sparkled as she tipped the cup. She hugged the cup and felt its warmth in the palms of her hands; the steam carried the coffee's aroma reviving her earlier thoughts. *Robert. my son; Jack, my grandson. Jack, so young, his youth gives him a chance to overcome all of this. A tragedy…how will this end? Oh, my son…*

Ruth sat her coffee cup and saucer on the small table beside her.

"Dr. Marshall, I'm thrilled with the progress Robert is making. I now know why they say this is the best facility in the Midwest."

"Thank you, we do work hard, and we're lucky with the staff we have here at the facility as well," answered Dr. Marshall, beaming with pride. "Nurse Bell, Robert's head nurse, is one of the best when it comes to successful rehabilitation. Even if Robert doesn't make a full recovery, if it's possible, Nurse Bell is the one to bring him through it."

"Yes, yes she is," said Ruth, smiling and nodding in agreement. "You know my husband and Elizabeth served together in WWII."

"Yes, I did know that," said Dr. Marshall, picking up Robert's case file. The conversation fell into a silent lull for a moment. To avoid acknowledging the awkwardness, Ruth took a sip of her coffee and manipulated the silence instead.

"Dr. Marshall, do you see Robert making a full recovery, do you see him getting his memory back?"

"Well, it's only been a few weeks and it's really too soon to tell," replied Dr. Marshall.

Ruth took a deep breath, and her self-preservation and self-sacrifice became one in the same.

"Dr. Marshall, are you aware that Robert has a violent past and served ten years in prison? He went to prison when he was fifteen for manslaughter."

She barely heard herself say those words, and she couldn't tell how she delivered them because she didn't believe them herself. For she knew those words weren't true. She could barely swallow her throat was so tight.

"No, I was not aware of that. What was the nature of the incident?" he asked.

Ruth licked her lips and swallowed hard. There was no turning back now.

"He had gotten angry at me one night and took a semi-automatic weapon and shot out the widows of my restaurant, and the result of that action ended with a man dying. I only bring this up because if his memories are coming back, I think you can see why I worry about any underlying issues," said the mother of her adult son who was down the hall struggling to recover, survive his nightmares, and reclaim his life.

Dr. Marshall rubbed his upper lip with concern. "I see. So, you're worried about an angry man leaving the facility and going back home and the interactions that may happen between him and his brother?"

"Yes. These past few weeks have been especially hard on me and my family, as I'm sure you can understand. I have one son fighting for his life and my other son accidentally shot him. I have doubts that Robert will be able to overcome this, and I wonder if you have any insight on this matter."

"How long has Robert been out of prison?" inquired Dr. Marshall.

"About four years now."

Dr. Marshall took his glasses off, set them on his desk, and rubbed his eyes. "Were Robert and Sean in an altercation when the shooting took place? Was Robert the aggressor?"

Ruth looked down at the floor before answering, "Yes, he was. Dr. Marshall for years my family has lived walking around on eggshells. I want my son to have the best care possible and for all of us to have the best quality of life that we can. In the past few weeks, I've come to terms with the fact that Robert may be institutionalized for the rest of his life; it hasn't been easy, believe me. That's why I wanted to speak with you and get your honest opinion. Do you think my family could be at risk if he makes a full recovery?" she asked with her innuendos and insinuations.

"Well, Mrs. Pointer, this sure is a lot to take in. I don't believe I have enough information or have spent enough time with Robert to make that determination," answered a perplexed Dr. Marshall.

Ruth quickly switched strategies. "I was hoping you'd say that. I feel better already. I still feel like we have hope.

"Dr. Marshall, I don't think I would survive another death or near-death situation."

Dr. Marshall maintained eye contact with Ruth.

"I can understand that, Mrs. Pointer. These are two very traumatic events that you and your family have been through. Do you think counseling would help your sons work through their issues together? It's quite a tragedy between the two, and it does seem that things escalated between them in a short time."

Ruth broke eye contact with Dr. Marshall for a moment, then faced him again and answered, "No, I really don't. We've tried that in the past upon Robert's release from prison."

Dr. Marshall put his glasses on. "Give me a couple of weeks to further evaluate Robert and see if we have any insight to this newfound information. Robert's situation is compounded by many variables as you well know. Let's talk after the Christmas holiday. How does that sound?"

Ruth dabbed her eyes with her handkerchief. "Thank you, Dr. Marshall." She reached for her purse, and he helped her with her coat.

"Oh, Dr. Marshall, each year at the Pointer Enterprises Christmas party and New Year's Eve party we collect for certain charities. I just wanted to let you know I'll be adding your name to the list for both parties. I'm so thankful for all of you here and for all the help and care that Robert and my family are both receiving."

"Mrs. Pointer, that's very generous of you, thank you. Merry Christmas."

"Merry Christmas," replied Ruth.

With that Ruth left his office, turned her back to the direction of Robert's room, and walked toward the EXIT sign. The wind had picked up, causing her tears to sting against her face. *What have I done? What have I put in motion?*

Through her tears, the lock to the car door was blurry, and her gloved fingers fumbled trying to unlock the door.

She sat in the car waiting for it to warm up and did her best to talk herself through it, reasoning and rationalizing. Today, in the present, she was the mother of two adult sons and a grandmother of a young and angry fifteen-year-old. The past and the present continued to crisscross with each other. One voice in her head was saying, *See they're right, you are nothing but new money, and the true difference between old and new money is the attitude and the voice you give your money.* The louder and stronger voice of her reason said, *Your money can buy things and change your situation, it may not be able to buy people per se, but it may be able to control them. Now, if you didn't have your money, you wouldn't be able to save yourself or anyone else. Without your money, there'd be no solution.*

There were newspaper headlines again flashing through her mind and they all led to the same story: "Pointer Enterprises New Scandal: Pioneers of Braxton Missouri spells: C-O-R-R-U-P-P-T-I-O-N!" If she was ruined over what happened in the past Pointer Enterprises would not survive and she would have no financial security. Pointer Enterprises was not built on a cornerstone, contrary to its presentation. Charles would fall. Sean would fall. Rose would fall. Cassandra would fall. What would happen to Robert then? Who would provide for his care? Everyone they employed would fall. She would be exiled from her society, and her legacy would be lost. Her loudest and strongest voice said, *You had no choice but to continue to tell that lie.*

CHAPTER THIRTEEN

"A Rich Man's Daughter and a Preacher's Daughter"

The town was becoming a winter wonderland. Ruth and Cassandra both left Springton that morning driving those same Ozarks roads, each traveling down different paths. Mother and daughter never caught sight of the other that morning, yet they both witnessed the holiday season coming alive driving through town. Christmas carols could be heard, and the Salvation Army bells were ringing at the entrance of every store. The Christmas wreaths were hung on all the doors and window fronts were sprayed with fake snow wishing "Merry Christmas, Joy and Peace." Santa was coming to town to visit with the children, and the town parade was scheduled. The main highway would be shut down to traffic and busy with only footfalls, so all could celebrate the season as a community. Pastor Whitney would officiate the events of the parade and stand tall next to the Nativity scene that sat on the church's float that proudly told of the birth of baby Jesus. The only store front business that was not decorated and bringing forth good tidings was the Station at 76; there were no bell ringers at its entrance. There was no one there, it was vacant. It was empty. It screamed of abandonment and brokenness, and no one seemed to notice except for Cassandra when she drove past the station.

An anxious Mary was waiting for Cassandra at the marina when she arrived. They greeted each other with a comforting embrace, so happy to see one another.

"How's Robert?"

"He's doing the best that can be expected," answered Cassandra, sinking back into the chair. "I don't think he'll ever be the same again."

Mary seemed to have mentally checked out. She wasn't prepared for any news other than to hear Robert was going to be okay and they were leaving.

"Mary, we've gotten through so much, we'll get through this too," aaid Cassandra moving to sit closer to her.

"Yeah, I know, I know," said Mary, wiping her eyes. "Isn't the Pointer Christmas Party this weekend at The Medallion?"

"Uh huh," answered Cassandra, giving Mary a disgruntled look, which she ignored.

"So, catch me up on what's been going on around here," said Cassandra, sitting down at her desk and changing the subject.

"Well, you can see the holiday decorations are up and we got the tree put up and decorated in the bar. The Christmas shows and headliners are selling out pretty quick, and the extra preparations you asked me to make have been made. There's an extra stash of Quaaludes and the last shipment of cocaine came last night, which was no easy task. Candi's a great negotiator and she got it done. The party favors and match books are already being filled for New Year's Eve. But look at this..." said Mary, showing her the after-party book.

"Oh, you haven't heard anything from the Frankie Group? Nothing from Alexander Frankel and my mom hasn't brought any new girls on the payroll, you know… young girls for Frankie?"

"Nope. Just the Pioneers and the Founding Fathers. I thought you'd be pleased not to have Frankie schedule his after-party this year. Maybe Frankie is getting too old…maybe he doesn't have that interest or drive any longer. Maybe he doesn't have a fetish to feed anymore," answered Mary.

"I am pleased," replied Cassandra. "Nothing would make me happier if Frankie was miraculously reformed or whatever it is you call it. You and I both know that as long as Mom has a bank account to feed she'll fill it by any means she can. It doesn't matter to her. Something's off, Mary. I'm telling you, something's off."

"Oh, shoot, I almost forgot, your dad dropped off the payroll today. I just haven't been myself, I'm sorry. And Cassandra, it's called a miracle, and miracles do happen!"

"Uh-huh," replied Cassandra, opening the payroll checks and then looking up at Mary. "Don't be so hard on yourself, none of us have been ourselves..." Her words trailed off, the payroll checks had her attention.

"Cassandra?" said Mary, walking around the desk to where Cassandra was sitting. "What is it?"

"Look at this, these checks aren't drawn of off Frankel's bank, isn't that strange? Have you heard anyone say anything about changing banks?"

Mary took her check and looked at the bank: it was Braxton Bank. "Would we know if your mom changed banks? Do we care if she changed banks?" asked Mary.

"No, I usually never pay any attention to this stuff. What happens on these boats is so hard to imagine, you know. On the outside it all looks so innocent, the wholesome family-run business. It's been easier for me to hide in alcohol and drugs, it's the only way I can do this job."

Mary looked over at Cassandra with a sideways glance and nodded in agreement. "I know, I know. Hey, are you going to the Christmas party at The Medallion?"

"No," answered Cassandra flatly. "I think it's best we stay in our own little world down here at the marina and make the yacht available for any after-parties. I just can't do those party events with my mother anymore."

She was still focused on her thoughts about Frankie, and a new bank name on the checks had her worried.

"It's just odd, though. What if Mom is no longer feeding Frankie and he's no longer her banker? Why would they end their relationship? It's been profitable for both of them for many years, ever since I can remember."

"I don't know," exclaimed Mary. "I'm still cashing it!"

The girls both laughed.

"Oh yes we are, we work to damn hard, my friend. When our friends were going off to college after graduation, getting honest work or getting married, we were *escorting*."

Mary got them both a glass of wine.

"We've never had much in common with the in-crowd, did we, Cassandra? Can you imagine if they really knew what went on around here and if they knew about their *own* fathers...?"

"And don't forget about some of their mothers as well!" said Cassandra in utter disgust, taking a drink of her wine.

"Hey, you don't think we got too old for Frankie, do you?" asked Mary, trying to keep a straight face, then bursting out with laughter.

"Oh, you know it!" said Cassandra, popping a lude and taking an unrefined gulp of her wine to wash it down.

"Here's to this year! The best year ever! Five years in the making. This year we'll be twenty-five and take control of our own lives. There will be no more PECC!"

"Cheers to that my friend!" replied Cassandra. "Well, Mary, I'm gonna crash. Tomorrow's another day. I'm exhausted."

"Cassandra, are you okay? Do you think Robert knows more? Do you really think Robert and Sean fought over those receipts about The Station at 76?"

"I do. Hopefully, when I go see Robert he'll be able to tell me more. Oh, by the way, what are you doing tomorrow? I need to make a trip to French Town and get this information to Uncle Joe. I promised Robert."

"I'll ride with you. We leaving in the morning?"

"Yeah. Will you wake me up? Oh, and then I want to stop at the bank on the way back and see if we can catch Frankie and find out what's going on with him."

"Yes, I will, I promise," said Mary, helping her into bed and covering her with the warmest blanket she could find. "Goodnight, my friend."

Cassandra fell asleep when her head hit the pillow, or passed out, Mary wasn't quite sure.

In her cabin Mary got herself ready for bed and made a hot toddy with a splash of bourbon. She grinned a little hearing Cassandra's words, *Well, Mary, a splash of bourbon still makes it an alcoholic beverage!* Sins were now scaled and prioritized. With everything that had happened and the corruption of her life here at PECC, even with all its sins, she wouldn't have changed a thing. She never expected to find true love when she came here. She never expected to find anything good here at all, she was just looking for better. Bearable. One night she was a stowaway on the showboat and the next night she lived here. She remembered it like it was yesterday, it was her story.

It was 1974. Mary and Cassandra were fifteen years old and even though they went to the same public school, they didn't know each other. Cassandra ran with a crowd her parents would never approve of. Just like Cassandra's family, her family buried their sins deep. The only thing Mary knew about Cassandra was who her parents were, and they ran a charity called PECC, and she was a little rich girl who worked at Mommy and Daddy's marina. They obviously didn't have anything in common, or so they thought.

Mary endured many nights of sexual abuse from her father, and one night he had gone too far and beat her while her mother was out. That night she stole her dad's car and drove to the marina; she was going to sign up for PECC and not be abused any longer. When the police arrived at the marina they found her father's car, but no Mary. They didn't look very good; she had hidden in one of the lifeboats. Just another runaway as far as they were concerned.

Mary was climbing out of the lifeboat and Cassandra was walking alone on deck with a bottle of bourbon in her hand and God knows what she had swallowed or snorted along with it.

"Hey, you! What are you doing crawling out of that lifeboat? Who are you?" yelled Cassandra, slurring and stammering her way to her.

"I'm Mary. I came here to fill out an application for PECC," replied a scared and beaten young girl in a nasally voice, with dried blood crusted in and out around her swollen nose.

"What the hell happened to you?" asked Cassandra. "You look like you lost the fight! I may not know much, but I know you don't want to be here! You don't want to fill out an application for PECC, you need to go home. This place is nothing but trouble. If you fill out an application for

PECC, you deserve to have your ass kicked," slurred Cassandra some more, pointing her finger at Mary.

"I can't go home. I can't!" wailed Mary.

"My dad did this and my momma doesn't help me. He does other things too…" she said, hanging her head in shame.

"So, that was your dad's car you stole?" asked Cassandra in a drunken, confused stupor. She didn't really care what was going on, she was on her way to pass out in one of the unoccupied cabins. She had her own troubles brewing just as soon as her parents realized she wasn't home at this late hour. It would be a couple of hours before her parents found her, and until then she would revel in this little game of hide-and-seek.

"Yeah, that was my dad's car," answered Mary, shocked by this obviously broken girl standing in front of her drowning in bourbon. Shocked she wasn't repulsed at the sight of her, but it was dark out. Shocked this obnoxious girl only seemed to understand she had stolen her dad's car!

"Hey, I recognize you," said Cassandra. "Aren't you that preacher's daughter? What the hell, man?"

"Please," begged Mary, "can I fill out an application for PECC and stay here? Can't I work here like you do?"

"If you're thinking you're gonna find God here, you're not. He isn't here," said Cassandra, with her ice-cold blue eyes looking directly at Mary.

"God lives in our hearts, silly, and he's in mine, so he's here!" replied Mary, returning her ice-cold stare with her green eyes, believing she was talking to a spoiled little rich girl with her made-up problems.

"Well, then take your God and go home, he isn't gonna wanna be here either," spat Cassandra, putting the bottle of bourbon to her mouth, tipping it high, and the liquor splashed and gulped its way to her mouth. Then, with her bottle in hand, she continued to stumble her way to the cabin. It was apparent to her this girl had no idea who she was talking to with such defiance and yet she couldn't help but admire the preacher's daughter a little. This girl had met her ice-cold stare stoutheartedly.

Mary fell onto the deck crying, screaming, and pounding the deck with her fists. Completely lost, alone, and afraid. She had just been raped and beaten by her own father and was being turned away, yet again. Mary felt that PECC was her last hope and going home just wasn't an option. She had no one and nowhere else to go.

Cassandra stopped dead in her tracks. "Oh for God's sake! All right, all right! If I help you, will you please stop crying? You're going to wake up the whole marina, and then we'll both be in big trouble!" she said in a hushed voice, extending her hand doing her best keep her own balance while helping Mary to her feet.

The two girls staggered and stumbled arm in arm to the cabin. Cassandra fell through the door of the cabin, tripping Mary in the process. Without much help from Cassandra, Mary finally found the light switch.

"Oh my God, girl, you need a doctor!" exclaimed Cassandra almost shocked sober, looking up at her from the floor.

Both of her eyes were still swelling and blackening right in front of her. One eye was blood red, where it should have been white. Her face was bloody, and her clothes were splattered with blood from her profusely bleeding nose that had swollen twice its size. "You may have a broken nose," exclaimed Cassandra.

In pain Mary shrieked, "No, No! No doctor! My dad will kill me. I swear he will!"

"You're a preacher's daughter!" antagonized Cassandra in disbelief.

"You're a rich man's daughter!" spat back Mary.

"Mary, is it?" asked a snarky Cassandra.

"Yes," she snapped back.

"Mary, I promise you, you're jumping from the frying pan into the fire if you go to PECC. It's not what you think it is. There's alcohol, drugs, and sex. That's what you'll find here. No Sunday school!"

"Will I ever have a choice if PECC does help me?" she whispered with a pout sitting on the edge of the twin bed, while Cassandra hadn't been able to get herself up off the floor.

Mary remained seated on the edge of the bed, refusing to help Cassandra up from the floor! This ungrateful little rich girl had no idea that she sat in the front pew at church every Sunday pretending everything was just like it should be. She had no friends and was an outcast at school. To make matters worse, she didn't know how to explain this beating. There was no way she would be healed by Sunday. What *was* her father going to say happened? What was her father going to say when she didn't show up at church on Sunday to assist with the youth department?

"Well," finally answered Cassandra, "you can choose not to do drugs, and you can chose not to drink, although I don't recommend it. Sometimes there just isn't enough drink and drugs to drown all this out." Then Cassandra mumbled to herself under her breath, "Like tonight."

"Okay," said Mary, ignoring Cassandra's last comment. "Where's the application?"

"Don't worry, my mother will soon be coming after me for borrowing her car tonight and she'll look for me here. I don't have any other place to go either…" Cassandra's voice trailed off; she didn't want to show any vulnerabilities to this girl she didn't know. She tried to take another gulp of her bourbon, and the bottle was empty; it had spilled when they fell through the door. Angrily, Cassandra made a failed attempt to throw the bottle against the wall.

Even though Mary thought she didn't deserve her kindness, she could no longer watch her wallow on the floor in her drunken state. Getting up from the bed and with her injuries from the beating, she extended her hand to help Cassandra up from the floor and sit next to her on the bed.

"This doesn't make us friends," said Cassandra, breaking the connection.

"Of course not," replied Mary in kind.

"You know, both of us did steal a car tonight, so we have something in common, right?" added Mary, optimistically, hoping to find something in common with her.

"Uh, no, you stole a car, I borrowed a car. So, no, we don't have that in common," said Cassandra, making sure she knew the difference.

"But I thought…" said Mary, and then she decided against saying anything else about it and just said, "Oh."

Like Cassandra said, Ruth showed up in a rage that her daughter had snuck out of the house again.

"Cas-san-dra," yelled Ruth, bursting through the door of the cabin, which reeked of bourbon. In her rage she didn't even notice Mary at first.

"I knew I'd find you here! One day you're going to take the car and I swear, I'm going to report that car stolen and not chase you down! That is stealing, Cassandra! You stole my car, again! You don't even have a driver's license! Do you know what would happen if you had an accident?" Ruth hadn't finished with her lecture and then she realized her daughter wasn't alone.

"We'll talk about this later, Cassandra," said Ruth, concluding the issue in front of prying eyes.

Although Mary received some satisfaction in knowing that Cassandra did in fact steal her mom's car, she hoped she had hidden it well.

"Mrs. Pointer," Mary cried. "It's all my fault. Cassandra was helping me. I want to fill out an application for PECC."

Ruth looked at her daughter. "Who is this poor child?" she asked.

"Don't you recognize her, Mom?" slurred Cassandra. "She's the preacher's daughter of that church that you and dad belong to, but never—"

"Cas-san-dra! Not now!" said Ruth, turning her attention to Mary.

Ruth gathered up both girls, marched them to the car, and took them back to the big house on the hill. Mary never saw such a big house and couldn't understand why Cassandra wouldn't want to be here. This place had everything! A housekeeper, a cook, and a swimming pool! Mattie was waiting for them and was devastated by the beaten child that walked through the door with Ruth and Cassandra. She was expecting to console Cassandra and play the part of a peacemaker like she had done many times before, not a nurse maid. Mattie was stunned when she saw Mary; she knew she was the preacher's daughter.

"I'm going to take care of this, Mary, okay?" said Ruth.

"Okay," answered Mary quietly.

Mattie took Cassandra and Mary upstairs and gently tended to her injuries from the beating. That night Ruth added a pastor to her list of those who were bought and paid for, increasing her portfolio. Cassandra and

Mary found they had more in common than they ever imagined and were inseparable from that night forward. With what little self-esteem each of the girls had, they shared it with each other.

CHAPTER FOURTEEN

"No Home for Uncle Joe"

The next morning was cold and windy when Cassandra and Mary headed to French Town. Mary drove and Cassandra talked. It was a four-hour drive to French Town, and Uncle Joe wouldn't be expecting her. It wasn't hard to find where he'd set up shop in that small, little town. When they reached Joe's Garage, the first thing Cassandra saw was the sign that was hung on the two-bay garage. She remembered Robert and her uncle taking that sign down; it was hard not to. The wooden constructed building he was working out of needed work: the paint was chipped, and the roof was so worn you could see that from the road. The parking lot was gravel and had a few potholes, it needed filling.

"Wait here, Mary. I don't think I'll be long." It took Cassandra a minute to get herself together to approach Uncle Joe, Robert knew him better than she did.

"Good luck..." replied Mary.

She grabbed the manila envelope with the receipts and contracts and headed toward the door with a sign that said, "Open."

When Cassandra entered the garage, she recognized the equipment that had once operated in The Station at 76. Uncle Joe had two cars in the shop and was standing at the welding table. She could see light coming in from the deteriorated spots in the wood from the far wall and the doors to the bays hung unevenly and were rickety. If the wind was strong enough, it would move the doors and sometimes the wind would whistle as it moved through the cracks. Even with a heater hung high and blasting heat through its coils, it was cold in the shop. When he saw her enter, he stopped and took off his welding mask. It was obvious that her presence brought about an uneasiness within him.

"What can I do for you, Cassandra?" he asked sharply, but not too harsh.

"I, uh, have something for you that's important. I promised Robert I would get this to you as soon as possible and he wanted me to hand-deliver it."

That seemed to put Joe at ease.

"I'm sorry about Robert. I heard about what happened. How's he doing?"

"He's doing as good as can be expected. He's been moved to a rehabilitation facility and is getting the best care that money can buy," she answered, still holding the manila envelope.

There was an awkward silence between the two that reminded them of the fact they barely knew each other and how strange it was.

"This is what Robert wanted me to make sure you had," said Cassandra, stretching out her arm with the envelope for Joe to take.

"Thank you," he said, taking the envelope.

Cassandra nervously cleared her throat. "Joe, Robert wanted me to tell you they're selling The Station at 76."

Cassandra watched Joe's eyes fill with worry and saw his heartbreak for Robert, his favorite nephew.

"I'm, um, uh, gonna get going now," said Cassandra nervously.

"All right, you be careful going home...and thanks," he replied.

Cassandra turned and closed the door behind her.

Joe opened the envelope and began going through the ever-so-familiar receipts and contracts. There was nothing that escaped him. He remembered the day he threatened his sister he was going to wallpaper the waiting area with all these invoices. He grinned remembering how angry she got. To him it was a win. *Oh, that joint bank account...* he thought. Then he came across the one propane gas bill he received in the mail from Ruth when he first arrived in French Town. Before he even had a roof over his family's head, a job, or even a home telephone, he ended up sending his last borrowed dime to his sister. In all his life he never wished misfortune on anyone, but for his sister Ruth, he hoped she choked on her money.

How naïve was I, he thought.

Joe flashed back to the day they finally had their two cars, his work truck, two full-sized U-Hauls, and a haul-behind all packed up and ready to go. He was angry and scared with nowhere to go but back to his mom and Alfred's. He was exhausted and had a four-hour trip ahead of him. It was a caravan that was leaving Braxton that day, and he was driving one of the bigger trucks. Alan, his most trusted employee and friend, drove the other one. Landon, his brother, drove his work truck with the haul behind and Anne drove the family car with their daughter Piper. His best friend James drove his very first car that would one day become the race car, The Viper.

Robert had a slick black GTO, and they would run races down at the dam. Robert loved it, considering he got his driver's license late in life and never thought he'd be able to do such a thing. It was another one of many things that bonded him and Robert. He was sad for Robert and knew that night they left Braxton, it was Robert who kept them safe. The only way they could communicate on the road was by CB radio. Joe thought Robert was a little unhinged when he told him to make sure that everyone had a loaded gun with them in the car, but was wise enough to listen to his young nephew. Robert had given his uncle the CB handle Viper. Robert, of course, wanted to be the Dark Knight, like it was some kind of a covert mission. Anne was the Silver Streak. Joe remembered telling Robert, "That's enough, now. I don't want this blown out of proportion any more than it already is, we're not giving everyone CB handles. We just need to be able to communicate so no one gets lost and make sure we don't have any breakdowns. And Robert, you don't need to go looking for trouble!"

"Uncle Joe, I know my mother, and she may be your sister, but you don't know her. I think you'll be lucky to get that equipment across the county line."

"You mean, you think they'll come for the equipment?" asked Joe.

"Yeah, I do."

"You mean like highjack us?"

"Yeah, and didn't Mom and Dad say that Piper could stay with them until you got settled?"

"Yeah, but I put the fear of God into Charles at the bank that day, and I was just hoping he would've given me a reason to knock him between his beady little eyes. I told both of them more than once that under no circumstances was Piper staying here."

"You gotta make sure Piper gets across that county line too. I hope I'm wrong. And if I'm wrong, we'll all be better off. Either way, Uncle Joe, Al needs a handle, being second in your caravan."

Joe remained quiet; the last thing he wanted was for anyone to get hurt, and the thought of not leaving peacefully caused him great concern. He plummeted into a dark place and a realization that his family was a tree of poison.

"Hey, Al," hollered Robert, "come over here for a second."

"Yeah," said Al, walking over to Robert and Joe, "what's up?"

"You need a CB handle, you're the second one in line of pulling outta here," answered Robert.

"Oh, right on!" answered Alan. "I'll be The Roadrunner! It's high time the record be set straight around here! No more making fun of my purple car!"

It was beginning to get dark when Joe pulled his caravan out onto that curvy Ozarks road. It was Joe, Alan, Landon, James, and Anne. Joe was leading by his headlights, and those following used the red taillights as a guide of the one in front of them.

It was late October back then, and the holidays again were right around the corner. Joe dreaded Christmas so much that year; he had a little girl who believed and was still full of hope. He was on borrowed money for him and his family; the wounds from his time here in Braxton were going to be fresh. Obviously, too fresh to be spending time with the family that did their best to destroy him.

His thoughts went back to Robert in the present; his family *did* destroy him. For the last three years Joe and Anne tried to escape their struggles of their time in Braxton.

That night Robert had lagged behind, following them in his GTO that he and Uncle Joe had built together. Robert had Sean's old shotgun from back in the day and put it in his car. About ten miles before the county line, two black Lincoln Continentals pulled out behind Joe's caravan. Anne saw them too and became gripped with fear. She saw the headlights in her rearview mirror getting closer and was feeling boxed in. The closer they got, the less she could think straight, and thankfully, Piper had fallen asleep in the backseat. *What if they hit me in the rear end? What if they get alongside me and run me off the road? What if they try to stop me and separate me from everyone else?* Continuing to follow the taillights in front of her as closely as she could, it proved impossible for her to let go of the steering wheel to make a call on the radio.

"Breaker, breaker, this is the Dark Knight, you out there, Viper?"

"Ten-four, this is Viper. Dark Knight, what are you doing?"

"You got company at your back door, Viper, two fancy Lincolns."

"Dark Knight, call the state patrol."

"No time, Viper, I think they're going to try stop you at the county line. You keep going. Everyone check in when you cross the county line. Whatever you do, don't stop. You all weigh enough to crush that caddy, you're gonna see at the county line, don't forget that."

Everyone in the caravan went silent trying to decide what to do; they had seen Ruth for who and what she was long before Joe had.

"Breaker, breaker, this is the Roadrunner. You copy, Viper?" called out Alan, loud and clear.

"I copy," answered Joe, afraid of what he was going to hear next.

"You ram 'em and I'll slam 'em and clear the way, ten-four?"

"Take it slow and steady, Roadrunner, ten-four," replied Joe.

Joe worried he may not be able to lead everyone safely to French Town; he began second guessing his decision to put Anne and Piper at the end of the caravan.

"Breaker, breaker this is Viper. Roadrunner, slow and steady, but we ain't stopping."

"Ten-four," replied Alan.

Anne was afraid she may not make it across the county line.

"Silver Streak," called out Robert, "you keep going. I'm right behind the Lincolns, they'll be off your tail shortly! Once you get across the county line it should be quiet the rest of the way."

Robert began to get closer to the Lincolns, threatening to tail-butt them, weaving recklessly from one lane to another and doing his best to distract them.

"This is Viper, county line and Cadillac in sight."

Robert heard that last call and he floored his GTO and got up right alongside of the Lincolns, and the drivers were stunned, obviously not expecting any interference. Robert raised his shotgun and pulled in front of them, his car turning sideways, tires squealing in a high pitch tone and smoke barreling out from his tires. In response the two Lincolns slammed on their brakes, tires screeching, coming to a hard and fast stop. The smoke came forward over the Lincolns, almost covering them in the dark limiting their vision, and then dissipated into the air rising upward.

When the smoke cleared it revealed they had nearly missed Robert's car. There were two in the front seat of each of the Lincolns. No one got out of their cars.

Robert heard over the radio, "This is the Silver Streak and I've just crossed the county line."

"Breaker, breaker, this is Viper. Dark Night, we all just passed the Cadillac at the county line, just like you said we would."

"Ten-four, keep going, Viper, I got all night. Let me know when you see the smokestacks on the right."

"Ten-four. Be careful, Dark Night, and… thanks."

Joe and the red taillights of his caravan disappeared into the night continuing to French Town. Joe carried his worries for his present and his family's future, along with the heavy equipment. Twisting and turning on those curvy roads in the dark of night, it was hard for him to determine which was heavier: the equipment or the uncertainty of how he was going to support his family. There was no home to lay his head and no job prospects. Where he was headed was darker than the night.

In the opposite direction Robert saw headlights coming his way. It was Ruth and Charles. They had been at the county line to hijack their equipment and who knows what else. Charles stopped the car on the road, leaving the headlights on, and angrily walked toward Robert.

"What the hell do you think you're doing, son?" fumed Charles.

Robert was standing behind the door of his car with his shotgun still aimed in the direction of the two Lincolns.

"Well, if it isn't Mom and Dad," said Robert in an all-knowing sound of voice. "Never thought I'd see you out here. I should be asking you, what the hell are *you* doing? Is the county line the new hang out spot for Braxton's finest? These fellas here friends of yours? I may know them! I've got friends too."

Charles and his son stood in a standoff in the middle of the road. Charles waited for his son to show him some respect and back down and Robert continued to stand his ground.

"Did you forget where I grew up, Dad?"

Before Charles could answer, Ruth got out of the car.

"Robert, this isn't your concern. Turn that car around and go home," said Ruth, angry the equipment had disappeared, no longer seeing any taillights of Joe's moving trucks. The loss of the equipment had killed the deal between Pointer Enterprises and the new buyer.

"Mom, you don't get to tell me what to do anymore. Last time I did what you asked, it didn't work out so well for me. Turn these guys around now. I'm not going home until I know Uncle Joe is safe in French Town, with all the equipment he bought and paid for in full. There's nothing he has that's yours!"

Charles walked up to the first Lincoln and exchanged a few words and they managed to turn their cars around after moving forward and backward, and then forward and backward again on the two-lane highway and headed back toward Braxton.

Charles walked straight toward Ruth, who was now sitting in the Cadillac, and made no eye contact with Robert.

Robert waved goodbye to his parents in a causal motion as they drove slowly past their son headed in the direction of home.

For the next few hours Robert remained on that curvy dark road and waited to hear Joe's call saying they had all made it safe and sound.

Finally, the call came across the CB radio. "Breaker, breaker, this is Viper, smokestacks on the right."

The yellow caution light was blinking its warning to turn around and leave. If you didn't heed the caution lights warning, eventually this little town would ensnare you. The prejudice and secret societies would destroy anything in opposition of the little town's backward ways.

"Ten-four, Viper. Stay safe. Tell little one I'll miss her."

Joe's caravan made the right hand turn onto the street of his parents' house and he signed off not knowing that would be the last time he'd ever speak to his nephew.

"Ten-four, Dark Knight, watch your back door."

"We'll do. Dark Knight over and out."

Joe sat in the rented U-Haul truck for a moment, lit a cigar, and couldn't believe the last few hours. That dead-end street he just turned onto was the end of his hopes and dreams. He had survived many wrongs from his siblings in the past, and there would be more to come in the future. A broken man he was, and this godforsaken town would lead him to his to death.

Once again Joe put those memories back in the past hoping they would stay there. He wasn't the same person he was when he first moved to Braxton, full of hope and excited about his new business adventure. Even though Robert may have been a little too cautious with the CB radio he knew what he was talking about, they would have been hijacked at the county line. He wished Robert hadn't gotten so overconfident and continued to challenge his parents over this deal. He wished more than anything that Robert would have just let it go. It had cost him so much.

Trembling a bit at the brutality of it all, he put the receipts and contracts back in the manila envelope, placed them in the file cabinet. When he closed the drawer, he tried to close that part of his life forever. Now at last, he was finally free from his sister. *There's a special place in hell for you, my sister, Ruth.*

CHAPTER FIFTEEN

"Whispers"

After leaving Joe's Garage Mary drove, and Cassandra was grateful; she was on the road a lot these days. It was the night of the Pointer Christmas party at The Medallion and the girls had one more stop to make.

"So, Cassandra, now we stop at the bank and talk to Frankie?"

"Yep, now we stop at the bank. I'm gonna comp an evening for him and take him out on a houseboat tonight if I can. We've got a couple of houseboats that can go out, don't we?"

"Yeah, there's a couple that've already had maintenance done and returned to their slips. Do you think he's going to the Pointer Christmas party?"

"I don't know. I wish I could talk to Robert," said Cassandra, looking out the window so Mary wouldn't see the fear that was beginning to consume her.

"I just wish I could see Robert," replied Mary.

The rest of the drive home was mostly quiet. Mary kept her eyes on the road, praying silently and thanking God that Robert was alive. Cassandra lay her head on the headrest and closed her eyes wondering if she'd be able to face Frankie.

It was about closing time when they pulled into the bank's parking lot, and Frankie was walking to his car.

Hurriedly, Cassandra got out of the car. "Frankie! Frankie!" she yelled.

"Why, Cassandra, what brings you here?" asked a smiling Frankie.

Commanding her biggest and best Pointer smile, she gave him a wink. "Tonight is the Pointer Christmas party."

"Yes, yes, I know," he replied pompously.

"Well," said Cassandra, "I was looking at the parties booked for the after-party tonight and I didn't see your name on the list. So I came here to let you know that your party is on the house tonight!"

Frankie was a distinguished-looking older man; he was tall and his full head of hair had perfectly grayed, complimenting his sophisticated but irresistible, rugged looks. He was sixty-nine, the same age as her father, and he didn't look a day over fifty. If Cassandra didn't know him so well, she may have believed all the ladies who said, *What a handsome man he is. All the good ones are taken, aren't they?* Before going to the bank, young girls and middle-aged women in crisis would make sure they visited the beauty parlor first, just to get a bit of attention from him.

He gave her that grin of his that most ladies would die for.

"Oh, you know you're a little too old for me these days, and now don't take that the wrong way," he replied.

Cassandra smiled big, and with the back of her hand on her forehead, played the dramatic one and laughed mischievously.

"Oh, the rejection I think is more than I can bear! Not one last night for old time's sake? You don't think you owe me that?"

Frankie went a little cold; after all, business is business.

"No, Cassandra, I don't think I owe you anything. If you must know, I'm not going to the Pointer Christmas party this year, so I didn't book an after-party on *The Crimson Rose*."

Cassandra pressed her lips together. "Okay, I just wanted to offer up a night comped on the house. I may not have a young girl for you this year, but there are other things that are your favorites just waiting for you and, of course, me! I'm still thirty years or so younger than your wife…"

Frankie was unlocking his car and seemed enticed. He didn't turn to face her or look up to talk to her, he only gave her a sideways glance.

"Are you willing to take a houseboat out?"

Cassandra knew she had just sold herself this time, and it sickened her. This was something her mother would do.

"Yes, of course, silly!" she answered quickly, putting those feelings aside.

"Uh, yeah, okay," he replied.

"Yeah?" responded Cassandra.

"Yeah, since you put it that way, see you around nine-ish," he replied with a wink and sexy grin.

"Well, what did he say?" asked Mary.

Cassandra was already answering her getting back into the car.

"He said he'll be there around nine tonight. Let's hope he shows and didn't just say that to get me to leave. He really had no plans to book an after-party."

"That's odd," replied Mary.

When the girls arrived back at the marina, they got the houseboat ready. Mary looked at Cassandra with worry. "Do you think this is going to work? Do you think he's going to tell you anything about him and your mother?"

Cassandra was unsettled by the day's events and struggling to stay away from the ludes and bourbon. She wanted to hide away, but this was too important.

"I hope so. I don't know how else I can find anything out. Help me get ready?"

"Of course," replied Mary. "Are you sure you should go out on the boat alone with him? You have to promise me to take it easy on the coke and the alcohol. And Cassandra, no Quaaludes whatsoever!"

"I will, I won't, I promise!" exclaimed Cassandra like she was talking to a chastising mother hen. Cassandra hated making promises she knew she might not be able keep. If it wasn't such a big operation, and with so many headliners performing on *The Eclipse*, she may not have had such an incentive to keep it all so classy. There was more in her life she wanted to forget than she wanted to remember. However, over the years she had been doing better, and one might say she *occasionally* partook these days.

Cassandra had chosen a royal velvet blue dress to wear for the evening. It had thin spaghetti straps and the back of each strap carried a wide strip of free-flowing silk that brushed against her exposed back. There was a thigh high side slit in the dress that teased just a little, leaving a man wanting more. It was a V-neck style and had delicate silver sequins that accentuated the curves of her breasts.

Mary helped her with her hair and make-up. Cassandra chose a dramatic style of make-up; shades of blue eyeshadows and a grey eyeshadow covered the outer corners of her eyes with thick eyeliner on her upper lids. It created an alluring, mysterious look with her full fluttering eyelashes. The blush on her high cheekbones gave her the elegance and sophistication that finished off her perfect porcelain look. She wore her hair loosely wrapped in a messy bun with thin free-flowing strands framing her beautiful face, begging to be undone. Once her make-up was done, Mary stepped back and adoringly gazed at her friend in the mirror.

"Cosmetics," said Mary, "a woman's way of keeping a man from reading between the lines!"

Cassandra giggled and winked at her. "Let's hope so!"

Her jewelry was kept simple, yet a sizable pair of round diamond stud earrings gave sparkle to an already breathtaking beauty.

Mary took one last look to see if she thought Cassandra needed anything else.

"Good luck, you look beautiful. Oh, I almost forgot," said Mary, bringing a jewelry case to her that held a diamond collar necklace. "Here, my friend," and she placed the collar around her neck and clasped it.

"This was a piece of jewelry given to me by one of my regulars from the *Pioneers,* a little something of mine for you to take with you out on the lake. I still don't like you doing this alone. Don't back him into a corner, Cassandra," she said precariously.

"I won't," answered Cassandra.

"Okay, good! Now, take a look. Is there anything else you need?"

Standing side by side they turned and looked in the mirror for a moment. In the mirror stood the alter egos of two beautiful young and innocent girls starring back at them, begging to get out of this place. Two beautiful innocent girls who hadn't yet met. Little Mary dressed in a beautiful, lacey emerald-green dress, white tights, and white patent leather shoes. Her long, auburn curly hair was in a partial ponytail so her silky curls could flow freely down her back. Young Cassandra was dressed in a satin blue dress with black velvet trim and a bow at the waist off to the side. Her tights were black and paired with black patent leather shoes. Her long black hair was tied in a ponytail that seemed to go on forever. The little girls' stares pierced right through them to the depths of their souls, like daggers. Neither Cassandra nor Mary ever spoke of their reflections in the mirror, what they saw, or what they felt.

"Well, this is it! I'll stop by *The Crimson Rose* before going home. You look beautiful too, Mary, you're absolutely stunning in green. I wish I could wear green!"

Mary blushed, her true shy and sweet nature peeking through.

"You can wear green, silly girl!" she replied.

"Maybe," replied Cassandra, "but not as good as you can."

"Well, I can't wear blue as well as you do, my friend!"

"Oh, whatever," replied Cassandra.

The two girls gave each other a hug. "Thank you so much, the necklace means a lot and I'll return it safely, I promise. Mary, I'm sorry for what you're going through."

Both girls blocked their feelings and controlled their emotions quickly, before they could control them. Cassandra thought Mary might have said a prayer. After ten years of friendship Mary was still a believer after all she had seen and been through.

"I'll see you later, you be careful," said Mary.

Mary turned and left to go to work on *The Crimson Rose.* Cassandra put on her silver strappy high-heeled sandals and took one last look in the mirror. It unnerved her, really, looking in the mirror. Sometimes she was afraid the person looking back at her not only confirmed she looked like her mother; maybe she *was* becoming her mother. The young and innocent girl hiding in the mirror would fade in the struggle of it all. For the first time in her life she thought about her future; she was getting older, Frankie was right. When she got too old to work here at the marina what would happen to her then? Was she expected to fill the shoes of her mother and take over PECC? She only had five years to go before she would be considered middle aged.

It was something she never thought about, until recently. There were many things she hadn't thought about, and then Robert got shot. Their futures were so perfectly planned and secured. Now that time was out of sync, their futures were in jeopardy. Cassandra did her best to drown out the hauntings of the silence that continued to whisper as it came and went, whispering of more tragedy to come.

CHAPTER SIXTEEN

"Pick Your Poison"

Cassandra and Frankie took the houseboat out to the middle of the lake that cold December night. Downstairs in the cabin was a champagne dinner for two. She chose to start dinner with a light salad of leaf lettuce topped with shredded provolone cheese and a hard-boiled egg served with bleu cheese dressing. The main course was a medium-rare porterhouse steak, roasted garlic parsnip puree, and honey-glazed baby carrots. Sitting on its own plate was a huge baked potato with a fancy dollop of butter in its center, beginning to melt. It carried its own comforting aroma promising to calm and sooth. In the small cabin below savory smells of light lemon, subtle garlic, honey, and a hint of cinnamon filled the cabin, teasing the senses. To top it off, in the center of the small candle lit table was the best bottle of merlot she could find partnered with two Bordeaux glasses. It was a meal fit for a king, and that was part of the plan.

Even though Frankie was into young girls, Casandra was still somewhat appealing to him. She was special to him, and he wasn't sure why he had this emotional attachment to her. Maybe because he was her first, maybe because she was given to him by her own mother. Maybe because she was the same age as his own daughter. The Pointers made his bank a landmark in the town, and the glitz and glamour were a bonus to his immense wealth and status in the community.

Frankie was dressed in a tuxedo, suggesting he just came from a party. He could have just lied to her and told her he wasn't going...but to her, that was neither here nor there. Cassandra played and teased with her food and picked up her wine glass for a toast, and Frankie followed her lead.

"Well, what are we toasting to, Cassie ole' girl?" asked Frankie, like he was talking to an old friend.

Cassandra grinned a little and her stomach turned upside down; she envisioned an emotional outburst by throwing her deep and rich red merlot in his face. The merlot would ruin his perfect hair and run down his face to stain his crisp white tuxedo shirt. It would wipe that smile right off his face! Instead, she commanded her Pointer smile, and once again it came on command.

"Funny, Frankie, funny!" said Cassandra.

"Cassie, c'mon! We're all getting older."

She held her smile, and to keep her eyes from betraying her she looked down at her salad and took a small bite.

"Well," said Frankie, trying to back pedal after being so insensitive, "you look beautiful *and* youthful, if that helps!"

She swallowed her salad and took a sip of wine, then smiled her beautiful smile.

"I see I've been reduced to arm candy, huh? Hopefully, I have a few years left before I'm put out to pasture!"

It was awkward sitting there with him. Usually the agenda was not hers, but tonight was different. She found herself in unchartered waters on the empty lake that evening.

"We've known each other for a long time, Frankie, and I think by now, you know your secret is safe with me. I'll take it to my grave, I promise. What's been done is done. So, let's toast to secrets and retribution, making something right, if only one thing as we go through this life," she said, looking directly at him with her big blue eyes meeting his gaze.

He really was a vision if you didn't know him to be the monster he was. Oh, he looked so sophisticated and slick leaning back in the booth. Sitting in a sway, with his legs and arms crossed holding his champagne glass. His perfectly gray, thick wavy hair and a smile that warned you and comforted you at the same time, drawing you in. His gray-blue eyes twinkled, and those who didn't know him would find him hard to resist.

"Cassie, why'd you comp this night for me, here on this boat, and bring out all the amenities?" he asked.

Cassandra thought for a long minute debating on how to handle this; he obviously wasn't interested in her, she was almost twenty-five years old. Should she just state the truth for her reason, or should she just dose his champagne with a Quaalude and stick to the plan to get the information out of him? Nothing would bring her greater pleasure than turning the tables on this monster. *Stick to the plan, there's too much at stake here. This isn't about you. Think about Robert, Mary, and The Lake Girls. Keep your shit together.* The twinkle in Frankie's eyes began to fade, becoming more intense, and she was afraid she took too long to answer his question. He wasn't an easy man to fool, and not one to cross.

"Frankie, if I shoot straight with you, will you answer my questions honestly? It's important?" she asked, deciding to start with the truth first.

If Frankie had a clear path to the deck, he would've left right then and there.

"Frankie, I was fourteen that very first night," she whispered. "And look at my life now. What do you think has happened to all those young girls that have come and gone all these years? Sure, a lot of us girls have retained our same clients and built a business of our own within this business. Then, as they got older, they sold their list or kept their business here on the yacht and houseboats for whatever reasons. Most didn't make it. Some had a choice, Frankie, some didn't. It's a vicious cycle and one hard to get out of. I didn't have a choice."

Frankie wasn't moved by her words and coldly replied, "Well, they had a safe environment to work. They would've gone to foster care or lived on the streets. Girls at those ages don't get adopted out and you know it. And you, my dear, you graduated high school a millionaire."

She began to boil with rage knowing she had to get through the bad to get to the good. Again, she was caught in the middle of good intentions and evil deeds. These lifelong lessons of "doing bad things to obtain good things makes it all worthwhile" had changed her. She found herself becoming more and more reclusive—the shame and anger had been devouring her over the years. Now she was afraid it would bury her.

Cassandra had to give him one more chance, but not really him. It was herself she was giving one more chance to find out what she needed to know. As far as the money, that was her compensation. Her payoff.

"Frankie, come on..." Her voice was frail and raspy, trailing off and betraying her. Her desperation was showing. The truth about that first night would come back to haunt her from time to time. The only memory she had was of her mother taking her to the marina for her fourteenth birthday party and then remembering nothing. When Frankie took little Cassandra's hand in his that night, she really believed he would be taking her back to her mother where she would be safe. Frankie ended up taking her back to her mother, but not until many hours later. It was a night to remember for Frankie, and for Cassandra it was a night she could only remember in pieces. A night that changed her life forever and still haunted her to this day. What she remembered of that night when the drugs wore off was Frankie's voice, "Come on...you have to get up and get dressed, you can't lay in bed all day." She knew she was naked and that was wrong, shameful in the presence of a man. Her mind was foggy, she was in daze. She tried get rid of that vision of Frankie and the sound of his voice as he grabbed her by the arm to lift her up from the bed. The vision never faded no matter how deep she buried it, and no new memories ever resurfaced to bring her the truth. Sometimes, at night, when she was sleeping alone in the dark, she would hear Frankie's voice in her head, see his cruel gray eyes and the evil smirk on his face. There were no other memories for her to find of that dreadful night.

"A toast to righting one wrong?" he said, leaning in toward her.

She met his glass with hers. "If it's righting only one wrong, I'll take it."

He was quiet for a moment and looked almost disgusted with himself.

"You know, it was your mother that got me through the ranks to become president of the bank. Your mother has made you and me a lot of money."

Cassandra spoke up, "Yep, she's made us both a lot of money, but who holds the ultimate control and who has made the most money? How easy do you think it is for me to access my trust fund? Look where I live, I live on a showboat, a riverboat in a cabin of four hundred and fifty square feet! Everyone thinks my life is so glamourous, if only!"

Frankie grinned knowing he'd been beaten a long time ago.

"You know your mother has this thing about her wealth, power, and influence; she knows how to protect her wealth. Times are changing, Cassandra, the way we've done business in the past, in the sixties and seventies is no longer as easy to do. After the war it was a feast, not famine society. Your mother and father set this town on fire and are two of the most prominent and influential people in this town. They're building this area into an entertainment capital of the Ozarks. Hell, even the main highway is being petitioned for a name change. People are actually able to live here and survive the winters."

Cassandra knew this was true; Braxton had become profitable for many people, but at the expense of those who were forgotten, and she was one of those. They were lost in the smoke of the glamour and in the mirrors of beauty, living in the underworld of the entertainment industry. Suffocating in its growth.

"Frankie, I know that's true, but I'm so tired of talking about money. Not everything is about money. People are people and deserved to be treated as such, not something that is *owned*."

"Oh, I agree, Cassie, people are people. There are people with money and people without money," he replied pompously.

"Frankie!" yelled an agitated Cassandra. "That's enough!" Thankfully, she heard Mary's words again, *Don't back him into a corner.* She was hoping she hadn't already done that with her tone of voice. She had to know what he knew.

"You know, Cassandra, you have this attitude about money because you have it. If you never had it, you might have a different perspective… but you've always had money, money and beauty. Money and beauty open many doors."

Cassandra had never lived without money, and there were plenty of doors opened for her, that was true. What everyone seemed to forget was that the price was too high and not of her free will. She snapped herself out of those thoughts, reminding herself to focus on the reasons she was here.

"Look, Frankie, this is about my brother, that's why I brought you here tonight. You know that my brother, Robert was shot, don't you?"

He perked up hearing about her brother; he did know that Robert had been shot.

"What I want to know," she continued on trying to heed Mary's advice, "is what happened that day at the bank with Uncle Joe and my parents. I want to know what happened with his eviction and why. Also, I noticed that our payroll checks are no longer being drawn on your bank, and I want to know about that too. Are you no longer handling Pointer Enterprises accounts?"

"Cassandra, there are things that are better left unknown," replied Frankie. He was surprised she had noticed what was supposed to be a subtle change over.

Cassandra had also noticed he had only called her "Cassie" a couple of times tonight, which was odd. And for now, they were both sober.

"Oh, believe me, I agree. If I hadn't found out some information, I'd be sitting in my room popping pills and chasing them with whatever alcohol I had a fancy for tonight. I'd be trying to escape this hell I've been living in for all these years. My brother was shot by my other brother, and although he's recovering, no one really knows if he'll fully recover, and I believe Robert and Sean got into a fight over the eviction of Uncle Joe."

Frankie sat his champagne glass on the table.

"It seems not much has escaped you. My, my, look at you, all grown up!" he said, now knowing that he was indeed talking to Cassandra Pointer. *It's possible she's come into her own.*

He ran his fingers through his wavy hair and gave her that swooning smile of his.

"Yes, it's good economics, Cassandra, and I believe you've proven that you're Ruth's daughter. Do you have anything stronger than this champagne?"

With that last comment of his, she was ready for something stronger too and thought to herself, *Why did he just ramble on about economics? All of this had escaped me. That's why we're here!* Hearing those words that she had proven she was Ruth's daughter was like hearing nails on a chalkboard and sent shivers down her spine.

"Yum, this steak is perfect. It melts in your mouth," said Frankie.

"Tequila, bourbon, or vodka?" she asked, getting up and moving over to the small bar in the corner, ignoring his compliment to the chef.

"Better make it your best bottle of bourbon for this conversation, and you'll want to join me," he said, taking a bite of his baked potato.

Cassandra cleared away the champagne and the merlot, poured two bourbons, and set them on the table. Frankie began to tell her what she wanted to know.

"It was a Saturday afternoon, and your mother had her lawyer draw up the papers to evict your Uncle Joe. We, of course, couldn't get it all together in one day, so we completed the eviction papers on that Sunday, and yes, a notary public notarized all the documents on a Sunday. That's perfectly legal, you know; questionable ethics maybe, but perfectly legal."

"I understand what *questionable ethics maybe, but perfectly legal* means Frankie," said Cassandra, looking straight at Frankie, who was enjoying a bite of his porterhouse.

"Of course you do," replied a snarky Frankie, still chewing his last bite.

"Anyway," he continued, "immediately after that your parents went to deliver the papers to Joe. Can you imagine getting served that paperwork with your Sunday dinner? There was already a signed contract contingent that all the equipment was to be included in the sale, between the new buyers of the station and Pointer Enterprises. Your parents said Joe had breached their contract due to the profit margin, but the profit was there, Cassandra. Pointer Enterprises may not have received it all in cash, but they received it in gas, kerosene, company vehicle car and truck repairs, personal car repairs, personal gas fill-ups, you know, those kinds of things. Then there was talk about how he breached their contract by having that highfalutin CPA take over his books. That really pissed off your mother and father, bringing in *old money* to count new money! I can't remember his name. It's ironic, but not important. Anyway, he wouldn't work with your parents for all the money in the world, but he'd work with Joe!" said Frankie, chuckling.

Cassandra remained quiet listening to Frankie and was imagining another emotional outburst seeing that he seemed to find this somewhat amusing. She had squeezed her glass so tightly it was a relief it hadn't shattered.

"You still with me, Cassandra? You following so far?"

"Yeah, I'm following."

"Just checking. Now, your Uncle Joe was lied to about the building being paid off and was more or less paying two mortgages, unbeknownst to him, of course. His rent payment was always paid on time, and I made sure the money that he paid for the mortgage was funneled into a designated account told to me by your mother. The plan was for Joe to leave and the station to be sold so that your mother could make good on the construction draws that she needed to complete the construction on The Medallion. Her construction draws were running short; your mother had overextended herself. Joe kept excellent records, and your mother, well, Pointer Enterprises owed him almost half a mil."

Frankie stopped for a moment and took a drink of his bourbon. Cassandra closed her eyes and took a deep breath.

"Robert found almost five hundred thousand dollars of receipts for gas between the construction and excavating company, the marina, and other things like you just said," replied Cassandra, taking a sip of her bourbon.

"They were from over the years that Uncle Joe had invoiced Pointer Enterprises and then I guess the money for the mortgage is what makes up the rest of what you're thinking?"

"Yep," said Frankie. "Over the course of the next few days I watched the most honest man I ever met be ruined by his own sister. She turned her own brother into a patsy and then, like a wet rag, would wring him dry. Over and over again, poor sap."

"Then sent him packing," Cassandra replied quietly.

"If you already know this, why am I here?" he snapped back.

Frankie took another bite of steak, washing it down with sip of bourbon.

She was afraid to reply to that, afraid he would clam up and stop talking if she told him the whole truth.

"Are you enjoying your dinner?" she asked.

"You know just how I like it! It's a perfect dinner. I can't wait to see what's for dessert!" he replied, dabbing the corners of his mouth with his napkin.

"I do know what you like, but we'll talk about dessert later," she said with a smirk.

They sat quietly eating their dinner, hiding in the candlelight. Both preparing themselves to accept the truth and face it.

"Frankie," she said quietly, breaking the silence, "I'm afraid of what I don't know."

"And you should be," he replied, making eye contact with her.

For a fleeting moment, she and Frankie seemed to be of the same sentiment.

"The next morning when my office opened, your uncle came in and paid the equipment loan in full," Frankie continued. "He'd borrowed the money from one of his brothers, I think. Anyway, on his way out, your parents showed up. I don't know how they knew he was there, but they stormed into my office and demanded to know what he was doing there. Joe told them he would be packing up the equipment and taking it with him. Charles said there was no way in hell he was taking the equipment, it wasn't his, and the note was a balloon note and it was due and payable on demand. Your father went to take a swing at your Uncle Joe, and Joe told him to go ahead looking for any excuse to flatten your father. Then your mother got in the middle of the two of them and asked me to explain what was going on and that the equipment was theirs to keep with the station. I informed her the equipment was now bought and paid for in full by Joe and it was his to do with what he wanted; it was out of my hands. With that your uncle turned around and left my office. I thought your father was going to chase him down, but your mother stopped him. It was that day, Cassandra, I saw your mother, really saw her. Hell, I guess I saw myself too," he said, looking down at his plate, taking a swig of bourbon.

"I guess we are who we are, huh?" he concluded.

"Is that why the deal didn't go through, because of the equipment?" asked Cassandra.

"Yeah, your parents lost the buyer on that contract and have had the building up for sale ever since. The loan on the equipment was structured to be damn near impossible to pay off."

There was something stirring within Frankie as Cassandra listened to him talk, and she couldn't determine what it was. His demeanor softened, and that scared her.

"I have my own demons, Cassandra, I know that. I guess I'm a monster in my own right, maybe. But I promise you, you were the last minor child I've ever been with. What reflected back to me that day in my office when I looked at your mother is an image that will stick with me forever. You've noticed I don't hang out here much anymore, right? How does one look in the mirror when you don't like yourself?"

Cassandra took a drink of her bourbon and didn't have an answer for him—she also struggled with her own reflection.

Cassandra thought she had seen some flicker of humanity in the man sitting across from her, but even that couldn't convince her otherwise. He was a monster, he was evil.

"Yeah, I've noticed, and that's another reason why I comped everything for you tonight. But I still don't understand, where's all this money at? Uncle Joe doesn't have it, he's in financial ruin, and Pointer Enterprises didn't pay it."

Frankie grabbed for Cassandra's hands, and she quickly went to pick up her drink to escape his touch. She slightly trembled lifting her glass to her lips. Frankie didn't pursue her touch.

"The construction and excavating company took over the completion of the construction of The Medallion," he replied. "Your trust fund, Cassandra, had been turned into your mother's personal slush fund. You, the beneficiary of the trust, have benefited greatly financially, have you not?" he said, making his point. "So, that isn't going to be a problem for your mother. Now, as far as those receipts, they'll prove your uncle didn't overcharge Pointer Enterprises. What they tell about your mother and your uncle is a different story! You know, predator and prey sort of story!" Frankie looked amused; someone else's dirty laundry being aired was always better than yours being told.

"Well, there you have it!" said Cassandra. "How amusing for you, I guess, relating a brother and sister to predator and prey. This is no joke, Frankie. I guess that's how you see me and my mother, predator and prey… How is the hierarchy set up in *your* family?"

Frankie laughed out loud, leaving Cassandra wondering what he found so funny.

"No, no, my dear, I don't see you and your and mother as predator and prey at all, that's another story. Your mother is like an eagle, the strongest eagle. A harpy, and we could say you and Rose are her two eggs seeing which one comes into her own first. Anyway, I guess you didn't invite me here to talk about Greek mythology, huh?"

"No, I didn't, but I get the jest of what you're saying," answered Cassandra.

Frankie rubbed his upper lip and nodded yes.

"Well, at the end of the day, the invoices aren't padded and will prove Joe didn't receive the money. Which in turn proves the Station at 76 is carrying a lot of uncollected debt. Does Joe have these invoices?"

Cassandra cleared her throat. "Yes, he has them."

Frankie took a deep breath and exhaled. "Joe'll be all right. If your mother would take any action against him now, she'd be a fool. And we both know that your mother is no fool," said Frankie, gulping down the last of his bourbon.

"So, let me guess, this is what Robert found out?"

Cassandra shook her head and a few tears escaped, running down her face. She didn't have the resolve or the courage to make it through something like this.

"Yeah, that is what Robert found out, and he confronted Sean. But why wouldn't he confront Mother?" she asked, dabbing her tears.

"Oh, Cassandra, I know this is confusing for you, it's confusing for me, but your mother recently made Sean trustee of your trust, and Sean holds the controlling interest in the marina. You didn't know, did you?"

"No, I didn't know."

Being born with such beauty *was* her first sin.

"What happens now, Frankie?" she asked.

Frankie got up and poured himself another bourbon, brought the bottle to the table, and poured another drink for Cassandra.

Without any emotion and an emptiness he couldn't hide, he asked the broken young lady he saw sitting in front of him, "Cassandra, do you remember the icehouses behind The Medallion?"

"Yeah, Mom had them rehabbed into small meeting rooms or something like that. I thought that *Daddy* was going to have a heart attack; from the arguing between the two of them it was apparently an expensive adventure. I never thought anything of it because our excavation and construction company did the work. Why do you ask about the icehouses?"

Frankie took another bite of his steak and then ate a couple of the honey-glazed carrots and washed them down with a drink of his bourbon. Then he smiled and swirled his bourbon around in his glass.

"Before the days that I began to embrace my fetish for young girls and found that Pointer Enterprises would provide me with many things other than money; it was in the icehouses I would meet your mother and we would hide away for hours. I used to keep myself in check, you know," he said like he could control his pedophilia and was pleased with his self-control.

Cassandra glared at Frankie, her stomach tied in knots. There he sat, casually leaning back in his seat. Enjoying the top shelf bourbon and his smile genuine. The twinkle in his eyes had returned.

"Well, anyway, I wasn't the only man she would meet in the icehouses to make such deals. It was kept such a secret because...well, you know why it was kept a secret, don't you? Because of who the people were. Even in our circle of those we knew who were making deals with the ever-growing Pointer Enterprises, we never spoke of it. There were even a few times that a couple of us met each other coming and going. There *are* two icehouses. I mean, if our wives, if my wife knew about this, I'd be ruined and so would many others. Our families, our children. Who knows, down here in the Bible belt we could be tarred and feathered! Your mother is the picture of absolute discretion, no doubt. I guess you got that trait from her."

"I doubt you'd be tarred and feathered as long as you belong the First Baptist Church of Braxton!" exclaimed Cassandra laughing.

"Oh, I see. Touché," responded Frankie.

His earlier words brought Cassandra back to focus and reminded her of the many reasons why she was here with him tonight. Then, it dawned on her the words he had said, and she shrieked, "Oh my God, you didn't, you weren't with my mother. I'm not sure I can hear any more!"

For a moment all she had done to pull herself together was lost in the realization of the truth that she had known deep down all these years and refused to face. It must have been another trait that she had gotten from her mother.

Now she knew exactly why he looked disgusted with himself. She was disgusted, and it was all for the love money. She couldn't help but wonder if there were other men who had a similar story to tell.

What am I doing? she thought. Her hand was jerky reaching for her bourbon.

"Cassandra, ole girl, to right one wrong. You said it not me, remember? Sometimes, you need to be careful about the questions you ask...you may just get the answers."

"I remember," snarled Cassandra.

She didn't know what she expected to hear when she started this little game of cat and mouse, but it wasn't any of this. She actually never thought about how or why this began at the marina. No longer did she try to speak to her mother about the first night on the boat when she was only fourteen. Many years after that, it had been just like nothing happened and she grew to question her own memories. Cassandra was afraid to challenge her mother; she had watched what her brothers had gone through all these years and decided it was just best to do what their mother said. Besides, who would want her after that dreadful night when she was turned into a party girl, stripped of her virtue and innocence. Escorts and whores aren't the girls you take home to meet the family.

Frankie continued bearing his soul, like he was on the path towards redemption.

"You need to hear this, Cassandra," said Frankie.

"Anyway, at a business luncheon one day at The Medallion, some drunks at the bar made a couple of remarks that unnerved quite a few us at the table. We couldn't hear the whole conversation, but these words 'icehouse hoppers,' or something like 'Going icehouse hopping...' was being heckled throughout the bar. Well, your mother quit serving them and had 'em escorted out. We never heard anything else like that again, and I don't ever remember seeing those two drunks ever again, now that I think about it," he said, shrugging his shoulders, seeming to say it was offered and he wasn't going to turn down free booze and drugs or free sexual favors.

"With your mother getting older, and if anyone was getting wise about the icehouse hopping, it was time to make a change. Your mother was at risk of losing the influence she had over the most powerful people in this town; they were beginning to feel exposed, and she couldn't have that. That's when all this business started going on here at the marina. But before the marina, it was the icehouses, and before it was you, it was your mother. Your mother needed you to secure Pointer Enterprises to continue to expand her wealth…you see, I was the banker."

"You son of a bitch!" hissed Cassandra.

"Beauty can be a risky business, Cassandra, but I think you already know that. Your beauty can confuse a man and make him do things he wouldn't normally do, and the marina provided entertainment out here on the lake at its finest." His eyes were gleaming, and she saw the same face in front her that continued to haunt her in her nightmares.

Cassandra pushed her plate away, taking comfort in her bourbon. Frankie, however, sat there inhaling his food, enjoying every bite.

Although the lake was still and calm, the boat would sway and bob. Just as these waters ran deep so did their secrets. The bobbing and swaying motions the boat made so subtlety, stirred their secrets closer to the surface. Secrets surfacing as they were being told. In the dark, where Frankie and Cassandra felt most comfortable, they could no longer count on the darkness to keep it all hidden.

Frankie finished his dinner and put his napkin in his empty plate and broke the silence for one last truth.

"Cassandra, this business with your Uncle Joe was an awful business. I told you all of this because, well, I don't know why. Maybe, because you asked and I felt like I owed you after all. Maybe because I've decided to retire at the end of the year and leave Braxton. As a matter of fact, I'm moving my family over the Christmas holiday, I'll be gone at the end of the next week. With the sale of The Station at 76, I fully expect an audit of Pointer Enterprises accounts and maybe even a subpoena. Hopefully not, but it's time to get out. Ever since the eviction of Joe, I've been minimizing my business deals with your mother, not taking on any new adventures with her. That's why you no longer see the name of my bank on your payroll checks, and honestly, I'm getting too old for this shit."

Cassandra had no words; she wasn't going to tell him thank you. He did owe her, and she could only hope he would go somewhere and isolate himself.

"Cassandra?" Frankie said softly to the young girl, who was now all grown up, sitting in front of him.

Her eyes didn't leave the downward direction she was looking in, she was just starring, and her expression was blank. She responded quietly with an automatic response, "Yeah."

"There's one more thing I know, do you want to hear it?"

She knew her answer was going to be yes, but she had to find the courage to actually say it. She reached for her bourbon and finished the last shot.

"Yeah, Frankie, I do wanna hear it," she answered, finally making eye contact with him.

"I know that Robert took the fall for Sean that night of the shooting at The Medallion."

"How…how do you know that?" she asked.

"I was the one who made the first transfer to the presiding judge's account: your mother paid off to try him as a juvenile for a light sentence with no jail time and for his record to be sealed."

Cassandra tried to speak, but the words didn't come.

"That's right, she had protected Robert, and there were a series of payments that were set up to be made to the judge for the next ten years so it wouldn't be noticeable. Oh yeah, that lucky bastard was headed for a nice and early retirement."

Cassandra poured herself another bourbon and topped off Frankie's drink.

"What happened?" she finally asked.

Frankie shook his head. "The judge that was supposed to hear Robert's case had a cerebral aneurysm and died on the operating table. Can you believe that!"

Tipsy and lightheaded from the alcohol, feeling betrayed and exploited, she looked up at Frankie with her baby blues. For a moment he found himself aroused.

"So, you going to finish your dinner? It was absolutely divine!"

Cassandra's eyes were heavy and sad. A cruel twist of fate once again had extinguished their hopes and dreams.

"No, I'm not really hungry," answered Cassandra.

"Are you ready to go back to shore?" asked Frankie.

She stood up, unsteady on her feet. "Yeah," she muttered softly.

He grabbed her fur coat and wrapped it around her, she didn't realize how cold she was. He kissed her on the forehead, and she stumbled backing away from him. On the upper deck he safely sat her in the chair behind him.

"I'll drive back, and hey, no regrets?" he asked.

Cassandra had no response for this monster. Maybe if she never had to see him or the marina again, she could begin to heal.

The throttle of the boat woke up the calm and still water. There was nothing left except the ripples and small waves the boat made on their way back to shore. The sound of the rustling water was calming to her, rippling out a sense of victory. A victory that fueled her quest for vengeance.

Frankie helped her out of the boat and onto *The Crimson Rose,* and he was gone.

CHAPTER SEVENTEEN

"Glitz and Glamour"

That same night while Cassandra was playing cat and mouse with Frankie, everyone else was looking forward to the annual Pointer Christmas party.

It took Ruth a little longer than usual to get ready for the event. She looked tired and was hoping her make-up would hide the worries she was carrying with her. There were many ways and many things that could mask a sin.

Her hair was in a mid-center, loosely pinned up voluminous up do. She chose a floor-length, gold-pleated off -the-shoulder ballgown with an empire waist that adorned emerald-green lace appliques. The lace appliques sat beautifully on her shoulders and accented her breasts creating a beautiful silhouette. The emerald lace sectioned off, extending mid-calf with the lacy wide pleats. It was sequined and shimmered elegantly. Her jewelry was never simple for these grand events: she wore a cascading emerald and diamond necklace with matching earrings. To finish off her look, in addition to her beautiful wedding ring, she wore her emerald and diamond cocktail ring. Her gold and diamond bracelets were ready to dance around her wrists while shaking hands gave and received warm embraces. Her shoes were dainty T-straps in a gold color with a medium heel height that would allow her to stay on the dance floor with ease. Ravishing and bewitching, she was ready to captivate the evening. Once again, she would take her rightful place in the center of the room.

Even though Robert didn't prepare the dinner for this party, the dinner was five star. Ruth couldn't help but think about Robert sitting at the table while everyone ate, drank, and chatted about this and that. No one seemed to have a care in the world. The majority of the party guests did take a moment to ask Charles and Ruth about their son and bring them well wishes. It was empathy tried at its best and sympathy given at its finest. The old money in the room didn't kindly give way to the scandal that loomed directly above cloaked in the glamour making it hard to see, and Ruth was aware. Ruth and Charles were happy to share the positive news they were receiving from the doctors about his recovery and how blessed they were. She used the word "Blessed" like she knew what a blessing was, giving the perception that she prayed.

From the table settings with linen tablecloths to the stemware and top-shelf liquor, it all provided the atmosphere of glamour and wealth. The band that was hired to play for the evening provided the atmosphere of sophistication. The annual black-tie event brought back the elegance of French rolls, up dos, and ballgowns. The sparkle of fine jewelry came from the gentlemen as well as the ladies, making it difficult to determine who the actual trophy spouse was. These were the reasons that old money attended the Pointer Enterprises events. Others just wanted to make sure they didn't miss anything. Everyone really likes a good scandal, they just won't admit it, and Ruth knew that too. It was the attitude of those with their new money that would clash in society with the old.

After dinner was finished the real party got started. Everyone gathered around in the banquet room to toast the holiday season. The toast was usually about how fortunate everyone here was and how important it was to give back to the community. The stockings that were hung on the fireplace mantle for charity collections; the Christmas trees and other decorations provided the reason and encouraged every one's best qualities to surface. This year it would be Ruth's voice they would hear for the official start of the party.

"Good evening, everyone," said Ruth to get everyone's attention. "Thank you all for coming. Once again, we come together to celebrate the season of giving and gratefulness. Charles and I would like to thank each of you for your well wishes, thoughts, and prayers for our family. It means a lot, it really does. This year we're adding another stocking to the mantle and it's for the Ozark Rehabilitation Facility." Handing the microphone to Charles, Ruth walked up to the mantle and hung the last stocking. The partygoers clapped and cheered.

Charles handed Ruth a glass of champagne and his last words to their guests were, "Let us celebrate good tidings and good times. Merry Christmas!"

The room was filled with raising glasses and voices gleefully exclaimed, "Here, here!"

Charles met his glass with Ruth's, and they each took a drink of their champagne to consummate their toast, and Charles sweetly kissed her on the cheek.

Charles and Ruth finally made it to the dance floor, one of their favorite things to do was dance with each other. It wasn't often these days people would go out dancing; times were changing and there were fewer places to go to hear ballroom music. It was nice to bring back a little of their generations way of life and celebrate in style. The Medallion's Christmas party was mainly made up of Charles and Ruth's generation; their children would rarely attend. For them it was too stuffy, too formal, and too old fashioned.

Ruth loved to see Charles in a tuxedo and all dressed up—he looked so suave and debonair. He matched his bow tie and cummerbund in the same emerald-green color of her dress. Even though he was considered short for man with his five-foot-five stature, he seemed to look taller in his tux. His hair was thinning and what was left of it was gray. Still, you put any man in a tux, a simple thirty-minute or so transformation takes place, and voila, a handsome and irresistible man stands before you!

Her smile was real when he brought her in closer to him and they waltzed some more. It was obvious to see as they danced how much Charles loved and adored his wife; after all these years he still couldn't take his eyes off of her.

He got lost in her on the dance floor and Ruth got lost in her worried thoughts. This was the wrong time of the year for even a hint of scandal, and she inconspicuously read the room. The season of giving and forgiveness may have provided the perfect emotional backdrop for Pointer Enterprises after all.

"Scouring the room, my dear, like the newspapers?" asked Charles while they twirled around on the dance floor.

Ruth gave a look to her husband and was thankful Charles preferred to be dismissed on a normal basis. Over the years she had mastered many ways to charm her observant husband.

"I'm sorry, I know. There are reporters here too," she said softly.

Charles swirled his wife out and around and brought her back to him. "Relax, I understand. I'm not judging, I promise."

When Ruth wasn't on the dance floor with her husband, she was circling the room. Guests were huddled and conversing according to their status and net worth. It was the top of the pyramid that concerned Ruth the most, those in the age bracket of Charles. There was little known about Ruth's family, but her family had been around town enough to create chatter. Occasionally, when circling the room she would hear mumblings of, *I remember when Charles came home one day from Rushing Springs and he was married to her.* Or, *Oh yes, Sean was a honeymoon baby.* Said with a "wink wink." Then, she heard the words she was hoping she wouldn't hear on this very night. *Isn't this the second shooting that Sean's been involved in?*

Before any additional chatter could commence about Robert and Sean, Ruth introduced herself.

Ruth observed the two couples were young, somewhat flashy, and too charming for their own good. However, this was in Ruth's favor, and she believed she was observing newcomers to town and possibly new money or no money.

"Mrs. Pointer, it's a pleasure to meet you. I'm Michael Malloni, and this is my wife, Grace."

They shook hands and Ruth's bracelets danced and her rings sparkled returning the niceties.

"Are you new to town? I don't believe we've met," stated Ruth.

"Yes, we've just relocated to town. At the first of the year, myself and Gabriel, my brother here, will be taking over the bank of Alexander Frankel."

"I know Alexander; together we've built a lot in this town. We worked together for over thirty years. I was sorry when he decided to retire, but we're all getting older and the time to pass the torch gets closer each day, I guess," answered Ruth with a smile.

"It's nice to meet you, Mrs. Pointer," said Gabriel.

"You as well, Gabriel."

"Call me Gabe, please. This is my wife, Joan."

"It's very nice to meet you all. Welcome to Braxton. Hopefully, in the near future we can do business together," Ruth stated while giving a congenial warning to Grace and Joan that it's not smart to bite the hand that may feed you. Michael and Gabe understood immediately.

"I'm guessing the four tickets that Alexander requested for tonight were for your party?"

"Yes, they were. Mr. Frankel had mentioned what an important client you were of his and how much you cared about the community," answered Michael.

"After the holidays we'll have to meet and talk business," replied Ruth.

"I look forward to it," said Michael, holding out his hand, and once again he and Ruth shook hands. Michael turned to his wife, his brother, and sister-in-law and gave them a disapproving look, hoping that Mrs. Pointer didn't hear them gossiping.

Ruth continued on, to sashay and mingle with all the party guests, paying special attention to those of old money.

The more the alcohol and champagne flowed, the more donations the Christmas stockings collected. Ruth felt that her position was strengthened, not weakened. It was comforting that Pointer Enterprises once again proved to be *the* last Christmas party of the year. Their New Year's Eve Party would certainly wrap up Pointer Enterprises in its security to move forward for a successful new year.

The party broke up around one thirty a.m. The old folks had broken curfew and felt exhilarated. The partygoers felt they were rightfully placed in their society, and each of them presented from their platforms to reinforce their positions. They had all been seen, and that was important.

The cloakroom was busy bringing out the fur coats, hats, and gloves. The valets were bringing the cars around while the partygoers prepared to make their way home. Ruth knew the exit was just as important as the entrance, if not more so. She and Charles made sure they thanked each guest for coming and wished them safe travels on the way home. Light kisses on the cheek, departing hug or handshake, each guest left believing they were part of something that was bigger than themselves. That was the bonus experience of the evening. As superficial as it was, it felt right, and it felt good. Ruth and Charles remained outside watching the cars pull out of the drive, waving them off until the last car drove out of sight. After gathering the stuffed stockings, they left The Medallion to head home. The Medallion wouldn't open to the public again until January 2, 1986.

CHAPTER EIGHTEEN

"Ambivalence"

For Cassandra, the next day came fast and furious. She woke with a horrible headache and still reeked of bourbon. Mary was already in her stateroom, with the curtains pulled back letting in the natural light that was announcing the new day. The large glass windows showed a panoramic view of the lake they both called home. There was no fog, and you could see clear across the lake; the water was calm and reflective like a mirror.

There were two breakfast plates on the table, and Mary looked like she was enjoying hers. The smell of fresh-brewed coffee that filled the small state room caused Cassandra to stir.

"Well, good afternoon, sunshine," said Mary, looking up from the newspaper.

Cassandra was groggy and hungover.

"What time is it?" she asked with squinty eyes.

Mary poured her a cup of coffee and handed it to her. "It's two in the afternoon."

Cassandra couldn't hardly believe it; she didn't remember much after boarding *The Crimson Rose.*

"What are you doing up so early, and why are the drapes open?" she grumbled.

She took a drink of her coffee and pushed her plate away; there was no way she could eat anything without hurling.

"Not hungry, huh?" said Mary with a little giggle.

"No, not hungry. What time did I get back to yacht? What happened?" asked Casandra.

"Well, you and Frankie came in about midnight or so, and you were wasted, which, by the way, you promised me you would take it easy on the alcohol and coke..." said Mary, simply making mention and not wanting any details. "I didn't really expect you back so early, I thought that was odd, and Frankie, well, Frankie was Frankie. Do you remember what happened? Did he tell you anything at all?"

"Yeah, apparently Frankie is a reformed man, found God I guess or something like that," answered a snarky Cassandra.

"Or maybe he can't you know...any longer, impotence?" said Mary mischievously and giggling. "Wouldn't that be justice? We're not the only ones getting older, you know."

Cassandra shrugged her shoulders. "That would be justice, but if I were younger, he wouldn't of had any reservations to feed his fetish, believe me. He's still a monster. And, just so you know, I did take it easy, you would've been proud of me. I didn't even bring out the eight ball," said a defensive friend making sure to set the record straight. It mattered to Cassandra what Mary thought. Mary mattered to Cassandra.

With the record set straight, Cassandra continued on, "He's retiring and moving his family away from this place. He said he's moving over the Christmas holiday and his retirement is being kept hush hush. And, get this, Mary, he's been distancing himself from my mother since the eviction deal with my Uncle Joe. So, as soon as Mom begins to find things to exploit with her new banker friends, we'll be seeing a new clientele here no doubt."

Mary sat stunned hearing these words from Cassandra. A new clientele would upset the balance they had created. Their clientele were in their late fifties, some early sixties. Even though repulsive, still a safer bet than the alternative. All of the girls including Cassandra and Mary had planned to be long gone before a new generation of bankers and politicians were to be introduced on the boats. If the Frankie Group was disbanding, how would that affect the shift of power to the second generations of the Founding Fathers and the Pioneers? How would that affect the girls?

"Oh, Cassandra, what are we going to do? This is bad, this is *very* bad."

"I know," said Cassandra, digging through her purse, pulling out a thousand dollars in cash and handing it to Mary.

"What's this?"

"Frankie paid for his night even though it was comped and told me to use this money to get out of Braxton. I don't know if he knew that's been our plan all along, but we toasted to making at least one wrong right, and I guess he meant it. Add this to the money we've saved up to leave. How much do we have?"

Mary took the money and tucked it away in her bosom, "I think this gives us about thirty thousand."

Cassandra leaned back and sighed a sigh of relief. "That'll help a lot to get us settled somewhere else. I hope the other girls are doing just as good saving. There's more bad news, Mary. My mother has turned the power of trustee of my trust over to Sean, and he now holds the majority interest in the marina."

"Oh my God, no!" replied Mary.

"Yeah, that's what I said when Frankie told me that. You know, Mary, check with the girls and find out where they stand financially; we all have to get out. I'm going back to the Springton house after Christmas at my parents and stay until our New Year's Eve party on *The Eclipse. The Crimson Rose* is now shut down for the season and all the houseboats are in. Hand me the phone, please. I'll call mom about getting a new car and ask for a draw on my trust fund if I have to. Mom can't know that I know Sean holds the majority interest on the marina and is trustee of my trust."

Mary had checked out, fearing that a new reality would be setting in.

"Mary!" said Cassandra in a raised voice, causing her head to pound.

"Where are you? Hand me the phone, please?" asked Cassandra.

Mary hadn't heard Cassandra ask her for the phone—she was lost in what she'd just heard and what it could mean.

"I'm sorry, Cassandra," Mary replied, reaching over and handing her the phone. Cassandra dialed her mom's number.

"Pointer Residence," answered a familiar male voice.

"Dad, it's me, Cassandra. Is Mom around by chance?"

Charles was always happy when he would hear Cassandra's voice on the phone asking for Ruth instead of calling to speak with him, though he'd never admit it.

"Ruthie, it's for you, it's Cassandra."

"Hi, Cassandra, everything okay?" Ruth asked hesitantly.

"Oh yeah. Mary and I are here working on the final preparations for the New Year's Eve party for *The Eclipse* and with everything going on we haven't really got to discuss the holidays for the marina and it's almost over. We're almost sold out on the showboat, so we're doing good. I don't expect any empty seats or tables at all. It's just that I've been out of town a lot with Robert, and we only have the one car here at the marina, and that leaves Mary stranded for the bank runs and any last-minute preparations or getting last-minute supplies. I was hoping to be able to purchase another car for the use of the marina in my absence. Robert has a long road ahead of him and I'd like to spend the majority of my time at the house in Springton during the downtime of the marina."

Ruth cleared her throat. "Oh I see. So you're planning to spend more time in Springton?"

"If that's all right, Mom?" added Cassandra, doing her best to choose her words wisely.

It wasn't all right with Ruth, but she was afraid of any additional friction with her children. It might be best to keep Cassandra appeased at the moment, and what she was asking wasn't illogical or unreasonable. Maybe Cassandra was growing up after all, and Ruth found it refreshing she was thinking about Pointer Enterprises.

"What do you have in mind?" asked Ruth with no judgment or reservation in her voice.

"You know…I really like your car, Mom. I was thinking about a Cadillac Seville!"

Ruth erupted in laughter.

"Oh really, I'm sure you do like that car. When you're my age, you can buy yourself a Cadillac! Besides, if you think you're going to drive a newer Cadillac than me, you're sadly mistaken!"

Cassandra replied with laughter, "I know, Mom, you can't blame me for trying! Honestly, I was just thinking about a Ford Taurus or something like that. I thought about a truck, but we already have trucks, and the most economical purchase would be a compact car. What do you think?"

"All right, meet me at the office tomorrow morning around ten and I'll have a check ready for you."

"Thanks, Mom, I'll see you in the morning."

Cassandra and Ruth both hung up the phone wishing all their conversations were so lighthearted. Cassandra wished she always felt that close to her mother. There was nothing she enjoyed more than laughing with her mother. Cassandra wanted to love her mom so much, but she couldn't trust her, and one or two happy moments didn't change their history. She just wanted a mom. Just as she knew Frankie was a monster, she knew she was not only Ruth's daughter, but also her ambition.

"Wow, Cassandra, was that really that easy? I remember a time when you would just steal her car!" said Mary, playfully asking and answering her own question.

Cassandra looked at Mary and rolled her eyes.

"Start looking for newer used compact cars…and Mary, I borrowed her car that night. I didn't steal it! Oh, and make sure to put that car in your name."

"Okay! So, we're stealing a car again!" said Mary, smiling that God-given innocent smile of hers.

"Yeah, you say okay! Just like a splash of bourbon is a drink!" said Cassandra.

"Uh-huh," answered Mary.

"Our place is ready you said?" asked Cassandra, dismissing the conversation of stealing and borrowing cars, shots and splashes, and snorting drugs or swallowing pills.

"Yeah, but it isn't close to Robert. We could stay at the hotel across from the rehab facility and go back and forth to our place."

"That sounds like a plan; we'll figure something out," said Cassandra.

Mary squealed like a little schoolgirl and hugged and kissed Cassandra. Upon on Mary's squeal, her head split in two and pounded like she'd just heard the high pitch sound of a trumpet. Holding her head with both hands and with barely a voice, "Mary, please…"

Mary poured Cassandra more coffee and whispered a sincere, "I'm sorry, I forgot."

The girls giggled and began to get ready for their day, going through the motions, waiting for it to be over.

The next day, as promised, Cassandra had the money from her mother to deposit into her account to purchase the new car as discussed. The girls began to feel even more confident in their abilities, getting closer to their new life. Now, they needed Robert to be okay.

Cassandra was still hoping that Robert and Mary would get married. Her twenty-fifth birthday was just around the corner. January fifteenth, the day she would come into her own and receive steady payments from her trust fund. The future was still uncertain as to Robert's recovery, but the time to leave this life behind appeared to be closer within their grasp.

It brought a sense of peace that neither Cassandra nor Mary had ever really experienced.

CHAPTER NINETEEN

"A Cold December"

The big house on the hill was decorated beautifully and welcomed all who visited with lights framing the roof of the house and its windows. Lights and garland hung from the large front porch and a lighted nativity scene was proudly displayed in the front yard. A large Christmas wreath of pinecones and red bows hung on the front door.

Inside, garland adorned the stair railing. The scene of a Christmas town was alive in the corner of the sitting room. The electric train went round and round the lighted ceramic town of little houses and shops. Special editions of Christmas Hummel's were proudly displayed on the fireplace mantle. The full spruce Christmas tree was decorated with handmade and store-bought ornaments alike. Over the years extended family, business acquaintances, and employees had given Ruth Christmas ornaments for gifts. The most precious to her were, of course, the handmade ornaments and ornaments given to her by her children. This year Santa brought everyone everything they wanted, except a fully recovered Robert.

At the Pointer household, it was a quiet Christmas compared to the ones in the past. Robert was terribly missed. The family gathered for Christmas dinner in the formal dining room, in an informal manner. Charles didn't slice the ham at the table to prove himself head of household. There was no talk about how successful Thanksgiving was, how successful the Christmas party was, or the amount of donations. Charles didn't even discuss any of his land purchase deals that were on the table. The tragedy was controlling them.

There were smells of pine and spice. Christmas holly berries connected by beautiful red flowing bows were imprinted on all the gold-rimmed holiday china with its matching mugs used for coffee, tea, and hot chocolate. The glazed honey ham brought mouthwatering sweet scents being passed around the table. The buffet was filled with colorful Christmas cookies, cakes, and pies of all varieties and shapes and sizes.

In the Pointer family, Christmas was celebrated for the children and to keep up appearances; their religion had already been bought and paid for.

Jack and Joshua seemed to be doing better, and you could see flickers of real smiles between them and Caroline. Sean wasn't as boisterous as he usually was, and that suited Cassandra just fine. Even Rose seemed to be more comfortable without any *healthy competition.*

They exchanged gifts, and Jack and Joshua were so excited to find that *Santa* brought them each fishing poles, rods, and reels galore and tackle boxes with all the trimmings. Each year Cassandra would give her parents a scrapbook of the events that had taken place at the marina and its milestones. Of course, choosing its show-and-tell presentation. She desperately wished that one year Ruth would realize what she'd done. Ruth never did see it that way and even took pride in the yearly scrap book. Rose and Charles snubbed the gift of the scrapbook, believing it was Cassandra's way of telling her sister she wasn't good enough or pretty enough to run such an operation. The two sisters would never know they were fighting similar demons, beauty versus intelligence.

Cassandra was struggling to find her own worth, being in the presence of Sean left her feeling exposed. Charles had gotten every one's attention and requested their presence outside; she was relieved the day was continuing to move forward.

Once outside, Charles opened the garage door and there were two brand new four-wheelers! Joshua was so sweet, he didn't know whether he should run to Grandpa, Grandma, his dad, his mom, or to his aunts. He made his rounds giving his hugs and his smile took up his whole face.

"Look, Jack! Look, there's one for me and one for you!" exclaimed Joshua.

Jack was already headed toward the garage to check them out and he was as excited as his little brother. This was a good day for the boys, and it was needed.

Jack came down the drive and Joshua ran to him and begged, "When can we ride, when can we ride?"

Jack didn't get a chance to answer!

Teasing the boys, Sean spoke up, "Not today, my sons! Don't you think it's a little cold to go out riding? We probably won't be able to ride for months!"

Joshua spoke up right away. "No, Daddy, it's not even snowing!"

Sean laughed and turned toward Jack. "Well, Jack, you think we oughta take Joshua out for a ride?"

"You betcha, Dad!" answered Jack, grinning from ear to ear.

Sean went to his truck and unloaded his ATV, and Charles motioned for Matt to take his. Matt grinned; this was one of the many things he enjoyed when visiting Rose's family.

"You don't wanna go ride, Charles?" asked Matt.

Charles chuckled. "No, Matthew, I don't think so. Don't tell anyone but I think it's too damned cold for an old man like me to be riding around on one of these things today! I'll build a fire in back and save you boys some brandy."

Caroline turned and looked at her sons and said. "That's gonna be hot chocolate for you two."

The boys seemed disappointed but were too excited about the bikes to hang onto that too long. The men in the family would bond through these manly men activities. Charles would "sneak" the boys a sip of brandy or a beer from time to time, it was their *thing*.

"Are you sure, Mom, just hot chocolate? It's Christmas and Jack will be old enough to drive soon!" said Joshua, protesting over losing a forbidden treat.

"Yes, Joshua. I'm sure!" answered Caroline.

Charles was shocked that Caroline would interject herself into a conversation that was between him and the boys, and he was going to voice his opinion on the matter when Ruth spoke up. "What did your mother say, boys?"

The boys suited up in layers and layers and disappeared riding down the driveway enjoying their cold, crisp ride. Charles continued toward the backyard to build the fire and was silently pondering what he witnessed. It was odd for Caroline to speak up and have Ruth's support.

They sat outside around the firepit waiting for the boys to come back from their ride; it seemed like an ordinary family Christmas gathering. From the outside it looked like a family coming together and supporting one another through a difficult time. The glimpses that Cassandra would see in the past of what could be were no longer visible to her. In her eyes, the Pointer family couldn't hide in the glamour any longer; reality had set in and hovered too long.

Cassandra poured herself another brandy, wishing it was bourbon. She sat by the fire and looked around. There was her mother, her sister, sister-in-law, and of course, *Daddy*. She wondered how they could be talking with each other and so much conversation buzzing about but saying nothing. It was Caroline that kept the conversation moving at every family gathering with the questions she would ask. Caroline and Rose would talk about Springton and Pointer's Inn, and she would let Rose know how each year she looks more beautiful and how marriage really agrees with her. While Cassandra was waiting for Caroline to coil up with her mother-in-law, it never happened. There wasn't any back-and-forth meaningless chatter between her mother and Caroline this year. The conversation had fallen into an awkward lull after Rose and Caroline had said all they had to say.

Cassandra got lost in her thoughts again and accepted that what had started as Robert's crusade had now become her cause, and it was consuming her. She wondered who this person was sitting next to her named Caroline. There seemed to be something different about her and she couldn't tell if it was a newfound confidence or arrogance. More importantly, why the change in her demeanor?

Rose was still the same person she had known all her life. The same girl that shredded her prom dress to threads in high school, and she was still the same girl that Rose's boyfriend ended up with at the prom's after-party.

Before the boys pulled into the driveway, you could hear them coming. Roaring loudly up the driveway and coming to an idle at the garage doors and then finally turning off their ATVs. Cassandra was happy to hear the roar of the ATVs breaking the awkward silence.

She spent some time with the boys after their ride, sitting around the fire while they got warm, still saying it wasn't too cold and the ride was just fine. They made s'mores and added more chocolate to that and drank their oversized cups of hot chocolate! Once the boys started settling down and the fire died down, Cassandra decided she was going to call it a night. Although the evening was cordial, the thought of Robert was weighing heavy on all their hearts.

That night the Pointer family was under one roof, and when the house went dark, the clouds were high and thin, like a veil. A veil that was growing thin and losing its ability to hold the emotional turmoil that was about to come.

CHAPTER TWENTY

"Ruth's Decision"

"Come in, Mrs. Pointer. I'm sorry we had to break up the holidays like this," said Dr. Marshall helping her with her coat.

"Thank you, Doctor, I am as well. Did you have a nice Christmas?"

"I did, thank you, and the rehabilitation center had a wonderful Christmas as well, thanks to your generous donation. How about you, did you have a good Christmas?"

"It was as good as could be expected. We all got together, but we missed Robert terribly. I'm hoping you have news since we last spoke?"

Dr. Marshall sat down at his chair behind his desk and picked up Robert's case file.

"Yes, I have discussed Robert's case in depth with my colleagues, including the information regarding his violent nature as a young boy, and we have come to the same diagnosis. I'm not going to try to not overwhelm you with his diagnosis in medical terms, so if you have any questions, please ask."

Ruth nodded her head yes and replied with an uncertain, "All right."

"I would like to say under the circumstances," Dr. Marshall began, "we all feel that Robert is responding really well. It's amazing to see how well he's progressing. However, Robert has suffered a couple of seizures since his stay here. Those with penetrating brain injuries such as Robert's will be at a higher risk for seizures for the rest of his life, and we still cannot rule out the possibility of a stroke. The frontal lobe on his right side was affected by the shooting, which is why you are seeing impairments such as broken speech and trouble with non-verbal functions, and little show of emotion. With his progress and his determination to regain or re-learn his lost abilities, it may be possible that he may be able to recover and have a good quality of life; in lay terms, his left side of his brain may recover from the weaknesses caused by the damage done to the right side of his brain.

"Now, the right side of his brain controls attention span, memory and recall of memory, reasoning and the abilities to problem solve. It also controls visual interpretations and its comprehension, imagination, and emotions. The right side of the brain organizes, so to speak, and the left side analyzes and brings logic. However, the emotions and feelings of anger, pride, and even though contrary to those feelings, happiness also comes from the left side of the brain. There are also lesions on the left side of his brain, due to the scattering of the lead pellets," he explained while using pictures of a healthy brain and comparing to scans of Robert's brain.

Dr. Marshall took a drink of coffee, flipping through a few pages in Robert's case file. Ruth remained silent soaking in everything he had said like a sponge.

"Although there is a left and right hemisphere of the brain, that doesn't mean the left and the right brain functions independently of each other. They work in conjunction with each other. In my opinion, the cruelness of this situation is his tendency for violence. In therapy, I have witnessed what I believe is the underlying anger, rage if you will, just as you said. That could come from the struggle of trying to remember or the whole struggle of it all. It's important that we interpret just where his rage is coming from so we know what form of treatment to administer. It is also important that we do not mistake rage for any frustration he could be feeling. I do believe that he remembers the day of the shooting, and for whatever the reason is not sharing those memories. Maybe he's not ready yet, and that isn't uncommon either."

Ruth took in a deep breath and slowly exhaled. She was fidgety, shifting from one side to the other in her seat. A tear ran down her face.

"Mrs. Pointer," said Dr. Marshall, handing her a box of tissues, "would you like to take a break?"

Dabbing her eyes with the tissues, "I think so," she whispered.

She stood up and went to the same window where she had stood just a couple of weeks ago. Dr. Marshall filled her coffee cup with a warm up and allowed her the time she needed to try and process this difficult and emotionally devastating information. For a few moments they stood quietly looking out the window. The steam from her coffee was easily seen against the windowpane, rising up.

It was beginning to snow. If she hadn't gotten up and walked over to the window, she would've never known. So illuminating, beautiful, and magical. Light, innocent single snowflakes falling from the sky that could become heavy and treacherous accumulating in layers on top of layers.

Ruth sat down placing her coffee cup on the table. Her movements were mechanical and precise.

Dr. Marshall sat down at his desk and gently spoke. "Mrs. Pointer, he's come a long way since he's come out of his coma, it's really miraculous. It's not uncommon, you know, that coma patients will be disoriented with strange memories such as the ones Robert experienced. He now knows that he remembered Optimus Prime from past memories, and the color *red* was significant because of all the blood at the scene."

Ruth continued to listen to Dr. Marshall's words and wanted to quash the day and continue on with his therapy. She wanted to hear more of the positive progress and more of the good things that may be coming Robert's way. Images of Sean, Jack, and their futures flashed through her mind.

"Dr. Marshall, I have to ask," said Ruth with hesitation.

"Take your time, Mrs. Pointer, I know how difficult this must be for you."

Ruth sat up straight in her chair, crossed her legs, and cupped both hands over her knees. "Doctor, please explain to me the injuries to my son and the process of his recovery. If you continue on with his therapy, how will that affect him? I know he has a lot to face, I worry about him being in pain, you see. Physically and mentally. Do you understand, Doctor?"

There was a flash in her eyes, and they went dark for a split second. Devastatingly enough, the good doctor didn't see it. In front of him sat a beautiful, distressed woman, full of much sadness worrying about her son. There also seemed to be a conflict raging within her that Dr. Marshall couldn't identify. This lady sitting before him was living a mother's nightmare that no mother should have to endure, and he could feel her pain.

Dr. Marshall continued on with what he believed was expected of him in light of the circumstances.

"The additional information that you have provided to myself and my colleagues regarding his personality and who he was before is a concern."

Ruth remained in her position and nodded to the doctor.

"Now with that said," he continued, "we believe that if Robert would make full a recovery, with the damage done particularly to the right frontal lobe, he would not be able to mentally handle the years of rehabilitation. It'll be difficult for him to organize his thoughts, so to speak. There'll be immense frustration for him, and along with the seizures he will have constant pain. Pain that will need to be medically managed; we believe he'll need a pain management regimen."

"Dr. Marshall, what are you suggesting?"

Dr. Marshall looked down at his desk, laid out the scans and pictures of Robert's brain for review.

"Mrs. Pointer, I'm afraid that if Robert doesn't regain his lost facilities, such as reading, writing, and basic physical abilities before he regains his memories, he could be lost. Trapped in his own mind so to speak. It's possible the memories he does regain may not be accurate either. Now, none of us doctors who have worked with Robert on a daily basis have a crystal ball, we don't have the tools to predict how long his rehabilitation will take and if that rehabilitation will lead to recovery. We can only determine when a specific treatment is not being responded to, not leading us to the results of rehabilitation that we are hoping for. Then we try a different treatment until we're out of options."

"I see," said Ruth. "And are you out of options?"

"With the damage done to his right frontal lobe and the weakness of the left side of his brain and then including the pain management, in the best interest of Robert's mental and physical health we're recommending a frontal lobotomy," answered Dr. Marshall in a familiar, unsettling, steadfast tone she had heard before.

Ruth physically gasped and collapsed in her chair almost falling to the floor. Dr. Marshall quickly got up from behind his desk and kept her from collapsing to the floor. "Mrs. Pointer, can I get you anything? I know this is hard to hear," he said, still kneeling at the side of her chair consoling her the best he could.

"Would you like to take another break?" he asked.

Sitting straight again and leaning on the back of the chair, she crossed her legs and let her arms rest on the chair. It was hard for her to hear. She and Charles could lose their son forever, and this would destroy Charles. There was no going back after this, and the hands of time would be unforgiving.

"No, please continue," she replied.

"A lobotomy is rare, and this type of surgery is only recommended if all other treatments have failed, and it's more of a delicate procedure these days. The nature of the specialty of this surgery has never disappeared, not really. In performing the lobotomy, some of the nerves in the brain are cut to sever certain pathway connections. For example, a frontal lobotomy is effective for pain relief and would add to his pain management program that he will need. Also, his violent nature would be calmed as well. The stigma that has been attached to this type of surgery leads brain surgeons away from this type of surgical procedure. On a positive note, there have been those who've had this surgery with great success. We've complied some information for you to read. You and your husband take the time needed to think about it and please contact me at any time with any questions."

With weak and shaky hands Ruth took the information from Dr. Marshall and nodded. She tried to speak, and the tightness of her throat prevented her from swallowing and kept any sound or words from being heard.

"If you decide to go ahead with the surgery, you'll find the forms that need to be signed by you and your husband in the envelope. I know you're a couple of hours away, and if you do sign the papers you may overnight the papers and we'll schedule his surgery as soon as possible. Even as soon as Monday, December thirtieth."

Ruth dabbed her eyes again with a tissue and her voice was raspy, "Oh, that soon, huh? Will he remember me, recall any past memories at all?"

Dr. Marshall shook his head. "It's hard to say. You've seen yourself the struggle your son experiences when he sees you and Charles, how he sees you both and knows who you both are, and then you notice the moment he puts it together who you actually are in relation to himself. He has to work to process his visual to reclaim the knowledge."

"But," exclaimed Ruth, "he recognizes Cassandra, and he's obviously comfortable with her."

Dr. Marshall hesitated for a moment.

"Cassandra is obviously a constant in his life, and one could say that she's in his heart, mind, and soul."

There were some things that hadn't escaped the doctor. Those were hard words for Ruth to hear, and even harder for Dr. Marshall to say, and he said them as gently as he could. Ruth accepted the doctor's answer and wasn't going to discuss any further matters with him regarding the Pointer family, she had resolved her inner conflict.

"Mrs. Pointer, please, if you have any questions day or night, do not hesitate to call me. I know this is a big decision and a not an easy one to make. No mother and father should ever be faced with such a dilemma."

Ruth stood up and grabbed her purse. "Thank you, Dr. Marshall, for all you've done. Can I see my son before I go?"

He helped her with her coat. "Of course, of course. You know the way to his room from here?"

"Yes, I do. Thank you again." Ruth turned to walk out of his office and stopped suddenly.

"Oh, Dr. Marshall, I almost forgot, here's the donations from the charity Christmas drive at our Christmas party. Please, no mention of this or my earlier donation; this is my own family, my personal business, and I would prefer as least amount of exposure as possible."

Gratefully he took the envelope and said, "I understand."

Ruth walked down the hallway and entered Robert's room. He was lying there; the bandages had been removed and only had a patch over his right eye. The closer she got to the bed she could see he was lying there awake. There was no definition to the right side of his face. Robert didn't have a cheek bone or any teeth. A single bandage held on with tape stripes covering the scabbing, gaping hole in his face.

"Robert, son, it's Mom." She could tell he recognized her, but it was still a little unclear if he recognized their relationship. He didn't try to speak. His eye was blinking rapidly and began to water.

"Robert, I love you, it's gonna be all right, I promise," she said.

Robert was unresponsive to her words; he couldn't verbally or physically engage with her. He needed to see Cassandra, and he wanted to see Mary. He remembered Mary. He remembered everything. He had heard his mother say these very words to him before. Robert knew things weren't going to be okay and that his time was going to be cut short, his mother had just told him so. He lay there and remembered how he'd once stretched out his arms for his mother's safe embrace, and he couldn't reach her. He didn't make one movement in response to his mother's words. He didn't know what was going to happen, but he knew he was as good as dead. He had overplayed his hand. His sense of right and wrong didn't factor in the new generation of his nephews that he never took the time to get to know. Ruth leaned down and kissed her son on the forehead. "I'll be back to see you on Monday. You just rest. I love you."

On the way home Ruth made a stop at the Braxton Post Office and took out the papers the doctor had given her to read. Rose's words came back to haunt her: *Oh, that's right, if we don't talk about it, it didn't happen.*

Ruth sat, nervously clicking the pen repeatedly and then signing her name first. She stared at the line that had the name typed underneath, *Charles W. Pointer.* It wasn't that she couldn't sign Charles's name, she had many times before without hesitation.

The snow was still falling, and the windshield wipers were chattering away. Possibly saying, *you can never look back,* wiping the fallen snowflakes from the windshield that melted to droplets of water by the heat of the Cadillac's blasting defrosters. There was fear and shame breaking through from her younger self to her older self. Her younger self afraid of being poor, and her older self afraid of being destroyed. If Robert remembered, it could mean complete ruin for her and for Pointer Enterprises.

Ambition said this was best for Robert. Ambition said she didn't have any control over this and if she suffered because of it, everyone else would too. Ambition said, with time, all would heal. Her ambition said she may have lost her children's generation, but she didn't have to lose her grandchildren's generation.

Without reading the rest of the literature Dr. Marshall had given her, she put pen to paper and perfectly signed Charles's name just like it was another contract, employment agreement, or land deal and put the signed papers in the envelope. Opening the car door, she was numb to the freezing cold and the fierce winds blowing the snowflakes about. She dropped the envelope in the Fed-Ex box. Her son's fate was sealed.

CHAPTER TWENTY-ONE

"Cassandra Learns the Truth"

Cassandra awoke freezing under the thin blanket that was on the couch and it was already dark. When she arrived at the Springton house late that morning she built a fire and grabbed a bottle of wine to help her relax from Christmas. The fuzzy numbers on her watch said six p.m. There were three empty wine bottles and an empty wine glass on the table. *Oh my word, how could I have drank three bottles of wine? Dammit! There's nothing worse than a wine hangover*, she thought, rubbing her eyes.

She hadn't meant to fall asleep; she wanted to go visit Robert, but now it was too late. To get a head start on tomorrow she decided to take a hot shower. It was nice to take a hot, steamy shower without a limited water supply of hot water. The mixed aromas of vanilla, white orchid, and the sweet smell of sparkling sugar helped her to relax, somewhat.

Dressing in a comfortable warmup suit, she left her long wet hair down to dry and decided to make herself something bland to eat. The brewing coffee smelled good and the lingering smells from the shower announced that an early night was the only thing now on her agenda. Today she couldn't help feel that she failed and let Mary and Robert down. Sadness and anger at the same time were still fighting within her to be dominate over each other, until the anger conquered and fueled her passion for vengeance. She was tired and needed some space, not to have to think so much. This pain she was feeling, she wanted it to go away. In her one day of quiet solitude, Cassandra had no idea what this lapse of time was going to cost her, Robert, and Mary in the near future.

The next morning Cassandra entered the rehab facility and was hoping she would see Nurse Bell. There was a sign on Robert's door: "No Visitors."

What's this? No one said anything to me at the front desk and they all know who I am!

"Ms. Pointer," she heard, and when she turned around, Dr. Carsman was walking down the hallway.

"I'm sorry, they should have told you at the front desk, Robert is not to have any visitors." Cassandra's piercing blue eyes made direct contact with his and she crossed her arms.

"And why not?" she asked, demanding an immediate answer.

"Uh, Robert, your brother, is, um, set for his first surgery Monday," he replied.

It was obvious to her that he was either nervous or doing his best to sidestep her presence by holding his silence.

"Well, I'm no doctor, but don't you think it's a little too soon?" said Cassandra in her demeaning "*daddy*" tone of voice.

"Ms. Pointer…"

"Cassandra, doctor, it's Cassandra."

Doctor Carsman took a step back at her demeanor. "Yes, of course, Cassandra," stammered Dr. Carsman.

"Are my mother and father aware of this surgery that is scheduled on Monday?" Cassandra demanded.

"Ms. Pointer… Cassandra, I'll refer you to your mother, she's in control of making his health care decisions and you know that."

Cassandra was showing no signs of confidence in what Dr. Carsman was saying, and he knew it. Her body had stiffened and the scowl on her face warned Dr. Carsman to brace himself for what was coming next.

"I demand to see my brother and I demand to see him now!" flared Cassandra.

"Cassandra, we just want to minimize any distractions. Surely, you want to do what's best for your brother."

Dr. Carsman's words left her reeling.

The audacity!

"I'm not a distraction, I'm his sister, and he needs to know I'm here. He's only been here for a few weeks, how can he be ready?"

"Cassandra, I am afraid I must ask you to leave. In cases like this, I understand how you feel. The uncertainty of it all, the injury itself, the recovery of the mind and body with more surgeries to follow. Then the process repeats itself over again. What you're feeling is perfectly normal."

Cassandra couldn't believe her ears, did he just really use the word 'normal'?" There was nothing "normal" about any of this. Dr. Carsman turned Cassandra away from Robert's door and she spotted Nurse Bell walking toward them.

"Dr. Carsman, can I help with anything?" she asked.

"No, no thank you, this young lady was just leaving," he replied.

"Very good," said Nurse Bell, and continued on her way past Cassandra down the hall like nothing happened. Cassandra pulled her arm away from Dr. Carsman and turned down the hall to show herself out. Her mother was next on her list. *Mother knew, and when did she know?*

With her keys in her hand, angry and upset she hurriedly walked to her car, stomping her feet with each stride. She wasn't paying attention to what was going on around her. There was no mention of this at Christmas and she wanted to know why.

"Ms. Pointer, wait… Cassandra, Ms. Pointer!" hollered Nurse Bell.

What does she want? Ms. Bell had begun a slight jog toward Cassandra, causing the crunching of the salt and leftover remnants of snow and ice to be louder and faster. She was a little out of breath when she finally caught up to her.

"Ms. Pointer," she said in her breathy tone. "I'm so glad I caught you. Can we go somewhere and talk?"

Cassandra looked at Nurse Bell and was confused. She decided that talking to anyone other than her mother would be better company.

"Okay, yeah, sure, want to come to the house?" answered Cassandra.

"Yes, what's the address?"

"It's 11780 Springton Manor Drive. Do you know how to get there?"

"Yeah, I'm familiar with the area," answered Nurse Bell.

When Cassandra arrived at the Springton house she made a pot of coffee and put the kettle on in case Nurse Bell preferred tea. Then she thought about dinner. *Oh no!* In the fridge was one bottle of wine, four Cadbury caramello candy bars, a half-gallon of milk, some orange juice, a pound of bacon, stick of butter, eggs, and a few slices of cheese. She closed the refrigerator door. That was it, oh, and a loaf of bread and a box of Cheerios on the counter. After all that, she decided it really didn't matter, she didn't invite her for dinner anyway…she hadn't invited her at all.

Nurse Bell arrived just as she expected.

"Come in, let me take your coat. Did you have any problems on the roads or finding the house?" asked Cassandra.

"Thank you," she replied. "No, the roads aren't too bad. The snow's still falling though. It's winter in Missouri, you never know if you're going to get two inches or two feet of snow, rain, or sleet."

"I know that's right," Cassandra agreed. "Would you like a cup of coffee or tea? I have both ready. I wasn't sure if you preferred coffee or tea."

"Yes, please, at this point anything hot to drink would be wonderful. I think I'll have a cup of tea."

The tea kettle began to whistle loudly, calling Cassandra to the kitchen.

"Have a seat, make yourself at home," said Cassandra.

Cassandra brought in hot tea for two and noticed Elizabeth looked nervous but still confident and was amazed how she could own a room.

"I want to apologize for this morning at the rehab center. I know it appeared that I walked right past you and didn't acknowledge you."

"What do you mean, Nurse Bell? I thought I had done something wrong," replied Cassandra.

"Please, call me Elizabeth, and no, you haven't done anything wrong," she replied, relieved the pleasantries had gone so well.

Cassandra decided that now was the right time to ask about her relationship with her parents and get more information on the Bordure family.

"I was so upset," said Cassandra. "I couldn't understand why I couldn't see Robert, and then Dr. Carsman tells me I have to talk to my mother? Nothing was mentioned about this surgery or anything."

Cassandra paused for a moment and decided she was going to ask her, she needed to know.

"Elizabeth, how well do you know my parents?"

Elizabeth took a sip of her hot tea and set the cup and saucer on the table, and nervously clasped her hands together.

"Cassandra, I haven't seen your parents in years, but I feel I know you mother pretty well, and please forgive me if I'm speaking out of turn. After watching you and Robert these past few weeks am I wrong in concluding that you and Robert aren't cut from the same cloth as your mother, so to speak?"

Well, now we're getting somewhere, finally, thought Cassandra. A stranger they didn't even know saw her and Robert as individuals, and knew they weren't anything like the parents they were born too.

"No, Robert and I are nothing like our parents, thank you for realizing that," she answered.

Elizabeth's shoulders relaxed and her eyes softened.

"This morning," she began, "when I came into work I had been removed as Robert's head nurse."

"Do you know why? You've worked there ever since the center opened, right?" asked Cassandra.

"Yes, and before that I was a private nurse to a patient who had suffered a heart attack, and that's what brought me to working in rehabilitation. I don't know why I was removed from his case, and I don't understand why Robert is being scheduled for surgery on Monday."

"Yeah, that's what Dr. Carsman told me this morning, and Mom and Dad never called me or said a word about it. It seems he's doing really well with you. Do you think it's too soon for Robert to take such a big step, is he ready? Do you think Mom had something to do with you being removed from his case?"

Elizabeth took another sip of her hot tea. "I'm not sure, but I've never been pulled off a case before and my gut says yes, I believe Ruth had something to do with it. I also agree with you, I think the surgery is coming too soon. Today I was shocked to see that Dr. Carsman wouldn't allow you to see Robert, and it causes me great concern, and that's the main reason

I'm here. All I'm willing to say is that I believe Robert's memory is coming back of that horrible day that he was shot. Since I've been pulled off his case, I cannot ethically access his records anymore."

"What about his seizures?" Asked Cassandra.

"His seizures are a concern and not uncommon for someone with his injuries," answered Elizabeth.

"Will he ever make a full recovery?" Asked Cassandra.

Elizabeth thought long and hard before she answered such a complicated question.

"Probably not, but how far he can go, we just have to take that journey. It's been my experience that you exhaust all possibilities first, but I'm not a doctor, Cassandra. We just don't give up. We can't. We can't quit. That, too, is part of the process. I just don't feel that we've been able to complete the journey, that's all. Robert hasn't had enough time in my opinion. For whatever reason, it all feels so rushed."

Cassandra poured her and Elizabeth another cup of tea.

"Am I right in thinking since you know my mother, you want me to know this information in case there's a reason I need to know this?"

Elizabeth was taking a chance and she knew it; she was already afraid she had acted unethically. For years she believed there was more to Bruce's death than what she was told all those years ago. The death of Bruce destroyed his father, Bryce. She knew Ruth Tarlson all right, and a beautiful woman she was still today. Years ago, she witnessed the flash of darkness that Ruth possessed.

"Yes," Elizabeth answered.

Cassandra and Elizabeth sat there for a moment in silence, no expression on their faces and no body language between the two. Cassandra was doing her best to gather her thoughts. The one thing she did know was at that moment when Elizabeth answered yes, she knew Elizabeth didn't believe the story that was being told. She didn't believe the shotgun went off when it hit the ground.

"Elizabeth, if Robert's regained his memory of the day he was shot, would his psychiatrist share that information with mom?"

"I don't know, your mother is his health care directive. I don't know what Robert's relationship is with Dr. Marshall. It seems to me he's slowly coming around."

"Me too, Robert is coming around, I can see him getting better every time I visit."

"There's one more thing, I heard that your mother came to visit Robert yesterday. Did you know that?"

Cassandra's eyes went dim, the corners of her mouth fell, and she slumped into the couch, hurling further into darker places.

"No. I didn't know that. Mom never said anything about coming to visit Robert after Christmas. She never said anything, nothing at all.

"Elizabeth, I have to see him if he's remembering I need to talk to him, but with the surgery coming soon and then recovery from that, he may not be able to talk for who knows how long. I can't wait that long."

Elizabeth sat remembering Bruce, wishing she could hear his voice or hold his hand one more time. The difference between her and Cassandra was the fact she wasn't able to move on from the past. She felt trapped by the past because she never got the answers she needed.

"I start the second half of my swing shift at two this afternoon and the receptionist leaves at five p.m. Come after five and I can get you into Robert's room without anyone knowing. I'm afraid that's all I can do, and even that's pushing it."

"I understand. You were right, there's a reason I need to know this. Thank you."

Cassandra walked her to the door, and again she couldn't help but be affected at this young woman she was looking at. It took her back; she looked so much like her mother. It brought back many memories for her.

"Cassandra, you're a lovely girl. I'll see you later," said Elizabeth in awe of her.

"Thanks, I'll see you later. Be careful driving in this weather," replied Cassandra.

"Oh, one more thing," said Elizabeth "you'll need to be gone by eight p.m. He'll be given his evening medications and probably won't wake until the morning."

"All right," replied Cassandra. "Thanks again."

Elizabeth turned and left. Cassandra watched her walk to her car and pull out of the driveway. With all the talk about Robert and his surgery on Monday, she forgot to ask Elizabeth about this Bordure name she had been hearing about, and it was too late to get her attention for her to come back. Finishing her tea, curled up on the couch, she tried to make sense of her mother coming to see Robert and not telling anyone.

At exactly 5:15 p.m. Cassandra walked through the front doors of the center. Elizabeth and Cassandra dared not speak. She followed behind Elizabeth to Robert's room, and she unlocked the door and disappeared in what seemed to have been all one motion. Cassandra went into the room and closed the door quietly behind her and locked it. She didn't want to startle Robert; his eye was closed and she thought he may be sleeping so she sat quietly and held his hand.

"Cassanda, is at u?" He was communicating better, even though he still spoke from the left side of his face.

"Where havvve u een?"

Cassandra squeezed his hand a little tighter. "Robert, they won't allow you to have any visitors, they say you're going to have surgery on Monday."

Slowly Robert spoke, "Oom os here. Ssshe tol ee it wasss going to ee all righ."

"Mom was here? When? Just recently?" inquired an even more curious Cassandra.

Cassandra knew that had to be yesterday. *It's true, Mom was here yesterday. Dammit! I should have been here! Why was she here?*

"Oh, I got those receipts and papers to Joe. Mary and I hand-delivered them. He's opened his own business in French Town, and I know about my trust too, that Sean is the trustee and holds the majority interest in the marina."

Robert had learned to communicate in many different ways since the shooting. Cassandra had learned his smile and his words. She knew when he would shake out of nervousness or frustration. She also knew if his shaking was the onset of a seizure. As Robert was getting stronger, he was also gaining new abilities, little by little.

"Oh, Robert! You squeezed my hand! That's wonderful!"

"U ust get ary and leavvv. I annnot goin to et theww this. I as goo as dead."

Silent tears rolled down her cheeks.

"Robert, you're going to get through this, and we're all leaving together," said Cassandra demanding it so. If she demanded it and wanted it bad enough, it would happen!

"When you leave this place, we're not going to back to Braxton. Mary already has us a place set up."

Robert got frustrated, and by trying to talk faster, he spoke louder, and that was heard in the hall. Cassandra could see shadows of footprints under his door and the key was turning to unlock it. Quickly she hid in the bathroom and Robert was able to act like he was dreaming, more like having a nightmare, and then calmed himself. He closed his eye and became still again. That seemed to appease whoever had checked on him. Cassandra stayed quiet until she heard the door lock again.

Once again at Robert's bedside, she held his hand and he opened his eye to look at her. "Soree," he said quietly.

"Don't be sorry. Nurse Bell snuck me in here to see you. I have to be gone by eight or we'll both be in big trouble!"

Robert's eye danced—trouble was all the two of them knew. It wasn't only their troubles they knew. It was their mother's, Sean's and now Jack's troubles they knew.

Robert began to speak in a whisper and Cassandra leaned up closer to hear him better. "Ja-Ja-Jac ssshot ee, I emer."

"What? Jack shot you?" She sat down hard in her chair and her heart was pounding.

"Oh Robert!" she cried. "I knew Sean was lying this whole time! I just didn't know what he was hiding. He's such a liar, he's just like Mom!"

She leaned up again to hear Robert's half words and slurs. He didn't want to talk about anything Pointer. He wanted to relive the few happy moments that he had in his life, and she didn't have the heart to deny him.

"You and ary do this fffar ee. U ember the tea arties with ierrr?"

It took Cassandra a second or two to figure out what he was saying. "Are you asking me if I remember the tea parties with Piper?" she asked softly.

His expression softened and his eye teared up.

"Yeah, u and ary nee to leavv now and livv tha lifff."

"Me and Mary aren't leaving without you!" said Cassandra.

"U and ary leavv now," he whispered.

Robert was doing well in rehabilitation; he was slow to remember and put relationships together, but he could do it and do it accurately. The trauma he was suffering was hard for him to cope with, and his memories were shattering to him. His pain was excruciating and disabling. Each fragment of memory that returned piece by piece brought him pain.

He knew that Cassandra needed a reminder of what life could be. He wanted to speak of those days in his own words. Since he couldn't, she would have to repeat those beautiful stories.

Cassandra brought him honesty and truth. In turn, that helped him to make sense of things. All he knew for sure is what he told Cassandra, the rest was still jumbled, and he was frustrated.

The cruelty wasn't his violent nature, it was the lie about his violent nature.

"Oh Robert," she said as the tears continued to stream down her face. "We can't leave without you. We won't leave without you. Those tea parties seem so long ago, don't they? We're going to live that life, Robert! You and Mary will get married, and eventually I'll move out. Maybe we'll be neighbors!"

Like reading a bedtime story to a child, she held his hand and they reminisced about Piper's tea parties.

"Well," she began, "you would tease me that you had a standing date once a week. I knew that was a lie, or I thought it had better been a lie! I knew Mary was out at the marina and you would walk to where you were going, *and* you couldn't be walking to the marina.

So, I followed you one day, and you walked down to Uncle Joe's garage. You went around to the back yard, and I'll never forget how hard

I laughed when I saw you sitting around a bistro set. Your legs were crossed, and you were wearing an old ladies' hat, with your nose in the air having tea with Piper and her dolls! You, this muscular manly man, a messy, bearded face and all tatted up, sitting there getting instructions from Piper on how to hold your tea cup. Then Piper gave special instructions that you had to hold your pinky a certain way when you tipped the cup. And YOU did it!"

Cassandra was laughing and crying at the same time. Robert's eye reflected joy and his mouth formed a crooked line that was now his smile.

"When Piper saw me she didn't know what to think at first, then she asked me if I'd like to come to her tea party. Remember that, Robert?"

For a moment both Cassandra and Robert were immersed in a conversation of good times and almost forgot they were in a rehabilitation center and that his quality of life was hanging in the balance. It felt like an ordinary day they would spend at the marina on the upper deck hanging out, drinking bourbon, and picking on each other as brothers and sisters do, with Mary playing referee. She checked her watch to make sure she still had more time with her brother.

"I told her I'd love to come to her tea party," she continued on, "and then Piper picked up one of her dolls and sat it on her lap and gave me her chair. You then asked her if you could hold her doll while she drank her tea. And there you were, with your silly hat, legs crossed, holding a doll and drinking tea! She poured me a cup of 'tea,' which was actually tea! Then she passed around the chocolate chip cookies and told us her dolls names and we talked about kindergarten…"

Robert was drifting in and out of sleep; the look on his violently disfigured face said he was as content as he could be.

Robert squeezed her hand, "Yeah, ore ea arties, omise ee. Tell ary I lovvv her."

Cassandra stood up; she was going to have to leave. It would be time for his meds soon.

"They'll be in soon with your pain medication. I'm sorry. I don't want to leave you. I promise I'll tell Mary you love her, and she loves you so much; you are her one and only. I promise I'm not giving up hope that we're going to take you out of here with us. Robert, tonight proves that you're getting stronger and beginning to think clearly. I'm going to try to come see you again tomorrow and I'll be here Monday, I promise. If you don't see me, I'll be raising hell in the waiting room trying to get in, you hear me!"

He tried to lift his arm to reach out to her, and he was weak; she took his hand and held it to her face, and he tried to wipe her single tear with his thumb.

"You keep fighting, you hear me! You're doing so good! It's our turn, Robert. It's our turn!" A tear escaped from his eye, and she wiped it away. She kissed him on the forehead and whispered in his good ear, "Goodnight, I love you."

CHAPTER TWENTY-TWO

"Pointer Resolve"

Cassandra was thankful the snowfall had let up, making her travels less daunting. When Cassandra arrived at the house, the first thing she did was get herself ready for bed, build a fire, and grab the last bottle of wine. She wrapped up in a blanket and curled up on the floor, propping herself against the chair closest to the fireplace. Robert's words played over and over in her mind when he'd said, *He was as good as dead.* She hung onto her anger for her strength, remembering how many times she'd heard her mother say, *Everything's gonna be all right.*

Robert seemed to be in a place where he knew his fate and was working toward its acceptance. They both had been scandalous for most of their lives and spent their time looking to Ruth for her approval. Cassandra and Robert were told everything they had done, was for the good of the family…and it was only the two of them who could save the family. Robert looked to his mother and grew up in prison. Cassandra looked to her mother and remained working and living at the marina. The marina was a big operation, and PECC had taken over the marina. Years ago, Cassandra and Robert believed for a time they had received their mother's approval, after all, they had saved the Pointer reputation and secured it financially. No one in the family had worked harder and sacrificed more than Cassandra and Robert. For they had sacrificed themselves. After Robert's release, he and Cassandra had been hiding in plain sight from their mother, making all their plans. Whatever had been distracting Ruth over the last year had worked toward their advantage. It wasn't just the shooting with Robert, there was something else going on with her. Physically she was slowing down and going to bed earlier than usual, at times she would slow to catch her breath.

She wanted to ask her mother what she was doing at the rehab facility the day after Christmas and why didn't she say anything about this. Was her mother too confident that she would continue to stay ensnared in her ambitions? The biggest question she had was, *Why is Robert having surgery on New Year's Eve?* There was no keeping this a secret; surely her mother knew word would get out that she was at the rehabilitation center visiting Robert.

She finished her glass of wine and poured another. Thinking about the confrontation between her and her mother that was inevitable; she knew she had to be ready.

The flames from the fire danced around the room and popped and crackled as they scattered about. The smell of fresh pine filled her senses. The only way Cassandra could bring this truth to light and maintain her resolve was to hold her emotional outbursts.

Sometimes, Cassandra felt like a tea kettle on the stove that was too full. The tea kettle would overflow, bubbling, hissing, and spitting as the water ran down the sides only to anger the flame. The only thing to prevent it was to take the kettle off the stove when it began to whistle. Cassandra's rage would overflow into rantings until they made no sense and her family had tired of the hysterics.

Her mind wandered, and she knew it was time for Mary come to Springton to see Robert before his surgery on Monday. Mary was right; it was time for the truth to be told. Cassandra dialed Mary's number and the phone rang and rang; maybe there was a bad connection with the weather, or maybe she was still working. Just as she was getting ready to hang up, she heard Mary's voice. "Hello."

"Mary, it's Cassandra."

"Oh, Cassandra, I'm so glad to hear your voice. How's Robert?"

Cassandra wasn't sure where to begin or what to tell and what not to tell. As hard as she tried, she could no longer make sense out of anything and was emotionally raw.

"That's why I'm calling," Cassandra stammered a bit. "I think you're right. I think it's time for you come to Springton. Robert isn't allowed any visitors, and he's having his first surgery on Monday. I can't guarantee we'll get to see him."

"I'm leaving here right now. I can be there in four hours!"

"Whoa!" exclaimed Cassandra. "It's late and it's been snowing. Don't leave tonight; get a good night's sleep and leave in the morning, and don't come to the Springton house, that's too far. I'll meet you at the hotel across from the rehab center and get us a room there. Oh, shoot! Did you get a car? I completely forgot, are you without a way to get here?"

"Oh yeah, I got us a 1984 Ford Taurus. It was a *steal*!" answered Mary.

"Oh, that's funny, real funny. You just be ready, we're leaving right after the New Year's Eve party!"

"Oh, thank God! We're leaving, Cassandra! I know Robert won't be with us for a while, but finally! And, yeah, I get a good one in every now and then!"

"Yes! Finally," said Cassandra. "Get a good night's sleep and I'll meet you around ten tomorrow morning at the hotel and we'll see if we can get in to see Robert, okay?"

"Yes! I'll meet you there in the morning," Mary said excitedly, and then in a softer voice she asked, "Hey, are you doing okay?"

There was silence on the line for a moment.

"I'm hanging in there, how about you?" Cassandra finally responded.

"Much better after talking to you."

"Me too. Goodnight, my friend."

"Goodnight, my friend," replied Mary, hanging up the phone.

Ruth and Charles were at the rehab facility that next morning when Cassandra and Mary arrived. Ruth subtlety expressed her displeasure in seeing Mary there.

"Cassandra, you're going to be hosting your New Year's party on the showboat tonight, aren't you?" asked Ruth.

Without giving her daughter time to answer, she turned to Mary.

"What are *you* doing here?"

In Ruth's mind, Mary should be working on such an important day instead of driving around the county gold digging.

Mary's eyes began to well up; she bit her lip to keep from speaking out of turn and looked down at the ground, wishing there was a place to hide.

"Mom, she's here to see Robert," snapped Cassandra.

"You know, Cassandra, Robert's not allowed any visitors, and I had no doubt that she was here to see Robert, *thank you*!" Ruth spat back.

Cassandra's blue eyes were deep and intense. "I know that's what the doctors are saying, but *is* that what the doctors are saying, or is that what you're saying? I could ask you and *Daddy* both what you're doing here if he isn't supposed to have any visitors! *And* why and how is he having surgery on New Year's Eve? That's unheard of!"

Charles was now on the defense with his daughter and the newfound admiration he had found for her left him.

"Cassandra, in case you've forgotten, we're Robert's parents and I am your father, don't take your tone with me, little girl."

Mary remained silent and a bundle of nerves; she just wanted to see Robert.

"Oh, *Daddy,* I haven't forgotten. Mary and I have every intention of being on the showboat tonight, but we want to see Robert before we head back to Braxton. Are you and Mom gonna be here when he wakes up from surgery? Are you serious that we have to throw these New Year's parties tonight while he goes through surgery alone?"

"Young lady, this is not the time or the place!" flared Ruth, putting her daughter in her place.

"Never is, Mom, never is..."

There was silence between the four of them walking to the front door of the rehab facility and the mood was as cold as the December day. The only sound heard was the crunching of the snow and salt under their feet.

At the reception desk it was relaxed and familiar. The nurse showed Ruth and Charles to Robert's room without hesitation. Cassandra and Mary followed closely on the heels of Ruth and Charles.

"Mary, I'll give you some time with Robert," said Cassandra, giving her a hug for reassurance.

"Thanks, uh, um, will you come in with me?" asked Mary, with her green eyes full of all the emotions that Cassandra knew too well. Mary was anxious to see him, but apprehensive if she'd be able to handle it. Her knees were a little weak and she was praying her legs would continue to hold her up entering Robert's room. Oh Robert, the love of her life. What she wanted to do was burst into the room and throw her arms around his neck and kiss him deeply.

Mary and Cassandra left Ruth and Charles in the hallway. Mary ran to Robert's bedside and was horrified by what she saw. The right side of his face was bandaged again. The wounds she could see on his face were scabbed over heavily and his head had been shaved. There was a deep incision from the back of his head to his forehead with stitches or maybe staples; it was hard to tell with the dried blood. He had a patch over his right eye and the right side of his mouth drooped and wouldn't open all the way.

For a fleeting moment it pained her to see him, and she barely recognized him. At the moment they made eye contact that all disappeared.

She grabbed Robert's hand and kissed it and then gently kissed him on the forehead.

Cassandra went to the other side of his bed. His eye teared up and his mouth formed that straight downward line. Cassandra held his right hand to help with his shaking. They gave him a minute to take all this in and he became calmer.

Cassandra saw Mary beginning to crumble. To Mary it looked like Robert was not happy; there wasn't a smile and no squeeze to feel from his hand.

"Look, Mary, he's smiling," Cassandra said softly.

"Oh, Robert, I've missed you so much. I love you," professed Mary. "I've found us a place to live in a nice, quiet little town, and when you get ready to leave here, that's where we're going. Away from here," she said, raising his hand to her heart.

Robert lovingly gazed at her with his eye and sweetly whispered, "I uve u."

Mary held on tighter to his hand. "And don't you worry about anything, I have it all under control, or I really should say, me and Cassandra have it all under control." She giggled softly, with a real smile on her face for the first time in months.

Ruth and Charles entered the room, and neither Cassandra nor Mary left his bedside for them to get any closer. It appeared their presence had caused Robert some distress. That came as no surprise to Cassandra. The only place in the room was at the end of the bed for Ruth and Charles to stand, and that's where they stood.

"Son, you're doing real good and it's only gonna get better. You stay tough, you're gonna get through this," Charles said with a genuine voice and a hopeful heart.

Ruth sounded as sure and supportive as Charles. "That's right, everything's going to be all right, I promise," she said.

An uncontrollable sadness tainted with darkness came and went in Ruth's eyes like a lightning strike. It was too quick to be noticed unless one was looking exactly at the right moment. Most believe that beauty can only beget beauty. Men wished they had her, women wished they were her, and young girls wanted to be her. Ruth's beauty could tell a lie and it would always be perceived as truth. Charles never saw it, and Cassandra didn't understand what she saw. Mary was focused on Robert. The only one in the room who saw the flash of darkness was Robert, and it reminded him that his end was near.

With those words said by his mother, Robert began to convulse. Cassandra thought he was going to come out of the bed, then his body stiffened, and he began to shake. His face turned red, his scabs cracked open, and blood was running down his face from the reopening of his wounds. Alarms and beeping noises filled the room, and they could hear Robert gurgling, gasping, and saliva spew and ran from his mouth. Sounds of Robert's crying and moaning pierced their ears and broke their hearts. Mary and Cassandra lost their grip on his hands as he seized.

"Oh, my God, he's having a seizure!" Cassandra screamed, running into the hallway to get the doctor or a nurse and they were already on their way to his room. By the time they reached him, he'd already pulled out one of his IVs.

"Nurse, clear the room!" yelled the doctor.

As the doctor commanded, another nurse entered the room and led Ruth and Charles out of the room and a shaken Mary followed, only being able to go where she was led. Cassandra immediately went to Mary and put her arm around her friend's shoulders and coddled her while waiting to hear from the doctor.

Red-faced and his beady blue eyes glaring, Charles spoke harshly to his daughter, "You think we don't know anything, but we know more than you think we do! That's our son lying in there and we do love him. This is the reason why we requested no visitors, so he could rest, remain calm, and heal. Have you forgotten he was in a coma?"

Their world had gone dark. Without emotion, walking like she was in a trance, Cassandra led Mary to two chairs in the hallway and they sat quietly. At that moment, Cassandra had made her mind up, that her *Daddy's* Father's Day was coming, and she was going to give it to him. *Daddy* could deny the truth or never tell it if he wanted to, but when she was done, there would be no doubt that he would know the whole truth.

Mary clung tightly to Cassandra.

"Cassandra, was this my fault? Did I cause this?" cried Mary.

Mary's eyes were closed, she was still holding Cassandra's hand, rocking herself back and forth in the chair.

"No, of course not. It wasn't your fault. For a moment he was truly happy, and that was because of you," Cassandra whispered in her ear.

Cassandra gave Mary a hug and she let her head fall on her shoulder once again. Looking at her mother over Mary's shoulder, Ruth and her daughter made eye contact. It was instinctual. Instincts of a mother and a sister to protect their own. Cassandra was stronger today than she was yesterday, and Ruth was weaker today than she was yesterday. Neither Mother nor daughter wanted to be the first one to break eye contact, in fear of showing weakness. Cassandra believed her mother knew that Jack shot

Robert. Cassandra let that uncomfortable silence between them carry her mother a message that she no longer lived in fear of her.

Turning her attention back to Mary, Cassandra wiped her tears, and she had calmed a little and was no longer trembling. Mary kept her back toward Ruth and Charles and focused on mimicking Cassandra.

The doctor came out of Robert's room and spoke to all of them, "Robert's had a seizure, and this is not uncommon. This seizure was unexpectedly violent and he's receiving medication to help calm him. He'll need to rest."

How cruel this twist of fate had been.

"Doctor, may I sit with him as he drifts off?" asked Mary quietly, turning to face the doctor.

Ruth and Charles were silent, and Cassandra could tell he wasn't sure how to answer Mary's question. Even though the seizures were common, Cassandra knew it was her parents' presence that caused Robert's anxiety that led to his seizure.

"Doctor, this is Mary, Robert's fiancé," said Cassandra. "It wouldn't hurt for her to sit with him, would it?"

"No, I guess not," replied Dr. Carsman. "Keep it as quiet and calm as possible. If you need anything at all, just let the nurse know."

Dr. Carsman turned and left the family once again. Ruth and Charles were stunned at what they heard Cassandra say, and neither one of them were going to ask any questions, and Cassandra offered no explanation.

By the time Mary finished her visit with Robert, Ruth and Charles were gone. Cassandra saw a broken-hearted Mary; her movements were slow and she appeared lost.

Cassandra drove back to Braxton that afternoon to give Mary some time to come to terms with what she had seen that day.

"Are you okay, Mary? I know that was hard to see."

Mary didn't turn her head, she just kept starring out the window.

"No, Cassandra, no. I know you did your best to prepare me, but my God. I know it was an accident. I have to wonder how can Sean live with himself? Does he even know what's happening?"

Her tears were coming faster than she could catch them, and in hysterics she shrieked, "I don't want to leave him, Cassandra, I don't want to leave him!"

"I know just how you feel. That's why after the New Year's party we're coming straight back here."

There was always something that kept them from leaving. They couldn't get their timing right. And now, Cassandra had a decision to make. Whether or not to tell her best friend that it was Jack, not Sean, who shot Robert.

"What about the after-party and the clients we have booked, Cassandra?"

"Right after that clock strikes midnight, we're coming right back here. I don't give two shits about the after-party or what's booked. The other girls can handle it, and if they don't want to, they can close the place down for all I care."

"Oh, but your mom and dad?" Mary whimpered.

"Don't worry, by the time they find out it'll be too late to do anything about it. I am…*we are*, done with this life."

Mary wanted nothing more than to leave and start a new life. They weren't living the life they wanted to, but it was within their grasp, and she was afraid to jeopardize everything they had planned.

"Do you think we should wait and see how his surgery goes? Everything depends on him being able to leave the facility. If we mess up now and he's not ready to go after this surgery, I mean, they said he has several surgeries to come. And now your parents know about me and Robert, which means my parents will know too!"

Cassandra stared straight ahead and kept driving, not wanting to hear her words. There were things they still had to do to get their place ready, and if Robert wasn't ready to leave the facility they wouldn't be able to make a clean break.

"I know… you're right. So, we stay for the party tonight and drive back here tomorrow to our hotel room?"

Mary nodded. The rest of the way back to Braxton the girls were silent, and Cassandra wrestled with what to do about her secret.

CHAPTER TWENTY-THREE

"New Year, New Beginnings..."

Cassandra and Mary sat at the bar the majority of the night watching *The Eclipse* filling up with partygoers. They were there physically, but mentally absent.

Each year *The Eclipse* was packed, and this year was no different. The bars on the upper decks could barely keep up, and the dance floor in the inside bar was shoulder to shoulder. If it had been any other time, it would've been a great party. It would've been the perfect send off for The Lake Girls and Robert to reclaim their lives and ring in not only a new year, but a new life.

Once everything seemed to be going as planned, the girls went to hide away with a bottle of bourbon on the upper private deck. This time of the year the private deck wasn't so private, but more so than any other place on the showboat. Everyone was preparing to get the fireworks displays ready. They sat amongst the chaos of all the activity wrapped up in their blankets, hats, and gloves. Even with all the hustle and bustle going on around them, Mary's mind wasn't kept busy enough to keep her from wondering about everything and nothing.

"Cassandra, how do you think Robert's doing? Do you think your parents and Rose and Matt are feeling the way we are? What about Sean and Caroline? I wonder what they're thinking. Are they in Springton?"

"I don't know, we'll know how the party at Pointer's Inn went when we read the society pages tomorrow afternoon."

"I do hope Robert is doing okay. I miss him so much. The holidays have been hard, haven't they?" asked a dismal Mary.

"Yeah," replied Cassandra.

The girls sat quietly for a moment, taking everything in. It was amazing what they had done with the cruel hand life had dealt them. Before this, they were beginning to feel like they had survived. They were seeing an end to this life and longing to be with Robert. The question *Will they make it?* was coming back to haunt them, and Cassandra's secret was stirring within her, festering.

"Hey, have you heard from Matt? I haven't seen him around here in a while," asked Mary.

"Nope, I haven't seen Matt since all this happened except at Thanksgiving and Christmas. Oh, and you know the funny thing was, with Robert being in the hospital, Matt and I sat next to each other on Thanksgiving," explained Cassandra, tipping her glass to Mary before chugging the last bit of bourbon.

Mary choked on her drink a little. "You're kidding?" She gasped.

"Nope, and it didn't bother me a bit, but I sure could tell it bothered Rose," said Cassandra, laughing.

Their reality was so real that sometimes the drugs couldn't help numb the pain they were feeling. It didn't really matter what they talked about now, everything was unmasked. Everything except the fact it was Jack that shot Robert. Their truths were right in front of them refusing to be ignored, demanding acknowledgement and reconciliation. This new secret was no different; it just hadn't been buried long enough to create its own wake.

Mary continued to observe the partygoers and they seemed so lighthearted and happy. It looked like everyone was so open to what was coming next in their life, even excited, while she was drowning in despair. She wondered some more…then she realized that, just like her, all these people believed another day was dawning and the only thing to do was to get up and face it.

"Do you think your dad knows what goes on here at the marina?"

Cassandra didn't have to think about her response and replied, "Do you think your mom knew your dad was molesting you?"

Mary closed her eyes and took a sip of her bourbon.

"Subconsciously maybe, but not consciously? You know my mom only let me stay here at the marina because of *PECC*."

"What kind of double talk is that?" spat Cassandra with disbelief at what she heard.

Cassandra didn't have the heart to tell her best friend she was allowed to stay because she brought an opportunity to PECC. The opportunity to control the town pastor. The pastor who was still preaching for the last ten years. The pastor who led the parades and stood tall next to baby Jesus on the day of his birth.

"Cas-san-dra!" Mary spat right back.

"Don't *Cas-san-dra* me! Oh! I know, I know. That made it all better, didn't it?"

"Yeah, it did make it all better. No one was really sure of anyone or anything when we first got here, and we were so young. If I hadn't met you I wouldn't have a best friend, and if I hadn't met you I wouldn't be in love with the most wonderful man. So, yeah, Cassandra, maybe not ideal, but better."

Cassandra finally faced her friend and smiled. "I'm sorry, I don't mean to be so harsh sometimes. I love you, Mary. I don't tell you that enough."

These were the moments that Mary lived for.

"Awww, thanks, friend!"

"Don't get mushy," replied Cassandra.

"What? You mean this doesn't make us friends, either!"

"No! It makes us best friends," answered Cassandra.

Over the years the "The Lake Girls" tried to make excuses for their fate, tried to make the bad good and the good bad. Doing their best to live somewhere in the middle. It didn't matter what they told themselves, they were always the dirty little secret. Mary continued to keep her thoughts on their future. Her and Robert's future. Cassandra's future and the future of The Lake Girls.

"Are we leaving in the morning?" Mary asked.

"Yeah, wanna leave about seven? We can get our things to the hotel, get some breakfast, and then go check on Robert?"

"That sounds good," answered Mary.

The rest of the evening Cassandra and Mary made their rounds to see how things were going and if the girls needed anything and just what kind of back-room parties were going on. Usually on New Year's Eve it was the locals, and the worst that would happen was a fight between two drunks, and the solicited favors were usually just a one-on-one action. For the most part, it was husband and wives and boyfriends and girlfriends anxious to ring in the New Year together and embrace the hopes and dreams it promised to bring.

The regular crowd had found the matchboxes filled with cocaine and the party favors filled with ecstasy and ludes for sale; by now they were happily ready to ring in the New Year. It was the regular crowd that brought the real money into the marina.

The closer it got to eleven p.m. the more of the inside crowd started making their way outside to see the fireworks. There were champagne fountains on the decks for everyone to fill their glasses to toast to the New Year. Each year the fireworks display became more flamboyant. The upper deck looked like it was filled with artillery. There were short metal mortars that had been set up for launching and electrical wires were everywhere. If it were up to Cassandra there would be no fireworks display and no dropping of confetti. In the beauty of it all, what stood out to her most was the heavy haze of the smoke that was left behind to linger and the burning smell of the sulphur and gun powder. Each year, her ears would ring, and her eyes would burn, and sometimes she even thought she could taste a residue of it all. All this did was remind her of the mess it left behind and the high cost of insurance premiums. Cassandra was the only one on the boat that thought about these things. Everyone else was filled with as much excitement as the party goers were.

The partygoers and surrounding area waited two times a year with anticipation like none other to see the fireworks display over the marina. People who had access would get on their roofs, and those who didn't would park their cars and trucks on the road that led to the marina to see the display. There was nothing like watching the fireworks going off over the lake. The sky was lit up in a vast of array of many colors and shapes. Huge circles of light were sent up to the sky, and with each explosion came a new color and then would twinkle and sizzle its way down to the water. Periodically, the night sky lit up like it was the day.

Lovers would sit on blankets with a picnic dinner and champagne. Tailgaters and coolers were everywhere. Children would do their best to stay up with their parents to see the whole display. From fur coats and blankets to insulated overalls and cooler cups, they were all there with their ooo's and ahhs. The reflections of the fireworks bouncing off the lake created beautiful prisms of light. The marina was alive, and it was magical. The sparkling, flickering lights from the sparklers of illuminated on the deck of the showboat, and at one time you could see their smiling faces if you were watching closely. It appeared no one had a care in the world and all was right and as it should be. If it wasn't, it would be after ringing in the New Year.

Cassandra and Mary didn't get any champagne, they just topped off their glasses of bourbon and went back up to the private deck. It was one minute till midnight, and the grand finale of the fireworks display had started, and glasses full of champagne were being held up ready for the toast. It looked like a lake of champagne on the decks with the lights playing and dancing off the glasses. Even though *The Eclipse* sounded her horn every year, it always brought the same, if not more expectation and excitement within the partygoers than the year before. It was like the first time they heard her horn and the anticipation mounted and the countdown began. Ten, nine, eight, seven, six, five, four, three, two, one… *ERNNNNNNN!*

The Eclipsed Entertainer had just announced the New Year had arrived and was heard throughout the marina. The whole crowd erupted in an attempt to announce "Happy New Year!" in one voice. Party favors were being blown and the sounds of the hand clappers, kazoos and rattling of the maracas could be heard between the booming fireworks! Corks from champagne bottles were popping and soaring through the air. Loved ones hugged and kissed and then extended their hugs to their friends and strangers alike as the confetti rained down from the deck where Cassandra and Mary sat. The showboat's horn echoed back over the lake, "Happy New Year!" The song "Auld Lang Syne" was playing over the intercom of the showboat bidding farewell to the previous year. The partygoers stood together arm in arm singing along and swaying back and forth welcoming the New Year. It was officially January 1, 1986.

Cassandra and Mary held onto their hopes, just as everyone else did, that something magical was going to happen at midnight and change their reality.

"This is going to be a mess to clean up. I swear every year you dump more and more confetti!" said Cassandra, taking a drink of her bourbon.

"No, Cassandra. Same amount as last year and the year before. Every year you complain about the clean-up before wishing me a 'Happy New Year'!"

"Happy New Year, my friend!" Then under her breath repeated, "This is going to be a mess to clean up."

"Cheers, my friend, Happy New Year! And I heard that!" said Mary with an openness Cassandra wished she had.

CHAPTER TWENTY-FOUR

"Robert's Demise"

The next morning came quickly and brought with it the left-over magic of the New Year and kept what little bit of hope Mary and Cassandra had left alive. To Cassandra's dismay Mary had decided not to make the trip to Springton. She didn't want to see Charles and Ruth and decided she was going to put her energy into more positive things, such as the house they were going to move into.

Cassandra waved goodbye to her friend that cold and blistery morning and drove the winding roads of the Ozarks. She had learned every twist and turn of the road ahead of her over the last few months.

She arrived at the rehab facility about ten a.m. that morning and there was no sign of Ruth and Charles. There had been little change in Robert's condition after the surgery. He couldn't speak and his eye wondered aimlessly. The right side of his face was still being treated, fighting an infection and again bandaged. Cassandra felt an unfamiliar distance between her and Robert, but once he was up and around, he would continue to gain his strength. It wouldn't be long, and they could resume their vocal charades that seemed to help both of them so much. It was expected he'd be groggy and incoherent after the surgery, it took a lot out of him. Right now he needed to rest.

"Robert, as soon as you're able if you want to go see Uncle Joe, we can do that too."

There was no response from her brother, he just lay there so still. Not even a squeeze from his hand that once felt so strong for his condition.

"Mary continues to taunt me with her little tidbits of information about the house and the surprises she has for us. And I tell you, Robert, the best part of the clues she gives is the sparkle in her eyes and that big smile of hers lights up the room. She calls it her 'labor of love!' Oh! *And* she dumped more confetti this year on *The Eclipse*! Each year she dumps more and more and thinks I don't know it! You should have seen it this year. Oh well, what do I care, it won't be me that has to clean it up this year because we're outta here! Anyway, I just act like I believe her after she denies it."

Robert would stir a little; he was heavily sedated and for the most part unresponsive. It made her sad; she thought the mention of Mary would get a hand squeeze or something, but there was nothing. She wondered if he knew she was there.

"You know, as far the surprises she has for us I don't even really guess. I don't want to ruin it for her. So, how much you wanna bet she has a grand piano in the living room and a state-of-the-art stove in the kitchen with a library of cookbooks for you! Oh, and of course, I can picture a fancy grill on the back patio. We're all going to get so fat!" she said, doing her best to fake a giggle.

Robert was still unresponsive. Cassandra remained unsettled. Another day had ended, and tomorrow couldn't get here fast enough so she could see him again.

"I'll be back tomorrow. I'm staying right next door." She leaned over and kissed him on the forehead. "I love you, my brother."

It was numbly cold walking across the parking lot to the hotel, and the crunching of the snow beneath her feet sounded louder than what it was.

Although lonely in the hotel room, she was happy for the solace she found being so close to him. She called for room service and sat herself down in front of the television. She ate a little bit of dinner and then crawled into bed and drifted off to sleep.

The wakeup call she had scheduled for the next day at eight a.m. was right on time. Room service provided breakfast and plenty of coffee. She remained in an emotional stupor. The paper was included on the serving table, and she drank her coffee, flipping through the newspaper. In the society pages, as expected, Pointer's Inn was the place to have been on New Year's Eve. From the pictures it looked like Matt had done a wonderful job putting the party together. There was a picture of Charles, Ruth, Matt, and Rose. It was a pretty picture. Living in the brokenness of the Pointer toxicity, it was hard to find it in this perfect picture. *How can one know and still not see it?* Rose looked striking in the photo. She stared at Rose in the picture for a moment and saw a girl who reminded her of a fragile porcelain doll. Funny how she never thought of her sister as "pretty"; no one did, really. Her hair and make-up were perfect. She was stunning in her own way. *Did Rose see that in herself at all? What if Rose saw her beauty in herself and I saw some intelligence in myself? Would things have been different between us?* Cassandra put the paper down, finished her breakfast, and got ready to make her walk across the parking lot to see Robert.

When she walked into Robert's room, Ruth and Charles were sitting and talking with the doctor. "Mom, Dad, is there any change?"

The doctor quietly excused himself from the room.

"No, not yet, but the doctor says this is not abnormal, it'll take time. He's heavily sedated. Are you staying at the hotel?" asked Ruth.

"Yeah, it's just easier being next door instead of on the outskirts of town, and I've been on the road so much these days."

The atmosphere was heavy in the room; it was awkward. The eerie silence had returned and brought it with a warning that another secret was looming.

"How did the New Year's party go on *The Eclipse*?"

"It was good, standing room only. How'd the party go at Pointer's Inn?" asked Cassandra.

"Every plate was sold," Ruth replied.

It was a relief the holiday season had finally came to an end. How Pointer of them to be discussing the success of the parties here and now in this place. That's what their family New Year's Eve party at the big house on the hill was all about. Cassandra wasn't sure she had survived the season yet.

Charles remained quiet and sat by his son's bedside looking lost. Cassandra never seen him look so pale. His movements were slow, and he seemed unsteady on his feet. Her father would be seventy years old this year and he always looked so young for his age, but today he looked a little older. This ordeal seemed to have aged him.

Her mother would be fifty-nine this year. Cassandra noticed that even though her dress, hair, make-up, and manicure were perfect as always, she looked pasty-faced and a little slimmer.

The nurses were coming in to take vitals, and the doctors weren't sure if he'd be doing much today and now would be a good time for them all to get some much-needed rest. Cassandra and her parents parted ways and did just that.

The next day, once again Cassandra made her way across the parking lot to the rehab facility, and, again, Ruth and Charles were already there. When she entered the room, she heard the tail end of the conversation as the doctor said, "…he should be ready to be transferred to the nursing home by the end of the week," concluded Dr. Carsman.

Robert was sitting up in a wheelchair and appeared to be in a vegetative state, catatonic. He was unresponsive and almost childlike. He was strapped into his wheelchair so he wouldn't slide down or slump. He didn't seem to recognize her.

"What home? Why is he being sent to a home?" said Cassandra, boldly entering the room. "He was talking and he was gaining his strength. What's happening here?" Cassandra's eyes went ice cold and glared at her parents, casting blame on both of them. Her cheeks were flushed with panic and her heart pounded high in her chest.

"Where are you taking him I asked!"

Ruth and Charles remained quiet.

Mother and daughter eclipsed again, both harboring a shared secret and a new secret just born.

"Cassandra, honey, Robert didn't come out of surgery as expected. The brain damage is irreversible."

"No! No," she cried. "That's not true. It can't be true!"

"Oh, honey, I'm so sorry," said Ruth, and began to cry along with her daughter.

Stammering, "Mom…does this mean…this is it? This is how he'll always be? He's going to live in a home for the rest of his life and not be able to speak, not remember any of us? I can't accept that, and you shouldn't either! You're his parents!"

Robert continued to sit in his chair, his eye wandering the room, unemotional and uninterested in what was going on around him.

In and out of reality, Cassandra whispered, "Not remember anything about his life? Not remember who we are?"

Ruth tried to comfort her daughter, but she was better at controlling than comforting.

"The doctors are saying he'll eventually be able to feed himself and he may learn to walk again, but his abilities will be no more than that of a nine-year-old child. He'll be living at the Monument Nursing Home only an hour away from us," said Ruth, clarifying Robert's existence was just that, existing.

The hope had just been squeezed out of Cassandra. The question *Would they make it?"* became, *Will they make it without Robert?*

Once her will had returned and she looked at her *daddy*, she almost felt sorry for him—it genuinely looked like he was just as lost as she was. Her mother seemed sad and heartbroken too but was cool and collected. Then she looked at Robert, sitting there so still, starring and unresponsive. She knew she had to finish what he'd started.

She faced Robert and looked him straight in his eye. "Robert, Robert, it's me, Cassandra. Oh, Robert!" The tears were streaming down her face, and they kept coming. "Robert, please, please!"

She knew if she willed it hard enough he would appear and she'd see a glimmer of recognition in his eye. No matter how hard she willed it, there was no emotion and no response from her brother.

"Mom, Dad, this isn't right, this can't be. This was a reconstructive surgery, how could it have gone so wrong? Did you ask the doctors, did you ask? You can't send him to a home. He had a longer road ahead of him and now he won't have a chance to complete his therapy! He was making progress, and you as his parents should have seen that! What the hell is wrong with you two? You forced him to move too fast!" she screamed at the top of her lungs.

Cassandra then hurled herself, kneeling in front of Robert's chair, and flung her arms over his legs, hanging onto him and crying. Charles tried to lift his daughter up, the daughter he found admiration for through all of this and ignored it, setting it aside. She refused to let Robert go. Hanging onto him and fighting her *daddy* every step of the way.

"NO! No! I'm not leaving him!" She wailed and cried out loud and began begging and pleading for things to be like they were a couple of days before.

"Cassandra, I know, I know," said Charles. "Come, let us take you back to the hotel."

Being gently pulled away from Robert, he showed no emotion.

"I just don't understand," Cassandra said to her dad. "He was awake and knew what was going on around him just yesterday! Just yesterday..."

It went unnoticed to Cassandra that her dad wasn't condemning her for an emotional outburst, but genuinely trying to bring her comfort. Her mother stood back like a spectator, reading the room like she'd been chosen to write the next newspaper article.

"If you want to you can spend the next couple days with us at the Springton house, or would you rather go back to your hotel?" Charles asked Cassandra.

All she could do was nod to her father, and her parents drove her over to the parking lot next door. Robert was going to live out the rest of his years in a home and never would remember her or Mary ever again. Those memories were gone, taken by a gunshot wound to the head, and he wasn't coming back to her and Mary.

Ruth and Charles offered to stay with their daughter at the hotel, but Cassandra didn't want anyone's company unless it was Robert's or Mary's. Alone in her hotel room her thoughts were jumbled and they made no sense. *What am I going to tell Mary?* Robert told her he wasn't going to come out of this, that he was as good as dead. *What did he know?* All that he had told her, his memories were coming back of that dreadful day. The seizure, their mother's words promising him it was going to be all right, caused this turn of events for the worst. She had to get back to the marina.

The ringing of the phone caused her to jump, and she didn't want to answer it. It could only be Mary or her parents, and she had just talked to her parents. All she had to offer Mary was the truth and that would destroy her.

"Hello," finally answered Cassandra.

"This is the front desk. Is this Miss Cassandra Pointer?" said a female voice.

"Yes, it is."

"We have a package here for you at the front desk. You may pick it up at your earliest convenience."

Cassandra thanked the receptionist at the front desk and took the package back to her room and plopped down on the bed in a state of exhaustion. The day of the shooting was never going to end. The day that had taken so much from her.

She opened the envelope and there was a medical pamphlet and information on a procedure called a "Frontal Lobotomy." She skimmed through it and saw horrifying words pop off the paper: "A more delicate procedure than in the past… severing connections to and from…prefrontal cortex. Spontaneity, responsiveness, self-awareness, and self-control may be reduced…emotionally disabled… restricted intellectually. Can become more childlike… Catatonic. Low memory recall of past events and persons unlikely to be able to recall…this procedure has had some successful results."

She had never heard of a frontal lobotomy. The words were too brutal for her read on. The truth was that if Robert remembered who shot him, their mother's ambitions would be in jeopardy. That was the final and absolute truth. *Mom knows it was Jack who shot Robert. She knows...but even still, there's no way that even she would say okay to something so inhumane and cruel. Could she? Would she? Is this what happened to Robert?*

The only one who could arrange such a surgery was his directive health caregiver: their mother. Robert was silenced forever. This was more than a scandal, this truth would surely ruin Pointer Enterprises, and if Robert was at least well enough to point the finger and explain his existence, then everyone would clearly see Ruth Wilma Tarlson-Pointer for who and what she was. The next to fall would be PECC, and then the marina. The downfall of Pointer Enterprises would mean judgment day for a lot of people and cause problems for a little town that no longer struggled. Cassandra knew this was not the intention of her brother because there was no way he would put her and Mary in such in jeopardy. He was trying to right the wrong done to Uncle Joe and protect those exploited by PECC.

There was a quiet knock on her door. For a moment she thought if she stayed quiet they would go away. Again, there was quiet knock on the door, and she sat the tear soaked pamphlet on the bed and got up to answer the door.

"Cassandra, may I come in?" asked a familiar voice.

She opened the door wider, and Elizabeth came into the hotel room. She could see that Cassandra received the envelope and had read its contents.

"I guess it was you who sent me this information?" asked an unsteady Cassandra.

"Cassandra, I…" she tried to explain and search for the right words at the same time.

There was so much she wanted to tell Cassandra, and now wasn't the time. This was about Robert, and if she were still Robert's head nurse, she would have demanded to complete his therapy. To continue onto the end embracing the small successes into major accomplishments.

"It's okay, I know not to say anything. You risked your career giving me this information, and it was even riskier for you to come here. Why did you do it?"

Elizabeth knew that Cassandra was in no state to comprehend her reasons why, but she would be able to comprehend the emotions.

"For many years I've not been able to reconcile with the past. The answers I needed were never there for me to find, and I don't want that to be your fate. I wish we had the time and I could answer all your questions, I really do. But this isn't about me, it's about you, and right now we need to take care of you. I know what you're going through, I do."

Elizabeth sat down on the bed next to her and picked up some of the papers that were sitting on the bed. "Do you have any questions for me?"

"I just, I just don't understand what happened. Robert was remembering and I know what he was remembering. Before the surgery he recognized me and Mary. We were going to take him away from Braxton and leave everything 'Pointer' behind. We were going to start a new life. I even had hopes that Mary and Robert would get married. At the very least we could all be together putting our lives back together, and now they're moving him to Monument Nursing Home. Will he ever remember us? Ever know that we're there to see him?"

"I'm afraid what you saw today is most likely how Robert will live out his life," answered Elizabeth.

Cassandra let go of all the pent-up emotion and confusion she had been carrying with her over the last few months and now the grief and pain. Elizabeth held her in arms and cried with her.

"Elizabeth, do you dislike my mother?" asked Cassandra.

She hated Ruth, and it was clear to her why. However, to underestimate Ruth's ambitions could be a fatal mistake. Elizabeth chose her words wisely.

"I wouldn't say I *dislike* her. I think I know her well enough to say that her ambitions can be unhealthy and toxic. Do you think that's a fair assessment?"

Elizabeth sure had a way with words that were much nicer than how she would describe her feelings toward her mother.

"Yeah, absolutely," said Cassandra. "I hate her. She had to know this surgery was taking place and that it wasn't a reconstruction surgery for his face. She's a liar and a thief. My father's no better either; he's blind when it comes to her, so blind."

Elizabeth wiped Cassandra's tears and then wiped her own. *How gentle,* thought Cassandra; the last time someone wiped her tears, it was Robert.

"I want you to promise me something very important, Cassandra. You cannot let this consume you. I've brought a list of names of some counselors in Braxton for you to go see if you want to."

"Thank you," she replied. Even though she had no intention of swapping ludes and bourbon for counseling. She politely took the list and put it in her purse.

"Are you going back to Braxton tonight or tomorrow?"

"I'd like to already be on the road, but it's getting late. I'll head back tomorrow, I think. I have to tell Robert's fiancé. How am I going to do that?"

Elizabeth hugged her shoulders. "With gentleness and compassion."

It was getting late, and Elizabeth knew Cassandra had a long drive ahead of her tomorrow and got up to leave.

"Oh, I almost forgot, I brought this for you to help you sleep. It's a mild sedative, nothing too strong. This is also our little secret. You need rest. Cassandra, the best thing you can do for Robert now is to live your best life. That's what he would want. Hang onto how he feels about you and what he would want for you," she said softly.

Cassandra walked Elizabeth to the door. "Thank you, I really appreciate all you've done."

"I'm sorry I couldn't have done more. Take care, Cassandra, and you know where to find me if you…well, if you wish to call me for any reason."

"Thank you, goodnight."

She closed the door and got herself ready for bed, keeping her eight a.m. wake up call. Swallowing the sedative, she crawled underneath the covers. She knew her mother would wake up tomorrow just as wealthy as she was today, if not more so, and Pointer Enterprises had evaded another potential scandal. She had rendered one silent, forever burying the truth. Her own son, and how her mother did it, she may never know.

Her eyelids were getting heavy, and before drifting off to sleep, the last thought going through her mind over and over were two questions: *Does Mother even know the brutality of what she had done? How am I going to tell Mary?*

CHAPTER TWENTY-FIVE

"The Tragedy Takes Another"

The marina was quiet this time of year; only the bar and dining room were open on *The Eclipse*, and the hours of operation for the restaurant were scaled back, leaving only the bar open until one a.m. The showboat wouldn't see any real action until Valentine's Day.

Mary was a walking zombie these days; her innocent smile and optimism had faded away when she heard the cold hard truths Cassandra had told her. Mary had been a saving grace for Cassandra all those years ago; the marina had made Mary's life better, even safer as confusing as that was to Cassandra. Mary had made Cassandra's life bearable. She was worried about her friend. Each morning they'd have breakfast in Mary's cabin, and it was difficult to get Mary to talk. Cassandra found they'd switched roles and she wished she could've purchased joy and faith from that religious grocery list of hers for her friend.

"Mary," said Cassandra, picking up an empty bourbon bottle, "I'm so sorry. And I know how easy it is to take ludes and chase them with this bourbon. I know I'm the last one to talk, but Mary, you have to be careful. *We* have to be careful."

Mary looked up at Cassandra and she could see the hopelessness overtaking her, and she remained quiet and still.

Sobbing quietly, Mary replied, "I know. I know. I want to scream and I can't! I want to make your mother and your brother pay, and even if I did, it wouldn't bring Robert back to me. It's over, Cassandra, it's over..."

"Oh, believe me, when I get done, everyone will know everything! I promise! We'll start over and live close to Robert."

"Yeah," replied Mary.

It was confusing to Cassandra; her responses didn't match her facial expressions or her body language. She almost wished that Mary would let go and just release the emotions she was feeling; surely that would be healthier than how she was dealing with Robert's current condition.

Cassandra's birthday was approaching, and her and The Lake Girls would usually take a shopping trip to Springton each year and stay at a hotel that was not owned by Pointer Enterprises. This year they decided to celebrate on the boat with a small celebration. It was hard to celebrate this year, and Cassandra would have preferred to have skipped it all together. In one way or another this tragedy had caused a ripple effect that affected many outside the Pointer family.

The night of Cassandra's party, the loss of her brother, and the loss of Mary's one true love weighed heavily on their hearts, and the way he was lost to them was inconceivable.

The lounge was moderately decorated with a "Happy Birthday" banner and some helium balloons. The clean-up from New Year's Eve was still in full force.

"Hey everyone!" Candace called throughout the room. "Grab your glasses! Tonight we're here to wish Cassandra a happy twenty-fifth birthday. Happy birthday to a smart and wonderful boss. Thank you, Cassandra, for giving us all hope and then a plan for a new way of life." All the girls cheered "Happy Birthday, Cassandra!"

It was a casual event and began with cocktails and appetizers. After the dinner salad came the main course of either a filet mignon or a porterhouse steak. The steaks were served with baked potatoes that were almost as big as the state of Texas!

There was a lot of small talk buzzing around the table until a loud "pop" was heard! The bartender had opened another bottle of champagne to fill their glasses. After realizing it was the opening of the champagne bottle, they giggled and went on talking about this and that.

Then in unison, "Speech, speech, speech!" was being chanted throughout the lounge.

With a full glass, Cassandra stood up.

"Thank you, ladies, for the birthday party and your prayers for my brother. Each year we get to spend time together and just be us. Thank goodness there are so many of us that we get to celebrate once or twice a month!"

Cassandra looked over at Mary and she looked almost plastic, drinking her champagne and joining in the small talk. There was a smile on her face, and it looked like it was painted on.

Raising her glass to Mary, she continued on with her toast.

"This year has been like none other, and I would like to celebrate individuality, and shortly we'll be embracing our individuality.

"Thank you all for spending this day with me and Mary, it really means a lot. Here's to new beginnings for us all!

"Here here!" they cheered. Hope for some filled the room and reality hovered over others.

Cassandra and Mary slipped away to the upper deck after the girls decided to call it a night and sat in the cold overlooking the lake and sipping bourbon.

"Mary, we're still going to leave here, and we'll go visit Robert. With my twenty-fifth birthday here, my trust fund becomes mine, and we're going to make a life for us, and all of the girls that are working here have been planning, just like we have. We're all going to make a new start." That didn't even bring a real smile to her face.

"Yeah, I'd like that. No one will ever love me like he did, accept my past and leave it there. No one is ever going to want me. Robert knew about me. Robert knew me. He knew my shame, and we'd overcome it and rise above it together. Robert made me happy."

Cassandra heard her words and felt the same way about herself. Tearing up and in a supportive voice said to her friend, "Mary, that's not true. You saved my life! Robert knew what true love was because he met you. Besides, when the day comes that we all leave here, don't forget you and I are going to stand up here and watch the girls as they leave to begin their new lives and toast to new beginnings!"

There was a little smile on Mary's face. "Yeah, a tea party, right?"

"That's right," replied Cassandra, "a tea party. Bourbon goes good with tea, right?"

The girls laughed and cried at the same time.

"Well, the bourbon will be our secret," replied Mary.

"Oh, absolutely!" Agreed Cassandra.

The girls laughed, and then the laughter faded as quickly as it came.

"You know," said Mary quietly, "Robert's gone to us, it's like his whole being has been erased. He sees but doesn't recognize and doesn't speak. Can you imagine, Cassandra, living that way? Do you think he's still in there and just screaming silently in torture what he wants to say and can't? It would be better if he was dead! Your mother was his Judas!"

Just like Cassandra had done, she let go of all her emotions and sobbed. Her emotions ascended from quiet whispers to excruciating screams. "Your mother was *my* Judas!"

Fate whispered and taunted them, *Dreams aren't for you! Dreams are for other people. There is no other life for you other than what you have here and that means you cannot escape it, no matter what you do!*

The fog was rolling in over the lake limiting one's sight, causing confusion between what was real and what wasn't. Confirming the uncertainty about the future was real. It wouldn't be until the sun rose to fight against it to bring the truth forward by the light of day, for all to see. It was one day, and for Mary and Cassandra it started like every other day, and that day still had not come to an end.

"I promise you, Mary, the truth will be told and my family will know what was done and why. I am going to tell everything at our family New Year's celebration."

"I know you will. There are many surprises that I left you in a quiet and quaint little town that you'll enjoy, my friend."

"We'll enjoy them," replied Cassandra.

Tattered and torn, they finished their bourbon in the freezing cold.

It was early afternoon when Cassandra woke the next morning. She made a pot of coffee and headed up to Mary's stateroom. There was no answer to her knocks at the door.

Knocking again, "Mary! Mary! Wake up, I have coffee," she said, trying to make coffee sound as enticing as she could. There was still nothing. Maybe she had gotten up before her, she couldn't hear any moving around in the room. She turned the doorknob, and it wasn't locked. Cassandra walked in and sat the coffee pot on the table, got two coffee mugs, and stepped into her bedroom and Mary was still lying on the bed asleep.

Gently, Cassandra tried to wake her by tapping her on the shoulder; there was no movement. "Mary, Mary! Wake up! Come on, my friend, you never let me sleep when you're up. My turn to return the favor!" Mary wasn't moving. Cassandra soon saw she wasn't breathing, her face was pale, and she was cold, so cold.

"Mary, oh my God, no! Mary, Mary!" she cried out again and gently shook her friend by her shoulders.

Cassandra ran out on deck and her crying screams were heard across the lake, "Help, help me, please, it's Mary, help!"

The girls came out of their cabins and ran to Cassandra. "You have to help me, oh my God, it's Mary, I think she's…" Cassandra ran back in to Mary's state room and took her in her arms and her body was limp. She sat on the bed cradling her in her arms rocking back and forth. When the paramedics arrived, they had to take Mary's lifeless body from Cassandra and she wouldn't let her go: the last time she was pulled away from Robert, he was gone, just gone, never to be in her life again, and she wasn't going to lose Mary too!

Two paramedics gently lifted Cassandra from the bed so they could examine Mary and see if she had a pulse. Cassandra's big blue eyes turned gray. The paramedics pronounced her dead and entered in their log suicide by drug overdose and based on what Cassandra had told them noted an estimated time of death between and ten a.m. and noon.

When Cassandra had set the coffee pot on the table, she never noticed an envelope with her name on it. One of the police officers handed it to her. With her trembling hands she took the envelope. It was a letter written in Mary's hand.

Dear Cassandra,

You're my best friend and you saved my life. There was just no saving me this time. I know that life at the marina wasn't a traditional way of life, but we made it better for each other. Bearable.

Robert was my life, and I loved him with all my heart and soul. He made me whole.

Without him, I don't want to go on. Please go to that quiet and quaint little town and leave all this behind. You're a wonderful person and I love you, never forget that.

I don't expect you to understand, but I hope that you forgive me. Live for me and remember for Robert.

Goodbye, my friend,

Mary.

With her same trembling hands she put the letter back in the envelope. She didn't realize how loud silence could be.

She was being looked upon with sympathy and pity. The paramedics had been given the authority to take Mary away. As they passed by with Mary's body on the stretcher, Cassandra began screaming and grabbed her hand and refused to let her go.

"No! No! Where are you taking her? You can't take her, she'll never come back if you take her!" wept Cassandra entering another realm of awareness.

The Lake Girls were sobbing and trying to tend to Cassandra so the paramedics could get the stretcher past her in the small space. Even the paramedics were having a hard time upon hearing Cassandra's last plea not to take her friend and slowed before they carried her out of her cabin.

Outside of the cabin they covered her whole body with a white sheet. Cassandra and the girls followed them to the shore where the ambulance was waiting, and Mary was placed in a plastic bag the color of death. Cassandra wouldn't leave her side. One of the paramedics spoke to Cassandra as kindly as he could, "Ma'am, ma'am, I'm sorry, she's gone, we have to take her now."

Cassandra had no idea he was talking to her, she was consumed with more grief and pain than she ever knew possible. One of the girls came and led Cassandra a few steps back and the paramedics zipped the bag closed. Cassandra heard nothing except the sharpness of the zipping of the bag that was left echoing in her head. One by one the links of the zipper connected and had eventually hidden her, forever. Mary was placed in the ambulance, and they drove away.

As the ambulance was leaving, Cassandra collapsed and fell to the ground with all her emotions of pain, confusion, and grief. All bundled together they escalated to anger and then an uncontrollable wave of rage overtook her. A couple of the girls helped her to her feet.

Cassandra began to stand and found her feet and slowly began to walk of her own volition. This time she wiped her own tears. Walking back to the showboat, she was determined that all who were responsible for this were going to pay dearly.

Cassandra turned to one of the girls. "Please let the rest of the girls know I'd like to see everyone in my stateroom as soon as possible," she said the best she could, swallowing the big lump in her throat.

She made another pot of coffee and sat at her small kitchen table looking out over the marina; the sun had already burned away all the fog and she could see clearly across the lake.

"I know we're all devastated by what happened today and we're all going to miss Mary terribly."

The Lake Girls remained quiet in the disbelief of the death of their friend.

"None of us were planning on staying here and for the last few years since Robert's return we've been doing what we can to get out of here. I just want you girls to know Mary had once said to me that life here at the marina was not a traditional one, but we all made life better for each other.

I hope all of you feel the same way. Robert and Mary gave us the encouragement to make our dreams a reality. Things didn't go as planned for me, Mary, and Robert, but that doesn't mean that your lives shouldn't go as you have planned. It means just the opposite. Mary's last words to me in her note were, *Live for me and remember for Robert*. That's why we must continue to do as we planned."

Cassandra was quiet for moment and took a sip of her coffee, looking out over the lake.

"Candace, do you have the money from the drug sales on New Year's Eve?"

"Yep, I have it all right here, and yes, we paid the suppliers upon receipt as we always do, so they're paid in full. Pure profit is what we have here."

"Count it out," said Cassandra, "and split it evenly among yourselves."

Cassandra turned toward the window again and stared across the lake while Candace counted out roughly ten thousand dollars. There were five girls that worked in the back room of the marina, not counting Cassandra and Mary.

"Cassandra," she said, gently putting her hand on her shoulder to get her attention, "here you are, this is your and Mary's share." She turned around and faced the girls once again.

"No, you all take this money. Oh, and girls, make sure you take all your jewelry and any other gifts that have been given to you over the years."

Candace spoke almost in a whisper, "What are you wanting us to do now?"

"Our time here is over. It's time for you all to make a new start," answered Cassandra handing out reference letters.

"Oh my," said one of the girls, "this is signed by none other than Ruth Pointer herself."

Cassandra grinned. "Why, yes, they are, aren't they?" The girls giggled.

"Good girl, you did it again!" exclaimed Candace.

Cassandra gave Candace a wink. It was good to see that some dreams could come true.

Cassandra stood up. "Now, I want you all to pack your things and get out of here and never look back. The time to leave has come as we hoped it would. You should have everything you need to start over and have the life you want, the life you deserve."

The room fell silent. Each one of the girls worried what was going to happen to Cassandra; they felt a loyalty to her and were conflicted in leaving her.

"Go, go, all of you, this has been years in the making. Run, don't walk!" said Cassandra, being able to smile a genuine smile.

"We have something for you, Cassandra. This is from all of us," said Candace. "We all had great pain and suffered abuse, and then when we came here, we thought it was all over, but it wasn't. When we got to know you, we realized you were just like us and afraid of the same things we were. We all had the same dreams."

Candace handed her several hard back books, they looked like journals. Cassandra flipped through each one and they contained a list of names of men and women alike who had been on the yacht or the showboat, and included their real names. The journals were full of dates, times, their ages, and even their fetishes. Each journal began with the girl's story of their newfound horror through *PECC*. The formation of their dreams to the disillusion. The girls who had become her family had written it all down.

"Use these as you see fit. We'll stand with you, and there's a trunk back by your bed that contains more of these journals. It was Mary's idea that we write our stories in case we needed them one day," said Candace.

"Thank you all so much," said Cassandra trying not to break down.

The girls said their goodbyes and wished each other the best and prepared to leave. There wasn't one dry eye, and with each hug, they hung onto each other a little longer. Even though they were filled with fear and uncertainty, they set out boldly to take their lives back. This was the moment they had waited and worked for all their adolescent lives, and with Robert's help, "The Lake Girls" were well prepared.

While the girls were packing Cassandra grabbed a bottle of bourbon and headed to the upper private deck and watched the girls one by one reach the shore and leave. She wasn't alone on the top deck, a vision of Mary manifested through her grief. And just as promised, they toasted to new beginnings. Cassandra wished she could stay there longer with her memories and the vision of Mary of standing beside her, as she had always done. She was afraid to blink, hoping the vision of Mary wouldn't go away. After The Lake Girls were gone, the vision of Mary slowly faded. This was supposed to be a day of celebration, a victorious celebration. The lake was still and silent. The misery of this endless day had left in its wake, Robert soulless and Mary dead.

The endless day had left her nothing to celebrate, except vengeance.

CHAPTER TWENTY-SIX

"One Truth, Two Truths"

Cassandra was paying special attention to her appearance getting ready for the family New Year's Eve party at the big house on the hill. She continued to apply her make-up until it began to hide the dark circles and minimize the puffiness. It was a mask, and beauty, being her original sin, would be her weapon today. She hadn't heard from her mother since they were in Springton and was told the date and time they would ring in the New Year as a family.

Being the last gathering of the year, it was always casual and relaxed. She dressed in nice blue jeans and a light blue sweater with a folded over neckline. She mimicked her mother when picking out her jewelry. Sapphire earrings played peek-a-boo through her long, silky feathered hair, and Mary's diamond collar necklace embraced her neck. Her mother had taught her there were many ways to hide one's sins, but Robert and Mary had taught her the only weapon against sin was the truth.

Living for Mary and remembering for Robert, with her gold bracelets on her wrists and ringed fingers, she gathered one of the journals, the tear-stained medical pamphlet, and placed them in her backpack. Throwing it over her shoulder, grabbing her purse she left. Today, she wouldn't be the one crying.

When she arrived at her parents' house, the family was gathered in the sitting room. "Hello," she called out, opening the front door. "Anyone home?"

"In here," Ruth called from the sitting room.

"Well, it's about time you got here!" said Charles.

Joshua went running to his aunt and gave her a kiss and a hug. Cassandra made her way to Jack and gave him a hug. "Well, there's my nephew, Jack! Such your father's son, you're just growing up too fast, kiddo."

Her comment was off color to all. Caroline quickly chimed in and said, "Happy New Year, Cassandra." Almost as if Caroline was issuing a warning of some sort. Cassandra paid no attention and went over and hugged her. She was hoping this new Caroline would take it one step further.

"Happy New Year, Caroline," she said trying not to sound too sinister.

"WOW! Sis, look at you! Looks like the marina's doing well.... What's in the bag?" asked Sean.

"It is, it is," Cassandra responded, glancing over at Rose.

Then looking to Sean, "Party favors, Sean, party favors! What did you bring for dinner tonight? It smells delicious," she answered.

Cassandra's comment didn't get pass Sean either and he hoped he imagined it. There was no way anyone other than his mom knew it was Jack that shot Robert. No way, he was just being paranoid.

"I smoked a prime rib," he answered dryly.

This year wasn't any different than any other year, except for the absence of Robert, of course.

It had become clear to Cassandra no one had been told about Mary's death, and if they had, no one seemed to care. No one seemed to care that Robert had found some happiness along the way. They didn't even know.

Charles wasn't real sure what he was picking up from his youngest: there was an air about her that was making him feel uneasy. To him it looked like she was a walking, talking emotional outburst just waiting to happen.

"Well, now that Cassandra's here, how about we all have dinner?" announced Charles.

The family went into the dining room and took their seats. Without Robert, Cassandra was once again sitting next to Matt. Mattie was going around the table with a tray of glasses filled with champagne. Charles stood up and was going to make his traditional New Year's "rah-rah" toast.

"*Daddy*," interrupted Cassandra.

"I would like to say a few words. Robert and I are close, and he's my brother. We'll be living on without him from here on out and I think we should do right and honor his life."

In anger, Sean replied, "What? He's my brother too! *And* he's Rose's brother!"

Ruth recognized this familiar feeling with her daughter and being on the edge of her seat, "Cas-san-dra, I understand, but now is not the time."

Ruth's adrenaline began racing through her veins, causing her heart to pound and bring her more breath to meet her youngest.

"We're all devastated," stated Ruth, doing her best to remind Cassandra that she wasn't the only one suffering due to this tragedy. However, she knew one rush of fear wouldn't bring her the strength needed to contend with her daughter, now turned adversary.

"Oh, Mother, it *is* the time!"

Cassandra reached into her backpack and pulled out the journal, slamming it on to the table. The glasses clanked, and the silverware rattled. Everyone sat up straight and were stunned at the startling noises of the slamming book.

"Cassandra, I'll have no emotional outbursts at my dinner table. You'll put that away or you'll leave! Do you understand me?" said Charles scolding his daughter.

Her cold dark blue eyes met her father's tired light blue eyes and she flared, "Oh, *Daddy*, everyone at this table is going to want to hear this!"

She grabbed her glass of champagne, looking like a vision from a painting, took a sip, and began on her path of destruction.

"I'd like to thank my mother and father for the opportunities I've had by being in charge of the marina," she said in what mocked of her mother's voice.

Ruth grew more anxious as Cassandra continued.

"I'd like to clarify just how I got that job at the marina, but first let's confirm how the loan to buy the marina was obtained. *Daddy*, do you remember when the icehouses were remodeled? Why don't you ask Mother about the 'icehouse hopping,' and did you know that sometimes she had so many 'meetings' the gentlemen callers sometimes ran the risk of running into one another on the way out? So, cheers to me for securing Pointer Enterprises its most stable financial asset that brought great wealth to this family. *You're welcome*!"

Charles looked like he'd been sucker punched and in a way he had.

"Cas-san-dra, stop this nonsense immediately!" said Ruth, desperately hoping everyone would disregard this as one of her rambling emotional outbursts.

"Charles, as usual she doesn't know what she's talking about," said Ruth looking directly at her husband.

"Really, Mother, I don't? What about how you bargained me off to the bankers in trade for money-making deals with the bank to secure the funding for the marina?"

Mother and daughter eclipsed again. Ruth tried to speak, and Cassandra outshined her. With her hands clasped together and a tight jaw, all Ruth could do was keep her seat at the table and bet on an emotional outburst and ramblings from Cassandra.

Cassandra then looked at her sister. "Rose, how old were you when you first had sex?"

A wide-eyed Rose looked up at Cassandra. She was embarrassed to be asked such a personal question. Then Rose looked over to her parents, begging them to make her stop.

"Fourteen, Rose. That's how old I was when I first had sex, still feel slighted by sitting in the corner office?" she said contemptuously to her sister.

Cassandra looked at Ruth. "Mother, do I know what I'm talking about? The wonderful *PECC*? Some charity there, huh? Cheers to Robert for being the catalyst for the startup of PECC to sooth one's guilt, and cheers to me and Robert for actually giving a damn!" blazed Cassandra.

"Cassandra, how dare you talk about such things in front of my sons. Come on, we're leaving! I'm sorry, Charles, Ruth, but I just can't sit here and listen to this outburst," flared a self-righteous Caroline.

Sean and Caroline were rustling up Jack and Joshua and heading out the door. Cassandra wasn't going to let this new Caroline get a word in edgewise.

"That's right, Caroline!" said Cassandra in her accusatory tone. "As if your sons have never witnessed Sean beating the hell out of you, sending you to the hospital more than once! Be sure to ask your husband to fill you in on the latest; he's the trustee of my trust and holds the majority interest in the marina, did you know that?"

Caroline hesitated walking out of the room. She did know that, but decided she wasn't going to get involved in this outburst of Cassandra's and kept walking toward the front door.

"Nothing to say, Caroline?" yelled Cassandra as Caroline was reaching for the doorknob to open the front door.

"What about you, Jack, nothing to say? How are you feeling these days after shooting your uncle?"

"I didn't mean to do it." Jack began to sob and screamed, "I didn't mean to do it. It was an accident, I swear!"

Caroline embraced her son and held him tight. Joshua stood still and quiet, looking down at the floor.

Enraged, Sean turned back toward Cassandra, and Caroline tried to grab his arm. "Sean, let's just leave. It's not worth it!" she yelled.

Matt turned to face Sean's direction, not sure if he'd be able to keep Sean from hurting Cassandra. Sean pointed his finger in her direction, moving quickly toward her with an intent focus on only her. His brown eyes blazed. "Cassandra, I'm warning you! You have no idea what you're talking about!"

"Oh, Sean, you're warning me?" said Cassandra, laughing. "That's funny!"

She seemed to be the only one in the dining room that wasn't afraid of Sean at that moment.

"Here in this journal is all the proof you need that the marina is nothing but a floating whore house!"

Mattie rushed into the dining room hearing all the screaming and yelling.

"Mattie, would you please take the boys into the kitchen for dessert? They really shouldn't be in here," asked Ruth.

"Yes, Mrs. Pointer. Jack, Joshua, let's go get some dessert, we have your favorite," she answered quickly, ushering the boys to the kitchen with Caroline following close behind.

It was too late; Cassandra had already exposed her nephew. Jack was old enough to know what he had done. He knew he'd never see Robert again, he knew Robert would need round-the-clock care. Robert was in that place because he'd pulled the trigger.

Jack sat next to his mother at the kitchen table and asked, "Why did Aunt Cassandra do that, Mom? Grandma and Grandpa won't love me anymore! Now they know!"

"STOP!" Charles yelled, standing up, and that was heard all the way in the kitchen. Even Ruth was still. Charles skimmed through the journal while everyone sat paralyzed in the horror of it all. After all these years, Charles now figured out where his relationship went wrong with his youngest daughter.

"Ruth, tell me this isn't true, that you didn't do this to Cassandra and that you didn't play me for a fool the majority of our married life," he asked his wife quietly.

"Charles, she's exaggerating like she's always done. I'll explain everything, later," she replied with her quivering lower lip, knowing she'd lost this bet.

"I'm always exaggerating?" screamed Cassandra viciously to her mother. "Is that what you tell everyone in the family to make them think I'm just an emotional wreck, a mental case like Aunt Dorothy? Let's talk about Robert."

Again, she reached into her backpack and pulled out the tear-stained medical pamphlet and handed it to her father. For everyone sitting at the table it felt like Cassandra had pulled all the oxygen out of the air.

"Do you know what's wrong with Robert? This is what's wrong with Robert, because he remembered that Jack shot him, and Sean and Caroline were scared for Jack. You all wanna know how I found out it was Jack that shot Robert? Robert told me himself, he *did* remember, and Mom did what she has always done, protect Sean. Just like all those years ago when you coerced Robert in saying he shot up The Medallion. So, cheers to Robert for sacrificing his adolescence for his brother, the golden child! And last but definitely not least, cheers to you, Sean! History has repeated itself, except this time it was Jack's anger that pulled the trigger!"

"Cassandra, why you haughty little bitch, you better watch your step!" fumed Sean.

"Cassandra, Sean, knock it off!" demanded Charles.

"Son," said Charles, turning to Sean, "did Jack shoot Robert?"

Sean glared at Cassandra, and she glared right back.

"Yeah, he did," answered Sean forcibly.

Charles then turned to Ruth. "And Ruth, did you know this?" he asked in disbelief of his wife's betrayal.

Cassandra was interested how this was going to play out between her mother and the golden child. The protective and valiant son that he was spoke loud and clear. "Dad, it wasn't mom's fault," he declared.

Cassandra mocked Sean and repeated arrogantly, "Yeah, *Daddy*, it wasn't Mom's fault!" Charles didn't seem to hear Sean or Cassandra and his eyes never left Ruth.

"Ruth, I asked you a question, did you know and not tell me? Did you lie to me and tell me that Robert was having a reconstructive surgery instead of some ice pick hack job on his brain? Do you know what you've done? Do you? What in the hell's happened around here and why? Ruth, these are your children, your flesh and blood, and I am your husband..." His voice turned raspy and trailed off.

"We'll finish this conversation later," Charles said flatly to his wife.

Ruth remained quiet, fearful she may have just been destroyed by her younger self.

Charles got up and went into the kitchen where his grandchildren were sitting and embraced both of them. "Jack, Joshua, we're Pointers and we'll get through this together. I promise and I love you both very much! Don't forget that, okay?"

Charles turned to Sean. "Son, take your family home and tell your son your story and begin to heal. Jack can only come to terms with this if he knows your story, and Sean, the whole story." Charles understood the change he'd seen in Caroline over the last few months and knew she was now a force to be reckoned with. Sean, Caroline, and the boys left.

It remained quiet when Charles went back into the dining room. Charles was overwhelmed with what he'd just witnessed and felt like someone had just ripped his heart out of his chest. He picked up the journal and began to skim through it again. Cassandra sat still, watching her father read all about "PECC" and the horrors the charity contained.

Charles faced his daughter, whom he finally saw as a broken innocent little girl and an exploited young woman. His face grew pale and sad, full of shame.

"Cassandra, I'm sorry," he said softly. "This is a father's worse nightmare. I swear I didn't know. If I had known, this would've never happened. I'd like to take a closer look at this if you don't mind. Can you leave it with me? We may not be able to change what happened, but we can change going forward, together."

Cassandra wanted to believe him, but his words were too late, and a single tear ran down her cheek.

"How could you have not known?" she whispered.

Grabbing the journal and the medical information back from her father, he struggled to hang onto it, refusing to give it back.

"This is mine. This was my young life. My nightmare!" she exclaimed with conviction, finally ripping the journal out of his hands, putting the information in her backpack.

"I don't mind if you read it, in fact I want you to read it, but it's not leaving my sight!"

Cassandra took her backpack and went into the sitting room to compose herself so she could leave. She didn't want to do that to Jack, but the truth had to come out, it just had too. These damned secrets had destroyed her life, Robert's life, and Mary's life.

Rose pursued her sister to the sitting room.

"Cassandra, I'm angry and repulsed by what I just heard. I'm so sorry, but do you think you could have handled this a better way? It's wrong to hold someone accountable for things they have no control over. Daddy isn't getting any younger. He didn't know! Did you think about what this would do to him?"

Cassandra turned to Rose. "So, you think this is all my fault?" she answered in a weak and defeated voice.

"No, no, I didn't mean that…" stammered Rose. She too saw a broken little girl and wounded young woman.

"What exactly did you mean? How would you have handled it, Rose? How would you have handled these last eleven years?"

Rose continued to stammer, chastising her sister. "I don't know, but I wouldn't put the blame and guilt on someone who didn't know what was going on, and, Cassandra, what you did to Jack, he's fifteen years old. Don't you think this has already destroyed him? Have you forgotten all those years ago? Did you ever think about telling someone? Did you ever think about saying '*no*'!"

"No, Rose, I haven't forgotten, but it seems that you have! Your high level of intelligence almost makes you stupid! I did talk to someone, I talked to my *mother*! Who should I have said *no* to, Rose? You think that *Daddy* didn't know what was going on? You don't think that Sean didn't know what was going on? Robert figured all of this out on his own and now he's as good as dead! And don't you dare throw any of this back on me, I was a little girl! How do you think a drugged fourteen-year-old should've responded?" she snapped back.

Rose stood there in shock and was sad for her sister. She wanted to reach out to her to comfort her, but Cassandra was inconsolable. It was too late, they had all cared too late.

"Like father like son, wanna deny that, Rose? Is that the way it is? Oh, wait, don't answer that. You get to run back to your own big house on the hill in Springton and leave all this behind for another year! So, whose fault is it, Rose?"

Rose's stare turned into a hard glare at Cassandra. Rose had her mother's eyes, and they reminded Cassandra the worst was yet to come.

"I'll tell you whose fault it is, Rose. It is everybody's fault who turned a blind eye to all this deception, and that includes *Daddy*!"

Rose didn't think she could feel so sorrowful and so angry with her sister at the same time.

"No, Cassandra, it doesn't. When things don't go your way, you start lashing out at those closest to you, looking for somewhere and someone to cast the blame. And although that's understandable—"

"Rose, don't pretend you know me," she flared, cutting her off in mid-sentence. "Those closest to me are dead! And you know, you're not innocent in this either!"

"What are you talking about? I don't even live here or work for Pointer Enterprises," answered Rose dismissively.

Cassandra raised her eyebrows. "You knew what Mom and Dad were up to with Uncle Joe, you know what happened with the eviction of The Station at 76 and you chose to just walk away and keep silent! Why would you do that?"

"I didn't stay silent! I asked the hard questions. It's funny how you think you're the only one in this family who has paid penance!"

"Come on, Rose, let's go," said Matt, entering the sitting room. "We can do no good here."

Rose rejected the thought of leaving her father amongst all this chaos. "I'm not leaving my father alone in the state he's in," Rose declared.

Matt was feeling closed in and he didn't want to be in between the two sisters.

"Cassandra," said Rose, "I'm sorry that happened to you, I truly am. As far as what happened with Uncle Joe, I know very little. That doesn't give you the right to be a little bitch and destroy those around you and involve yourself in Sean's life! There are better ways to handle things. That's all I'm saying."

"I see, I tell the truth and I'm a bitch. You've got your nerve telling *me* what I should do! I'm not the only one living a lie!" spat back Cassandra.

Matt gently reached for Rose's hand to lead her out of the sitting room.

"Come on, let's go home. There's so much to be done here and we're not part of it. If you're worried about your father, he can stay with us if he wants to until all of this calms down."

"No, Matt," said Rose, breaking free from Matt's grasp, "she should be the one who leaves, not me!"

Charles came into the sitting room, just in time to hear Rose tear into Cassandra.

"You know, Cassandra, maybe you got what you deserved. You were always a haughty little girl anyway! You show up here today all decked out like you're going to a ball instead of a causal party. You're just like mother, you look like her and you act like her! Icehouse hopping, boat hopping, whatever the hell it is!"

Cassandra slapped her sister hard across the face and before Matt could grab Rose's arm, she had doubled up her fist and bloodied Cassandra's nose. Once Matt had separated the two sisters Charles stepped in between them.

"Cassandra," said Charles sternly, "Rose is right, you need to leave!"

"Oh, I'm leaving!" said Cassandra, wiping her bloody nose like it was a badge of honor, ignoring the pain. "So much for changing things as we move forward, huh, *Daddy*?"

Then Cassandra turned to her sister and angrily spewed the last the bit of venom she had left.

"Oh, and by the way, Rose, why don't you ask your husband whose bed he was in when he wasn't in yours and see if you can go back to your perfect life then!"

"You vengeful bitch!" screamed Rose, and then falling to ruin as Cassandra slammed the door behind her.

CHAPTER TWENTY-SEVEN

"The Crimson Rose Turns Dark"

"Matthew, please tell me Cassandra was lying," Rose said quietly, having to face her *insecurities* once again. "Matthew, please?"

Charles looked at Matt in disbelief: there's no way this could be true. He put his arms around his daughter to comfort her.

"Tell my daughter, your wife, that Cassandra's lying!" demanded Charles. Charles desperately needed something to be true in his world.

Only Rose's crying could be heard while Matt struggled for his words. His silence exposed the truth that her intuition had been right all along.

"You bastard!" screamed Rose.

Matthew's face fell; everything that ever mattered to him had been ripped away. Rose slipped away from her daddy, blindly grabbing her purse and keys. Matt followed after his wife and stood between her and the front door.

"Rose, Rose, wait, let me explain."

"Get out of my way, Matt! There is no explanation."

"Rose, sweetheart. It isn't what you think. Let's just talk," he replied, refusing to move.

"Get out of the way, Matt. This is over!"

"All right, all right. Let's just go somewhere and talk, please?"

"I'm not going anywhere with you. Not now, not ever!" she screamed in his face.

Rose left the big house on the hill, speeding out of the driveway, going nowhere.

"Charles!" yelled Matt. "Give me the keys to your car, I need to go after her and make this right!"

"You son of a bitch!" screamed Charles. "You think you can make this right? Have you not been paying attention, have you not heard the devastation that has ripped through this house? I trusted you, Matthew. I treated you like you were my own son! I thought you were good for my daughter! I believed in you and her. I'll go after her, you have no idea what you've done!"

Charles left in a rushed state of wildness to find his daughter and Matthew was met again with a slamming door. He was left alone in that sitting room, to do just that and wrestle with his indiscretions. He knew Ruth was home, but she wasn't anywhere to be found, and the house was quiet.

Matthew had always wanted Cassandra; he, too, was good at hiding things he didn't want to be seen. He was no different than any other man that Rose had met, and now, his wife knew him, his true wants and desires. He desired Cassandra, and always had. He yearned and ached for her, he couldn't wait until he could be with her again. "*Dammit*!" he grumbled, furious with himself and with Cassandra.

He truly loved Rose, but he came alive when he was with Cassandra. She had a way about her, he could let go with her. Cassandra didn't need saving and Rose did. Rose was the day and Cassandra was the night. If you didn't know the two of them were sisters, you'd never be able to tell seeing them standing side by side. Ambition said you could have it all, that struggles and sacrifices were for others.

Matt made himself a drink; there was nothing left for him to do but wait for his father-in-law to bring his wife back to him.

For hours Matt paced the floors waiting for Charles to return. Around midnight he saw a car drive up. It was Charles, and Rose was nowhere in sight.

"Charles, did you find Rose? Where is she? Is she okay?"

Charles looked right through him and walked past him. Matthew wasn't even sure if Charles heard him. In the sitting room Charles poured himself a shot of whiskey, drank that down, and then poured himself a drink and sat down in front of the fireplace. Sitting on the table next to him was the chess set where he and Rose would sit for hours at a time. He leaned toward the fireplace with his elbows on his knees, holding his eyes closed with one hand and his drink in the other.

"No Matt, she's not okay," he choked.

"There was a car accident, and in her state of mind, I know she couldn't think straight. She ran through a red light and was hit by a delivery truck and was pushed into the lane of oncoming traffic. When I got there, the police, an ambulance, and even two fire trucks were there. You know, Matthew, I must have ran ten car lengths to get to her. They couldn't get her out of the car, they had to use this big piece of equipment and the intersection was closed off. She was pronounced dead at the scene. I watched them take my baby girl away in a body bag and I wasn't allowed to see her. I identified her body by her wedding ring, the necklace I gave her years ago, and the shoes she was wearing. I did that, Matthew, me! Her father. My sweet Rose died alone and never knew I was there for her, that I was chasing after her. The woman who loved *you* and trusted *you* with all her being, the woman who centered her life around *you*!"

From Charles's hand the heart of the diamond necklace he had given Rose when he gave her away to Matt on their wedding day was dangling. Rose never took that necklace off, and Matt focused on the heart pendant.

"Charles, NO! Please tell me this isn't true and she'll be walking through that door any second…please, please say that Rose will be walking through that door!" wailed Matthew.

"Shut up, Matthew! You don't get to speak my daughter's name! We were supposed to be ringing in the New Year and taking a break from all this year's hard work. Rejuvenating for the upcoming season, just like we do every year!"

He couldn't look Charles in the eye, so he looked into the fire.

"I'm so sorry, Charles, I'm so sorry."

He cried for the loss of his wife, she loved him more than anything and he knew it. Charles had no consoling words for his son-in-law.

"Matthew, I want you gone first thing in the morning," said Charles, finishing his whiskey. "And I never want to see or hear from you again."

"Charles, she's my wife, and whether you believe me or not, I loved her. I made a mistake, and that's something I have to live with, but this is my responsibility as her husband. She'll be in Springton with me!"

"HA!" replied Charles. "If I were a younger man I would tear you apart piece by piece. She will not be buried in Springton, she'll be buried in our family plot. Your office will be cleaned out and your things will be sent to you. If you want to keep your career, you'll make this decision wisely." Then he walked up the stairs to one of the guest rooms, and without breaking his stride, he walked right past the bedroom he shared for years with his wife. Getting ready for bed he wasn't sure what to think about. The floating brothel and PECC, the frontal lobotomy of his son, the icehouse hopping, and the jet-black-haired beauty down the hall or the sudden death of his sweet Rose. He couldn't control his thoughts. Frazzled and in shock, he laid his head down on his pillow, fighting his emotions, engulfed in his grief. He tossed and turned all night, and it was pure emotional exhaustion that led him to fall asleep. He heard Cassandra's voice over again and he cried out in his sleep, "I didn't know, I didn't know!" Visions of his dead daughter, visions of his son not recognizing him, not responding at all. Robert was in front of him as a young adolescent and then in the blink of an eye, a grown man with blood running down his face and falling to the ground. Then he heard Robert's voice as that of a fifteen-year-old crying out, "Dad, Dad!" Charles tried to reach him, and he remained just out of his reach. There were visions of his one true love, that jet-black-haired beauty, but she didn't have a face. His nightmare jolted him awake, and he sat straight up, sweat rolling off of him and he could barely breathe. Then he would try again and close his eyes, only to see the same images again and be plunged back into the madness.

Just as Charles instructed, when he awoke in the morning Matt was gone. Ruth had already made her way downstairs and was sitting at the kitchen table. She had a pot of coffee made and hadn't dressed for the day. Charles poured himself a cup of coffee and sat down.

"Charles…I," Ruth began to speak to her husband.

"Ruth, I know we have a lot to work out, but there's something you don't know." Ruth closed her eyes. Maybe if she tried to ward off whatever it was, he wouldn't have to speak it. Ruth's words were no longer magic, and Charles was no longer spellbound.

"There was a car accident last night and Rose was killed," he informed Ruth as a matter of fact.

"What? No! What happened?" she replied, gasping.

"Apparently, Matt was sleeping with Cassandra behind Rose's back, the girls fought, and Cassandra ended it by telling Rose. Rose left here like a bat outta hell, I went after her, and I couldn't catch her."

The words Charles spoke bounced off Ruth. Like her husband, she could handle no more grief. Even though it was little consolation, she had said her goodbyes to Robert. In her mind, a cause or reason of why things had to be the way they are could provide closure. There was no reason and no cause for Rose's death. She was lost in a whirlwind of devastation. She wouldn't stand, because she couldn't. She wouldn't speak, because she couldn't. Surely, the past had nothing to do with Rose's death. She was angry that Rose was gone, and Cassandra was to blame for this. Ruth began to bargain with her "had to's" only to find that ambition had turned its back on her, to save its good attributes. Maybe ambition could also make one devious.

Charles offered no comfort, there was no gentleness in his voice, no warm, comforting embrace, not even a pat on the hand. He could barely stand to look at his wife, and being in the same room with her was exasperating.

Ruth sat there looking out the window through the barren woods that backed up to the house; all the leaves were gone for the winter, and there were patches of snow and ice on the ground. Icicles hung from the barren branches, glistening a cold beauty. Nature knew the trees weren't dead, and the grass was still under the snow waiting to grow. Ruth had gotten lost in her thoughts, and she heard Charles's voice, only to hear his words in midsentence, "…this house is big enough for the two of us to live here without having to cross paths, I believe we both need some time to ourselves.

We have just lost three of our four children. I'm getting older, and, honestly, Ruth, I don't know if I'll survive this. You've destroyed our family, and over what? Wealth, money, status, and power. I don't even really know why. I can't talk to you about this right now. We have to bury our daughter."

Ruth covered her face with her hands and rubbed her eyes, wondering if she was going to survive this.

"Oh, by the way," said Charles, "if your sister Lydia and her husband John are still in need of work, the marina is going to need new management."

"When do you want them here?" she hurriedly asked, realizing what he said.

"As soon as possible!" he yelled, slamming the door.

The day of shooting had not ended yet, just as it promised. It was still dragging on. Drudging up history and drowning all of them until it took their last words, their last breath. First Robert, then Mary, and now Rose.

She curled up in the kitchen nook nursing her coffee. The snow fell silently and was pure in its untouched beauty.

CHAPTER TWENTY-EIGHT

"Cassandra Comes into Her Own"

Cassandra woke up early that morning and she had really slept that night; it wasn't a peaceful sleep, but it was restful. Not everything was right in her world and never would be, but now all was known. She went into town to the penthouse and began going through Robert's things. She gathered mementos and things that would remind her of him. She found his release paperwork from prison and took that with her.

Going through his closet she found an old broken-down box. On top of the box was a note written in the handwriting of a first grader. It read, "Cusen Robert, I will miss you. Love Piper." Inside the box was Piper's plastic tea set. She had forgotten what the tea set looked like. It was painted with delicate pink blooms, and instead of a gold rim, it was pink. It included the tea pot, sugar bowl, creamer, four teacups and saucers with a tray for serving. Robert's words came back to her, "Have more tea parties." She took the two boxes she had packed up and headed back to the marina.

Once she had finished loading all of Mary's things into her car, she saw her father pull in. She didn't acknowledge him and kept walking back to her state room.

As she expected he bulldozed his way into her room. "Oh, hey, *Daddy*, come on in," she responded in kind.

"I do own this place, Cassandra, in case you have forgotten!"

"No, *Daddy*, I haven't forgotten, but I think you did."

Cassandra could see that yesterday had an effect on him, and it didn't faze her one bit. It wasn't ideal but the truth had made it bearable, and it was time this life affect someone else other than her. It was time someone else had their dreams crushed, their life ripped away from them, and their heart torn out and stomped on. It was time someone else experience the intense sorrow and rumination she had felt for most of her life. It was time. *Live for Mary and remember for Robert.*

"What do you want, *Daddy*?"

Charles looked straight at her. "Cassandra, get your things and get out. Don't ever come back here again," he demanded from his place of grief.

Cassandra grinned a little. "I'll be gone just as soon as we work out the payments from my trust fund. I want sixty thousand a year and cost of living increases figured in with each new fiscal year sent to this post office box. I don't care if you send it in a lump sum or if you send it monthly, and I also want a yearly salary from Scenic Waters and my retirement. Then you'll never have to see me again. Then as you say, *Daddy*, we can change and move forward, right?"

"That's ridiculous!" he screamed.

"Well, then I'll go to the newspapers and turn all these journals in for publication and be paid handsomely either way and the whole world will know you sold your daughter so you could buy this place. And what do you think will happen to PECC? Do you think Mother could stay out of jail? What does one do with their money in prison, *Daddy*? And lastly, what about Sean, he holds the controlling interest in this place and he's the trustee of my trust. I want to be the trustee and beneficiary of my own trust, and I want PECC shut down. Then and only then will I go away. It's mine and I worked for it!"

"Fine, Cassandra, I'll take care of it," said Charles, turning to leave, not telling her that her sister had died.

Cassandra continued to pack her car and didn't tell her dad that Mary had taken her own life because of PECC and because of the brutality this family brings.

"Cassandra!" she heard from an open window of a car pulling up next to hers.

"Well, Pastor Whitney, Mrs. Whitney. What brings you by? I haven't seen or heard from you in almost ten years, and neither has Mary. Let me guess, we're in your prayers?"

"Now, Ms. Pointer…"

"Cassandra, it's Cassandra," she said.

"Cassandra," said the pastor in a meek voice, "we don't want any trouble, we just want to collect Mary's things and give her a proper burial."

"Oh, I see, doing things the proper way these days, huh? Well, she doesn't have anything, and she already left her wishes in her Last Will and Testament and everything's already been done. You're about ten years too late," she said, sneering.

"Now, look here! You have no right to keep us from our daughter in her death like you did while she was alive!"

"Pastor Whitney, do you really want to discuss this? Because we can, it was your abuse that kept her away from you in her life," she said challenging him.

Mrs. Whitney, the ever so graceful and prominent first lady of the Church, gasped when she heard those words. Cassandra wasn't sure if it was because she had never heard such words spoken out loud or if she was truly living in denial.

"Do you need the details to remind you of her horror? You are a sanctimonious prick and you, Mrs. Whitney, are the biggest hypocrite in this town. I suggest you get the hell off my property!" she demanded, feeling somewhat vindicated and it felt good.

"Why I oughta…" raged an angry man of the cloth.

"Why you oughta what? Pray for me? You don't pray for people like me, do you?" seethed Cassandra.

"It looks like someone already punched you in that sinful mouth of yours!" responded Pastor Whitney, obviously reveling in Cassandra's swollen nose and cut lip.

"HA!" She laughed. "Don't worry, the person responsible for this will still be suffering long after I'm healed!"

"William," said his wife with her nose in the air, "I'd like to leave now."

Pastor Whitney and his wife left with what they had brought to Mary throughout her life: Nothing.

CHAPTER TWENTY-NINE

"Knowing the Truth, Realizing the Truth"

Ruth and Charles arrived home to an empty house after Rose's funeral. They both struggled for words, they'd become strangers. Charles poured them both a brandy and had finally found some words for his wife.

"Ruth, you know I've loved you since the moment I set eyes on you, but you were dating my best friend. I was so proud the day we were married. I think it's time you tell me what happened the night Bruce died. You know, it didn't matter to me why you chose me. Just that you chose me. You did choose me, right?"

"Charles, do we have to talk about this right now? I've already told you!" she responded, swirling her brandy.

"Yes, dammit!" he answered, slamming his fist on the table. "Yes! We have to talk about this!"

"Oh, Charles! You're Sean's father!" she replied weakly.

Ruth met Charles with her dark brown eyes.

"You're his father in every way that matters. We brought him home from the hospital together and we raised him together and..."

"Well, this explains why you protected Sean when he shot up The Medallion and sent my only son into a life of pure hell. Do you know what you've done? Do you! Robert is my rightful heir and Pointer Enterprises was his legacy! You've destroyed him to protect Sean, *your* son! Again! Sean was all you had left of Bruce, and you weren't going to lose that, were you? You weren't going to give up the one connection to Bruce that you still had in this life," said Charles with his beady blue eyes raging at his wife.

"No! Charles, no! You know that's not true!" said Ruth, beginning to cry. "We made that decision together to have Robert say he did that, because he was fifteen and we thought he would've been tried as a juvenile and there wouldn't be any jail time, remember! Robert's my son too!"

"You manipulated me, Ruth. If I had known the severity of what Dorothy was implicating to Sean and if I had known the truth myself..."

Ruth stood up and raised her voice, "Oh, if you had known for a fact that Sean wasn't *your* son back then you would've made a different decision? You would've let Sean face the consequences of the shooting and still remain in prison today? Did you ever think that maybe this frontal lobotomy was the only choice, Charles? Did you ever think that maybe I wanted to protect you from having to make that horrible decision?"

"I don't know, Ruth! I was never told the truth from the day we were married! You wanted to protect me? Is that because you love me *so* much! This is what I know, and that is you've taken everything from me! You've taken my legacy and made it a *Bordure* legacy. Did you ever love me, or was I just a stand-in for Bruce all these years? For God's sake, Ruth, what would've made you happy? Didn't you have everything you ever wanted? There was nothing you didn't have! Except Bruce..."

"Charles, you're the only father Sean knows, and you are Jack and Joshua's grandpa, they love you and adore you!" cried Ruth.

"Yeah, and I adore them, and I adore Robert too. But that is no more, Robert is gone to all of us, Rose is dead, and Cassandra is dead to *me*. You know, Ruth, had I known you were pregnant with Bruce's child, it wouldn't have made a difference to me. I loved you. Why didn't you just tell me the truth? I'll tell you why, because it made a difference to *you!*" stated Charles, making his final judgment.

"The night that Bruce died," began Ruth, quietly sobbing, "he came to the apartment to tell me he no longer wanted to see me and that he was in love with Elizabeth and wanted to make a life with her. He told me it would be best if I resigned my position with Bordure's and follow my family to French Town."

"I see. Then what happened?" he asked.

"He thought he could completely erase me, then I told him I was pregnant. We began fighting and I pushed him out of the apartment, he tripped backwards and fell against the railing. The railing broke and he fell to his death. It was an accident," cried Ruth.

"I remember the day Bruce met Elizabeth; he fell in love with her that very first moment. He fell head over heels for her, just the way I fell for you. This lie about Sean is the original sin, the lie that bore all the other lies."

"I'm sorry, Charles," cried Ruth. "What do we do now?"

"I don't know. I don't think I can get over this. I look at you and I see someone I don't know. I'm lost in grief and can't sleep without nightmares. I just buried—*we* just buried our daughter Rose today."

"I understand," stammered Ruth weakly. The stress over the last few months had taken its toll and she had grown weaker. She stood up to go to her room and collapsed on the curved staircase.

"Ruth, Ruth!" said Charles, gently shaking her, and there was no response.

The ambulance came and Ruth managed to regain consciousness. There was no one following the screaming sirens of the ambulance through those curvy Ozark roads.

CHAPTER THIRTY

"Resolution and Reflection"

After going through the cabins, making sure every trace of The Lake Girls was erased, Cassandra gathered up the last of her things.

Today was the day, she was leaving the marina. It was still bitterly cold. There was no snowfall, sleet, or rain, and the grayness of the sky blocked any sunlight.

Cassandra saw the sign for Monument Nursing Home well before she needed to turn. From its outside appearance, it had more of a commercial look to it and a heavier presence of an establishment than a residence.

A loud buzzer sounded, and the doors unlocked for her to enter through the front doors. Walking into the lobby there was only one direction in which she could walk. At first sight there was a large circular, round desk managed by two receptionists who were sitting there chatting.

"Hi, I'm Cassandra Pointer, here to see my brother, Robert Pointer."

"Oh, sign in right here," said one of the girls. "I'll find out where he is and take you to him."

"Thank you," Cassandra replied.

This place made her uneasy, it symbolized this was going to be a permanent situation. There were no plans to take Robert back their new place, that hope was gone.

The receptionist made a call, and it wasn't long when the phone rang back.

"Ms. Pointer…" said the receptionist.

"Cassandra, it's Cassandra," she replied before the receptionist could finish.

"Cassandra," she said, "he's in the TV room, follow me."

They walked down a short hall and Cassandra heard the loud buzzing sound again, and that door could now be opened. There was a fleeting odor of urine and defecation that slapped Cassandra in the face. An orderly came right away to help the resident and took him for a bath and a change of clothes. None of the other residents seemed to notice, and the receptionist leading her to her brother didn't flinch.

"Cassandra," said the receptionist, placing her hand on Cassandra's shoulder and giving her a reassuring smile, "that happens sometimes. Please be assured that all our guests are given not only a bath and new garments to wear, but we do our best to maintain and return their dignity at times such as these."

Cassandra wanted to take Robert and run away. *Could I care for him, could I tend to him and keep him safe?*

There was a *smell* in this place, and it wasn't unpleasant, it smelled musty, and Cassandra found herself faced with the fact that death is inescapable. She wondered if this is how it ended for most people, living in a nursing home. Waiting for death, day after day once you'd been marked.

Cassandra saw her brother before the young girl standing next to her and she ran to him. "Robert! Robert! It's so good to see you!" she said, bending down and giving him a kiss on the cheek. She was uncomfortable in this room they called the TV room. She noticed the strap that once held him in his chair was no longer there and he was sitting up on his own without slouching.

"Ma'am, do you think I could visit with my brother in private and see his room? I have some things for him," asked Cassandra.

"Oh, sure. Of course, I'm sure he would love that," she answered.

"Robert," said the receptionist, "look, your sister is here to see you. I was so excited to get meet her today. I bet you're happy to see her too, huh? We're going back to your room so you can visit, okay?"

There wasn't any response, but his eye seemed to acknowledge that he knew he was going back to his room.

His room wasn't as homey as the room he had at the rehab facility. When Cassandra walked into the room the first thing she saw straight ahead was a picture window along the far wall, with heavy golden yellow drapes. The color reminded her of a puke yellow, just blah. The floor was just like the floor of a hospital. To the right was his bed and there were straps hanging from a canopy of sorts that worked mechanically to help lift him. There were stainless steel metal railings on each side of the bed. His sheets, pillowcases, and blankets were white. A television hung from the ceiling for easy positioning. The bathroom was close to the bed, and the walls were painted a light tan color. The bathroom was just as drab as his room.

"I brought him some sweatsuits, socks, T-shirts, and underclothes and some things from home for him, if that's all right to put them in his room," said Cassandra.

"Yes, that's perfect!" the young girl answered, showing her his closet and the six-drawer chest that sat perfectly against the wall to the right towards the picture frame window.

"How's he doing? Is he beginning to talk or eat on his own? Does he walk at all?" Cassandra asked while she was putting away his things.

"Well, he's on a level-three ward, and that requires routine and continuous supervision in most of his daily living," she answered. "He does have a pain management regimen, and we have ten registered nurses on staff, so he's well looked after."

"I'm sure he is," said Cassandra.

She was still feeling uneasy but reaching some kind of a comfort level while she tried talking herself through it. She didn't have much of a choice and was forced to accept this and needed to, so she could do her best for her brother. What that was, she wasn't sure yet.

"I'll leave you to visit with your brother. If you need anything at all just pick up the phone and press *nine*."

Cassandra wheeled his chair over to a small sitting area and sat next to him and held his hand. He looked at her like a child would look upon someone with wonder or in awe.

"Robert, I miss you so much," she said, trying not to cry, he didn't need to feel her pain.

"I wanted to let you know, that PECC is no longer. You'll see Mary soon..."

She stopped suddenly, she didn't know what to say and she didn't mean he would see her soon, that he was going to die *too!* What if Mary was right and he was in there and he could tell what was going on around him but couldn't communicate. Left to suffer in his own head, struggling with paralyzing emotions and limited physical abilities, helpless to do anything. She couldn't tell him that Mary was gone, she couldn't allow Robert to suffer any more than he already was. Could she ever tell him that Mary was gone? If he was in there, he would want to know why she wasn't here, but if he wasn't in there, he would never know the difference.

"Mary loves you very much, and she's so excited to see you." Those were the words that Cassandra managed to finally say.

He didn't respond to her words, and she wondered if he knew what she was talking about, he had always responded to the mention of her name. Mary's suicide was so out of character for her, it wasn't something she would do. So how could she explain it? She talked about God and the future; she was the bright light on the lake. She talked about faith, hope, and love. Then it dawned on her, maybe that night when she went to bed, she thought about Robert and how this lobotomy may drive him to madness. Maybe it drove her to a moment of madness when she swallowed those pills. Maybe it was the fear of going mad that rocked Mary to her core and only for a moment she lapsed. A fatal moment.

"Anyway, the whole truth is out there. About Uncle Joe, about PECC, about the icehouse hopping, and they all know, Robert, they all know it was Jack who shot you." She waited for a response from her brother, and still nothing. Not even any familiar movements.

"Oh, Robert, the whole family is scattering like cockroaches when a light switch is flipped, they have so much explaining to do to each other!" Still nothing, maybe a nod, she couldn't tell if he was nodding to her, getting tired, or if he was in pain.

"I'll tell Mary you love her, she knows that you do, but I'll tell her again," she said quietly.

"Hey, Robert! They told me you came to your room," said a woman who had entered his room with a stainless-steel rolling cart. "Oh, please forgive me, they didn't tell me Robert had a visitor. I'm Barb, the RN on duty."

"It's nice to meet you," replied Cassandra.

"It's time for his pain medication," said Barb, dousing a cotton ball in alcohol and rubbing his arm, then picking up the vials of medicine and a needle. "It won't take but a minute and then you can continue your visit. Now, he may get groggy, so I'll have him moved to his bed."

After he received his pain medication, two strong young orderlies moved Robert to his bed and made sure he was as comfortable as he could be. His eye looked to be filled with gratefulness.

"All right, Robert, you tucked in there nice and comfortable now?" one of the orderlies asked and even seemed to expect an answer.

"He may fall asleep, ma'am. His pain medications will sometimes make him drowsy."

"I understand. Thank you," replied Cassandra, not mentioning that had already been explained.

"No problem at all, we all think a lot of Robert here," he said, smiling.

Cassandra smiled thankfully, wishing Nurse Bell was his nurse.

"Robert, I have some things I'm going to put on your shelves for you, okay?" she asked, awkwardly turning to look at him over her shoulder, and he had drifted off to sleep. She placed Piper's tea set on top of his dresser with a few pictures and then she took out the urn that held Mary's ashes and placed them on one of the shelves. It brought great comfort to her knowing that Mary would be here in this room with Robert for as long as he stayed here. She didn't mention anything about this as she sat next to his bed, holding and caressing his hand while he slept. The staff would peek in periodically checking on him, them, but didn't enter the room and left them to just be together.

A couple of hours later Robert had woken and the first thing he saw was his sister's face. It meant so much to her, and she hoped it meant as much to him. He looked at her with kindness, but there was nothing else.

"Ms. Pointer," said a nurse entering the room, "it's time for dinner; we'll be taking him to the dining room. Would you like to stay and have dinner? I can have a plate made for you. We have several options."

"That would be nice, and I'll just have what he's having," said Cassandra.

"Oh, no! We're still making his food in the blender. I'll get you a plate," she replied on an upbeat.

They sat in a dining room that was a level-three dining room. There was an orderly that sat with them, helping Robert get his nutrients from a straw. Cassandra was shaky and not sure she could eat. She wondered if Robert would ever be able to bite into an apple or a nice juicy steak. Fate had been cruel and evil in so many ways, he was a chef! He was the baker, broiler, griller, and chopper of the vegetables. He knew nutrition and his palate was second to none. This place didn't seem evil, it was just evilness that had brought him here.

Cassandra sat with her brother and his orderly and the feeling of not wanting to leave him was creeping in. She could stay with him, in his room and do his activities with him. Sadly, she knew that wasn't how it worked. On her plate there were two salmon patties, cooked carrots and peas, mashed potatoes, and another kind of a vegetable melody of cucumbers, a tomato wedge, and Brussel sprouts.

After dinner and once back in Robert's room he received his nightly meds, and again two strong orderlies lifted Robert into his bed.

"All right, my man, there you go, we'll be close by checking on you, okay? So no sneaking out and chasing the pretty nurses!" said one of the orderlies.

"Robert, what a lovely lady! Is she your girl?" the orderly asked seeing the picture of Mary that Cassandra had placed by his bedside earlier.

There was, of course, no response from Robert, as heartbreaking as it was.

"She was…uh, she's Robert's fiancé," answered Cassandra.

The orderly was careful with his words, and didn't ask any obvious questions such as, "Where is she?" Or speak words like, "We can't wait to meet her." That would be for another day.

She sat with him again, holding his hand until he seemed to peacefully drift off into a never, never land. She kissed him on his cheek. "I love you. I'll be back to see you soon," she whispered.

She sat in her car bereft and beaten. This was her mother's fault, her mother did this! Jack did this, a young man who had grown too big for his britches! The little morsel of peace she did find was the satisfaction she had finally exposed her mother and Jack.

She took the map from the glove compartment and located the address of the house Mary had set up for them. A house that was now going to be a lonely home for one. Maybe fate had run its course, maybe Mary stowing away on the showboat was all part of a bigger plan and no accident, a part of her legacy. What was Robert's legacy? What was her legacy? Did they each have a legacy or did fate cruelly rip that away from them too?

The sign on the side of the two-lane road said, "Now entering Rushing Springs. Population 4,357."

Oh my God, Mary! You've got to be kidding me! Hill people live here! Cassandra pulled over to make sure she hadn't made a wrong turn. There was no way Mary could have known that Ruth was born here, in this very little town. Shivers ran down Cassandra's spine and she feared that fate was not done with her.

She was looking for Hide-A-way Springs Lane. Even the name of the street, Mary sure did have a sense of humor! It was in a subdivision and each house sat on at least five acres, and that gave Cassandra some hope for this property.

Finding the house, the driveway was huge and perfectly landscaped. There was a three-car garage and a cobblestone sidewalk that would wind you around to the covered front porch. It would be adorned by beautiful bright colored flowers in spring. A little further out in the front yard were two trees, and one was surrounded with a flower garden. The main floor was handicap accessible; Mary had really thought of everything. Just like Cassandra knew all along, there was a large chef's kitchen that led to a back porch with a grill for use with charcoal and a state-of-the-art gas grill. In one of the large living rooms, positioned perfectly by the large windows, sat a black grand piano with shiny black keys. *I knew it!*

There were four bedrooms and three baths. It truly was a labor of love. This was Mary's legacy, this is what Mary and Robert had poured their money and dreams into while Cassandra provided a smoke screen.

Everything was here and it was fully furnished. Everything was here except Robert and Mary. Cassandra didn't know what do with herself. She had never been alone, not really. She always had Mary, The Lake Girls, and for a short time she had Robert.

Cassandra sat on the front porch and noticed there was pile of papers thrown in the front yard. Mary must have subscribed to every Braxton newspaper there was! She picked them up and sat them on the wicker table that sat between two large matching wicker rocking chairs. She could hear Mary's voice telling her, *This place I found us, is as close to heaven on earth you'll ever find! You just wait and see my friend. Can you guess where it is?*

For Cassandra, the day Robert was shot had finally ended. If finding pleasure in these acts of vengeance makes her selfish, then so be it. If you could ask Robert and Mary about it, they would say Charles, Ruth, Rose, Sean, and his little family of four got off easy. It was Robert's story to tell, but he wasn't able to tell it. Justice should have allowed him to tell it, but vengeance forced it to be told and rightfully so. *How would Robert tell his story?* thought Cassandra, rocking back and forth in that wicker rocker alone with her own voices in her head. There was no drink or drug to keep her in a fog.

The cruelest demon of all that Cassandra had to fight was her own unanswered questions that came back to haunt her time and time again. *Did I lose my resolve? Was I worthy of Robert and Mary's love and trust? I had the means to destroy Pointer Enterprises, but instead I secured my trust fund and ran? Were Daddy and Rose right?*

Cassandra's daily routine was changing, and she began to get settled in, one day at a time. Getting settled took up the majority of her days, and when she started to find some time on her hands she would play the piano, taking comfort in Chopin and getting lost in the madness of Mozart. Some days she banged and clanged out her anger and grief, and some days she would gracefully and elegantly glide her fingers over the keys, dancing and swaying with each key stroke.

The weather warmed and spring was slowly arriving; some days she would find herself wandering through the house or wandering over the five acres. Mostly, she would make a pot of coffee, collect the many newspapers, and sit on the covered front porch finding herself scouring the papers for everything and anything that was Pointer. There must have been about three or four months of newspapers she had yet to read. It was her mother's habit to scour the newspapers, and that caused her to hesitate when picking up a paper, there was plenty of time to catch up on current events. She was nothing like her mother. She had no fear of being anything like her mother; how could you be like someone you didn't even know? *It couldn't be possible.*

Here in this sizeable piece of heaven on earth is where Cassandra would grieve and mourn the loss of her brother and the loss of her best friend. Wishing it would've been her that was shot instead of Robert, there wasn't anyone who needed her or anyone to miss her. Then Mary and Robert would be here, together, as it should have been. As it should be. In her solitude she couldn't help but wonder about the Bordure name. All of the secrets had been told, hadn't they?

CHAPTER THIRTY-ONE

"Death Without Grief"

While spring was bringing awareness and reconciliation to Cassandra, her father was still reeling in all he'd been told that dreadful New Year's Eve.

Charles didn't spend much time at the hospital; however, he did make sure that Ruth received what she needed.

"Mr. and Mrs. Pointer," said Dr. Skien, "we have the test results from the X-rays, blood work, and smears."

"What's wrong with my wife?" asked Charles. He heard his own voice and when he used the word "wife," it sounded strange to him. He loved her so much in life, in death he didn't know her. She was looking frail, this hadn't happened overnight, but it was the first time that Charles had noticed.

"The CT scan shows a mass on the lung. It's not lung cancer. It's stage IV cervical cancer that has metastasized to the lungs. There are new advanced platinum chemotherapy treatments available for such an aggressive cancer. The chemo treatments will work in conjunction with the radiation treatments to try and shrink the tumor," replied Dr. Skien.

"Doctor," said Ruth, "will this chemo treatment kill the cancer in order for me to survive?"

"It's hard to say, but in my opinion at this stage, it's terminal. It may prolong your life, but not save it," he said in a familiar matter-of-fact tone.

"Then no treatment," said Ruth with certainty.

"Ruth, are you sure?" asked Charles. "I've never known you to just give up and quit."

"I'm sure. What is it that you say when you play chess and you're losing?"

Charles remained quiet and the doctor quit taking notes. Dr. Skien and Ruth were waiting for Charles's answer.

"Charles, do you remember?" asked a breathless Ruth.

"There will always be a winner and a loser, it's inevitable. When losing you can still maintain some power by determining how you're going to lose," answered Charles.

"I believed Robert would beat all odds. You must believe me when I tell you that Charles," replied Ruth.

Her judgment day had come, and she would stand in judgment of her family, what was left of her family. It was a harsh judgment, and she had no choice but to accept it. She had made one deal too many, and when that eerie silence would find her, she heard its warning. She had nothing left to give and no one realized what she had given. Her husband became a pioneer of a town, married a trophy wife, and became a father of four beautiful children. His pride was bountifully fed. Sean did receive all the glory and would have been chosen to run the empire she had built, and it was a Bordure legacy after all. If things had gone the way she planned, Cassandra and Robert would never be sacrificed again and would enjoy an early retirement, the fruits of their hard labor. And Rose, sweet Rose, would take her rightful place at Pointer's Inn in Springton and be a matriarch in her own right. Time had run out, and fate had other plans on the day that Jack shot her son. Her only ambition now was to secure her legacy, and she could only hope she had preserved all that she had built. A legacy of two generations with the promise of a third, and hopefully their platform would one day become old money.

She would be judged by only four, and those four knew how to keep hidden what they didn't want to be seen.

The phone rang early one morning in the Pointer household that again was a lonely household of one, and Charles was jolted awake. His heart leapt to his throat picking up the phone.

"Hello," he answered, clearing his throat.

"Mr. Pointer?"

"Yes."

"This is Braxton Memorial, and I am sorry to inform you that your wife, Ruth, has taken a turn for the worse through the night. We suggest you gather your family."

"Okay. Thank you, we'll be right there."

He gently placed the phone back into its cradle. Getting dressed he moved slower than normal, his arms and legs felt heavy. For a moment he wondered if he really had to go to the hospital and then realized, for public persona, he had to go. He knew the woman he was to going to see he really didn't know. Since New Year's Eve he had been questioning whether or not he knew himself. In reality it was just him, Robert, and Cassandra. That's what was left of his family. Surely, Sean *and* Caroline would be a joined force to be reckoned with in the future. A future he had to gain control over.

Charles and Sean arrived at the hospital and sat by her bed as she struggled to breathe. Hospice was offering their support, and the doctors were administering medications to do their best to keep her calm and manage her pain. When Charles saw her lying there in the bed, her rib cage protruding and managing to take a few breaths, he found no love for her. To him, there lie a woman who had been an acquaintance or a business partner. By this time, she had lost her ability to speak and what she was thinking, no one really knew. One would think he plunged deeper into his madness, but in his mind she died New Year's Eve.

"Mr. Pointer," said a nurse entering the room, "I'm sorry to bother you, but we have a call for you at the front desk. Shall I put it through here?"

"Sure. Thank you."

"Hello."

"Mr. Pointer?"

"Yes, Lauren, is that you? You're not at the office already, are you?"

"No, sir. How is Mrs. Pointer?"

"She's doing the best she can, but we're afraid she doesn't have much longer. We've been told to gather the family, so that's what we did," he answered.

"I see," said Lauren. "I'm so sorry for you and your family. I can't imagine how difficult this must be for you. Which makes it all the harder for me to call you. I'm over at The Hotel at 76, and, Charles, the station is on fire, and they've closed the highway. They can't contain the fire, and two other counties are being called in to help get it contained."

"What?" responded Charles in a whisper.

"I'm sorry, Mr. Pointer. Even if you wanted to come down here you wouldn't be able to get through. I got here just before they closed the highway."

"All right, Lauren, thanks for the call. Just manage what you can and hold off the news crews if possible."

"Yes, Mr. Pointer. I'll do my best, and again, I'm so sorry, for everything. Goodbye."

Charles and Sean sat next to Ruth's bedside and turned on the television in her room and the news was reporting the closure of the highway and The Station at 76 was a raging inferno. Black smoke was billowing up to the skies, snuffing out the daylight, and while the smoke rose, it looked like there was a hidden ball of fire in its midst. They sat quietly listening to the reporter tell of the horrific event.

"We're bringing you breaking news here on Highway 76 this morning. A gas station here on the strip has caught fire and is causing a concern due to the underground gas tanks, and businesses in the area are doing their best to evacuate. Traffic is being redirected; the fire chief is reporting the highway will be closed until further notice. So if you're traveling down the strip, you'll need to find an alternative route. We've been told by Tanton County's fire marshal that Ridge County and Greenco County fire departments are being called in to help contain this raging inferno that you see behind me. The fire apparently started around four a.m. this morning, and fire crews do not have a time frame as to how long it will take to get this fire under control or when the highway will reopen. Stay tuned for more breaking news as our crew remains here on site to bring the latest breaking news."

"Oh my, look at that, Dad," Said Sean.

"Yeah. Well, they can't drive up and down the strip to point fingers at the shingle today," replied Charles numbly.

"No," replied Sean, "it can be seen from right where they are."

"Yep."

They watched their station burn to the ground and witnessed Ruth taking her last breath. It came hard and fast, she was gone. From this day forward, Ruth was gone from his life. For all the days to come his heart would mend with each fading memory.

While they waited for the funeral home to pick up Ruth, they remained quietly at her bedside. It was time Charles faced his truth to decide what he was going to do. The fact that his daughter Cassandra was his only living competent heir hit him hard.

"Dad, what are we going to do?"

Charles was still a proud man, and Cassandra, who was dead to him, would not inherit his legacy. When he looked at Sean, he now saw a Bordure. Charles made his decision, and like his late wife did all those years ago, he buried the original sin of Ruth Tarlson Pointer with her. Charles wasn't left with much choice, this woman he called his wife had the last word even in her death.

"Nothing we can do, son," answered Charles. "Your mother is gone, and as far as the station, it's going to burnout eventually."

They held a small memorial for Ruth with immediate family and it was officiated by Pastor Whitney. Charles no longer questioned his decision to bury Ruth's original sin with her, it was necessary to protect Pointer Enterprises from its rightful heir, Cassandra Marie Pointer. He brought a huge bouquet of flowers for Rose's grave and gently placed them on the ground, centered with her newly placed headstone. Then, he stood up and took a couple steps to his wife's freshly dug grave and let a single rose drop from his hand to the dirt.

Looking at Sean and Caroline was like looking at two familiar strangers. Charles now saw resemblances of his long-lost friend in Sean's features. Sean had thick, curly ginger hair, his was thin and straight. Sean could grow a beard, he couldn't. Subtle things he'd never paid attention to before. Charles didn't know who Sean was, he only knew who he wasn't. But Jack and Joshua…they were Pointers.

CHAPTER THIRTY-TWO

"Out of the Ashes"

Charles woke early and went into the office every day; he no longer had Ruth, who basked in the glory of running Pointer Enterprises. Just like always, Mattie set his breakfast setting with love and adoration. Now, it was accepted and appreciated.

These days he had to read the papers himself. There was no one to scour the papers on his behalf and indiscreetly manage any public relations. This morning the Tri-Lake newspapers had a whopper of a story to tell, and he wasn't prepared.

All the Tri-Lake newspapers had reported on the fire at the station. One headline stated, "Body Found During Investigation of Braxton Gas Station Fire."

The pictures showed the once busy gas station in a heap of rubble. The parking lot shone like glass, still being wet from all the water. The article reported the body was badly burned and could not be identified, but they were inclined to believe it was a male. Another newspaper article reported that it appeared the body found at the station had been there for some time and that an autopsy would be conducted.

"Charles, can I get you anything else?" asked Mattie, popping her head in the dining room to check on him.

"Yeah, why don't you join me for breakfast?" he replied.

"No, thank you, I've already eaten," Mattie responded.

"Join me for a cup of coffee, then. Have you seen the morning papers?"

Mattie poured herself a cup of coffee and joined him.

"Yes, I'm sorry, Charles. I've read the articles," she replied and thinking to herself, *Even to the end, what a selfish woman she was.*

The phone rang and Mattie got up to answer it.

"Pointer residence."

"Hey, Mattie, it's Sean. Can I talk to Dad?"

"Hang on, let me see if he's still here. Charles, it's Sean," she said, covering the mouth piece of the phone.

Charles shook his head. "No."

"I'm sorry, Sean, he must've already left for the office; may I take a message?"

"No message. Thanks, Mattie. I'll try him there," replied Sean, hanging up the phone.

"Thank you, Mattie. Now let's finish our coffee, shall we? It's going to be a long day," said Charles, motioning for her to take her seat at the table.

"You're welcome. If there's anything I can do, please let me know. I'm so sorry, Charles."

"Well, Mattie, I can tell you this: there are going to be some changes around here. Do you think you're up for it? It's going to get pretty intense. I'm sure there will be many questions throughout the investigation of this man who was found in the rubble of the fire," he said.

"I'll be just fine," answered Mattie.

Charles got up from the table to get his day started and gently patted Mattie on her shoulder. "Good, glad to hear it. Wanna have dinner around six?"

"Sure, dinner will be at six," answered Mattie.

"See you then, and Mattie, set two places. One for me and one for yourself."

There were only two decisions Charles was sure of as far as Pointer Enterprises was concerned. The first was that it had to be Jack to lead the company for the remainder of the nineteenth century. The second was to keep Cassandra's trust fund fed as she asked to keep her away.

Charles was anticipating Jack's college graduation; it brought him peace in the midst of the heartbreak all around him. It seemed like a way to reclaim his life and legacy. He was ready to serve in an advisory capacity at Pointer Enterprises and pour all of his knowledge into his grandsons so they could successfully embrace their Pointer legacy.

What he didn't know was Jack's secret. A secret that bore bad blood between the brothers, and he didn't know that Cassandra was living in Rushing Springs, where it all began.

Printed in the USA
CPSIA information can be obtained
at www.ICGtesting.com
LVHW021659240924
792026LV00012B/239